Expeditions

Circle for the Earth Book Two

Expeditions

A Time Travel Journey

Daphne Singingtree

All proceeds from this book will be donated to Zaníyan Center, a nonprofit 501c(3) that promotes health through plants and connection with the earth.

Eagletree Press
Eugene, Oregon
www.eagletreepress.com

Dedication

For the ones who ask, *"What if?"* and then pick up a shovel.

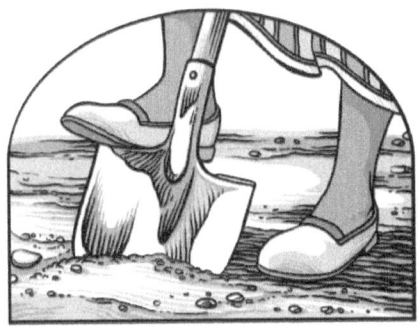

Important Note About Language and Content

The terms *Native American*, *Indigenous*, and *Indian* are used interchangeably within tribal communities. In this book, *Native* refers to those from the twenty-first century who were brought back in time. *Indigenous* refers to the people who lived in these lands in this time period. The term *Indian* may be used by characters from either group and reflects common historical usage.

Lakota words are written with full diacritics (pronunciation marks) the first time they appear, for those who wish to learn them. A pronunciation guide can be found on page **i**. After the first use, simplified English spellings are used, with occasional accent marks retained for clarity.

In dialogue, there is an occasional racist slur or offensive language reflective of the 1790s. These words are included to portray the brutal reality of that time. If you find them disturbing—*good*. They are meant to be.

Some readers may be impacted by content that includes profanity, racism, slavery, sexual violence, mild sex scenes, and LGBTQ+ themes.

This book is unashamedly political, with a strong progressive and anti-colonial stance. It advocates for Indigenous sovereignty, climate justice, and a better world for future generations.

Contents

Lakota Pronunciation Guide

Consonants

IPA	Examples	English approximation
b	bló	about
tʃ	wašíču	check
tʃʰ	héčhena	choose
tʃ	šič'éši	check, but with a pause afterwards
g	ógle	again
g	ǧí	French parlor
h	wóžuha	hat
x	ḣóta	Spanish jota
k	ská	skin
k'	k'éyaš	skin, but with a pause afterwards
kʰ	wakhéya wakháŋ	cab
kˣ		like cab, but sharper
l	hokšíla	life
m	makes	man
n	iná	neighbor
p	tópa	spot
pʰ	ophíye pḣeží	pot
pˣ		like pot, but sharper
p'	p'ó	spot, but with a pause afterwards
s	tiyospaye	sun
ʃ	tóške	shoe
t	witkó	stand
t'	t'élanuwela	stand, but with a pause afterwards
tʰ	mathó	torn
tˣ	tḣáwa	like torn, but sharper
w	tuwá	well
j	wíŋyaŋ	yes
z	wazí	zip
ʒ	maǧážu	measure

Vowels

IPA	Examples	English approximation
a	akézaptaŋ	hat
ɛ	iye	bed
s	iš	bit
ɔ	kȟolá	thought
ʊ	táku	push
ə	waŋží	huh
ĩ	siŋtésapela	bit, but nasalized
ʊ̃	uŋkiye	push, but nasalized

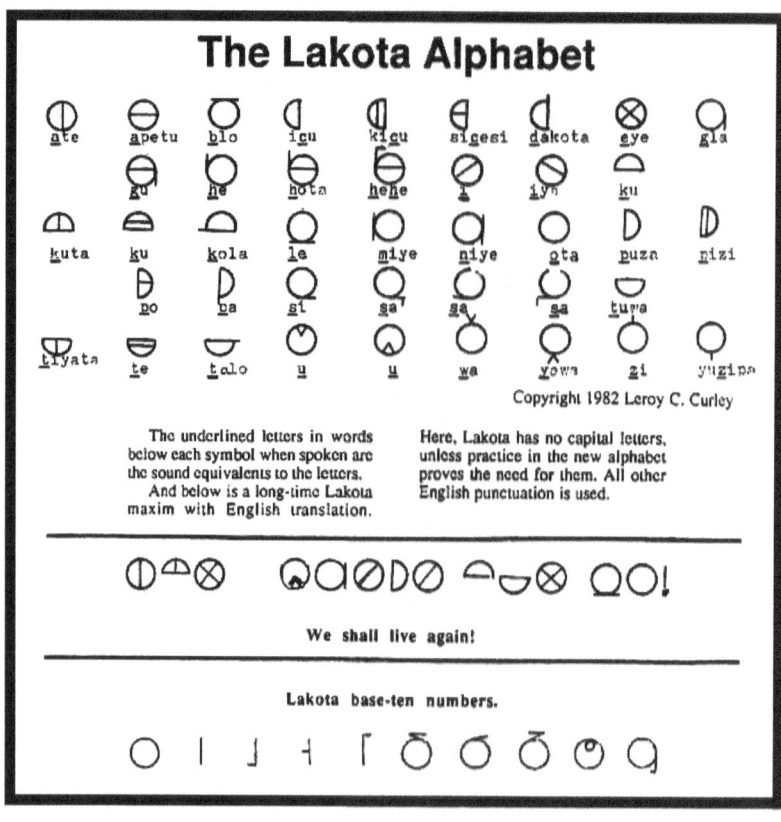

The Lakota Alphabet

Copyright 1982 Leroy C. Curley

The underlined letters in words below each symbol when spoken are the sound equivalents to the letters. And below is a long-time Lakota maxim with English translation.

Here, Lakota has no capital letters, unless practice in the new alphabet proves the need for them. All other English punctuation is used.

We shall live again!

Lakota base-ten numbers.

Cast of Characters

Changleska Coalition Executive Council
Duane Nelson – Minister of Communication
Jerome Brown – Minister of Agriculture
Mary Landrau – Chair and Minister of Education
Oliver Jackson – Minister of Defense
Richard Russo – Minister of Infrastructure
Shawn Caris – Minister of Human Services
Theresa Martinez – Minister of Medicine

Changleska Coalition Officials and Staff
Andrea Richter – Second in Command at First Shield Command
Charlotte Evans – Assistant to Oliver Jackson
Elliot Gray Owl – Attorney General
Phil Gallo – Chief of First Shield Command

Omímeya Staff and Their Families
Billy Fast Dog – Security Chief at Omímeya
Bruce Milsham – Attorney at Omímeya
David Kim – Information Technology at Omímeya
Doris Stewart – Administrative Assistant at Omímeya
Gift of Thunder – Adopted daughter of Hotah
Hotah Chasing Hawk – Rose's ex-husband, father of Kimi
Jenny Abrams – Events Manager at Omímeya
Joseph Chasing Hawk – Father of Hotah Chasing Hawk
Julian Bradley – Department Head, Guest Services
Kimímela Chasing Hawk – Daughter of Rose and Hotah
Kyle Ward – Resource Director at Omímeya
Leon Bauer – Former IT staff at Omímeya
Rose Chasing Hawk – General Manager and CEO of Omímeya
Wayne Becker – Facilities Manager at Omímeya

County Residents
Clyde Folsom – Former South Dakota State Senator
Ed Robinson – Brule County Commissioner
Kenneth Harris – Brule County Sheriff

Changleska Guard
Cheryl Tigard – Commander of the Changleska Air Guard
Ed Tilson – Sergeant, California Expedition
Elijah Walker – Formerly enslaved, now a corporal in the Changleska Guard
Joe Dunning – Sergeant and second in command of Jamal Alston platoon
John Dunphy – Commanding Officer, Expedition Base
Jonathan Gardner – General Changleska Guard
Lou White Mountain – Commander, Changleska Guard Marines
Mateo Rodriguez – Lieutenant, later Colonel; commander at Oca Landing
Ryan White Mountain – Honor Guard assigned to Mary Landrau
Thomas Parker – Lieutenant; commander of the Changleska Navy.

Expedition Members
Andrea (Andy) Dunphy – Member of the California Expedition; daughter of
Andrew Morrison – Captain (eventually Major); California Expedition
Darren Iron Cloud – Lieutenant, California Expedition
Harold "Bones" Rogers – Militia member California Expedition
Jerry Dunphy – Sergeant; son of John Dunphy
Jody Landrau – Lieutenant, California Expedition
Karl Bauer – First New Orleans expedition, presumed lost
Tom Chandler – Road crew, California Expedition
Jack Tilson – Lieutenant, California Expedition
Jamal Alston – Private (later Lieutenant); Boston Expedition & Oca Landing
Nels Hansen – Private; medic-in-training, Boston Expedition.

Maps

Location of Thirty-mile Circle Brought Back in Time

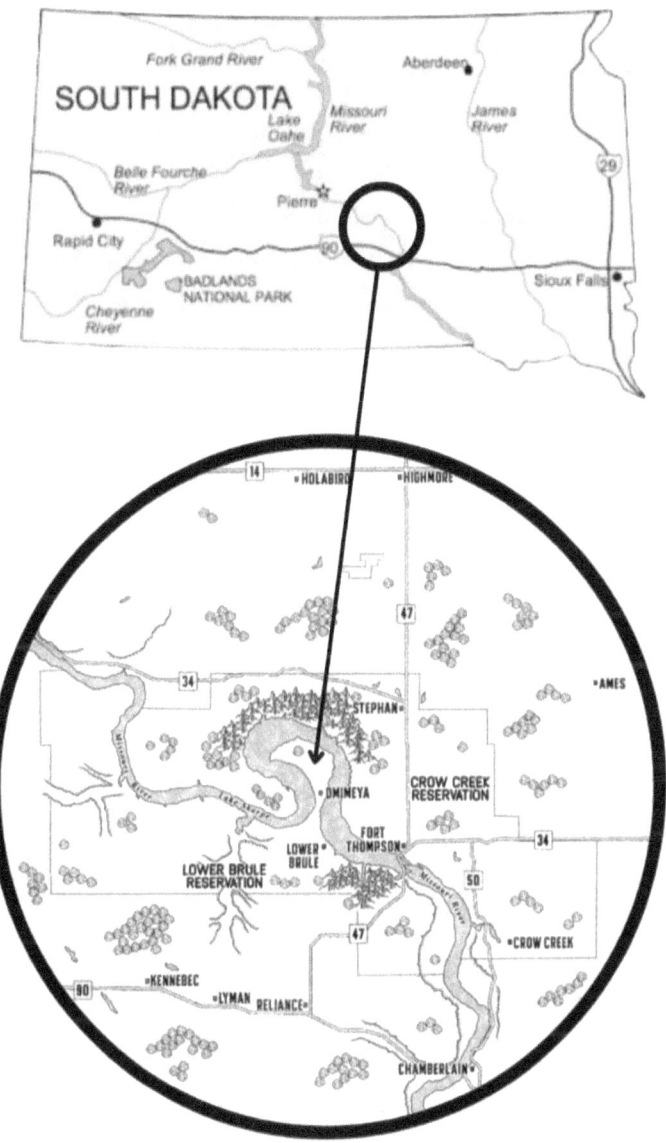

Omímeya Casino and Resort

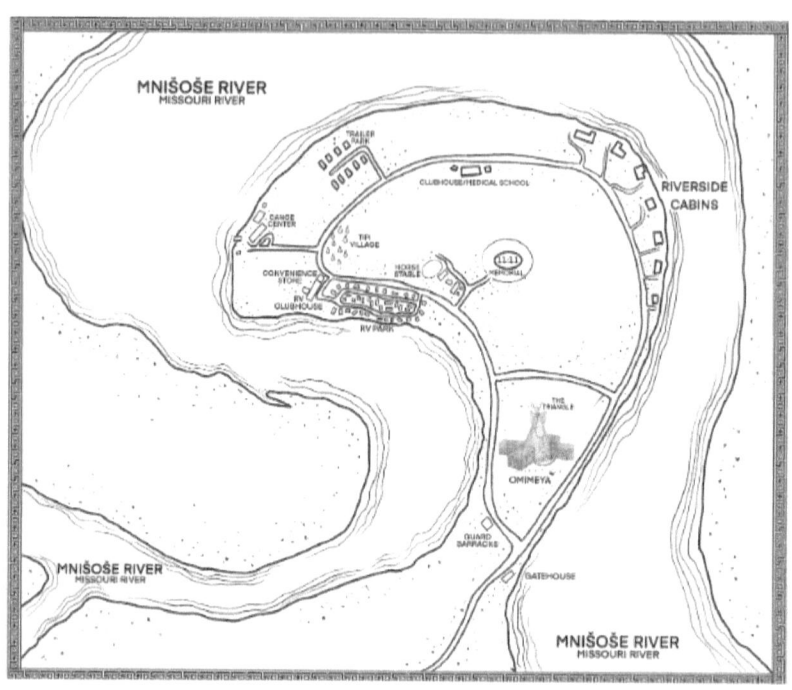

Lands prior to Changleska's Founding

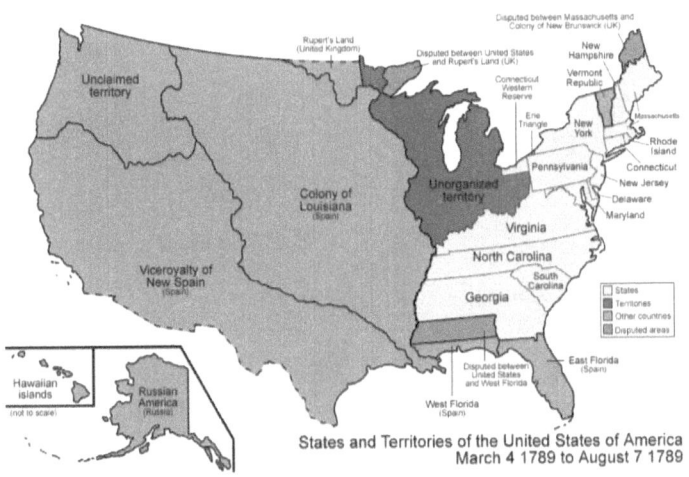

States and Territories of the United States of America
March 4 1789 to August 7 1789

Borders and Settlements
CHANGLESKA

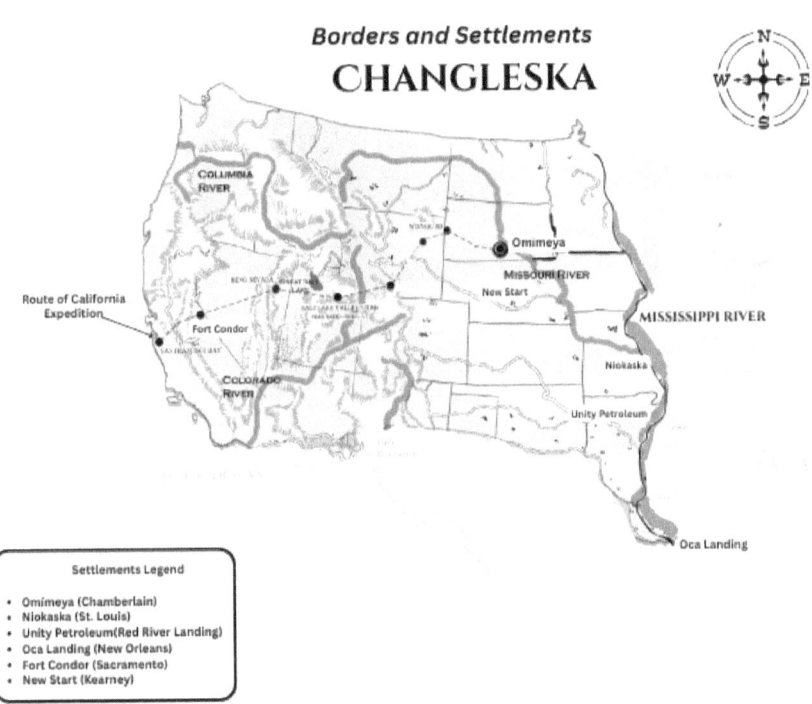

Settlements Legend

- Omímeya (Chamberlain)
- Niokaska (St. Louis)
- Unity Petroleum(Red River Landing)
- Oca Landing (New Orleans)
- Fort Condor (Sacramento)
- New Start (Kearney)

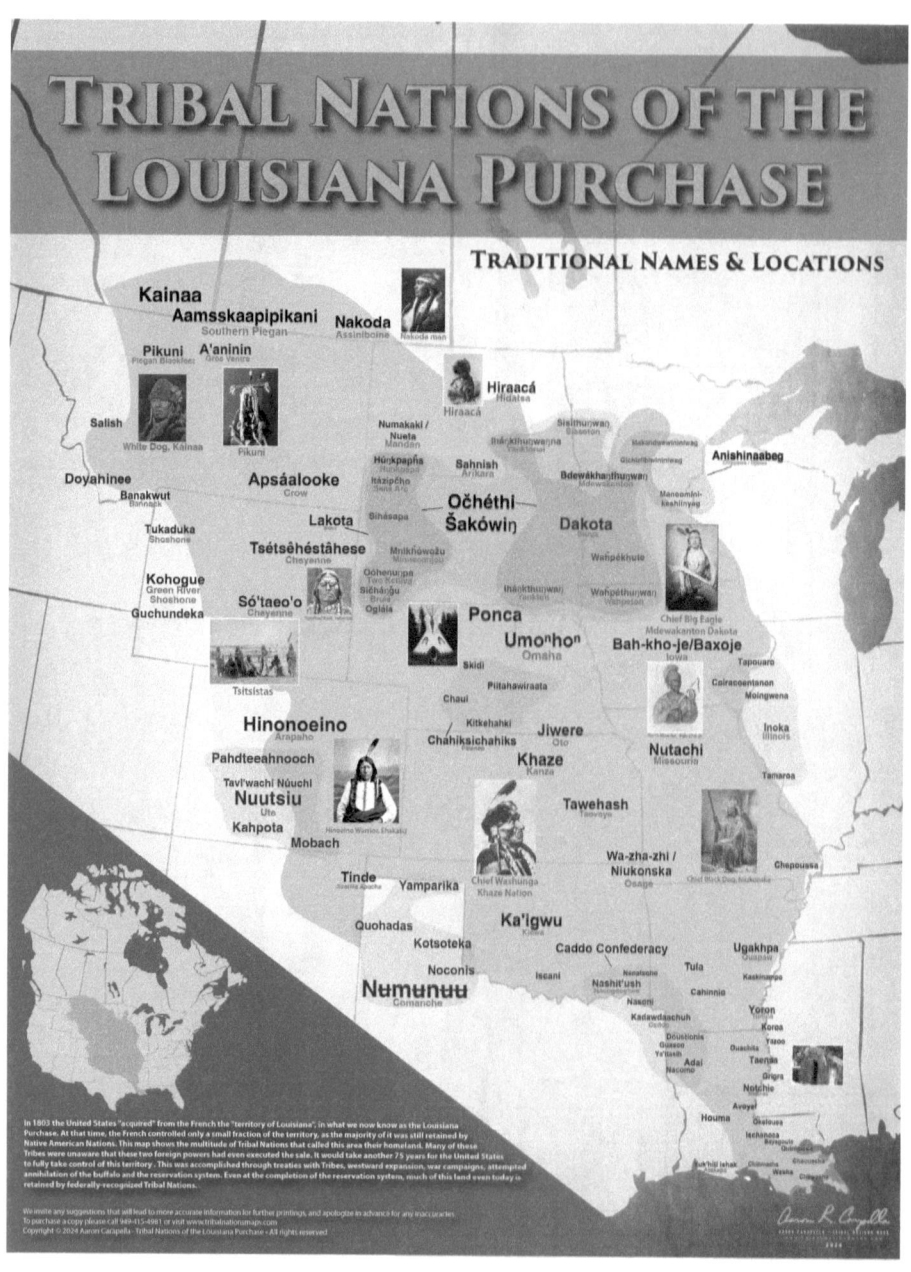

PART I
Spring
(wétu)

Let us put our minds together and see
what life we can make for our children.
—Sitting Bull (1831-1890), Hunkpapa Lakota Leader

Chapter One
Rose

SIX MONTHS AGO, a deafening thunderclap shattered Rose Chasing Hawk's reality. The Omímeya Casino and Resort, along with everything inside a perfect thirty-mile circle, was hurled back to 1791. No one knew what had caused their return to the past, or how they might ever return. One moment, she was the Assistant Manager, juggling staff schedules and corporate bureaucracy. The next moment, her boss was left behind in the twenty-first century, and she was suddenly in charge, responsible not only for a resort but for a community uprooted from time. With no warning and no escape, she became a reluctant leader in a world unmoored from everything she knew.

Before she was transported to the late eighteenth century, her life thrown into chaos, she excelled at her job. Most of the time she even loved it, despite having a difficult boss and a frustrating corporate office. The demands were hard as a single mother of two teenagers, but after earning her degree in hospitality management, she dedicated herself to her career, working her way up for thirteen years. However, it was ultimately just a job; she could always quit and probably find a better-paying position elsewhere. Because her previous boss was left behind in the Circle, presumably in the twenty-first century, she became the General Manager and CEO of Omímeya. Now she held a powerful leadership position over more than the resort—its hundreds of staff and guests now displaced in time—and was helping to shape the course of history.

The pressure of leadership chipped away at her confidence, leaving her constantly second-guessing every decision. More than a job, now it was her life's work. There was no going back and no quitting.

Before she was transported to the late eighteenth century, her life thrown into chaos, she excelled at her job. Most of the time she even loved it, despite having a difficult boss and a frustrating corporate office. The demands were hard as a single mother of two teenagers, but after earning her degree in hospitality management, she dedicated herself to her career, working her way up for thirteen years. However, it was ultimately just a job; she could always quit and probably find a better-paying position elsewhere. Because her previous boss was left behind in the Circle, presumably in the twenty-first century, she became the General Manager and CEO of Omímeya. Now she held a powerful leadership position over more than the resort—its hundreds of staff and guests now displaced in time—and was helping to shape the course of history.

The pressure of leadership chipped away at her confidence, leaving her constantly second-guessing every decision. No longer a job, now it was her life s work. There was no going back and no quitting.

Rose barely saw her kids before Big Thunder, the name they gave the event that changed everything. Now, leading Omímeya consumed nearly every moment, leaving even less time for her family. Not only was she busier, but her family had grown.

Her thirteen-year-old daughter, Kimi, had asked to be called by her full name, Kimímela, which means Butterfly in Lakota, but her nickname, Kimi, stuck. She now had an adopted sister, Gift of Thunder. Gift, sixteen, had been rescued on the first day of their arrival. She was Arikara, captured by the Lakota as a child and later sold to a fur trader. Later, she'd been taken from the same fur trader by local fishermen. Rose s ex-husband had formally adopted her last fall. The two girls were inseparable.

Rose intended to spend more time with them, but something always came up at work, fires only she could put out. Though guilt clung to her, she managed to step back and view the situation as a whole, finding justification in the bigger picture. It didn't always help.

Luke, her fifteen-year-old son, had struggled through a rough year, caught up with the wrong people and got into serious trouble. But he had finally turned a corner. His probation came with strict conditions, including no video games, a part-time job, and finishing high school, and surprisingly, it had helped. Now he was working on the construction crew, making friends with older, more responsible guys. They were building a new medical school, originally planned as a golf clubhouse for the resort. Since much of the work this time of year was interior finishing, he was getting valuable training. He was even learning Spanish along the way.

Kimi had always had an unexplained awareness of events before they occurred. She had warned Rose about Big Thunder hours before it happened. She had done the same right before cartel gunmen opened fire at a public gathering last fall. Now could predict the weather, but it was more than that. She seemed to have a relationship with thunder itself.

Rose didn't know what to do with Kimi's growing abilities.

One evening, Kimi and Gift sat outside on the deck. The sliding glass door was open, and Rose, working in the kitchen, could hear their conversation.

Kimi pulled her shawl tighter, her gaze on the horizon. "Mom says I should write it down," she muttered.

Gift glanced over. "Write what down?"

"When I feel the thunder before it comes." Kimi tapped her temple. "Like keeping track will make it normal or something."

Gift tilted her head. "The Thunder Beings speak to you. Listen to them."

Kimi let out a short laugh, but Rose could hear the frustration beneath it. "I wish . . . I don't know. I wish it wasn't weird. That I wasn't weird."

Gift nudged her shoulder. "You're blessed, not weird."

Kimi let out a breath. "Then why doesn't anyone else hear it?"

Gift placed a hand on her shoulder. "Others hear the spirit. Our *Wičháša Wakháŋ* (holy man) can help you. They also hear the Thunder Beings."

Kimi's voice dropped. "If I feel these things, I should be able to warn people. I didn't listen the day of the attack and look how many people died."

"Your warning saved us," Gift said softly.

"Not enough," Kimi whispered. "How will I ever know what a real warning is or just my fears?"

Rose felt bad for eavesdropping, but she was glad she had. Now, she understood how much guilt Kimi carried.

She made a mental note to talk to her daughter about it—soon. But not now. Right now, Kimi needed her friend, not her mother hovering over her.

=..=

Rose gazed out the window, watching the sky darken over the river. How many others carried the same weight of guilt? They had all been thrown into this world without warning, without a guide. Although it was a burden, it could also be a gift. They'd been given a second chance to get things right.

In the wake of the time-travel event, the Tribal Councils of the two Lakota reservations, along with leaders from the small towns caught in the shift, realized they had an unprecedented opportunity: to avert the colonization of Indigenous lands, the erasure of cultures, and the ecological destruction that would follow.

At a meeting with local businesspeople adjusting to the new reality, Rose stood to explain the stakes. Public speaking still made her palms sweat, but it was getting easier. The words came more readily now, shaped by purpose.

"We were thrown back to 1791," she said, "just twelve years before Jefferson would have bought this entire region in the Louisiana Purchase. He wanted New Orleans, a port he could not afford to lose, and land for settlers already pouring west. Spain controls it now, but we know how this ends. Every Indigenous nation will be overrun. Many erased." She looked around the room. "We've been given a second chance to stop that. That's why we declared independence. That's why we wrote our own constitution. And it's why we need allies now."

In the version of history Rose came from, Spain would soon trade this land to France in exchange for a slice of Tuscany. By 1803, France would sell it to the United States for fifteen million dollars, doubling the nation's size overnight. That was the history Rose once knew. Now, Changleska was rewriting it. Declaring independence was the first step, but survival meant diplomacy. They needed recognition from Spain, France, Britain, and the United States. Without it, they were a target waiting to be conquered.

To change that future, the group declared independence and created their own country, *Čhangléska* Coalition, a Lakota word meaning "circle" or "hoop," symbolizing unity. They wrote a constitution and a bill of freedoms and rights. They elected a seven-member Executive Council with expertise in various areas and had committees propose laws. It was a simple and effective form of governance, but not without growing pains. Although called a coalition, it was more like a confederation, with each sovereign tribe having autonomy, but exactly what it would look like was still being negotiated. Changleska claimed all lands from west of the Mississippi to the Pacific Ocean on the borders of the old United States. If they could pull it off, this new government would preserve the land for the Indigenous tribes, although most tribes were unaware their future was being decided.

Changleska, recognizing that France was the more resourceful adversary, although Napoleon hadn't yet come to power, wanted to bypass France and buy the territory from Spain. Spain was struggling to maintain its many distant colonies and might be willing to sell the lands without significant resistance. They d need the cooperation of both France and Spain to recognize their independence without a fight.

After arriving and realizing how limited their modern resources were, they understood survival beyond a basic eighteenth-century lifestyle required sharing their modern knowledge with the rest of the world. Declaring independence and creating your own country is one thing. Having the rest of the world recognize your claims is quite another.

Rose, though not part of the Council or a member of a committee, had a unique position as CEO of Omímeya. The resort was largely self-sustaining by geothermal and solar energy, solidly built with 320 guest rooms and many large meeting spaces. Built by a consortium of Indian casinos, it was larger and had more resources than such a small reservation justified. What few knew was that the corporation had also built it as a luxury retreat for natural or man-made disasters. There were secret stockpiles of supplies, weapons, and technology, including critical backups of internet data.

Although Rose had influence, she didn t control Omímeya resources. The Board of Directors had the final say: she and the four others who knew the level of secret resources. Her expertise was hotel management, not international diplomacy and global finance. Figuring out the next steps to achieve a nearly impossible goal was a challenge Rose was not sure she was capable of.

Soon after they created the Changleska Coalition, they sent expeditions out with letters and copies of their founding documents. When they could, they sent laptops or phones with videos they produced showing modern wonders. They invited officials and businesspeople from Spain, France, Britain, and the new United States to come to Omímeya this spring to witness everything firsthand and attend the First Summit to begin the process of negotiations. There was much they needed from the outside world, and knowledge about science and technology to share.

This meeting represented the first step in a long process with much at stake. Providing meeting spaces was normally what Rose and her team did, however since Big Thunder, it was proving more challenging. Rose was anxious since she was ultimately responsible for the hundreds of details needed for the First Summit to go smoothly.

As she entered the lobby of the Omímeya, she felt a familiar knot of tension in her stomach. She couldn't shake the anxiety about the upcoming visitors, the first significant meeting with eighteenth-century people. Hosting and negotiating with the leaders of Indigenous tribes who had been arriving over the last months was stressful enough, but this was a whole other level.

=..=

On the way to the staff meeting, Rose walked by the server rooms. She could hear the hum of the machinery, a sound that now unsettled her. The server room's hum sent a chill through Rose. *So much power in these machines. They could change the world for the better or destroy us*, she thought.

Thinking about the upcoming visitors brought her concerns back to the forefront. These officials, and what they brought back to their nation's leaders, held the fate of Changleska in their hands. They had no leverage, no sticks, only carrots. No one knew if it would be enough, but they needed to start somewhere. They didn't know if the powers of this time would view them as an opportunity or a threat.

Entering the staff meeting, everyone's mood was upbeat and cheerful. It had been a long, hard winter; it was the Twentieth of March, the first day of spring, and the feeling of renewal permeated the air. Small groups chatted excitedly, with smiles and laughter. Rose could not help but feel better; hopefulness is contagious.

Jenny Abrams started as the Events Manager, in charge of conferences, weddings, and other hotel events. Now she was Assistant Manager, Rose's right hand. Promoting her put a few of the department heads with more seniority noses out of joint. She was smart, young, and attractive. She was talking animatedly with Julian Bradley, the department head of Guest Services. He was an older White man with gray-white hair, a fastidious dresser, and one of the few openly gay men Rose knew.

"Are you looking forward to eighteenth-century guests?" she asked.

"I'm grateful we can start going back to our regular jobs. Catering to people from this time will be different, but I'm looking forward to the challenge."

The staff were used to running a hotel and resort, not the emergency shelter and government office building that Omímeya had become. Geothermal provided unlimited heat and hot water; however, it couldn't extend beyond the radius established on the day of Big Thunder. Most buildings outside that area use natural gas or propane for heating. While the natural gas pipes still existed, they were neatly cut off in the perfect circle created by the Big Thunder event. The lack of natural gas left many vulnerable to deadly Dakota winter conditions, as not everyone had access to wood-burning stoves or electric heating.

The Changleska government paid Omímeya for rooms for emergency housing. While Rose was happy with that income, as there were practically no other guests, it brought a host of problems staff needed to address. They were used to well-off vacationing guests who stayed a few days or a week or two at the most, not people living long-term without resources. Everyone was looking forward to becoming a hotel and resort again.

Wayne Becker, the Facilities Manager, who knew the geothermal system best, recommended shutting down unused hotel floors to save wear and tear on the parts that ran the system. Although geothermal energy was limitless, the parts to run it all came from the twenty-first century. While they had spare parts and 3D printers, it was unclear how long those would last. Rose knew he would be happy to see some floors closed again, to have less stress on the system.

Once she got to the meeting room, Rose announced, "Everyone, let's get started. Is everyone here?"

Billy Fast Dog, Omímeya's Security Chief, spoke up. "Phil is on his way, picking up the latest reports from the St. Louis station."

He was referring to Phil Gallo, originally the Casino Manager. The Casino ran as a separate department from the rest of the resort. Following the casino's downsizing, his assistant assumed most of his responsibilities. Now he was the Changleska Intelligence Chief, on the Security Council, and the Omímeya Board of Directors. Rose's relationship with him wavered between utter frustration and mutual respect. He was arrogant, smart, and capable. Phil had run the casino for years, overseeing everything from high-stakes games to internal security. He knew how to manage people, spot deception, and protect sensitive information. Those skills served him well in his new role as Intelligence Chief

"We'll start without him," Rose replied.

Rose settled at the head of the table while the staff finished grabbing their tea—wishing for coffee, which was still in short supply—and sat.

"This is our biggest influx of visitors since Big Thunder," Rose began. "The *Endeavor*, our steam barge, was designed for cargo. Our team has done wonders transforming shipping containers into passenger units. While not luxurious, they'll offer some comfort."

"How many guests are we expecting?" Neal Suttle, the Food Services Manager, asked.

"The *Endeavor* now carries eight crew and eighty passengers—sixty in third class, sixteen in second class, and twelve in first-class cabins. Not sure what the breakdown is between our invited guests, their servants, and other passengers. Phil will have that information when he arrives," replied Rose.

Julian raised a question. "Servants usually get lower accommodations. Which rooms should we use for them?"

Jenny suggested, "Rooms on the shelter floors as they are gender segregated. It's important to people from this time."

Rose heard a sigh around the room. No one was happy that they needed to create separate floors for men, women, and families. With both staff and vulnerable community residents needing shelter from the cold, issues arose. Tensions flared between unfamiliar groups, and maintaining safety became a challenge. Women didn't feel safe. While there were no rapes, sexual harassment and unacceptable behaviors were happening before they instituted the change. It was worse when alcohol was involved. The rate of alcoholism on the reservation decreased by a large percentage, with less access to alcohol and meaningful work being significant reasons, but it hadn't gone away completely.

There were upsides to creating separate floors. Initially, the end of each floor had featured a small area with vending, ice, and slot machines, along with a couple of comfy chairs. Following the removal of the machines, the area became a space for socializing. Subsequently, they opened the adjacent room to enlarge the common area to include a bathroom and small kitchenette. The women s floor common area often hosted crafts, while the men played video games and watched recorded sports games on tv. The family floor had toys and board games. Having common areas helped create a sense of community, important for long winter nights with an uncertain future.

"Julian," Rose said, "what have you learned about customs and manners we need to be aware of for our guests? Specific things to avoid unintentional offence?"

"Michael Dubray, our historian, will hold a training tomorrow to cover proper forms of address and other courtesies. For example, handshakes are rarely used as an initial greeting. Attendance is mandatory for all staff; it is easy to cause offense. It is quite involved. Bows and curtsies are expected when interacting with those of higher rank."

Jenny interjected, "We're Americans, or Changleskans now. Do we have to cater to nobility?"

Julian shrugged. "If we don't want to offend, we follow their customs. People reject anything too far out of their norms. If we want our values to be adopted, we need to take the first step and accept compromises for now."

"Good point. This training will be essential for staff," Rose said.

"Neal, what is the plan for food?" Looking at the next item on her agenda.

Neal replied, "Red Oak will keep the basic cafeteria menu, catering to the Walleye Room for some meals, but we'll open Prairie Abundance."

There were murmurs of approval. Prairie Abundance was the fine dining restaurant that closed right after Big Thunder. Reopening felt like a step toward normalcy.

Neal added, "Room service will remain closed, mini bars empty."

Julian asked, "What about the bar?"

It will now be open every day but Sunday from four to midnight serving wine and beer, but with the hard liquor cabinet unlocked. Twenty-first century liquor prices will be high, but the moonshine is not bad, made into cocktails. Hopefully, we ll have enough wine. The French and Spanish are big wine drinkers. Kyle?"

Kyle Ward would know. While his job started as Emergency Preparedness Director, he was now in charge of the new Resource Department. Part of his old job involved purchasing emergency supplies, mostly all kept secret. Now, his expanded department inventoried and processed all incoming supplies, with only a couple of staff cleared to know the extent of the hidden supplies.

Kyle answered, "Enough wine for this visit. We'll need wine shipments from New Orleans soon. With the new brewery opened in Chamberlain, there is plenty of beer. I'm not sure if they drink beer."

Julian said, "The British and Americans do."

Just then, Phil Gallo arrived.

"Sorry I'm late; it took longer than expected to get all the messages from St. Louis sorted."

"At least we have the radios and don't have to rely on couriers," said Kyle.

Kyle had helped set up the radio towers between here and the new settlement called Niokaska, an Osage name for middle waters, a few miles south of St. Louis. They brought a limited number of shortwave radios that had about a 1000-mile radius but worked better at night. Because of the limited numbers, and because it was unclear if they could be replaced, they were building telegraphs for Morse code.

Phil continued, "Profiles on incoming guests will be on your devices, with space for notes. You can add things like preferences, but if you have information useful for security, be sure to fill out the online form. We'll have more information after they arrive, but from passenger manifest, the principles are in first class: four Spanish, three French, three Americans, and two British. In second class: three priests and the rest high-ranking aides or servants. Third class has eight soldiers, twenty-two servants, fourteen formerly enslaved people, and sixteen others, mostly craftsmen and merchants. There are also twelve children and three infants."

Billy asked with concern, "Are the soldiers armed?"

Phil answered. "With swords and flintlocks. They had stored their firearms in the weapons locker for the journey, but we'll return them. The soldiers are mostly an honor guard and aides. They wanted to send more, but with such limited space, they had to choose between soldiers and servants. They chose servants. Someone must care for their fancy uniforms."

Everyone laughed, relieved.

Jenny asked Phil, "Is there a Henry LaChamp on the manifest?" her voice tight.

Phil looked at the list and nodded. Rose caught Jenny's expression and made a mental note to ask about it later. Henry LaChamp was a Hudson Bay Company (HBC) clerk sent last fall to verify the seemingly wild claims of an entire area arriving from a different world. The twenty-first-century wonders wowed him, but he lacked the authority to make trade agreements. He became smitten with Jenny, who acted as a tour guide. His departure had left Jenny visibly upset, though Rose didn't know the details.

Phil continued, "Of the four Spanish nobles, the highest ranking is Don Sebastián de Alarcón, the envoy for the king of Spain. Don José de Esquivel is the Captain-General of the Spanish territories in the Americas. Marquis Alejandro de la Vega is a noble whose family owns sugar plantations in Cuba. Sending a woman surprised me. Doña Isabella de Villalobos, is a Marchioness and Advisor to the Spanish Court. She has ties to Louisiana through her late husband, a Spanish colonial officer."

"The French sent Baron Étienne de Villiers, a Military Attaché; the diplomat Claude-François de Malet; and another woman, Madame Henriette Dupont. A prominent French businesswoman in New Orleans, with deep ties to the revolutionary French government. She came with two school-age children."

Rose asked, "Did they have time to travel from overseas?"

"The Spanish and French were already in New Orleans, except Vega. He came from Cuba. The British envoy and the HBC representative sailed directly from London to New Orleans. The Americans sailed from the eastern seaboard: Charles Cotesworth Pinckney, a retired Revolutionary War general; John Laurens, also military, retired as a major, was an aide to Washington during the war; and..."

He paused, with a big grin, and said, "Benjamin Tallmadge."

He waited expectantly for a response but received only blank stares.

"Did anyone watch the miniseries *Turn* about Washington's spies during the Revolutionary War? Ben Tallmadge was a main character. Based on a true story but fictionalized for TV."

A few people said yes or asked if it was available in their online library of films.

Jenny asked, "Does he know he is portrayed on a TV show from our time?"

"Not sure, but if he thinks we don't know he led a major spy ring, we won't tell. I'm sure he'll find out eventually."

Kyle said, "They must have been pretty motivated to travel in the middle of the winter."

Phil replied, "Normally it takes four or five months this time of year, but if they arrived in time to meet the *Endeavor*, it took two to three months off their travel time. We sent persuasive formal invitations. No one wanted to be left out of the negotiations, or the chance to case the place, in case they think we can't keep it. Plus, because we invited them to a formal summit, we pay most of the expenses."

Rose interjected, "They also wanted to see the steam barge in action. They know the power of fast river travel. There are few roads. Most goods travel by water."

Phil said, "Weren't steam engines already invented?"

Kyle replied, "By 1792, a few steam-powered boats had been tested, like the *Pyroscaphe* in France, but nothing practical for river use. We used 1880s riverboat designs, built from salvaged parts and modern knowledge. It's a century ahead of its time, and every mile it runs reminds us just how fragile our edge is."

Jenny asked, "Are any of the servants' slaves?"

"No slaves can come on board. All passengers have been told Changleska automatically frees every slave that steps aboard or crosses west of the Mississippi. If they tried to bring slaves, they'd lose their 'property' without compensation. We check for freedom papers. If lacking, we issue before boarding."

Phil added, "They won't be required to be quarantined at the Welcome Center like other arrivals. Medical staff cleared them before they received their IDs; they've been on the barge long enough to complete quarantine."

"Did that create any problems?" Rose asked.

"Not sure. I get very little information in the initial reports, but if they went through delousing, same as everyone, I'm sure it ruffled a few feathers of our wealthy visitors."

Everyone was relieved to hear the precautions taken. There was a small outbreak of typhus during the winter, which is spread by lice, extremely prevalent in the eighteenth-century. Consequently, they set up the Welcome Center, a converted motel, as their own Ellis Island. The first stop was the delousing station, where clothes and belongings were steam-cleaned to kill the bugs. A four-day mandatory quarantine, with medical checks, an orientation video, and ID were issued.

Because room and board were free for the four days of quarantine, there wasn't much complaining, despite being confined to their rooms. They could stay longer for the cost of the usual inn of the time, if there was room. What was unusual was that fur traders, newly freed slaves, and wealthy people were all housed with equal quality rooms and food. They ignored any complaints from the wealthy; the others had never seen such fine accommodations.

The Changleska Guard, their military, had border patrols both on the river and overland routes. Visitors lacking proper ID were led, sometimes at gunpoint, to either quarantine or the border. Locals were unhappy about being required to carry ID, but they understood the necessity of quarantine. The threat of epidemics, especially spreading to the Indigenous population, trumped civil rights. When locals encountered unfamiliar faces, they pulled up the kerchiefs nearly everyone wore as masks until they could see the stranger's ID. Most people also kept their hair covered.

The system worked well over the winter because visitor numbers remained low. Quarantine protocols were only required for individuals who arrived independently rather than as part of organized expeditions. To minimize risk of disease spread, medical staff took a proactive approach by traveling directly to Indigenous camps to conduct health screenings and offer care, rather than requiring tribal members to come to the Welcome Center.

Everyone was concerned about the genuine risk of a smallpox outbreak. Smallpox devastated Indigenous populations. Its eradication in modern times resulted in only pre-1972 individuals having received the vaccine. Edward Jenner developed smallpox vaccination in 1796, although a less precise method called variolation existed prior to that time. Creating a safe smallpox vaccine was a top priority, but the process was not simple or fast. Even with 153 doctors, there were no virologists or anyone specializing in vaccines. Luckily, a veterinary pharmaceutical center in Chamberlain, which produced animal drugs and vaccines, repurposed its facilities for human use.

Rose noted the upbeat energy in the room. Despite the weight of their responsibilities, the team's dedication inspired her. The meeting addressed logistical challenges and preparations for the visitors. Many previous staff had moved to other jobs. Staff shortages would have to be addressed to return to being a full-fledged resort.

After the meeting, Rose approached Jenny. "Want to talk about Henry?" she asked gently.

Jenny sighed. "He broke my heart. Then sent a letter apologizing. It's complicated."

Rose smiled. "You don't have to tell me, but I can listen."

"We hit it off during his visit. I'm not sure if he was so enthralled with me or a modern woman who was free to speak intelligently."

"For the weeks he was here, you sure spent a lot of time together."

"I thought we really had something. I still had birth control, it had been a long time, so..."

Rose nodded. No more needed to be said. "What was the problem?"

"I didn't realize during this time, men sleep with prostitutes or wives, not women they are dating. He took things seriously. He told me he'd return as soon as he could. Which made me happy."

"Then what happened?" asked Rose.

"The topic of religion came up. He told me he preferred if I converted to Catholicism. But he could accept it if any children we have were raised Catholic."

"Children? You only knew him for weeks."

"That wasn't the problem. It was when I told him I was Jewish. Even though I'm non-practicing, and my parents were reform, I still am and will always be a Jew."

"What did he say?"

With tears glistening in her eyes, she said, "He dropped his hand from mine and physically stepped back, got angry, saying I should have told him. He didn't quite call me a whore, but that was the implication."

"How horrible. I can see why you were hurt. An apology letter won't cut it. This kind of cultural prejudice is deep. I don't know if he can overcome it.

"I don't think so either, but I feel stronger about him than any man before, including my ex I moved here from New Jersey for."

Curious, Rose had to ask, "What did the letter say?"

"Not a lot. He let me know he was coming back, received a promotion, apologized for his behavior, hoped I would forgive him, and we could still be friends."

"Ignore him and make sure you are seen with a hot guy."

"Great advice." They laughed and departed the conference room.

Along the way, Rose asked, "Are you coming to the ceremony this afternoon?"

"That's right, it's today. Are your girls helping organize it? I enjoyed the winter solstice ceremony they helped with."

"No, it will be very traditional, but they invited Kimi to participate."

Rose was uneasy about the belief that her thirteen-year-old daughter had sacred insight or powers. But she had known for years Kimi was different, knowing things before they happened. Hours before Big Thunder, Kimi had warned Rose it was coming with the words she translated from Lakota, 'Big Thunder strengthens the circle; the circle protects the Earth.'

Rose added, "Red Eagle's tribe will host the ceremony at the Lower Brule powwow grounds."

"They came for the big meeting. I heard they're fierce."

"Not sure about that, not as friendly as the Two Elks tribe, and larger. Everyone is looking forward to the ceremony. It may differ from the modern one we do. The *Wakínyan* (Thunder Beings) or Thunder Ceremony celebrates the returning of the Thunder Beings, who will bring the rain to wake up plants, hibernating animals, and people."

"I don't want more Thunder Beings doing anything," Jenny joked. "The last ones did a number on us."

"Be sure to wear a skirt," Rose advised.

"I'll change," assured Jenny.

Jenny was wearing slacks, an Omímeya polo shirt, and a cardigan, her everyday work attire. In the twenty-first century, nontribal women rarely understood that not wearing a skirt for a sacred ceremony was disrespectful.

Women from this time didn't wear pants. Slowly, women in the Circle were changing their attire. No one wanted to be perceived as a prostitute to outsiders. Many adapted the full-length, wraparound pinafore aprons like what Rose had made as uniforms for the female service staff. Using bolts of indigo-dyed sturdy hemp cloth from New Orleans, they created aprons that could be worn over uniforms or other clothing. They became a very popular side business for the shop Rose contracted with. Laundry soap had run out, and parts for broken washers or dryers were low on the priority list. With people washing their clothes less, aprons were a great solution. The shop even designed a hemp work-apron for men.

After Rose and Jenny parted, Rose read a text from her son Luke letting her know he was getting a ride to the ceremony from his friends from work. She smiled. Having friends was important at this age, and the young men Luke worked with were good influences.

Rose headed home; she had time to change and pick up Gift and go to the powwow grounds for the ceremony. She'd meet Jackson there. Rose's heart quickened when she thought of Oliver Jackson, the beautiful man she loved passionately. Jackson was the blessing that Big Thunder brought to her life.

Jackson had been a Sioux Falls cop in Chamberlain giving an in-service training to other police on nonviolent interventions when Big Thunder occurred. The tall, handsome Black veteran's commanding presence and excellent communication skills secured his overwhelming election to the Changleska government's Executive Council. Each of the seven Council members specialized in a different area; his was defense. The new government's structure meant the Executive Council Chair wasn't automatically Commander-in-Chief; that role belonged to the Council's Minister for Defense. Jackson was a firm believer in nonviolence; the role of the head of the military chafed at his soul.

A good-looking alpha male in a position of power, he was the most eligible bachelor around. Many young, beautiful women vied for his attention. Rose still couldn't believe he chose her. She was a thirty-seven-year-old, plump, recently divorced mother of teenagers, with a demanding job that took most of her time. Jackson, by loving her completely, gave her a sense of self-worth she needed to face her doubts. The intensity of their love was the fuel that propelled her, gave her strength to face the challenges ahead, and filled her with a sense of wholeness.

Chapter Two
Mary

—⬧◇◇⬧◯⬧◇◇⬧—

MARY LANDRAU LOVED complex challenges. Her role as the Chair of the Executive Committee of the Changleska Coalition wasn't much different from her previous positions of overseeing a teacher training program at a small community college or serving as the Chair of the small Lower Brule Lakota Tribe. Now, things kicked up a notch. Changleska, her new country, was hosting the First Summit. This first meeting was preliminary, setting the groundwork for either an agreement or, if that failed, a future conflict. They expected that proposals would need approval from their leaders. Given the slow communication, finalizing would take another six months to a year.

They needed to create agreements regarding port and river passage rights, recognition of Indigenous sovereignty, freedom of slaves, and negotiate access to modern technology. In addition, representatives of two of the largest and most powerful corporations in North America were going to be present, as well as leaders of several Indigenous tribes in the area.

The rest of the world did not recognize Changleska Coalition as a sovereign nation. Their Declaration of Independence angered Spain. The US and France felt threatened, considering their slave-labor economy depended on slave labor. Changleska's offer needed to appeal to nations wanting money and military technology. They hoped the promise of significant improvements in medicine, agriculture, and manufacturing would balance their refusal to trade weapons and higher-level tech. Despite the refusal to trade weapons, many items, including radios and enhanced maps, offered substantial military gains. The first navy to adopt their improvements in ship design and navigation would gain a profound advantage—leaving other nations in the dust, or at the bottom of the sea.

Control of ports and waterways was essential for the US plans for expansion. The threat of military intervention would exist if diplomatic efforts were to fail. Changleska needed to offer persuasive financial and technological incentives to avoid war. The competing interests of colonial powers, each with their own ambitions and demands, had to be carefully managed.

Many outsiders confused Omímeya with Changleska itself. But the resort was a single corporation. It was wealthy, well-prepared, and now vital to the new nation's survival. It held property, businesses, contracts, and much of the stored knowledge, but it was not the government. Political power lay with the Executive Council and the sovereign tribes of the Coalition.

Mary had been intensely studying for months, preparing for this meeting. She had a dedicated and smart team providing invaluable help and insights. After Big Thunder, satellites disappeared, cell service became limited, and modern communication throttled; however, inside the Circle, they had basic internet access. NewNet ran on DSL landlines and Wi-Fi was only available in a few places. Internet ran slowly at an early 2000s level. Omímeya as part of their emergency preparations downloaded Wikipedia up to the day they came back in time, as well as other technical, engineering, medical, and historical databases. Very little was open to the public. A cooperative of software and hardware owners decided what to release and when. They knew future knowledge was a powerful weapon capable of bringing about great change. It gave them their strongest leverage, and was likely the key to achieving their goals and liberating themselves from the grasp of colonial powers.

NewNet hosted old style bulletin board forums. Committees, work groups, teams, and various interest groups had discussions that often led to solutions, plans and policies. For people from the information age, forums became not only a substitute for social media, but a way forward out of an unfathomable situation. Seeking solutions, people found a constructive activity. The wide variety of topics ensured almost everyone could find a forum of interest. With limited entertainment options, especially in the winter, it was very popular.

Mary was active in the Foreign Affairs forum. Reading late eighteenth-century treaties and the politics of the time was overwhelming. Crowd-sourcing research, sharing links with relevant articles, made an enormous difference. The forum began as public, became invitation only, but didn't require security clearance. No one realized until later what a mistake that was.

Forum discussions were opinionated and sometimes voluble. A small but vocal group wanted a closer relationship or annexation to the United States government, now only nine years old when the official treaty was signed. Opposition to Changleska lingered, fueled by racial prejudice and unease over the Natives' role in a nation perceived as excessively liberal and at odds with their values. Apart from a few, all within the Circle were citizens; most taking the oath as a solemn commitment to create a better world. Others mouthed the words to get healthcare and other benefits awarded to citizens. By now, everyone understood life couldn't return to the way it was, but some believed the fledgling United States of America was the answer. Mary staunchly defended their new constitution's right of dissent. Still, she couldn't imagine anyone actively betraying Changleska.

Mary had dismissed some of the dissenting forum chatter as harmless venting at first. But then a quiet intelligence report arrived. In the past two weeks, several regional distribution hubs experienced unusual delays. One vaccine shipment was temporarily rerouted without explanation. Another facility had a break-in, though nothing was stolen or damaged, only oddly rearranged. All of them were managed or staffed by people with links to Clyde Folsom's church compound. There was no proof of sabotage, just a pattern. And patterns, she had learned, were often the first signal of something deeper stirring.

=..=

Endeavor docked at the river port they were building in Oacoma, just outside Chamberlain. The new port was loud with construction noise, muddy, and chaotic. Passengers looked around with disappointment, expecting modern marvels but seeing only cranes, shipping containers, and a couple of trucks. Doubled as port officers, the Changleska Guard insisted on checking everyone's papers after debarkation; however, lacking adequate space, they forced everyone to stand in long lines in the cold. The dignitaries were offended to be treated the same as anyone. Those going on to Omímeya required an extra shuttle due to unexpectedly large amounts of luggage. This caused delays and frustrations because no one wanted to be separated from their luggage. It wasn't an auspicious start.

The freed slaves, many with children, stood huddled back in a group, looking frightened. The promised jobs, housing and settlement assistance seemed too good to be true. They were free, but also free to starve.

"Don't worry," one of the Guards said, his voice calm and reassuring, "someone will be here soon to escort you."

Not long after, a short Black man and a tall White woman approached. "We're from the Freedom Assistance League. Let's get you sorted and take you to your new home."

The relief was palpable. The former slaves had heard of this group; they raised funds and bought slaves in the south with valuable skills, like blacksmiths, carpenters, masons, or textile workers, providing them with freedom papers and explaining repayment would allow them to free more slaves. Some walked away without paying the debt, but most did. Those who promised repayment received jobs, housing, and transportation to Changleska. The program would also buy enslaved family members. A small percentage of their wages went back to the League. The news spread rapidly, but the League could only free those with needed skills. They were raising funds and hoped to free more in the future. The waiting list was already years long.

Some passengers looked in askance at the former slaves. News of the League spread, arousing resentment, particularly among the wealthy who profited from slavery.

Once everyone was sorted, those staying at Omímeya got on the shuttles. The smooth roads, warm comfortable seats, and the speed of the thirty-mile journey astounded everyone. The drivers made a detour through Chamberlain to look at buildings, streetlights, and storefronts. Chamberlain's population, nearing 2,500 when Big Thunder arrived, was rapidly growing due to freed slaves and those seeking work. Larger than St. Louis, Chamberlain was a big city for this time.

Mary later learned with both amusement and consternation about the arrival of the group for the meeting. Forty-three VIPs, servants, and a couple of children, with heaps of luggage, all arrived in the lobby at once. The group gawked at the lobby in both awe and confusion. The designers of the Omímeya lobby had created an earthy, elegant space resembling a tipi's interior, featuring a seventy-foot-high ceiling and wood-like poles converging in a cone at the top. A huge skylight with a reversed teardrop shape let in light. The large stone circular fireplace in the center of the room was not lit. Comfortable seating was located around the room. Beautiful rugs covered the stone floors. Four wide circular staircases with polished wood led to the second floor. The nobles were not strangers to grand palaces, but this differed from anything anyone had ever seen. The first dignitaries stepped out onto the Omímeya drive as twilight colored the river sky. Lanterns cast warm light across the entrance, catching glints of glass and polished steel. For most, it was like stepping into a waking dream.

Doña Isabella de Villalobos, her skirts brushing the stone walkway, paused beneath the portico. Her gloved hand slid along the smooth glass doorframe, mouth ajar. "It is... a palace of light," she murmured in Spanish, to no one in particular.

Inside, the British envoy, Sir Edward Havilland, scowled as a motion sensor activated, opening a door in front of him. He halted, eyeing the panel beside it suspiciously. "What devilry is this?" he muttered.

His aide, a boy of perhaps thirteen, darted past him with a grin, clearly delighted. "Magic," he whispered.

Across the lobby, Baron Étienne de Villiers craned his neck upward at the high conical ceiling. "The architecture evokes both cathedral and tent."

Those who could read English saw the sign over the main desk: Welcome to Omímeya Casino and Resort. Below it, a large monitor displayed event schedules and meeting rooms. At the top was the bold heading: Changleska Coalition First Summit (Thókáhe Wičháho).

A child pointed at the screen. "Maman, the painting moves," he said, eyes wide.

Julien raised his voice to be heard over the crowd. "Pardon me. May I have your attention, please?"

Many of the group looked at him without comprehension, as they didn't speak English. The military interpreters had yet to arrive. Once Julien realized this, he motioned for Manuel Torez, the shuttle driver who translated for him in Spanish.

"Welcome to Omímeya Casino and Resort. My name is Julien Bradley. I am the Guest Services Manager. This is Phil Gallo, the Casino Manager, motioning to the well-dressed man at his side, and Rose Chasing Hawk, the General Manager of the whole resort."

Phil gave a slight bow, Rose a little bob. She wore a longer skirt than usual, with a blazer jacket, and native jewelry.

Manuel translated the introduction into Spanish. He could hear someone in the crowd translating it to French.

"Please, everyone, including servants, line up and check in here, pointing to the front desk."

There was a bit of a gasp at this, twitters and giggles. A few looked offended. It was obvious something was wrong. Manuel spoke modern Mexican Spanish, different from the formal Castilian of the late 1700s, but he assumed the meaning would be clear despite his accent.

A well-dressed woman in her thirties approached. In perfect but accented English said, "Perhaps I could be of assistance. I am Madame Henriette Dupont. I speak French and Spanish. It looks like you need some translation help."

"Yes, please, there's obviously a problem, but not sure what."

Madame Dupont looked more amused than embarrassed. "The words 'check in' sounded like another term, a double entendre, for sticking something in, understand?"

The Omímeya staff looked mortified. They realized Manuel had just asked everyone to line up and fuck the hotel, please.

=..=

Two days later, when Mary entered the room where the intelligence briefing was being held, everyone in the room stood up respectfully. She wondered if she'd ever get used to it. Phil Gallo now headed the second largest department in the new government, called First Shield Command, or FSC. One agency combining CIA, NSA, FBI, Cyber Defense and Homeland Security. He argued persuasively that intelligence could prevent wars and was necessary to win them. The success of George Washington's army against the more powerful British forces was in part because of the crucial intelligence gathered by his network of spies. All expeditions, both underway and in the planning stages, had military personnel with intelligence training. His cyber force teams protected their new nation's most valuable assets, information in their computers that could unlock the future.

Twenty-five people attended the meeting, including half a dozen FSC officers, Rose, Omímeya staff, military personnel and a few others. Mary wondered why Changleska's attorney, Elliot Gray Owl, was there. Martin and Anna May Worthington's presence surprised her. Martin was an older insurance executive displaced with his wife during Big Thunder. Mary was pleased to see they had the security clearance to attend. Martin was active in the Foreign Affairs Forum, making valuable contributions. While Anna

May presented herself as an airhead socialite only interested in fashion and culture, Mary knew she was smart and ambitious.

Phil began the meeting by saying, "We sent everyone the full dossiers to your secured devices, but before we begin our briefing, we've experienced our first major security breach, one that's potentially treasonous."

Uncomfortable murmurs filled the air. Phil gestured to a young woman in a housekeeping uniform to join him at the front of the room.

"This is Sofia Piaz; she's a FSC officer, because we can't have her coming into the resort in her actual uniform, she's wearing her 'work uniform'," Phil said, making air quote marks.

He looked fondly at her. "Sofia is one of our superstars. She noticed something fishy, investigated further, and uncovered the breach. I'll let her tell you."

The small woman, maybe nineteen or twenty years old, began her formal report confidently with a slight accent. "I'm assigned to the Spanish contingent, cleaning their rooms, and the Walleye Room after meals. They have little awareness of operational security." She said with disdain. "They may not know I speak Spanish or ignore servants routinely."

Phil added, "Her observations are in the dossiers you received."

Sofia continued, "I finished the lunch cleanup. While walking back, I noticed John Montgomery from our watch list entering the room of an American envoy with a small box." She gestured about the size of a small book. "When he left not long after, he didn't have it with him."

Martin interrupted, "Sorry, I am new to this. Explain the watch list and who you spotted."

Phil answered, "The domestic watch list are those who pose a threat, usually from their publicly stated opinions opposing Changleska or their association with those who do. Montgomery is an active member of Clyde Folsom's church and lives on his compound."

People in the room nodded. Their views on privacy and civil rights had changed when faced with existential threats. Folsom was an ultraconservative state senator caught inside the Circle while visiting a relative. He tried to take over as governor when they first arrived, using his standing as the highest elected official in South Dakota. When that tactic didn t work, he ran for the Executive Council and had a humiliating defeat. He rebranded himself as a religious leader. His popular radio show and growing church brought him many supporters and substantial funds. He often suggested that Changleska give the new United States its technology and let them run the government. Folsom clearly opposed Changleska, and all it represented, while never publicly saying anything actionable.

Mary felt chastened. She was familiar with John Montgomery's political philosophy from his posts on the Foreign Affairs forum, but had never taken it as a serious threat.

Sofia began again. "Charles Cotesworth Pinckney is a former Brigadier General from the Revolutionary War and a wealthy planter and slaveholder. Although sent as a diplomat, he strongly opposes us. Seeing that mystery box sent up some red flags. After consulting Mr. Gallo, when he was away from his room, I went in and searched. He hadn't hidden it well. The box contained a phone and a small solar charger."

There was a gasp around the room. The solar charger was worth a fortune. Phones, computers, and advanced technology were illegal to sell to noncitizens. People sold tech illegally, but if caught, they received a heavy fine and probation for a first offense; a second offense resulted in a loss of citizenship and exile. The new justice system had those convicted wear bright yellow vests with words like 'Thief' or 'Wife Beater' or 'Tech Betrayer' on them in public as part of their probation. The fear of public humiliation was a huge deterrent.

Sofia continued with a smile, "I was told to leave the phone in place, but I heard it 'got' a virus."

Phil said, "We swapped it for an identical phone loaded with spyware. We'll now know who they're talking to and where they go if there is Wi-Fi. The new phone has limited functions, and it'll look like the video and data on it got corrupted. It'll take time to analyze the data Montgomery sold them. We'll continue to watch the entire group and gather more information and who they are communicating with."

Elliot Gray Owl interjected. "The phone will be evidence in Montgomery's eventual criminal trial. Depending on the data, it may be an illegal tech sale, or treason."

Mary asked, "What are we doing to prevent more incidents?"

Billy Fast Dog, as resort Security Chief answered. "We don't have video surveillance in the rooms, only in the halls and common areas. After this, we assigned someone to review all the footage, past and present."

Mary thought, *I bet they'll bug the rooms after this, but I don't need to know.*

Phil looked up from his notes. "Have you seen the latest transcripts from Folsom's radio programs?"

Elliot Gray Owl, flipping through his own notes. "He's calling the treaty a betrayal. Says we're trading sovereignty for survival."

Phil noted, "And some people are starting to echo him. Not in public meetings yet, but it's showing up in the forums and the churches."

Mary tapped her pen once on the table. "I've watched movements like his grow before. At first it's all talk. Then it spreads to people who used to believe in the vision. And suddenly you're defending something that shouldn't need defending. This treaty has to be more than ink. If we lose the people, we lose the foundation we're trying to build."

After Phil announced the start of the regular briefing, names and photos appeared on the overhead screen. A woman FSC officer started the presentation on the twelve primary subjects. They compiled the extensive dossiers on each from available historical records, reports from New Orleans or *Endeavor* on the journey here. She noted they had information on staff and servants, listing their names, duties, and their daily routines, but didn't include it in this briefing. One maxim in intelligence is there is never too much to learn about someone; you never know what information might prove useful.

=..=

The Spanish sent three priests. *At least they were Jesuits, not Franciscans,* thought Mary. Jesuits, known for their intellectual rigor, were educators and often scientists of the day, whereas Franciscans had a history of inflexible and sometimes fanatic missionary work. Mary felt the Jesuits might bring a more thoughtful and measured approach, hopefully avoiding the harsher tactics that had traumatized Indigenous people in the past. Franciscans were leaders in the Spanish inquisition. Although the inquisition had changed, heresy remained a significant worry, since the Catholic Church had enormous wealth and political power. Mary genuinely feared Changleska would be branded heretics.

Although Mary was Lakota from the Lower Brule Tribe, she had been raised Catholic. She was devout but not ignorant of the historical harm the Catholic Church had done to Indigenous people. As had happened to almost as Natives, authorities had forced many generations of Mary's family into boarding schools, cutting their hair, punishing them for their language and culture, and frequently abusing them physically and sexually. Mary had engaged in long discussions with her parish priest, Father Murphy, who believed God sent them to this time to prevent the abuses of the church. He tirelessly penned letters to every priest and church authority, meticulously detailing the benefits of a different approach, learned only with hindsight. He was hopeful Rome would send a papal envoy, but it took time. Mary hadn t talked to Father Murphy since the priests arrived, but knew they were staying at St. Agnes with him.

As an active conference center, Omímeya was well-prepared. On arrival, participants received tote bags filled with pens, notepads, and penlights, branded by different future companies. Packed with printed materials, including a recent edition of the weekly newspaper with the stock exchange listings and classified ads, including ones for companies looking for investors. There were also menus, a spa rate sheet, and brochures from companies wanting to sell their products. There was a movie guide for the Omímeya theater they created from the old sports bar, listing plots and showtimes. The carefully curated films included *Dances with Wolves*, *Twelve Years a Slave*, *Even the Rain*, *The Mission*, and several powerful environmental documentaries. The printed program covered meeting topics, times, and rooms. There were sessions on everything from medicine to the stock market. The names and titles of all participants were listed alphabetically. This was completely unlike diplomatic meetings of their day.

Mary was excited about the two events opened to the public over the weekend, designed to impress the visitors. Saturday was the Trade and Technology Fair. Vendors would demonstrate their products or prototypes. Students from the area high schools showcased their science fair projects on how to reproduce twenty-first century technology with eighteenth-century resources. The kids proposed innovative solutions that even adults hadn't come up with. One student team had built what they called a "living battery" a shallow planter box layered with moss, wetland plants, and electrodes. It used two systems at once: electricity harvested from photosynthesis in the moss and from bacteria in the root zone of the cattails. They ran a wire from the planter to a small LED light and a slow-ticking clock, proving that the layered soil could generate a constant trickle of power.

"This could work in remote outposts," one student explained. "We're still testing how long it lasts, but we think the plants will keep feeding it as long as they're healthy."

Another created natural refrigeration using underground storage and evaporative cooling. One team even designed a simple battery-powered radio using scavenged copper wire, charcoal, and vinegar. They would announce the winners at a special ceremony that evening. Sunday was the

Changleska Guard's Field Day, the military exercise and demonstration which was turning into a big event with people from all over the Circle taking part.

Mary got a report from Rose about the conversation with the emissaries after their arrival.

"These chambers," remarked Don Sebastián de Alarcón, "are beyond anything I have encountered in the finest palaces of Madrid. The furnishings, the warmth. It is most agreeable." He gestured toward the welcome gift basket with a faint smile. "And such attentions. It speaks well of our hosts."

Others murmured their assent, though some voices carried a note of discontent. Sir Edward Havilland, the British envoy, spoke up. "It is curious, however, none of the Council saw fit to greet us upon our arrival. In my experience, such matters of protocol are not lightly set aside."

The French diplomat Claude-François de Malet nodded. "Indeed, to have us wait three days before the meeting commences is most irregular."

Rose was practiced with privileged guests. "I assure you; the Council values your time. We're waiting for more Indigenous leaders to arrive."

If fact, they'd been here for weeks. The delay was intentional to give time for backdoor discussions and wrangling. They also staged the introduction to the Council as a formal event.

She continued, "While you wait, you'll find the tours enlightening. There are advances in both tools and methods to build them. For example, McCormick Reapers and plows improve farm productivity. Sorry, there can be no farm tours this time of year, but we can show you the silos and how much farms can produce with our methods. We also have a tour of the hospital planned. We are building only a small fraction of what our old world offered, but Omímeya has many plans they can sell for you to take home and manufacture yourself."

Pinckney, the American envoy, grumbled, "I am confused by Omímeya and Changleska, not sure where one begins, and one ends."

Rose explained, "Your confusion is understandable. Omímeya Casino and Resort was here first, the name is Lakota for circle, the shape. Because we are in the circle like loop of the Mínšóše River, the Missouri, in English. Omímeya is a separate business, a corporation. Following our arrival, the people living here created Changleska Coalition, the country. Changleska is the Lakota word for hoop, symbolizing unity. The government, Changleska, has different finances than Omímeya. For example, the government paid most of your expenses for this summit to Omímeya. But they are a government and will not pay your bar bill. Omímeya owns much of what we call information technology, the plans for many of our inventions. That is why we can offer them for sale. We are a business, after all."

=..=

The official opening of the First Summit marked the culmination of months of planning. Mary reflected on how much had changed in the past six months, like survival, their unity, and their vision for the future. Mary stood in front of the mirror, carefully examining her appearance. She envied the Executive Councilors who'd wear business suits they already owned, with their sash of office, while her outfit took months to make. Being a Native woman and a head of state, she needed to make a statement. Her usual look, a grandmother in pantsuits, wouldn't cut it. At least she had lost weight over the winter. No more fast food worked wonders.

The design of her dress, a long mahogany velvet ribbon skirt, matching sleeves, and a white deerskin bodice with elaborate beadwork, took a lot of effort and incorporated a place for her sash of office. She wore a cap, adorned with beads, fringe, and a single eagle feather given by the elders, over her modern, easy-care haircut. Rose gave her a beautiful set of matching amber, amethyst, and turquoise earrings, bracelet, and necklace from the Omímeya gift shop, worth thousands. She'd face smart opponents experienced in diplomacy and negotiation, ruthless in trying to gain the most advantage. Like a chess player, she needed every edge to both impress them and throw them off balance.

They scheduled the first meeting in the newly remodeled Council Chamber. Mary had been uncertain about Rose's proposal for converting the previously boring conference rooms. It seemed extravagant and a waste of resources. After the last few months of studying the late eighteenth century, Mary realized she was wrong. This wasn't just a remodel. It was a declaration of power and wealth. The new Council Chambers turned out beautifully, even majestically. The people of this time knew the Lakota Sioux nation as powerful warriors, but saw them as poor, always asking for rifles and trade goods. They needed to challenge those assumptions. It's always best to negotiate from a place of strength.

Mary thought of her granddaughters and their friends. What kind of world would they inherit if this treaty failed? Would they grow up with their lands contested, their sovereignty reduced to negotiation backed by threats? Or could they know what it meant to live as a free people, building something new? That was the future she was fighting for. It gave her resolve, and maybe, without her realizing it, a touch of impatience.

The envoys waited impatiently in the hallway until everyone arrived; the door swung open, and twelve VIPs, with aides trailing behind, stepped into the Executive Council Chambers. A hush fell as they looked around in stunned silence. Exquisite art filled the room. A huge monitor took up the entire back wall of the room, currently displaying a realistic map of North America, with the Changleska boundaries, overlapping New Spain, in one color, the American colonies and various tribal territories marked. The map was extraordinary at this scale. It combined Google Earth and historical maps to create a genuine work of art.

Don Sebastián de Alarcón's eyes widened as he took in the map and room, "Incredible," he murmured, a mixture of awe and unease flickering across his face.

Under the monitor, a beautiful wood semicircular table on a raised dais drew all eyes. The seven Councilors, seated behind their name plates, stood as the visitors entered. In the center front of the dais was a small, circular wood table with a carved cross that could also be a four directions symbol. On the top rested a čhaŋnúŋpa, the sacred pipe, and other medicine items, and a beautiful small statue of the Virgin Mary. An abalone shell with burning sage and sweetgrass filled the air with fragrant smoke. Tribal leaders who had joined the Changleska Coalition sat in places of honor at the front and sides of the room, in full regalia, some in chairs, and others seated on buffalo robes on the floor.

The long table facing the Council was where Committee members usually sat to present proposals for voting. Today it was prepared for the twelve emissaries with printed name tags, and pitchers of iced tea and a set of blue-tooth headphones, which staff demonstrated how to use. Translators at the media booth in the back of the room tested the headphones to ensure everyone could hear the proceedings in their preferred language. Surprised but not shocked, they were quickly becoming familiar with technology. Some had even used headphones before, listening to music. Yet it continued to amaze them. The audience was sitting behind in standard conference chairs. The room was at capacity, the 400 invitations highly sought after, a chance to witness history in the making. Only about a dozen were from the visitors' staff. Other than the few tribes, they were Omímeya and Council staff, county officials, military, Committee members and prominent businesspeople.

After drumming and singing from Native teens, a small group of children entered and sweetly sang a hymn.

The priest from Cuba, Father Spinosa, stepped behind the altar and addressed the gathering in Spanish with a measured tone. "Our hosts requested an opening prayer representing the beliefs of all participants; besides myself, a local Protestant pastor and a tribal elder will offer blessings."

Father Spinosa prayed, "Almighty Father in Heaven, we beseech Thee to grant us Thy divine guidance as we face these troubling times that have shaken the foundations of all we know. Endow us with patience to listen before acting and allow us to align our actions with Thy holy will. May we find solace in the infinite mercy of Thy Son, our Lord Jesus Christ, and marvel at the boundless wonder of Thy creation. Guide us to understand how to move forward in the light of everything you have shown."

The Lakota elder and the Protestant pastor offered equally brief prayers. Everyone was directed to be seated.

Looking magnificent, her hands resting lightly on the table before her, exuding a calm authority, Mary said, "Hello, my name is Mary Landrau. I am the Chair or leader of the Changleska Coalition's Executive Council."

The visitor's expressions shifted from curiosity to focused attention, their postures subtly straightening as they absorbed her words.

"We're glad to welcome you to the Thokahe Wichaho or First Summit, which lays the groundwork for future collaborations. We hope to create a peaceful and prosperous alliance with each of you. My portfolio is education, the key to society's advancement. Emphasizing education is the core of our belief in sharing knowledge. You will find us to be an open and generous people who want to improve the world. We invite your young people to study with us; upon completion of their studies, they will return home possessing our most valuable gift, knowledge."

The diplomats looked surprised. In this time, nations jealously guarded valuable knowledge. They were suspicious; the offer was too good to be true. The tension in the air was palpable, each delegate weighing the implications of such an unprecedented gesture.

With brief descriptions of their portfolios or areas of expertise, the six other Councilors introduced themselves. The tribal leaders described where they lived, the number of warriors and horses they had. The Lower Brule and Crow Creek tribal leaders were pleased to find their previous small tribes were large compared to others in this time. Both tribes retained their sovereignty, in fact they strengthened it, since the Circle took place on their land. Their tribes were now both rich and powerful.

At the long table, beginning with Don de Alarcón the highest rank, the rest following precedence, the envoys and key businesspeople introduced themselves with great formality and length. The delay was effective. The tours and demonstrations humbled the visitors, and all enjoyed the comforts of the twenty-first century. Hot showers, flush toilets, and movies were a special hit.

Both parties exchanged gifts. It took all morning, but everyone seemed pleased, and the seeds of diplomacy were sown. The emissaries presented highly valued items, showing clear forethought, though they reserved trade goods like blankets, rifles, knives, and metal tools for the Indigenous. Spanish Envoys brought a large ornate silver bejeweled cross, beautifully embroidered silk and fine wool mantillas, Spanish wine, olive oil, and coffee. The French sent perfumes, glass beads, small paintings, wine, champagne, and aged brandies in ornate glass bottles. The British sent high-quality woolens and linens, Chinese tea and fine porcelain tea sets. They also sent law books, appreciated by the Law Committee. The Americans sent tobacco, rice, indigo, many constitutional and other legal documents, fine whiskey and rum.

The envoys received many books, including medical and math texts, color photo prints, various minor items sure to thrill anyone from this era, from plastic toys to spinning light wands, or pencils with emoji-shaped toppers, items no one valued before, irreplaceable today, sure to grow in value. The gift of solar calculators with instructions had the potential to significantly advance mathematics in their countries. Most were impressed by very detailed maps of their home countries, both topographical and historical maps of cities and roads if available. These were backhanded presents as they showed the detailed reconnaissance Changleska had on them. The military leaders were at first delighted, then they paled once they realized the significance. Gifts for the envoys also included generous loads of furs, tanned buffalo, and other hides. The primary trade good of both the French fur traders and Indigenous was pelts and hides. The Changleska government had bought the surplus from the trading posts to keep the prices stable. They had warehouses full.

There was a short benediction given by another Spanish priest. They ended with directions to lunch and a reminder of the formal banquet scheduled for the evening, ending early enough to watch the movie for those not wanting to stay up late and drink. Over the next two weeks there would be presentations from each Councilor in their areas or expertise, private meetings with each of the powers for preliminary negotiations, more tours and on Sunday, the military exercise and demonstration.

Mary s shoulders relaxed as the dignitaries filed out of the room, their expressions a mix of approval and guarded fear. She allowed herself a deep breath, a small smile creeping onto her face as the tension eased. For the first time in days, she felt a flicker of hope this summit might truly succeed. Her anxieties about a disastrous cultural misunderstanding proved unfounded. There were good conversations going on, and over the next weeks, they hopefully would lay the foundation for recognition of their sovereignty and the tribes they represented, as well as valuable trade agreements for all sides.

Six months ago, they faced an unfathomable situation and reacted by forging ahead, working to create something better. What seemed impossible now looked barely possible. Mary gave a prayer of thanks and headed to lunch.

Chapter Three
Jackson

JACKSON THOUGHT ABOUT Rose. He knew he should focus on his tasks for the day, but his thoughts kept returning to her. He couldn't believe he could fall in love again so soon after losing what he had imagined was the love of his life. Denise had been left behind the Circle when Big Thunder transported him in 1791. It was the wrong place, wrong time. Life before was fading like a dream. Looking back, things seemed so simple. He had planned to propose to Denise, maybe have a kid or two. He'd been tired of his job as a Rapid City police officer; it seemed like all he did was wrangle alcoholics and the mentally ill, people who needed a social worker more than a cop. Jackson enjoyed teaching nonviolent intervention techniques to other police departments so much he considered a career change. Denise was supportive, which was another thing he loved about her. Rose was so different, yet so much like Denise. Both were competent, focused career women: Denise, an emergency room nurse, and Rose, now the general manager and CEO of Omímeya. Jackson and Rose shared something unusual: the overwhelming responsibility and burdens of their work.

Jackson went from being a cop, a former army sergeant who served in Iraq and Afghanistan, to Executive Councilor in the defense seat. That meant he was the commander-in-chief. General Gardner, the leader of all Changleska military forces, reported to him. Only Rose understood what it felt like to be thrust into such a powerful leadership position you didn't plan or train for. Jackson remembered their late-night conversations when they both confessed how overwhelmed they felt by the weight of their responsibilities.

Rose had smiled, though her eyes betrayed her exhaustion, and said, "Sometimes, I feel like I'm holding this whole place together with duct tape and prayer."

Jackson had laughed, replying, "Welcome to the club. At least we've got strong tape."

That shared moment of honesty solidified the trust and connection between them. Having someone with whom to share concerns and fears honestly deepened their connection. Changleska, their newborn country, was like their child, one they worried over, nurtured, and shared hopes for. It didn't hurt he was physically attracted to her; their strong sexual connection deepened the more time they spent together.

They longed for more time together, but the demands of their separate responsibilities kept pulling them in opposite directions. Jackson only spent the night at Rose s occasionally. One thorn in his otherwise blissful bed of Rose was her kids. Being a stepfather to teenagers was not in his life plan. Not that he did not like them. Even Luke was growing on him. Gift was a sweet girl, but Kimi made him uneasy. Mature beyond her thirteen years, she would gaze at him steadily like she understood him. He knew she had warned Rose about Big Thunder hours before it happened. He remembered her warning cry get down!" moments before the shooting started, when armed cartel gunmen started shooting people in the Big Bear Room a few weeks after Big Thunder. Her action saved her family s lives. He knew she felt horrible because she hadn't given others an earlier warning. Jackson wasn t good with spooky, strange things, especially a potential stepdaughter. Because of the kids, he spent little time at Rose s house. He lived in the hotel. Rose visited his room as often as they could get away with it. They were in the honeymoon phase of their relationship, after all.

His assistant, Charlotte Evans, interrupted his pleasant thoughts of Rose.

"Phone meeting with General Gardner in five minutes. Anything you need before then?"

"You uploaded the agenda?" She nodded, annoyed.

It was a stupid question; Charlotte was very efficient. Too efficient sometimes. He wasn't sure if he could do the job without her.

Because of fuel shortages, in-person meetings were rare, which Jackson appreciated. He was uncomfortable being saluted by a general. Jonathan Gardner had been the Colonel of the National Guard unit stationed in Chamberlain when Big Thunder happened. His willingness to support the new country of Changleska had been a near thing. If he had turned over his command, with an armory filled with modern military hardware, to George Washington and the new United States, Changleska might not have survived. Gardner later told Jackson that his argument against slavery helped persuade him. Also, he thought Clyde Folsom was an idiot.

The first item on the agenda was a discussion of the intelligence brief they received about John Montgomery selling a phone and charger to the American Envoy, Charles Cotesworth Pinckney. More than the phone, the information was the true prize. Although they had intercepted the data transfer, they knew the next time it might be successful. In addition, as a Foreign Affairs forum member, Montgomery knew valuable strategic information, including negotiating points, which could prove beneficial to the Americans. Like closing the barn door after the horses escaped, the FSC immediately limited that forum to those with security clearances.

Jackson exhaled. "How do we stop internal leaks?"

"Time-consuming surveillance. The FSC is monitoring everything, public forum posts, MilNet emails."

"Can we do that legally?"

"Public posts are fair game. Emails are property of MilNet."

"Are we capable of filtering all that data effectively? The First Shield Center is not the NSA. I know we didn't bring back AI."

"Gallo engaged the old lady brigade to sift through the data."

"Old lady brigade?"

"Not all women, not even sure if they're all old, but it's what Gallo calls it. He enlisted retirees to read all the posts in specific online forums. Provided with a list of what to look for, secessionist politics is one. He pays a small amount for each piece of information submitted, regardless of whether it pans out. Funny thing, he pays a dime, people getting reported are 'dimed out'."

On January 1, all currency values switched to reflect 1792 prices. Ten cents could buy a loaf of bread or a dozen eggs. Circulating coins and paper bills were still legal tender; the value adjusted. US coins were only recognized in Changleska as they were not pure metals; even pennies were no longer made from pure copper.

Looking over his notes, Jackson asked, "Still no word on that early expedition?"

"Just the usual whispers. Some Spanish soldiers reported trading with a White man who spoke French and German. Might be nothing, might be something."

"Keep a note on it," he said. "Three people don't just vanish in 1792 without someone noticing. Eventually something will turn up."

Gardner brought up a new issue. "Gallo says they're tracking a rise in coordinated disinformation. It's not coming from fake accounts since NewNet requires verified IDs, but some of Folsom's supporters are using subtle language to distort facts in public forums. The messages look like normal posts, but they repeat claims we're hiding executions or denying medicine to people who oppose the government."

Jackson leaned back in his chair. "They think it's organized?" "Not exactly cells, but it's too consistent to be coincidence. They're using coded phrasing, quoting scripture, and sharing unverifiable stories. Enough to stir up fear."

Jackson was quiet for a moment. "If fear takes root, truth won't matter. Not to the people whose confidence holds this place together."

He straightened in his chair, setting aside the thought for now. "What are we doing to address internal security, with the envoys all here?"

"I posted on MilNet we uncovered a breach, reminding people treason is a capital offense, selling tech constitutes treason, and we will charge anyone failing to report a security breach with conspiracy."

"That'll have to do for now. Let's move on to Sunday's exercise. What more do we need to do?"

They spent the next two hours reviewing the logistics of the planned military exercise, the largest they had ever done. Demonstrating military power without revealing military secrets was challenging. Jackson was advocating for a big show, maintaining that fear of powerful weapons was a deterrent that led to peace. Gardner wanted surprises he could pull out if it came to warfare. Jackson deferred to Gardner; he usually did. He rarely asserted his authority. Without experience, he picked his proverbial battles.

Before the meeting ended, Gardner asked, "Did you read the after-action reports from the New Orleans engagement?"

"Just glanced at it. You have a meeting this afternoon with one private for a full debriefing."

"Pretty intense; I have to admit, people are pretty excited about capturing a pirate ship; it looks like we are starting our navy early."

Pirate ship? Jackson thought, *I really should read the report.*

=..=

After the meeting, he needed to tackle the mountain of paperwork that had become his life. Not actual paper, it was in short supply. Everything was digital, which came with its own set of challenges. The dependence on computers raised concerns. Eventually, hardware would fail, and microchip technology was unattainable in the foreseeable future.

He dealt with a couple of priority items and had just started on the reports. Charlotte asked him if he was ready for the meeting with a Private Pedro Hernandez, who arrived with the envoys. He was surprised to find the meeting was in person, held in the Defense offices on the third floor of the north wing. Omímeya's designers had prioritized form over function. He would have to walk down four flights of stairs, cross the lobby, and walk up to the third floor. They no longer used the elevators for everyday use, wanting to preserve the irreplaceable parts. He didn't mind the exercise, but noticed that Charlotte was a bit winded. On the way, she filled him in on Hernandez. When not deployed, he lived with his wife on the family floor, two south of the hotel. He had been working in the kitchen at Buffalo Burger, one of the Omímeya restaurants; she worked in housekeeping. Both from Honduras, they had worker green cards and jumped at the chance to become Changleska citizens. He enlisted right away and was sent with the maiden voyage of the *Endeavor* for a six-month deployment to New Orleans.

When they arrived in the meeting room, everyone stood, and Hernandez saluted. Jackson motioned for everyone to be seated and saw someone from Media Services setting up the video camera. In addition, an FSC officer was there. He had met her several times. Andrea Richter was a nondescript woman, mid-forties perhaps, of mixed heritage, either Mexican or Native. Before Big Thunder, she worked in casino security, reviewing video footage for patterns to catch cheaters. Her new job looking for patterns was not too dissimilar. She was second in command at FSC; they must have thought this meeting important. He knew Gallo interviewed Hernandez when he arrived days ago and wondered about the reason for the second review.

Jackson started, "Private, please start from the beginning and tell me everything. Pretend I never read your report; don't try to put it in military terms; use your own words and impressions."

Andrea Richter got out her pen and notebook and looked approvingly at Jackson's words and tone.

Hernandez was nervous at first but warmed up as he began his story.

"We had some hiccups on the trip down. I don't know the details, but the engineers did a great job. Nothing blew up; we just had to stop and float while they fixed or changed something. I heard they worked out all the bugs, and the second trip went better."

"I heard the same thing. Go on," Jackson said.

"The first expedition was supposed to be three weeks ahead of us, smoothing the way, delivering letters, finding us a place to dock, finding grain buyers, and identifying land to buy or lease. But as you know, they disappeared."

"Did I read something about finding twenty-first century items?"

"Yes, in the warehouse."

"Yes, sir. I just heard about it, still on the injured list. Found during inventory; I believe it was sent back here, with all the letters and paperwork."

Jackson looked at Richter, who nodded. He'd have to ask later; he was curious.

"No, sorry for the interruption. Tell your story from the beginning."

"After we arrived, it was chaos. We sent the boats ahead as planned to meet with the first expedition. They weren't there, and the boats drew a lot of attention. They found us a spot on Algiers Point near what would become the French Quarter. It was rural but industrial with shipping, so we docked there. Not long after, we were met by Spanish soldiers wanting to board the vessel or arrest us. Not sure, but they were mean and pissed. Lieutenant Rodriguez and Mr. Dillon told them they'd be happy to meet with port officials to pay any fees and their commanding officer could tour the vessel, but they wouldn't be boarded."

"Mr. Dillon?"

"Kevin Dillon, he was assigned to negotiate with the Spanish officials, but he didn't speak Spanish. I interpreted for him often."

Charlotte added, "Dillon's a lawyer from Chamberlain, handling real estate and wills primarily. His house was outside the Circle; he was in town at the hardware store. His wife and three children were left behind. Omímeya hired him to manage their commercial interests in New Orleans."

"Oh, I never knew about him losing his kids. Anyway, when the senior Spanish officer arrived, Lieutenant Rodriguez saw them staring at the guns pointing at them and asked if they wanted a demonstration."

Jackson couldn't help interrupting again. "What were you armed with again?"

"Besides our M4s, we had a M240B machine gun. On top was a M119A3 Howitzer for long range and the M2 Browning .50 Caliber. That was my girl," he said fondly.

"After they found safe targets and didn't believe us about the M11's range, we shot off a few rounds. We didn't want to waste ammunition, but Lieutenant Rodriguez said it was better to waste ammunition than lives."

"Quite right."

"Scared the shit out of them. Sorry, sir, for the language," he said, glancing at the women.

Jackson was amused; eighteenth-century mores were creeping in, or maybe he was raised to not curse in front of women.

"That's fine, Private; continue."

"They were happy we had no plans to shoot them and wanted to pay our dock fees and custom duties. Mr. Dillon told them they could inspect the cargo, but putting value on the unusual items would be difficult. Not sure what he said, but he wangled an invitation to meet the governor the next day. After that, it went according to plan. They didn't have a suitable wharf, so the engineers set up a pontoon-style floating dock, which impressed the hell out of the locals." He looked sheepishly at the women.

"Later, when we bought the land, we built a really good wharf, the best on the river."

Jackson remembered the first reports: they'd purchased a 100-acre plantation with warehouses along the west side of the Mínšoše River. Although small, the wharf was well equipped with warehouses and other structures. The owner had recently died. The widow wanted to return to Spain and sold the whole thing, including furnishings, tools, and twenty-five slaves. They immediately freed them, which angered the neighboring plantation owners so much they had to start patrols. A few shots in the air with the automatic weapons did the trick. At least Jackson didn t hear of issues. Most of the slaves stayed and worked for slightly higher wages than other free people got. Improving their living conditions was something the whole crew got behind. The crew started a school for the children in which they all worked and ate together and told them all about Changleska. Most people were excited about gaining citizenship in two years, although they remained suspicious.

Hernandez continued, "Things were going well. After the clinic was set up, the doctors were super busy. They even had the medic they were training seeing patients. Some people were calling us devils. The lieutenant brought in a priest for a blessing, and we put a cross in the medic tent. That helped. The canopies we set up to sell goods looked like a flea market. People went crazy for the junk we sent. A few locals wanted to get in on the action and started selling things. There was even a food stall after the medics did a health inspection."

Andrea Richter had been quiet and taking notes furiously. She looked up and asked, "What were your duties at this time, Private?"

"Before *Endeavor* left and returned with the second crew, there were only sixteen of us. We had to do about everything. After the second crew arrived, I went back to gunner and patrol."

"Let's skip ahead to the incident where you were wounded, please."

"One of the doctors and a Guard were doing a house call in a bad neighborhood. But it's only bad and worse neighborhoods in New Orleans. Turns out the house call was fake, a lure so they could be robbed. Dr. Brown was stabbed but survived. Casey died from his wounds. The doctors were all pretty upset, and felt he could have been saved with more supplies."

"I'm very sorry for your loss. With a group that small, I'm sure you were close."

"Yes, I didn't know Casey too well. He'd only been there two weeks, but Doc Brown is great. He returned with me. I don't know if he will ever go back."

"How did you find out who did it?" Jackson asked.

"People told us. By this time, we were popular because the clinic only charged what patients could afford to pay. They were surprised to be treated with respect. You wouldn't believe how badly people of color are treated down there. Multiple people ratted out the scum who did it. It was a gang of thieves, smugglers, and pirates—super bad guys. The leader scoped us out for a while, planned to kidnap the doctor, but didn't expect Casey would shoot three of his guys."

"I know the next part is hard, but please go over it again, please."

"After the attack, both the lieutenant and Mr. Dillon said we needed to show nobody fu... messes with us. We got permission from the governor. They don't exactly have police there," he said somewhat defensively. "We took a couple of days to reconnoiter the warehouse the leader lived in and plan the mission."

"Did the governor sanction this in writing?" asked Richter.

"Don't know about in writing, Mr. Dillon would know, but the governor sent a few Spanish troops to observe."

"We went at 0400, with night vision; they didn't have a chance. The night guard got a musket shot off, the one that winged me." He pointed to his arm, still in a sling.

"What is the status of your wound, Private?" asked Charlotte.

"Musket balls are huge, about .70 caliber. The doctor said that if it had been an inch closer, I might have lost the arm. They fixed me up good, but I needed an x-ray, possibly more surgery, so they sent me home. It turned out to be only a slight fracture. It has been three weeks now; I get out of this in a week." Pointing to his sling.

Jackson smiled at him, saying, "You'll get your purple heart at the ceremony Sunday at Field Day. Specialist Casey will get a posthumous Silver Star."

"My wife gets to pin on my medal; she is looking forward to it."

Jackson asked Charlotte, "Final count for the action?"

"Four casualties on our end, none with major injuries. Eighteen enemy KIA, twelve from the ship."

"Prisoners?"

"Not in the warehouse. Five on the ship."

Jackson looked at Hernandez, who squirmed a bit.

"Private, did you have orders to take prisoners?"

"If it could be done safely without endangering the team."

"It was crazy, sir. The first shot woke everyone. They were yelling, jumping up, some had knives. We did what we could."

Collateral damage?"

Yes, sir, four of the KIA were Black, probably slaves, two women. We didn t know; we couldn t see what color they were with night vision." He looked like he was going to cry.

"I killed the one who shot me. He was Black, but he was armed; they don't give slaves guns, do they, sir?" He looked at Jackson pleadingly.

Jackson was pissed. He clenched his jaw, forcing himself to inhale slowly to calm himself. "Look," he said, exhaling, "sometimes they do. But the man was shooting at you. You defended yourself." He met Hernandez's wary eyes. "You're not in trouble. We're not here to assign blame. We're here to figure out how to stop this from happening again. What happened on the ship?"

"The ship wasn't in our plans. It must have arrived that night. When the shots were heard from the warehouse, men ran out of the ship, shooting. The perimeter guard shot one and radioed. By the time we got outside, they were firing at us from above on the ship. Once we killed them, we boarded the ship. I heard it was bad. We were lucky that our guys were only wounded. I didn't board the ship because I lost a lot of blood. The medic patched me up, but it hurt like a motherfucker." This time the cursing didn't bother him.

I should have read the whole report before this meeting, Jackson thought. He was glad to see Richter take over.

"We have reports from the ship's action," looking at her tablet. "It says here after shooting the twelve on the ship, five surrendered. The first mate, a sailor, and three boys aged eleven, thirteen, and fifteen."

"Do you know what happened to them?" she asked.

"The first mate and sailor were handed over to the Spanish. They'll probably hang. The lieutenant told the Spanish we'd take custody of the boys, as they were minors. They wanted to hang the fifteen-year-old."

"Were they slaves?" asked Jackson.

"No, sir, mixed blood, from the Caribbean, cabin boys; the older one was the ship carpenter's apprentice."

"Where are they now?"

"Taken to Oca Landing, still there when I left. They all wanted to go back to the ship."

Jackson knew they named the riverside property they bought, Oca Landing. Pronounced okay, there was a little joke that further upriver they would find a place better than just okay. Oca was the Houma, the local Indigenous tribe's word for river. Upon arrival, they contacted the local tribes. The Houma were small and isolated, but happy for contact and trade.

"What happened to the ship and the warehouse?"

"Legitimate prize of war, approved by the Spanish. Mr. Dillon said since the warehouse was on the east side of the river we didn't want it. We turned it over to the Spanish with a lot of the contents."

"No wonder why they approved it."

"What do you know about the ship?"

"Nothing other than it is a very old, very dirty, smelly pirate ship."

Richter, reading from her tablet the report Jackson hadn't read yet, added, "It is a sixty-foot sloop, eighteen-foot beam, carried twenty to thirty tons of cargo, eighty-ton displacement, eight cannons, crew complement, twenty to thirty."

Knowing nothing of ships, he looked at her with a quizzical expression, his brow furrowed as if trying to piece together what the numbers and descriptions meant.

"It is small enough to navigate the Missouri River. With a good pilot and our depth finders, it could go to St. Louis; that is a big cargo load for this time. Not so good for ocean crossings, but suitable for seasonal Caribbean runs."

"What kind of shape is it in?" asked Jackson.

"Not sure; they moved it to Oca Landing. They asked French naval engineers to inspect it. The carpenter's apprentice was very helpful," answered Hernandez.

Jackson knew everyone would consider this a success, wiping out smugglers, and pirates, sending the message that no one fucks with Changleska Guard, and gaining a grand prize to boot. But four innocent people died, including two women, probably young. This troubled him, and he wondered if Gardner and the other leaders would feel the same. He needed to change the subject.

"What do you think of Lieutenant Rodriguez? You can be honest. I know he is your superior officer, but if there are issues, we may be able to help."

"The lieutenant is great. He really cared about the crew. He got into it with Mr. Dillon a bit."

"Explain."

"Little things mostly. The LT insisted everyone eat the same food; former slaves, hired workers, and crew all ate from the mess. He ate with us. Mr. Dillon wanted to eat fancy meals at the big house, and the LT said he'd have to pay a cook from his own wages."

"Did he?"

"Yes, the former cook at the house had left with the family. He went into town, bought a slave who could cook with his own money, freed her, and paid her the same wages as everyone. And paid for better food himself. He was sure to tell everyone. Mr. Dillon acted like he was better than us. He was always telling us he wasn't military; he worked for Omímeya."

Jackson wondered how much Omímeya paid him. With his education and background, he'd be upper management.

"He was generous, though; after everything had been inventoried, he set out tables full of goods from the raid and let the guys select what they wanted. Gave me and the other wounded guys beautiful Spanish swords, and I picked a gold and ruby necklace for my wife. Mr. Dillon said prizes of war were customary, and sometimes they were the only pay soldiers got."

"Correct, Private; that's why modern armies don't allow it. Looting is still theft."

Hernandez looked alarmed. He had probably already given his wife the necklace.

"Not your fault, Private. We must create our own policies and rules. None are in place now. We'll be making changes in keeping with our own values. We don't want to become like them, do we?"

"No, sir."

"Mr. Dillon's girlfriend got some nice jewelry, too."

"His girlfriend?" Jackson asked, both Richter and Charlotte scrolling their tablets, obviously news to them too.

"Maria used to be a lady's maid, but he didn't need one. Said she didn't want to work the fields or a brothel, her other choices. Mr. Dillon found her a job in laundry."

"How old is she?" Jackson asked tightly.

"Not sure, legal age, maybe early twenties."

Jackson turned to Charlotte. "Doesn't the military have rules about this?"

"Wouldn't matter. Dillon is a civilian. They are legal consenting adults," she answered.

"There is a power differential," Jackson replied, still visibly upset.

"Ahh, sir, him and the LT argued about this, so Mr. Dillon sent out a memo. He was always sending memos."

"That said?"

"Mr. Dillon said as an employee of Omímeya, he and Maria would send the human services form that dating employees had to fill out with the next run. He also hired an older woman, a former slave, as a personnel manager, and said anyone dating a former slave or employee had to check with her to make sure there was no coercion. Lieutenant Rodriguez gave us a lecture about how women from this time view us as rich saviors, and being unequal didn't make healthy relationships. I'm just glad I am married."

"Was dating locals a problem?" asked Richter.

"No women were sent the first two runs, and the medics scared everyone away from the brothels with really gross pictures. Even with a condom, no one wanted to take a chance. So, they made a rule that no one could buy a slave and make her a girlfriend or wife."

"At least there is that," said Jackson, disgustedly.

"Interracial relationships were frowned on, but not illegal in the Spanish colonies," Richter informed him.

Richter continued to ask Hernandez questions to help clarify the reports, checking for inconsistencies from different viewpoints of those who sent the reports. Jackson was beginning to think this was more of an interrogation than an interview. His relief was palpable when it was over. He was more upset than he thought.

He texted Rose to see if she was free for dinner. They'd been too busy recently for their usual weeknight dinners at the cafeteria at the Red Oak, often the highlight of his day.

She couldn't get away for dinner but said she would come to his room later. It was for the best. Jackson was still angry about the whole situation in New Orleans and didn't want to take it out on her.

He wondered what she knew about Kevin Dillon. He was Omímeya's representative. Jackson realized he'd need to talk to Mary and the Council. They would need to send the Changleska ambassador, or was that after Spain officially recognized them? There was much he didn't know, with so much at stake.

After he calmed down a bit, his mood improved when he realized, it being late, Rose would stay for a *visit*.

Chapter Four
Jamal

JAMAL FELT BOTH anticipation and anxiety as he looked at their ship to Boston. Relieved the day was finally here, seeing their ship, the *Anna Marie*, a typical merchant brig of the era, did little to assure him they'd arrive in one piece. It was a little over 100 feet long, 26 feet wide, with two square-rigged masts and a wooden hull reinforced with iron bands around the bow. The decks held tarp-covered crates and a couple of small boats. There were four small cannons and two swivel guns mounted near the helm and bow. Very few ships braved the gulf storms in winter to go to Boston. They'd waited three months in New Orleans for this one. They had little choice.

"Oh my god, this is the ship we're taking? It looks decrepit," Jamal exclaimed when they first approached.

Dan Clemons, the corporal in charge of their crew of four, said, "I'm assured it is seaworthy, and more importantly, the captain and crew are experienced."

"Don't worry, people travel on these types of ships all the time," said Nels in a vain attempt to comfort Jamal.

Jamal was grateful his romantic partner Nels would be his mission partner, despite the risk. They had to be very careful. Homosexuality during this time was a hanging offense. Initially, the plan had been for Nels to stay in New Orleans. He was training as a medic and was needed in the clinic. They intended to match Jamal with another member of his Guard unit, but an injury from using unfamiliar farm equipment a few days prior to their departure left no other options available.

He'd met Nels in Boulder, where they were both college students. Jamal studying engineering, Nels, forestry. Jamal was originally from Chicago. Knowing he'd never see Boulder or Chicago again didn't bother him as it once did. They were visiting South Dakota, attending a permaculture conference when Big Thunder brought them to this time. Since they arrived, Jamal's life became unrecognizable. He went from being a privileged student who had never known hardship to joining the Changleska Guard, working to end slavery and now posing as a servant. Unlike in New Orleans, where laws allowed free people of color, he had to pose as a servant to stay safe. Many Whites would not accept a Black man traveling openly on equal footing.

Pretending to be a servant, even for safety, felt like betraying his family s legacy of dignity and pride. A cold knot formed in his stomach. Was survival worth sacrificing pieces of himself? Although he had to admit, posing as a valet was a safe cover for Jamal. Higher-level servants received better treatment. The valet role amused Jamal. Before they met, Nels didn t pay attention to his clothes, owning only jeans and T-shirts, many of which were torn or stained. Jamal often bought him new clothes and hid his old stuff. Jamal, raised to dress impeccably, wore designer labels and expensive shoes. Making sure Nels looked the part of the adventuring son of a wealthy landowner came naturally.

Finally, their mission to combat the horrible institution of slavery was beginning. Besides supporting the growing abolitionist movements in Boston, they would meet with Eli Whitney. Eli was twenty-six years old, had just graduated from Yale, and was currently living back home in Westborough, Massachusetts. He would soon move to Georgia for a job as a tutor on a plantation, where he would invent the cotton gin., This invention caused cotton to become a valuable cash crop using slave labor. Prior to this, the use of slave labor had been declining for economic reasons; the cotton gin changed that. Jamal planned to offer him a better-paying job at Changleska. Not only would he get better pay, but Changleska would use his future work designing interchangeable parts at the new firearms factory they were building. Jamal hoped to wow him with modern engineering and manufacturing techniques.

This expedition marked the first trip to the East Coast for those brought by Big Thunder to this time. Jamal and Nels were going to Boston. They'd combine their visit to Eli Whitney with other crucial mission objectives. They needed to meet with shipyard owners, printers, watchmakers, fine artisans, abolitionists, church leaders, and newspapers. The other team, Corporal Dan Clemons and Private Brad Walters, were going to Philadelphia to get messages to George Washington, Thomas Jefferson, and members of Congress. In addition, they'd have the same or similar tasks as Jamal and Nels. They hoped to connect with Quakers who were leaders in the abolitionist movement in Philadelphia..

Jamal and Nels felt at home in New Orleans, despite having been there for just three months. Home is about people; both Jamal and Nels developed strong friendships with others in their Guard unit. A special camaraderie existed between those from the twenty-first century sharing the challenges of eighteenth-century life. Hard work with the same goals united them. Building Oca Landing, freeing the slaves that came with the original plantation, setting up the clinic, all created bonds unlike anything they had experienced before. Both were required to serve in the Changleska Guard for two years and were surprised to enjoy it. Nels, having a religious exemption from carrying a weapon, concentrated on becoming a medic. Jamal s engineering background kept him busy, although he finally got qualified to carry a weapon. Being in the engineering unit meant he could avoid most of the usual military duties such as patrol. Jamal thought he d hate being in the military, but he found comfort in order and discipline. The Guard in New Orleans was small, but increasing all the time.

Arriving in New Orleans on the steam barge *Endeavor* in December 1791 was thrilling. As they approached New Orleans, along the river, curious throngs of people watched them float down faster than any craft they had ever seen. With the accompanying colorful bass boats, the barge with its strange configuration of steel shipping containers, a paddle wheel in the back and pickup truck strapped down in the front, elicited excitement and wonder. People craned their necks, pointing and chattering. By the time they pulled up to the riverbank, crowds had formed. It wasn't until the Spanish soldiers arrived they felt any hostility.

After they docked, Jamal's stomach clenched. On the wharf, a group of enslaved men hauled cargo under the sun, backs slick with sweat. A White overseer stood by, tapping a cane against his leg. No whips, no shouting, just quiet, orderly suffering.

Jamal looked away, his fists curling at his sides. He'd read about this in history books, seen the sanitized versions in old paintings. But the sheer normalcy of it—how no one so much as blinked—was what sickened him most. He swallowed hard, forcing himself to breathe. *This is why I'm here. This is what we must stop.*

Despite this, Jamal found New Orleans exciting. Vibrant people of all races spoke many languages with no one rushing anywhere. While the smells of humanity were present, the air also smelled of molasses and indigo cooking vats, smoke from fires, and cookshops serving the river traffic. The slavery was as horrible as he imagined, but he didn t expect so many free people of color. Many owned businesses, and some were wealthy. Many women had elaborate high hairdos he found fascinating.

After they bought the land that became Oca Landing, curious onlookers stopped by, but only a few showed open hostility. The Medical Corps setting up the clinic first thing helped. They brought four physicians, two of which would leave soon on the Cherokee expedition. At this time, people believed foul humors, or bad air caused disease. The doctors had their hands full, both teaching and working. They charged the usual fees for the times, but took barter, including labor, and didn't turn people away. After some deliberation, they decided a free clinic would require too many resources and might alienate the current medical practitioners they were trying to reach.

They kept the print shops in New Orleans busy producing copies of all the materials they had brought original versions of. Eventually they'd modernize the printing process, for now the eighteenth-century presses preserved their scarce ink and paper. The Omímeya marketing department wrote the Changleska Story. This booklet contained their Declaration of Independence and founding documents, along with a vague account of their arrival.

The Medical Corps wrote health pamphlets described how clean water, improved sanitation, and handwashing could prevent cholera and other infectious diseases. Pamphlets offered instructions for lice removal, and explained how mosquitos, not bad air, spread malaria and yellow fever, providing herbal mosquito repellent recipes and describing bed nets. One pamphlet included the recipe for the oral rehydration solution for diarrhea and other conditions. It saved countless lives after being introduced in the 1970s by the World Health Organization; they hoped to do the same here. Diarrhea was a leading cause of death, especially children. A simple treatment of a half teaspoon of salt, six teaspoons of sugar in one liter of boiled water, drunk copiously, could save lives. The pamphlets included illustrations for those with low literacy or limited English.

Changleska paid expedition members to have era appropriate clothes made. New clothing was almost all custom made. A tailor in New Orleans outfitted Nels in suitable clothing for a wealthy young man and Jamal in clothes suitable for high placed servant. Jamal paid for an additional set of fine dress clothes from his own funds suitable for a well-to-do gentleman.

The tailor's excitement grew when they entered his shop in their twenty-first century clothing. "Gentlemen, I am delighted to see you." He exclaimed, "Do you know where I can get more of these?"

They both gasped, seeing him hold up a pair of jeans with a zipper.

"Where did you get these?" Nels exclaimed.

"A German gentleman, a month or so ago, traded in part for clothes he had made."

The tailor was disappointed they didn't have zippers, but they assured him that someone'd would sell him some eventually. Nels reported the tailor's comments to Lieutenant Rodriguez, who sent someone over to further question him.

Jamal asked Nels excitedly, "Do you think there are other time travelers here? Where else would he get jeans with zippers?"

"Weird, I know. I don't think the missing expedition had any Germans. Maybe he found it or bought it somewhere. Rodriguez will investigate." They left before solving the mystery. Their busy schedule prevented them from thinking about it again.

=..=

Boarding the ship didn't relieve Jamal's anxiety. It was dirty and smelled terrible. They had two small cabins, and since he couldn't share with Nels, he was paired with Brad.

"This is our cabin? It looks like a rabbit hutch and isn't much bigger," Jamal said, to Brad as they brought in their belongings.

The room was about eight feet by eight feet, with low ceilings and a small porthole. The walls facing the deck had slats, giving it the look of a cage. Two narrow wood beds hung hammock style on each side, with a fold down desk, a stool, chamber pot, and a tiny mirror over a fold down shelf holding a wash basin. They'd have to take turns using the desk or wash area. There were oil lamps on the walls. To Jamal's horror, he realized they burned whale oil.

"More space than the crew bunks on the *Endeavor*. We'll have to make the best of it, otherwise it will be a long two months," said Brad.

They met the others on the deck, feeling the motion of the ship as it sailed with the tide. Leaving New Orleans behind felt like letting go of the twenty-first century. Oca Landing, the Guard, and their friends represented a familiar world, offering the comfort of a shared culture. They'd be heading into the unknown without any kind of support system outside of the four of them.

One of the crew members was assigned to assist them. He gave them a tour, mostly telling them where not to go. The ship had a crew of fifteen, four officers, including the captain. Jamal was surprised to see several mixed-race crew members, including a very dark, large Black man with African tattoos. They were all free. The large man had been captured in Africa as a teenager and had escaped from the Caribbean by stowing away. The captain had immediately freed him. He was the bosun, a position of authority on the ship. Jamal didn t need to pose as a servant on the voyage but was told that at some stops, it was best to stay on the ship.

Later, the captain invited them to dine at his table. The captain, George Harrigan, received them warmly in his well-appointed cabin. As an incentive for an early departure, he'd received twenty-first century items as fees for their passage. The nautical maps showing hazards like shoals and reefs thrilled him, making their route safer and faster. But the biggest prize was a watch that kept perfect time and worked in any weather to assess longitude. While marine chronometers existed, they were expensive and not as reliable. Jamal and Nels warned him the battery would only last a couple of years, but hopefully they would have better navigation tools for sale by then.

Captain Harrigan also received what would be cheap trinkets in the twenty-first century but held enormous value now. The packet of photographs, mostly vacation photos donated by Changleskans, proved popular, as color photography and printing were unheard of. Pens were a popular item. Jamal wished they'd brought the fountain pens he heard someone in Changleska was making before they left.

They met the other five passengers, two going to Charleston, two to Philadelphia, and one going to Boston. The other men drank a lot and told jokes they didn t understand but seemed amiable enough. One man gave off uncomfortable vibes, asking too many questions about Changleska. While they were told to be as honest as possible, they were given a list of things to not talk about. They used the phrase the world we came from , not mentioning time travel, but saying it was a miracle from God. The passengers heard a few wild stories about Changleska from their time in New Orleans. Evidently, pornography was of great interest. One merchant had bought, at great expense, two pictures from a Playboy or Penthouse magazine from a Guard member. They were told they could view it for a price. They declined, laughing, with lots of inside jokes later.

Jamal had been feeling nauseous during dinner with the captain, which only got worse. By evening, he was throwing up and miserable. All four of them were seasick, but Jamal and Dan had it worst. Although the herbal tea Nels brought, made with ginger, peppermint, and chamomile, helped Dan, Jamal ended up throwing it up. Nels also brought sea bands, soft cloth bands worn on the wrists, with small pieces of wood that put pressure on acupuncture points. Used by Chinese sailors and midwives at home for morning sickness. Between the tea and the sea bands, everyone else was fine in a few days, but Jamal could barely move. He'd never felt so sick in his life. Nels felt helpless: he knew there were stronger antinausea drugs, but didn't have any. There was not a ship surgeon, but one sailor who acted in that capacity recommended paregoric if it didn't improve. It contained opium, camphor, anise, and benzoin. Nels carried it, as it was good for diarrhea and cough, but he hesitated to give it to Jamal because of the opium. Jamal's condition worsened, so they administered the paregoric. It helped him keep the tea down and allowed him to get up on deck, which provided further relief. It gradually improved, but whenever the ship hit rough seas, it came back.

Jamal brought his laptop but left Nels' behind as a backup with Jamal's files. Jamal continued to work on his patent projects, but the solar charger could rarely get a full charge. Nels continued his medical studies. The Kindle used less power. Before Big Thunder, preparing to attend the off-grid permaculture event, Jamal spent a small fortune on high end camping gear, including solar chargers. They were lucky they owned theirs. Changleska sent a laptop and LCD projector with the Philadelphia crew to show movies to George Washington, but fearing loss or damage, everyone used their phones. Brad wanted to play video games to ease the boredom, but Dan said the risk of damage was too great. Computers were irreplaceable. They had to be used sparingly. Instead, they played cards, among themselves and the other sailors. They learned whist and taught the sailors poker. They all lost the small sums of pocket money they brought except Jamal, who was good enough at math to count cards. He stopped playing, as he didn't want to cause resentment among the crew.

Once Jamal was feeling better, fascinated by the mechanics of the sails, he spent time with the sailmaker, learning as much as he could. He had some improved sail designs on his laptop, but the captain didn't want to risk the spare canvas for an experiment. He said once they got to Boston sail makers, they'd make a deal for new canvas in exchange for the drawings.

On the second week, they learned why Captain Harrigan had worried about the Gulf storms. It announced itself with a low, ominous growl in the distance. The sky, once a pale winter gray, now boiled with heavy black clouds that swallowed the horizon. *Anna Marie* groaned as the first strong gusts of wind hit her sails, making the ropes creak and the mast shudder. Waves, dark and menacing, rose, their white-capped crests slamming against the hull with the force of an angry fist.

Captain Harrigan stood firm at the helm, his hands gripping the wheel like iron clamps. His oilskin coat flapped violently in the wind, and rain lashed his face in stinging sheets. His voice boomed above the chaos, sharp and commanding.

"Reef the mainsail! We'll lose her if we don't lighten the load!" he shouted, his voice cutting through the deafening roar of the storm.

Sailors scrambled across the slick deck, working the sails. The captain ordered all passengers below, but Jamal volunteered to help. Even in good weather, the height of the mast terrified him. Despite his interest in sails, he never climbed the mast. The sailors' bravery amazed him as the strong winds high above the deck tossed them about.

"I need another set of hands here!" one sailor yelled.

Jamal, soaked to the bone and gripping a rail to stay upright, hesitated for a heartbeat before darting over. His eyes darted nervously to the monstrous waves crashing over the gunwale, each one threatening to drag them overboard. He was directed where to pull to help. The ropes burned against his palms, but he gritted his teeth and kept pulling.

"I'm not much of a sailor!" he admitted, his hands shaking as he grabbed the rope.

"Well, you're about to learn!" the man snapped, though there was no malice in his voice—only urgency. Together, they hauled on the line, their combined strength slowly pulling the sail tighter.

Above them, the wind screamed like a banshee. The mast bent precariously, and the rigging rattled like chains in a gale.

Captain Harrigan's voice rang out. "Wave on the port side. Brace yourselves!"

The warning came too late. A massive wall of water crashed over the deck, sweeping crates and barrels into the churning sea. Jamal clung desperately to the mast as water surged around his legs. He remained petrified even after the water receded over the side. He slowly made his way below, figuring if the ship sank, he would rather be with Nels.

For what felt like hours, *Anna Marie* pitched and rolled, her crew battling the storm with every ounce of strength they had. The wind howled, and the waves roared, but slowly, almost imperceptibly, the fury subsided. The sky lightened to a dull gray, and the waves became less violent, their rhythm steadying as the storm relented.

Following the storm, a pale sun fought its way through a patchy sky. The sea was calmer now, though the waves still rolled in heavy swells, rocking *Anna Marie* as she advanced slowly. The crew was weary, but relieved to have survived. However, their respite was short-lived.

"Captain! You'd better see this!" one sailor called.

Captain Harrigan climbed up from the quarterdeck, his keen eyes narrowing as he followed the pointing hand. The mainmast, the very heart of the ship's propulsion, bore a jagged crack halfway up its length, right below the topmast.

"Damn it," Harrigan muttered, running a hand over his beard. "The storm must've done it, but it held long enough to see us through."

Jamal joined them, wiping salt spray from his face. "Is it bad?" he asked, eyeing the damage uneasily.

"Bad enough," Harrigan replied. "We're not waiting for it to fail. We'll jury-rig it before it gets any worse."

The work began immediately. The crack wasn't deep enough to warrant replacing the entire mast, but it needed reinforcement to survive the journey. Harrigan directed the crew to wrap the damaged section in heavy tarred canvas. Over this, they lashed sturdy wooden splints salvaged from spare spars, securing them with thick ropes that bit into the mast like tourniquets.

Nels said, "This is like splinting a broken leg," his tone half-joking to mask his nerves.

Jamal grinned despite his stress. "A leg that carries the whole ship, no less."

Harrigan climbed the mast himself to inspect their progress. "Tighter!" he barked down. "It needs to hold against the strain of the sails."

By midday, the crew had completed the repairs. The splints gleamed with fresh tar, and the lines hummed under tension. The crew stood back, their faces streaked with sweat and dirt, watching as Harrigan gave the order to unfurl the sails. Under the strain, *Anna Marie* groaned as the wind caught the canvas. All eyes turned to the patched mast as it shivered but held. A collective cheer rose from the crew, their spirits buoyed by the small victory.

Jamal leaned against the rail, catching his breath. "Will it last?" he asked Harrigan.

"It'll get us to the next port," Harrigan said confidently. "After that, we'll need a proper shipwright. But for now, she'll hold."

=..=

A week later, battered and defiant, *Anna Marie*, with her patched sails flapping weakly and her splintered mast groaning, limped into the Charleston harbor, the salty air thick with the smell of brine and decay. All Jamal wanted to do was feel the ground under his feet. They were stuck in Charleston for two weeks for repairs and all passengers were ordered off the ship.

Unlike in New Orleans, people assumed all Black people to be slaves. When they first arrived, Jamal was waiting at the crowded harbor, keeping an eye on their luggage while the others looked for an inn. His unease grew with every glance cast his way.

Two men approached, their coarse clothing marking them as dockworkers.

One pointed at Jamal. "Hey, boy! What are you doing?" he demanded, his voice rough and accusatory.

Jamal stiffened but forced calm into his reply. "I'm off the *Anna Marie*. Just keeping an eye on the luggage."

The second man narrowed his eyes. "Do you have a pass?"

"Do I need one? I'm a free man, a valet for an important gentleman," Jamal said firmly, his fists clenching at his sides. He had his forged papers, but he didn't want to show them to these assholes.

The first man sneered. "Big words for a nigger without papers. Maybe we oughta bring you to the constable, see what he thinks."

Before Jamal could respond, Nels approached them with a confident stride. By his clothing, they knew him as a wealthy man.

He turned to the dockworkers with a polite but cold smile. "I trust there's no misunderstanding here?"

The men exchanged glances, grumbled something unintelligible before shuffling off.

Jamal exhaled, his shoulders slumping. "Now I understand why they said not to leave the ship."

Afterwards, Dan gave one of his few orders as a corporal. Jamal couldn't go outside of the inn alone. They set up a duty roster. At first Jamal felt stupid, like a child needing protection. After several incidents during their stay, he was grateful for their protection. He was safer if people assumed he was a slave. He had to shut up and suck it up.

The inn also served as a tavern, as was common at the time; there were no hotels in the modern sense. They didn t allow even free Blacks to stay inside, so he had to sleep with the other slaves above the stable. It wasn t as bad as it might have been. There were fewer bugs, and they used fresh straw for bedding. The women had their own side, which he understood they kept very clean. He d never had a real chance to talk with other slaves until now.

Most were young and their stories were heartbreaking. What made him angry was when he asked them about their dreams. If they had hopes for the future, they were small and muted. Slavery not only stole their freedom but also stole possibilities. A different life seemed unimaginable to them. They listened to Jamal wide-eyed when he told them any slave who could make it west of the Mississippi would automatically be free by law. They knew to be careful while passing on the tales, but Jamal knew word would spread.

Over drinks, the other ship passengers related stories of the strange people arriving from Lakota lands, with fast boats, horseless carriages and various wonders. They confirmed the tales when asked, even letting a few farfetched stories go. Jamal particularly liked the one where Changleska was the hidden city of gold and riches long sought by the Spanish that suddenly appeared from thunder and fog, but only those who were worthy could visit. Or the one where the magic city remained hidden for so long because the Lakota warriors that protected the lands killed all trespassers. This story often came with gruesome tales of killing and mutilation.

In Charleston, they continued their antislavery activities, including distributing abolitionist literature, organizing secret meetings, and aiding enslaved individuals seeking freedom, despite their efforts to maintain a low profile and their fear of arrest before the ship s repairs were complete. They gave out all the written materials they had printed in New Orleans and needed to print more at their final destinations. Besides the Changleska booklet and health pamphlets, they distributed abolitionist tracts, some religious in nature, calling slavery a sin, others highlighting the inhumanity of slavery.

Everyone was relieved when the ship s repairs were complete and they could finally leave Charleston, none happier than Jamal. The pervasive slavery clung like a foul smell he could not remove. He would carry it with him for the rest of his life. The discomforts of the journey and the terrors of the storm would be worthwhile if he could do something, even in a small way, to end this misery. He was grateful that he was not alone. Not only

Nels, but all of Changleska supported emancipation with words and deeds, including the funds that paid for this journey. Their unwavering commitment to the cause reminded him that the fight for freedom was not his alone. It was a collective endeavor, bolstered by a community that believed in justice and equality. As the ship sailed onward, he found solace in knowing that their shared purpose would guide them through the challenges ahead.

Chapter Five
Gift of Thunder

GIFT OF THUNDER stood motionless, watching the Minsose River s brown water slowly flow by. Despite the sub-freezing temperatures, Gift barely noticed the cold, her cheeks flushed and breath misting in the air. The river calmed her; she felt its presence like a good friend. The people brought by Big Thunder had rescued her from the life of a slave, adopted and loved her, and taught her their ways. However, as much as she admired them, they didn t understand the land, water, and everything that walked, swam, or flew belonged to itself, with its own unique spirit. They thought nature was to be harnessed for their own use. Her people understood, on a deep level, that the earth could not be tamed. By listening and respecting life, they lived in reciprocity with the earth around them. She didn t know if it was a lesson those from the future could learn. They all lived so disconnected from the earth, in comfort and plenty.

Although Gift felt loved and protected living here, it never felt like home. She didn t want to return to the Two Elks band. Two Elk had stolen her from her people, the Arikara, after the *wašíču* (White man) illness, called smallpox, decimated her village and left her scarred. While Two Elks and other men in the tribe ignored her, others, including his wives, mistreated her. After Two Elks sold her to a fur trader, the big stinky man brutalized her, stealing her innocence, leaving behind blood and pain. The day Big Thunder came, it brought the fishermen from the future, horrified by what they saw. Not wanting to buy a human, they'd traded an old hide for her under the condition she was given as a gift. Her name, Gift of Thunder, was bestowed that day, by the first people who cared for her.

A circle of land, a long day's ride from the center to the edge, brought back a world filled with wonders and people unlike any other. She was now a part of Changleska, her new tribe. Gift loved her new family, especially her adopted sister, Kimímela, her best friend, yet she still felt apart, having life experiences so different.

The machines, despite the noise, thrilled her at first. What they called modern conveniences saved people's time, but they filled it with busyness. She craved the beauty of stillness, the peace of the prairie, and simple village life. Gift missed the company of women working many hours to make a meal over a fire, instead of minutes pouring cans in front of a stove. She missed elders telling long stories on winter nights. After a while, TV stopped captivating her, turning to a distraction leaving her unfulfilled.

Kimi, quiet at first, knowing Gift was troubled, soon joined her at the river. Gift could feel her hesitation, her desire to speak, while waiting for the right moment.

"You're listening again, aren't you?" Kimi finally said.

Gift nodded. "The river speaks, if you know how to hear."

Kimi let out a slow breath. "I hear the thunder. It whispers before it comes."

Gift turned to study her. Kimi's connection to the thunder was something even Gift didn't fully understand. It made her both powerful and fragile. Storms stirred something deep within her—not the wind alone, but the sense of danger rising. Sometimes, the Thunder Beings spoke through the rumble.

Kimi's voice tightened. "I should be able to control it better."

Gift hesitated, chose her words carefully. "Power isn't about control. It's about understanding. If you fight it, you will only lose yourself."

She looked away, her jaw tight. "I know that. But sometimes, I just wish I was normal."

Gift answered softly, "The strongest trees grow where the wind is harshest." For a long moment, they stood in silence.

Kimi kicked a small rock into the river, watching it disappear beneath the current. "You sound like my mom."

Gift laughed. "Maybe she's right."

As Gift stood in the cold at the river, she wondered if she should share her troubles with Kimi. She had a hard decision to make. Kimi had her own struggles; she did not need to add Gift s to the pile. Gift had a chance to return to the Arikara the people of her birth. She was nine winters old when taken, and barely remembered her life before, other than the innate sense of home she felt nowhere else. Her first language had been Arikara, but she felt Lakota. She had lived so long with them, her moon ceremony had been Lakota, and her beliefs and customs Lakota. She feared she would not fit in with the Arikara, like she did not fit in anywhere, and was always the outsider. All she ever wanted, as far as she remembered, was a home she belonged to. She wanted her own lodge, children, a sister wife to share the burdens, and a husband who cared for her. Now she could have that home with the Arikara but would need to leave Changleska. This was the most difficult decision she ever faced.

Gift longed for Ciwaku, the man who wanted to take her away. Although they had only touched hands, she yearned to feel his arms around her. She desired him to touch her private places to take away the hurt and bring pleasure. Gift had heard the other women talk about how wonderful sharing robes could be. They promised her that the pain of her memories of her first horrible experiences would fade, replaced by joy of connection with a man that cared. She never had a man pay special attention to her, smile at her, or listen to what she had to say. Gift wondered if this was love. She watched movies about love and heard stories from girls at school, but romantic love was not anything she thought she d ever experience. For Lakota, attitudes about love were vastly different. Sometimes two people, usually young, had an instant powerful connection, but it was unusual. Love was quieter, gentler, developed slower. The passion in the movies and books from the old world was rare in hers.

She had met Ciwaku, the son of the Arikara leader, when he arrived with a contingent of Hidatsa and Arikara invited to join Changleska. Elliot Gray Owl, the attorney for Changleska, was leading the negotiations and asked Gift to translate. He needed permission from her adopted father, Hotah Chasing Hawk, who gave it reluctantly, concerned that it would take too much time away from Gift s schooling. Gift would never show it, but this angered her. She hated school. Gift felt telling him how much she hated school would seem ungrateful, so she persevered, hoping it would get better. Even after six months, the school still placed her with the younger children. She struggled to learn to read and write, both in English and in the new Lakota alphabet. Most of what was taught didn t make sense to her. Gift understood why Kimi, who wanted to be a midwife, had to learn certain things, or her friend Darla, who wanted to be an electrician like her parents. Having her own family was all she had ever wanted. Nothing taught in school would teach her what plants to eat in which season, the best way to remove hair from a hide, how to cook over a fire if there were no metal pots, or anything she needed to know for the life she wanted.

In Changleska, at sixteen, she was a minor child, her father in control. In the Two Elks tribe, she was a slave, but after she had her moon, was considered an adult. If a new law hadn't been written for Changleska yet, the old laws of South Dakota applied. In the old world, the legal age for marriage was eighteen or sixteen with parental consent. She doubted she'd be given permission; she had never heard of anyone around here getting married at sixteen. Without it, returning with Ciwaku to his village would be breaking the law, severing ties she didn't want broken. She needed to decide, for the first time in her life, if she would do something just for herself. She had always served others. First as a slave and even in Changleska, she did what was asked of her. Following her own path, fulfilling her own dreams seemed beyond her grasp. Until now.

As Gift was the only one in the area who spoke Arikara, Elliot needed her to translate. It took too much time going back and forth from where she lived with her new father's family to the resort's meeting rooms. With her father's permission, she moved to his first wife Rose's house full-time. Usually, she spent only an occasional weekend there with Kimi. At first, she missed Kimi, the comfortable chaos at the house, the new baby, even the rowdy small cousins. Rose and Luke were rarely home. For the first time in her life, she was often alone and found she enjoyed the quiet. The house was beautiful, with tall ceilings and big windows with river views, always warm and clean. At first, the openness was uncomfortable; she was used to small living spaces but grew to love it. She knew a traditional Arikara earth lodge would be dark, smoky, and crowded in comparison, but it would be her home.

Ciwaku told her about the lodge they would share with his first wife and baby. He was twenty-two winters old. The son of the leader brought prestige, but not wealth. They farmed corn, beans, squash, and sunflowers, just as she remembered from her childhood. The Lakota often raided in the fall, stealing the harvest, so hunger stalked the village. They wanted a treaty to protect them from the raiding Lakota. The Hidatsa and the Arikara were happy to join Changleska. Giving up slaves was a small price to pay, as they rarely had them. But the protection Changleska offered was theoretical. They admitted they could not send their Guardians with their fantastic weapons so far away. They would get a few muskets, with better ones promised next year, but they would return home with as much corn as they could carry, as well as other useful gifts. The few Lakota tribes who joined agreed to stop the raiding; they were negotiating boundaries and territories now. But they needed agreements with the whole of the *Očhéti*

Šakówiŋ (Seven Council Fires), made up of the seven bands of Lakota. If the new alliance was to protect them, they might have to war on the other Lakota bands if they refused to join Changleska or honor the other s treaty.

Gift had mixed feelings, as she considered herself Lakota. She knew they couldn't live on buffalo alone. A sickness would develop from too much protein. They needed carbohydrates like corn to live. Farming involved staying in one place, but the Lakota followed the buffalo, so raiding became a way of life for survival. Changleska wanted to change this. All the tribes needed to know that the greatest threat was the wasichu, which some called who ate the fat , or greedy people. The tribes needed to be united, not fight each other, or the wasichu would win. The old world the thunder people came from suffered sickness from greed. Most believed the Creator sent them here to prevent it from happening again. The first step was uniting the tribes. They d set up trading networks, with no need to fight for resources. She translated this in talks with the Arikara and Hidatsa. She accompanied them on tours, showing the wonders of the Circle brought by the Thunder Beings.

Ciwaku, whose name meant fox, showed wily intelligence in his questions. He was quick to embrace the thunder people, unlike his father and older members of the contingent, who remained wary. Ciwaku saw Gift s value with her knowledge of the language and the ways of the thunder people. Since the birth of his first child a few months ago, he'd wanted a second wife but could not provide for another. With the new riches promised by the thunder people, he could have as many wives as the Lakota. He lacked horses to offer her father, but if she asked to accompany him, he might permit it. She had been stolen from the Arikara; it was only right to return her. He went out of his way to pay attention to her. If she returned with him, he would be in a position to gain wealth and status in the tribe. He needed to figure out a way to convince her, even without her father s approval. His father couldn t see the potential in everything the thunder people offered, but he could. Ciwaku saw that this small, pockmarked former slave could be the key to unlocking the riches of this place. He knew she was kin to Rose, one of the leaders. He would need to treat her well, like a prize mare.

Gift heard Rose calling her name from the deck. She barely heard her standing next to the river, but started back up the trail to the house. She did not realize it had gotten so late. Rose was here to take her to the Wakínyan ceremony. The Spring equinox ceremony would welcome the thunder and rain that would nurture the earth with songs and prayers. It was a joyous celebration of the winter ending with food, singing, and dancing. Gift was looking forward to it, wondering how the Red Eagle band s ceremony would differ from Two Elks'.

=..=

They drove Rose's little electric car the seven miles to the powwow grounds where the ceremony was held, despite it being only an hour on horseback. Saving time was important to Rose.

Rose said, "What is troubling you, sweetie? Do you want to talk about it?"

Gift mumbled, "No, thank you."

"I have seen you with Ciwaku and the Arikara. I can guess why you are upset. Have they invited you to return with them?"

Gift nodded. Her head hung low, feeling like she did something wrong, although she knew she had not.

Rose gently said, "We love you, want you to stay with us, but you are free, an adult by your tribe. If you want to go, Hotah Chasing Hawk will not hold you back against your will."

"More than anything, I want a home of my own, a husband, a family, where I feel like I belong."

"I understand, but let me tell you the story about me and Luke's father. I wasn't much older than you, just started college, got a scholarship. Do you know what that is?"

Gift nodded.

"I wanted to leave home but stayed to save money. Hated living with my mother. I'll spare you the details, but you know how bad alcohol and drugs can be. I had little experience with men, but when I met Luke's dad, he was funny and charming, paid me a lot of attention, I fell for him hard. When his roommate moved out unexpectedly and he couldn't pay the rent on his own, he invited me to move in with him, even though we had only been together for two months. Between my feelings for him and wanting to get out of the house and live on my own, I jumped at the chance."

Gift was aware Rose's parents were divorced, but she still mentioned her father occasionally.

"Did he talk to your father before you moved in with him?"

"No, that's not how we do things. If you are over eighteen, you don't need your parents' permission for anything. Anyway, after I moved in, I had to get a job to pay the rent. He lost his job, and I had to work more hours. I lost my scholarship and had to drop out of school."

"That's not good. I know about college."

"Things got worse when I got pregnant with Luke, but that's not the point of this story. My biggest regret is rushing into living with the first man who showed me attention, so I could leave home. I didn't get the freedom I wanted, just traded one set of problems for another. What Luke's dad wanted was not me, but someone to cook, clean, and pay the bills."

"Ciwaku is not like that. He is a good man."

"I'm sure he is, but why rush anything? If he loves you, he'll wait. Why not take it slow? Spend more time here with us, with Kimi. You can visit his village later; the next expedition will be in a few months. I don't want to see you make the same mistake I did and rush into something without understanding all the implications. They say love is blind, that happened to me. I didn't take the time to see clearly. I don't regret Luke, of course, but if I didn't rush, it would have saved unnecessary heartache."

They arrived and started looking for a place to park. Gift was quiet, thinking about the conversation. Rose surprised her. She was always busy, seemed distant, but when she talked to Gift, it was obvious that she cared deeply.

It was still cold outside, but the sun shone from the cloudless sky. It was crowded; they had to carry the food a long way in. Fortunately, Kimi and her dad had reserved a spot up front, and she could see Jackson, Luke, and other family members. Gift couldn't see Kimi. She joined her family and waited. Not long after, the ceremony began.

The singing and drumming transported her back to growing up in the Lakota camps, bringing happy memories. At the end of the winter, there was little food. For weeks before the ceremony, the women combed the riverbanks for the foods they loved, like čhelí (cattail), pȟaŋǧí (Jerusalem artichokes) and pšiŋšíčamŋa (wild onions), as well as various greens just coming out. Most prized was čhaŋíčahpehu (nettles). The women harvested it, bearing the stinging cheerfully. They dried it for its medicinal value, good for many illnesses, and used the fresh plant to relieve the elders' joint pain. Carefully hoarded acorns brought or traded for were soaked and ground, sometimes mixed with corn and made into bread. The feast was a reminder that the abundance of the earth would return.

The scent of burning sage and sweetgrass wafted over Gift, grounding her, filling her with peace. Helpers brought burning bundles of sage so everyone could smudge themselves, cleansing and praying. After songs and prayers, several young girls walked towards the center, carrying sacred items for the ceremony. Kimi was wearing a beautiful white buckskin dress

Gift had never seen before. She wondered if the Red Eagle tribe had given it to her. Her hands trembled slightly as she brought the *čhaŋnúŋpa* (sacred pipe) forward, its stem intricately carved with symbols of the four winds, the bowl carved from red pipestone in the shape of eagle claws.

There was a moment of silence when the drums stopped. Right then, clouds rolled in like they were alive. A deep, resonant rumble began, like distant mountains shifting. Everyone looked up as the clouds formed a circle over the ceremonial grounds, the blue in the sky still visible at the edges at a distance. The sound of thunder softly surrounded the gathering, growing louder and more insistent, as though the very sky was speaking. Kimi did not look around. She closed her eyes, still holding the pipe, listening to the thunder, sounding like the heartbeat of the earth. The power she emanated was palpable, as though she were a conduit for something immense and unyielding. She stood still and silent, while moments stretched and warped, each breath drawn by the crowd feeling heavier than the last. The thunder seemed to vibrate through the earth, up her legs, and into her body. Kimi opened her eyes, looked around surprised everyone was staring at her, and smiled, stepped forward, offering the pipe to the elder. As soon as he took it, the thunder ceased, cutting off abruptly, leaving an eerie stillness in its wake, as if the sound had never existed. The clouds dissipated, blue sky returning, leaving behind the hint of the smell of rain. The ceremony continued as if nothing had happened. As the elder lit the sacred herbs packed into the bowl, the first tendrils of smoke spiraled upward, carrying prayers to *Wakȟáŋ Tȟáŋka* (Great Spirit). The pipe was a bridge between the earth and the sky.

When the thunder was the loudest, Gift felt a whisper threaded through the noise. It wasn't a voice so much as a feeling, a surge of emotions and fragmented words slipping just out of reach. She strained to hold on to it, her breath catching, her hands curling involuntarily at her sides. She didn't know what the Thunder Beings were trying to tell her, but she felt their guidance as surely as she felt the drumbeat of her own heart. The warmth of their presence lingered, a flickering ember in her chest. She knew that if she listened deeply, with her whole heart, she could decipher their message.

=..=

After the ceremony concluded, murmurs rippled among the twenty-first-century people, their voices chattering with amazement. Many didn't believe what they heard with their own ears, seeking a rational explanation. Those from this time knew Thunder Beings brought a sign. They accepted the mystery unquestionably, as if expected.

Gift hurried to Kimi, who looked overwhelmed, surrounded by people bombarding her with questions. The Thunder Beings had clearly sent a message. Everyone wanted to know whether it was a warning or a blessing. Last fall, hours before they were brought here, she was given a message, now part of the song they sang. 'Big Thunder strengthens the Circle; the Circle protects the Earth.'

Gift noticed one man, wearing paint, scalps, animal skins, and bone rattles, a leader of the ceremony, an important holy man from Red Eagle's band named Bear Walking. He glared at Kimi, radiating menace, obviously upset she had literally stolen his thunder.

Bear Walking was directing people away from her, "Go eat now, I will pray and fast, meet with others, and in time will share the meaning."

Kimi said to Gift quietly, *"Don't need to wait, I know now."*

Gift, surprising herself, risked irritating Bear Walking further by saying loudly to Kimi, "Sister, what did the Thunder Beings say to you? Is there a message?"

Everyone who had begun to wander off came in closer, listening intently. Bear Walking looked annoyed.

Kimi said calmly, "One simple message. If we share, there will be plenty."

"That's it?" scoffed Bear Walking. "You know nothing, you silly girl. This may be a warning. Interpreting the thunder took years to learn the right prayers and rituals. It will take time to find out exactly what the warning is, but these new people bring nothing but chaos. Already people run to their 'doctors' and do not listen to those who have been taught the healing way."

Gift said loudly to the people curiously leaning in to hear the argument, "Did you hear what my sister heard from the Thunder Beings? If we share, there will be plenty. It is both a blessing and a warning."

People walked away, repeating the phrase; awed murmurs passed it along, while Bear Walking looked on angrily.

"We don't know that is the message. Do not listen to her. She does not know the right prayers. We will tell you what it means later."

Almost everyone ignored him and walked away, leaving him more frustrated and furious.

Gift glanced back, concerned for Kimi. *"Don't anger him, you threaten his position of authority. He could curse you."*

Kimi shrugged, like she did not care or believe in his curses.

Gift felt a wave of protective love for her. Although she was bigger than Gift, she felt small, young, naïve, but determined.

"Don't go back to the Red Eagle camp. Stay away from Bear Walking. Return home with me. Your mother drove her car. Or we can go to the Arikara camp."

"No, I have *Skúya*, let's go eat, then decide."

Skuya was the name of Kimi's horse. It meant sweet in Lakota.

"I can ride with you; we'd have to ride double."

"Ok, but it will rain later."

Gift believed her; she always knew the weather. She didn t understand why more people did not ask her.

"Let me go tell your mother. I'll be right back."

Kimi stayed in the group still surrounding her, and Gift returned to her family. She saw Luke and the cousins and a bit further away she saw Rose and Jackson and stopped cold. They were standing close together, not exactly touching, but almost. You could feel the energy between them as they looked at each other, talking quietly. The moment felt intimate, and Gift was embarrassed. She wasn't sure why exactly. They were in public, only talking, not even touching. But even at a distance, the chemistry between them was undeniable. The love and desire were palpable. Gift wondered if Ciwaku would ever look at her like that. Watching Jackson and Rose, she recognized something rare and precious. It made her a little sad, thinking no one would ever look at her like that.

Gift tried to remember the whisper from the thunder, guiding her to the path to choose. But the words were fading, slipping away. The noise of the gathering pressed in, voices overlapping, pulling her away from the message she was supposed to understand. Was this a sign? If she returned with the Arikara, she could finally belong. She needed time for silence and prayer. Gift didn't know if she should become a wife and mother, fulfilling her lifelong dreams, or stay in Changleska. She understood on a deep level, if she stayed, she would sacrifice her needs to protect and serve Kimímela. But if she stayed... she wouldn't just be Kimi's sister, but her protector. Was that her true purpose? The weight of the decision settled deep in her chest. One path was hers; the other was duty. But which was which? She had to choose. Remembering Rose's advice, she realized there was no rush. Today was for celebrating. She'd get Kimi, and they'd ride to the Arikara camp for the feast. The women made corn cakes like her mother did.

Chapter Six
Jackson

JACKSON WAS BOTH excited and anxious. Changleska Guard Field Day was finally here after months of planning. Some argued this demonstration would only paint a target on Changleska as the richest prize in the world. Some hoped by demonstrating this level of military power, others would realize the costs would be too high to take it by force. It showed how the balance of power shifted to the owners of such technologies. It could also expose vulnerabilities and weaknesses, of which Changleska had plenty.

He knew there were people inside the Circle who resented the new order. Some missed their old lives. Others had never supported it to begin with. Most just grumbled, but Folsom had followers, infrastructure, and a plan. Folsom s compound was quiet lately, but that didn t sit right with Jackson. Surveillance reports showed increased shipments of fuel, preserved food, and medical supplies to the compound. Two new antennas had been installed. The prayer meetings were still public, but locals reported smaller, private gatherings afterward. No laws were being broken. But it looked like preparation, not just worship. Jackson had seen this pattern before. Quiet wasn t always peaceful. Sometimes it meant someone was getting ready.

As soon as they arrived at this time, General Gardner wrote plans to prepare for an attack by Lakota forces. His motivation stemmed from a mix of strategic caution and historical knowledge. He knew the Lakota had a formidable reputation as a military force and sought to mitigate any potential threat. In 1792, Lakota was the most powerful military force west of the Mississippi. Their mobility and superb horsemanship were unmatched. Many carried large-caliber muskets capable of killing with a single shot, and the few with rifles were expert marksmen. They could shoot either guns or arrows accurately while mounted at speed, a skill they spent a lifetime learning. Conflicts with American and European powers had not yet reached the west. Much of their fighting was with other tribes, driven by competition for resources, territory, and alliances. These conflicts were complex, shaped by shifting dynamics and the need for survival in a challenging environment. They were a feared enemy known for courage, battle prowess, and utter ruthlessness.

While planning the military exercise, the general integrated his old plans with studies of historical cavalry battles, including the Battle of the Greasy Grass, also known as Custer's Last Stand. However, his plans also reflected underlying biases, as he relied heavily on his own assumptions about Indigenous warfare. His reliance on historical battles revealed modern arrogance, assuming past knowledge would ensure present success. He also believed modern weapons would easily overcome Indigenous tribes. This belief overlooked how much a force multiplier that knowledge of the terrain, superior horsemanship, and the fighting for one's homeland was.

The number of his new Guard troops with horses was enough to begin a small, fifty-strong cavalry unit, primarily scouts, for now. They were a long way from being adept at fighting from the saddle. Without roads, rivers and horses were the only ways to travel any significant distance. Even with veggie oil-powered vehicles, the military needed to integrate horses more and more.

For the demonstration, the Guard wanted to portray an accurate battle against Lakota forces. To create an opposition force of horse riders, Gardner recruited from the community. Nearly every rider in the area volunteered. The group was predominantly White, spanned a range of ages, and included a notable number of women. They needed little training because they wouldn t be shooting anyone. All thrilled to play at warfare.

Field Day turned into a public event with thousands expected to attend. There d be various competitions, speeches, and vendors. Everything would have to be staged in advance, from portable composting toilets to command tents, first aid stations, water, and comfortable viewing for the VIPs. Fortunately, locals would bring their own canopies and chairs used to attending powwows and sporting events. They constructed a new road for military vehicles and the expected crowds.

Two Elks was keen to participate, now a formal ally with the marriage of his son to a Changleskan woman. Kinship ties had many layers of obligation and reciprocity. He had lost most of his warriors last fall in what could only be called a massacre. The poorly trained Neighborhood Watch militia had failed to hear the ceasefire order, resulting in thirty-five deaths and eight serious injuries. Jackson still carried guilt over that one. Gardner had moved on. Two Elks hoped to recruit more warriors from the tribes attending the summit, as his tribe was now wealthy with trade goods from Changleska and widows. He had many women he needed to find husbands for.

For the last six weeks, weather permitting, volunteer riders practiced. Afterward, Jackson would reflect that practicing had forged bonds between the groups, even among those who normally kept their distance from the Indigenous. A few weeks ago, warriors from Red Eagle's tribe started arriving, joining the training. Red Eagle and Two Elks took over the planning with glee.

Between the Lakota leaders' intimate knowledge of the land and Google Maps, they picked a battle site on the prairie, close enough to Omímeya to drive easily. A flat area of prairie with a creek and wooded area on one side, small hills on the other. Red Eagle's tribe camped nearby. The Guard had over 800 participants, bolstered by neighborhood militia, opposing 500 horseback riders. Only about 200 were from the Indigenous tribes. The rest of the riders were community volunteers, both Native and Whites.

The Guard had big guns, military vehicles, Bearcats, SWAT tank-like vehicles, and so-called 'technicals,' small pickups with automatic swivel guns on top, with the operators in the open back. It would be trucks against horses. The Guard had a limited supply of blanks for ammunition. Both sides would use paint guns. Those without paint guns or blanks would carry unloaded weapons and shout 'bang' repeatedly. All weapons were unloaded and checked by range officers, marked safe with tape over the barrel.

Because there weren t enough paint guns, they improvised by making potato guns. The guns shot wads of cloth soaked in dye in different configurations with sizes up to a cannon ball. Building them became a craze all over the Circle. Forum users shared designs and posted photos. Contests popped up, and winners were determined by online votes. The winners would be announced at Field Day, the event unofficially dubbed Paint Wars. Rules were simple: guns could not injure, and must use nontoxic, washable paint, but could not use any material on the Limited Resource list. This prohibition included modern paint and PVC pipes. People got creative using hollowed-out wood, bamboo, or repurposed various tubes. They made paint or dye from beets, sumac, or black walnut bark, cornstarch, and vinegar. Blown eggshells filled with homemade paint became makeshift grenades. The Guard colors were blue or indigo, while everyone else used brown, red, or yellow. Regular bows worked with cloth-tipped arrowheads, but making compound bows safe proved too difficult.

A Changleska victory was the foregone conclusion. It would be a poor demonstration for the visitors to see the Guard defeated by a smaller force without modern weapons. However, Red Eagle and Two Elks had decades of battle experience. Horsemanship, wily tactics, and actual battle experience would prove formidable. While the Changleska Guard had a few military veterans, most were new recruits or militia. No one had ever fought a battle against horse warriors. The stakes were high on both sides: the Guard needed to showcase its strength to reassure visitors of its dominance, while the opposing force aimed to prove that skill and strategy could overcome modern technology. The predicted Changleskan victory didn't stop bets being taken, with many areas ripe for betting, like the number of warriors who would be 'injured or killed 'on each side or the number of vehicles or big guns taken out. There was even a long shot bet that the Indigenous forces would win.

=..=

Field Day dawned crisp and clear. The scheduled opening was Sunday at noon. Buses transported visitors to early church services, then returned to the resort for a lovely brunch. While everyone was finishing eating, Jackson approached the microphone. He was glad he didn't have to wear the sash of office he wore for the opening ceremony; it made him feel like a tinpot dictator. He wore his Guard uniform of black slacks, a button-down shirt with epaulettes and a black cravat instead of a tie. The military ribbon racks, called fruit salad, had been recreated for those Big Thunder caught without them. One of his Purple Hearts, he thought was silly, for an injury that only took four stitches. At least the other was for the injury that sent him home. A chunk of bone was still missing from his hip. He received the Silver Star for being blown up by an IED and rescuing five of his platoon while injured. He believed anyone would've done the same. Jackson didn't feel heroic. He knew genuine heroes.

Jackson had the translators standing by and tapped the microphone for attention. Hello, I m Oliver Jackson, Minister for Defense and your guide to our first Changleska Guard Field Day. While this started as a troop exercise to show our esteemed visitors some military capabilities, it has become a special event for the entire area. General Jonathan Gardner is at the site now to lead his troops. I ll be available to answer questions. I expect you ll have many. We ll meet in the lobby in thirty minutes to shuttle everyone out to the site. Please dress warmly and comfortably."

They arrived at the site a bit late. Horse-drawn wagons slowed the traffic on the one-lane road, some cobbled together from broken trucks. The ingenuity of people adapting to life in this time surprised Jackson. His aide radioed their arrival. Nothing was going to start until he had the dignitaries settled.

The site had changed radically since Jackson had seen it a week earlier. The viewing area on the hillside was now filled with spectators. In an actual battle, one side would seek higher ground. Brightly colored flags marked the boundaries of the battlefield. Makeshift barricades, constructed from fallen logs and hay bales, dotted the area, creating strategic choke points. The side with the wooded area had a small creek protecting the 'enemies' firing positions. Centered, but off to the side, were the stage, media tent, and performers' area.

Gardner didn t want to reveal modern war maneuvers of movement, surprise, and initiative. They wouldn t show drones, aircraft, or much in the way of radio communications. The demonstration would resemble historical battles when two armies faced off directly against each other in enormous groups.

They invited the envoys to view the military vehicles parked neatly on the side of the field. A Guardian answered questions and showed anything unclassified. Months before, after lengthy forum discussions, the Council had approved, by vote, which twenty-first-century knowledge would become public. Almost anything nonmilitary that was reproducible with contemporary resources was available. Detailed 'How To' manuals were available for sale to allies or approved trade partners. Better to sell the information than worry about it being stolen. Becoming an ally offered substantial benefits, with preferred allies receiving discounted rates.

The men eagerly explored the vehicles, lifting hoods to inspect engines and climbing in and out of trucks like children. The announcement of the show's start from the stage cut it short, sending everyone to the hilltop viewing area. A canopy, camping chairs, an outdoor heater, and a table with snacks and drinks awaited them.

Although the command-and-control tent was off-limits to visitors, they 'accidentally' caught a glimpse inside with video and communication gear while walking by. The visiting military men knew the demonstration would not reveal Changleska's full capabilities but still found it impressive.

Once they got settled in their seats, the voice coming from the stage startled them; they could hear it clearly from far away.

"Welcome one and all to Paint Wars, oops, I mean Changleska Guard Field Day," joked William Andrews, the announcer, a popular radio host.

"I want to offer a special welcome to our esteemed guests from distant lands. They came from far away to witness what wonders our arrival brought. No one knows whether a rip in the spacetime continuum, space aliens, or a miracle by God brought us, but we're here now, and by golly, we're going to make the best of it. I've never been so proud to see how many people came together to make this event a reality. It took a lot of blood, sweat, and tears, plus gallons of beet juice and tree bark, to make this happen. This is a testament to what we can do when we work together. Before we get started, please stand for the opening prayers."

The speech didn't translate well. The visitors didn't know what spacetime continuum or aliens were, and exchanged puzzled glances. After the prayers, they opened with singers and a short powwow dancing exhibition, and a few marksmanship contests with both guns and arrows. Pageant princesses handed prizes out, including several in the potato gun category. A formal Guard ceremony gave out medals, a few Purple Hearts, and one posthumous Silver Star. Last was some impressive trick rodeo riding. Then a brief break for everyone to visit the restrooms, the vendors, and get settled before the main event.

It began as people were directed to look up on the top of a hill to an enormous boulder. Moments later, a sudden, thunderous boom sending a plume of smoke into the air. A cascade of rubble resulted as the boulder shattered, astonishing the hell out of the visitors, the locals—not so much. No cannon or gun was visible, which made it more frightening.

General Gardner said, "This was the work of our M777 Howitzer. It's twenty miles away."

The Spanish Captain-General exclaimed, "This is a trick. Our best ship's cannon has a range of one mile, two at the most. Twenty miles away is not possible."

"We assumed you may think that. That's why later we will take you to where the gun is. You can leave someone here to verify. We'll give them a radio, shoot again and prove it is possible." Gardner responded with a smile.

All the military envoys looked frightened and were quiet.

After the big gun demonstration, everyone moved and got settled into the viewing area. They watched as both sides moved into position. Horse riders that'd been milling about the periphery began coming inside the marked areas. Military vehicles entered the area noisily, smelling of the veggie oil that now ran their diesel engines. The Guard marched in smartly, lining up in columns, looking impressive with their mismatched camo uniforms and modern weapons or strange-looking paint guns. The opposition wore a combination of war paint and feathers from both Indigenous and Native riders; other locals wore farmer caps and cowboy hats.

With a blast from a signal horn, it began. Within minutes, the engineering crew built a bridge to cross the creek to access the 'enemy'. The speed of the bridge construction amazed the visitors, just as planned.

Baron de Villiers, the French Military Attaché, remarked, "Remarkable efficiency! Our engineers would envy such speed." Genuine admiration filled his tone.

Guard forces drove across the bridge with the Bearcats, technicals equipped with paint-firing launchers, and other vehicles to swiftly secure the field. The enemy horses emerged from the woods to flank the vehicles, using numbers and their superior maneuverability to launch an egg grenade assault, removing a few key vehicles from the field of play despite taking many paint casualties.

The big guns in the back responded by taking most of the riders out. Loud battle noises erupting from the loudspeakers, realistic enough to scare horses, added to the thrilling spectacle. The visitors glanced around nervously; Jackson had to explain they were movie sound effects. Smoke bombs erupted from the big guns, but produced less smoke than a real battle of the time. Realism had to be balanced with spectator visibility.

Anyone splattered with paint was supposed to sit down in the field to play dead or injured. They could hold their horse if it didn t run off. Yells of triumph and curses of defeat filled the air. Not everyone went down when they were supposed to. People shouted angrily, and some threw punches or delivered slaps. Paint splattered everything—horses, trees, barricades, and the occasional unlucky spectator were all streaked with blue, brown, and yellow paint.

Soon, casualties became obstacles for horses and trucks to maneuver around. Other riders, or sometimes the horses, reacting to the noise and chaos and threw people off. The numbers of riders racing through such a relatively small space resulted in a few nasty collisions. The sounds of people and horses screaming in genuine pain filled the air. Medics, carrying stretchers, quickly moved through the field to help those seriously hurt.

One warrior leaped off his horse, jumped in the back of a technical, 'killed' the operator, turned the gun around, and started shooting the Guard.

Captain-General de Esquivel asked Jackson, "Amazing. Was that planned?"

Jackson replied with a grin, "Improvisation from a true Lakota warrior. An automatic gun in real life would've decimated us. We asked them to attempt to defeat us for a true contest."

"Not a good demonstration of your power if you lost, despite your powerful weapons."

"No, but an excellent demonstration of our allies' abilities."

Jackson tried to keep up with questions, but things were happening fast, and translations were slow. The dignitaries didn't know how to address him, all highly uncomfortable with a Black man in a position of authority, responsible for such a powerful military force. They seemed surprised at how knowledgeable he was as he talked about tactics and specifics.

Most of the combatants were men, but enough were women that Baron de Villiers, the French Military Attaché, said to Jackson in shock, "There are women soldiers on both sides out there. What kind of army lets women fight?"

"Women are often victims of warfare. Should they not defend themselves, their homes, and their children?"

"To defend their children when attacked is one thing; a mother's ferocity is understood. But women as soldiers are another matter."

"Peace is better; we don't want to send women to war. If war is necessary, we plan to win and will use every resource we have."

"But surely, the presence of women on the battlefield diminishes the morale of their male counterparts."

"Morale is strengthened by competence, not gender. Every woman out there has earned their place through training and skill."

The baron looked uneasy but refrained from further comment.

The opposition led by Two Elks and Red Eagle, even outnumbered, with over-matched weapons, made a fantastic showing. They used feints, encircling maneuvers, and swarm suicide attacks on vehicles and big guns. Hundreds of reddish-brown and yellow paint-streaked casualties littered the battlefield.

The exercise ended with a big gun coming from the rear, mowing down horses by the dozens, forcing the opposition to surrender. With the loud horn announcing the end, the crowd erupted in applause. General Gardner, Red Eagle and Two Elks came up on stage to shake hands and speechify.

Gardner said, "I want to thank our worthy opponents today. This was a close call. If this was a real battle, we could've lost. We learned valuable lessons, including how courage and adaptability can overcome superior weapons. We are thrilled to welcome our new allies from the Lakota, Arikara and Hidatsa tribes. Changleska's strength is the sum of its tribal parts, each new tribe adding strength like a link in an unbreakable chain."

Two Elks and Red Eagle gave brief speeches thanking their hosts. Red Eagle boasted, "We are looking forward to next year. We will win. The Guard does not have a chance, unless Thunder Beings bring better horses and riding lessons."

Everyone laughed and cheered.

Despite the Guard losses, the demonstrations were highly effective, leaving the visiting military leaders stunned.

British envoy Sir Edward Havilland said, "A fascinating display. Still, you must admit, the losses would be catastrophic if this were real."

"True. Which is why we're here. To make mistakes now, so we don't make them when it counts."

Benjamin Tallmadge, Washington's spy supposedly here for business opportunities, asked an astute question, confirming communication from Folsom's side.

"I understand it will be difficult, or impossible, for you to make new ammunition or repair your powerful weapons. Soon you will have the same weapons as the rest of us."

Jackson was pissed. He thought whoever revealed that secret should be hanged for treason. They counted on the fear of their weapons as a deterrent to preventing war. That was the point of this entire exercise. He took a breath and smiled.

"While it may be true for a few weapons, only good for hundreds of times, but we have 233 years of accumulated knowledge of warfare, that is the real weapon."

The military men looked subdued and thoughtful.

Captain-General de Esquivel quietly said to the French Attaché, de Villiers, "fighting these upstarts wouldn't be easy, probably suicidal, but an ally with access to those weapons would be formidable."

Despite the visitors' discomfort with the unprecedented level of military power, this was the completion of a successful battle. The festival atmosphere persisted. There was a victory to celebrate. It was time to party.

Crews started dismantling the venue to return it to a prairie. The women, children, Sir Edward, and the older people returned in the first resort shuttle to beat the traffic, already clogging the small exit road.

The Captain-General asked Jackson, "Would it be possible to talk to General Gardner and the Lakota leaders? I have worked with Indios amigos often and have great respect for their abilities."

"I am sure it'll be no problem; let me check," Jackson answered, calling over his aide to radio a message.

"Aren't you the commander? Could you not order him to come here?"

Jackson thought, *stepped in it now*. Instead, he smiled saying, "Sir, Lakota are allies, not under my command, and General Gardner is busy with all of this," he gestured to the beehive of teardown activity, "it is simple courtesy to ask if he is available."

"Of course."

Following a radio exchange, Jackson and the VIPs moved to the front of the stage area so crews could dismantle their observation area. The military men met with the general and the Lakota leaders, having animated conversations, keeping the translators busy. Others peppered Jackson with questions.

While the stage was being dismantled, others were setting up tents and tipis, circling the field. Everyone was rushing about as it was getting dark. Food vendors were doing a brisk business and a beer garden was being set up. Volunteers received a dollar for their participation, enough for several beers or food from the vendors.

Talmadge asked Jackson, waving at those setting up tents, "What is this? Isn't it over?"

"Chamberlain is thirty miles away; Two Elks' camp is almost fifty. Everyone will leave by morning."

Talmadge nodded, knowing that distance was at least a full-day journey by horse. "Not everyone has cars?"

Jackson could see the spy's rationale behind the question. "No, most people do; we're making the switch to new fuels, but it takes time. Riders who didn't truck their horses are staying the night to leave first thing in the morning. Besides, they wanted to celebrate." He waved around.

All around the field, people started to congregate, building campfires. The sounds of laughter and animated conversations filled the air. Jackson led the visitors over to the beer garden, the aides fetching beer for those who wanted.

"Sorry no wine," he said. "They've made this beer locally since Big Thunder. A beer distributor turned its facility to a brewery. We've got plenty of grain for beer, but wine is all imported. Which is why we appreciate your gifts," nodding to the French and Spanish.

"I apologize for not having wine here. I assumed you'd want to be back at the resort by now."

"And miss all this?" Talmadge retorted.

Seated by a campfire set up in front of the stage, listening to stories from both sides, they noticed uproarious laughter emanating from the nearby media tent, with onlookers peering in. Curious, Jackson excused himself and walked over.

"Sir," loudly exclaimed one Guardian, alerting the others who jumped up and saluted.

"Rest easy guys, wanted to know what was so funny."

"Werther here," someone pointed him out, "put together a few really hilarious reels."

Jackson knew they'd be organizing video from multiple cameras and cell phones for a while. He was surprised they already had something up. He saw a paused video projected on the inside of the tent.

"Corporal, can you set this up to show outside on the tent walls so everyone can see it? It looks like you have an appreciative audience."

The young man looked uncomfortable. "It is pretty raw; I just pulled some funny clips."

"Is it possible?" In a tone that meant it better be.

"We can put the power cord under the tent; we may have to bring the battery bank outside. But quality won't be great at the bigger viewing size."

"I'm sure it will be fine."

They quickly set it up, word spread, and a crowd gathered. They rewatched the battle from different perspectives, angles, and with close-up shots. This method of battle debriefing obviously impressed the military envoys.

Everyone laughed as spills, falls, and paint splatters reduced the serious exercise to a game. A young woman dodged an incoming volley, only to trip and tumble into a bush. Her grin as she scrambled back to her feet drew applause.

The highlight was an older woman in a cowboy hat who rushed her horse towards a Guardian fumbling to get his weapon up in time and was splattered with brown paint.

They heard him clearly say, "Shit grandma, why did you do that?"

Afterwards, as Jackson gathered up his charges to return to the resort, he noticed the change in mood. Before they had been serious and cautious, the different groups rarely spoke to each other, but on the drive back, everyone was joking, happy, translating for each other, and sharing battle stories.

Jackson realized this became more than a military exercise, designed to incite fear of their military prowess. It revealed their humanity—people who laughed, partied, and fell down a lot. In that shared vulnerability, bonds were forming. It was the first step of peacemaking, aligning with Jackson's vision of building alliances not through intimidation, but through understanding and mutual respect.

Chapter Seven
Rose

ROSE SCREWED UP. She realized this after looking over the stunned and silent faces of all the men in the meeting. For days now, she'd been quiet and unassuming, smiling sweetly and being non-threatening. She accepted their patronizing comments and subtle belittling. She preferred being underestimated. Rose had Bruce Milsham, Omímeya's attorney and chief negotiator, take the lead. The men had essentially ignored her up to this point. Then she got in their face and punched them right in the ego, and there was no going back.

For days, Omímeya's negotiators had met with county businessmen, tribal leaders, and representatives from the Hudson Bay Company (HBC), the Northwest Fur Company (NWC), and European trading firms. The first meetings were all about posturing. Each side carefully weighed what the other had to offer. Now, the real work began: private negotiations. Today, Rose faced HBC directly. The company was a titan, the Amazon or Walmart of its time. Not as vast as the East India Trading Company, but powerful enough to dominate the region's economy. They wanted a deal. So did she. But only one side would walk away with the better bargain.

John Alastair Mackenzie, the chief factor from HBC, came from the London headquarters determined to maintain HBC's traditional trade monopoly in the region. Changleska had the potential to disrupt established fur routes. He viewed the Summit as a crucial opportunity to secure agreements to protect HBC's interests. He wanted exclusive rights to certain trade corridors and waterways. With these agreements, he hoped to dissuade the NWC's aggressive expansion efforts.

Henry LaChamp, who had visited before, stood at the whiteboard in front of the room. On one column were items offered by the HBC: rifles, blankets, pots, knives, all the typical trade items for Indigenous tribes, with an estimated cost total at the bottom. In the other column was what Omímeya offered: licenses to reproduce things easily made in this time, like farming tools. Each initial license fee wasn t expensive, considering that it came with samples, schematics, and detailed instructions. The royalty fee of three percent seemed small, but Rose knew how quickly it would add up over the years. Steam engine plans were the most sought after because they promised to revolutionize transportation and industry. Steam power had just been invented, and the plans promised to avoid years of costly mistakes. The ability to power riverboats and machinery efficiently would drastically reduce travel time and labor, giving any company a significant competitive edge in trade and production. Those in the room recognized their value. The journey upriver by the *Endeavor*, which cut five to seven weeks off the travel time, convinced everyone. Steam engine licenses, even with royalties, would be expensive. Everyone wanted exclusivity, but that was unlikely. But who got what, and when, was the question. Items the visitors really wanted, like communication gear and advanced weapons, were off the table.

The group had spent hours going over the list on the board, adding and subtracting, until it looked like the totals at the bottom of each were starting to even out. Rose and Bruce had their laptops out, Rose texting her questions. She found it amusing that "mouthpiece" was another term for a lawyer, and the men in the room attributed her questions to Bruce as his questions. He was her mouthpiece until he wasn't.

He kept ignoring her texts, then stated, "It seems we're close to an agreement; the items are roughly equivalent in value."

Rose felt each slight as a physical jab, her patience fraying as Bruce repeatedly ignored her messages. The accumulated frustrations of the past few days finally pushed Rose over the edge. She had spent hours listening to veiled condescension and watching negotiations inch forward without resolution. Tired of being dismissed and underestimated, she decided enough was enough. She was tired of acting like an airhead.

She strode up to the board and said, "Not sure if you don't know what you are talking about or can't add, but these figures are wrong."

Everyone gasped at both her words and tone.

"Where we come from, FOB means freight on board; the seller pays for the transportation costs. When you added fifteen percent and stated it may change due to weather conditions, I realized that these figures are incorrect. For example, if you look at goods transported by Voyager canoe, each canoe can carry about 3,500 lbs. Figure four canoes at a time, and after paying food and wages that comes to," and she quickly wrote a number. "That is just transportation costs. Now if they were being transported via ship along the coast..." and she went over the numbers, this is what it would cost overland," writing again. In addition, market conditions need to be addressed. Was the hurricane season factored in? And losses due to ice, accidents, hostile tribes?"

She was rattling off numbers and adding up so quickly no one could keep up. John scribbled on paper with his new pen, Bruce, on his laptop.

Bruce asked, "Did you do all that math in your head?"

"Of course," she said, the implication being, *Can't you?*

John Mackenzie looked at her. "I did not know you were so knowledgeable about these things, Mrs. Chasing Hawk, and so good with figures." He studied her intently for a moment, as though reassessing his earlier assumptions.

"I'm the Chief Executive Officer of the Omímeya Corporation, as well as the General Manager of the hotel and resort. Mr. Misham works for me. I'm responsible for over 200 employees, hotel guests, and our new facilities in New Orleans. I know all these things because I'm ultimately responsible for all of it—from who cleans your rooms each day, to the source of the coffee you're drinking, to the cost of a massage I know you've all enjoyed. The entire budget falls under my purview. And I'm telling you: your estimated FOB is dead wrong. We're not even close to parity. Our licenses will bring you a fortune. A close business relationship with us will create incredible wealth for your company for generations. Don't try to take advantage of us. Tomorrow, we meet with the NWC. We gave you the courtesy of the first meeting because you sent Henry to us last fall. Don't waste the opportunity."

The uncomfortable silence that followed her rant lasted a few moments, with Rose regretting her outburst immediately.

John Mackenzie broke the silence, laughing, and said, "I wish my late wife had met you. She was half Iroquois, and in her people's councils, women often hold authority. She was strong-willed and spoke her mind, but I dare say even she could not match your fire. I can only hope my daughter might grow to have a measure of your spirit."

Rose smiled and asked, "How old is your daughter?"

"Fourteen, but very mature for her age."

"Send her to school here. She could be anything she wanted. She could be an engineer running steam engines or learn to be a Chief Executive Officer. She could even run your company someday."

"What an interesting notion."

No one had any idea whether he was serious, but the exchange lightened the mood. Rose looked at John; maybe she underestimated him as well.

Rose explained that, while trade goods were useful for Changleska, as they took the lead in Indigenous trade, access to trade routes and waterways was their domain. They needed to meet with the Council representatives at a different meeting. Omímeya controlled copyright databases; most licenses had to be purchased from them. While they wanted foodstuffs, certain minerals, and chemicals, they mostly wanted gold, silver, or other specie easily traded globally.

By now, everyone at the negotiating table knew the history that might have been in a world without Changleska. France would have sold this land to the US for fifteen million dollars. No one knew what would happen now, of course, but Changleska and its chief economic engine, Omímeya, needed to raise a large sum in hard currency in a relatively short amount of time. The question of which country was still up in the air.

As the meeting literally went back to the drawing board, more realistic numbers started appearing. No one made firm agreements, no one expected any—but everyone knew their position. With the threat of competitors hanging over their heads, the HBC wanted a firm agreement before the summit ended.

=..=

Rose's next meeting involved a debriefing with Council and Committee members about what happened in their discussions with the French and Spanish. She was glad to miss that meeting; she had enough on her plate and didn't need to learn the intricacies of global politics. It was early in the French Revolution. Spain was in a severe economic depression, struggling with crippling debt and a decimated military and navy. Calls for independence across Latin America were gaining momentum, fueled by widespread dissatisfaction with colonial rule and the weakening of Spanish control in the region. The Louisiana Purchase in 1803 gave Napoleon the funds he needed for war. If Spain chose money instead of Tuscany, it might prolong its control of Latin America. Spain's long decline could be reversed, potentially making it a global power once more.

It was a complex situation requiring considerable time to fully understand, which they did not have. Rose was glad all she had to do, essentially, was write the check. Technically, Omímeya's board of directors decided, but they listened to her. She had to rely on the Council to figure out who best to write it to—the French or Spanish. They needed to decide what colonial power would be best for the long-term well-being of the planet. Since the area was Spanish territory, Spain could recognize their independence sooner. However, the French had been in charge for a long time, had vested financial interests in these lands, and wouldn't just go away. They'd need to work with both.

Omímeya could fund the purchase with technology, including access to maps of undiscovered gold and other valuable mines all over the world, if Spain would accept that in lieu of hard currency. However, it remained uncertain whether the Spanish would perceive such offers as helpful tools for rebuilding their economy, as disruptive innovations threatening their traditional systems, or perhaps even as suspicious ploys from a modern power they barely understood. While Omímeya had some gold, it was not nearly enough, considering the costs for the expeditions, buying land in New Orleans, and donating funds to the Freedom Assistance League. It d take many years to mine significant amounts of gold, even from the rich California fields. After long consideration, they decided against actively mining the Paha Sapa, or Black Hills. The land was sacred to the Lakota people, revered as the heart of their spiritual traditions. Beyond its cultural importance, the Black Hills were also a delicate ecosystem, supporting unique plants and animals crucial to the region s biodiversity, including buffalo. Mining was destructive. It could not only desecrate sacred land but disrupt its fragile balance. They issued a few panning permits, if accompanied by the Lakota, but most permits were now issued for California. A large expedition, planned all winter, was ready to depart for California in a few weeks.

As soon as she was out of the meeting, Rose got a text from Kimi. It read Making dinner, invite Jackson, pick up tortillas and dessert. She texted Jackson and wondered whether he d accept. She saw him last night, but he was in a weird mood. Something was bothering him and he didn t want to talk about it.

All three kids weren't often at her house on Friday nights, but tomorrow was the High School Science Fair, held at Omímeya. Although none had submitted a project, their friends had, and they were excited to attend. Sunday was Changleska Guard Field Day, with all three kids taking part. They had been practicing with the Red Eagle warriors for weeks. Luke loved to tell Jackson how much they were going to beat their asses. They were making buffalo tacos for dinner. Rose brought some pastries made for the VIPs. She had access to foodstuffs others did not. She tried not to abuse the privilege but felt she had earned the right to indulge her kids.

Rose was still upset about her day; it probably showed.

Kimi studied her face. "You look mad." Rose let out a tired laugh. "Mad? No. Just exhausted."

"Gift says when you're mad, you get a line between your eyebrows."

Rose raised an eyebrow. "Ah, you and Gift analyze my expressions now?"

"Only when you stomp around like you want to throw things."

Rose sighed. "Men are bad enough, but 1792 men are impossible."

"Then go yell at them."

"It's not that simple. If I push too hard, they dig in deeper. Sometimes it's better to let them think they have the upper hand... until they don't."

Kimi tilted her head, considering this. "Like tricking a horse into thinking it wants to walk into water?"

"That's... actually, a good comparison."

Kimi grinned. "So, you're training stubborn men instead of stubborn old horses."

Rose's heart softened. Kimi had a way of seeing things, even when she didn't say them outright.

"Thanks, Kimi," she said.

She shrugged again, but didn't pull away. "Guess someone's gotta look after you."

"Oh, now I'm the kid?"

"Maybe." She hopped up. "C'mon, let's eat. You look like you need food before you turn into one of those stubborn horses."

After dinner, as the kids settled into their rooms, Rose brought Jackson a glass of his favorite bourbon. She had stashed every bottle of his preferred twenty-first-century liquor she could find months ago.

Her home, the Riverside Cabin, had once been where the former general manager entertained high-roller casino guests. He'd been an unsavory character who'd left behind a safe filled with money and drugs, along with a hidden room stocked with luxury goods and premium liquor. Other than the drugs and money, she kept the rest as gifts for special occasions.

Rose didn't drink alcohol, but nowadays, fruit juice is rare and indulgent. She hoped someday they'd have access to tropical fruit again. She snuggled on the couch in front of the fire with Jackson, his glass in hand. The warmth of the fire and his steady presence eased the tension of the day. For a moment, she allowed herself to exhale, leaning into the quiet comfort of the evening.

Rose turned to look Jackson in the eye. "Now, will you talk to me? I know something is bothering you."

"I didn't want to unleash my frustration on you, but I'm still pissed." Jackson carefully considered his response, aware of sensitive security matters he couldn't discuss with Rose. He also knew Rose had Omímeya security matters she didn't disclose.

"I trust this'll go no further, but there was collateral damage. Four civilian casualties in the raid in New Orleans last month."

"The pirate raid where they captured a ship, Guardians killed and wounded?" asked Rose.

"I wish people wouldn't call it a pirate raid. It makes it sound noble or romantic. We went in and shot people in their sleep with night vision. It was an execution because they killed one of us, pure and simple. The ship was unexpected. It led to the firefight, resulting in more casualties, three wounded, and one dead."

"And you feel..." Rose prompted.

"Like our military is repeating the mistakes of the past. I saw this in Iraq. You don't know how much collateral damage they covered up," Jackson burst out. "I wonder if others saw their lives as less valuable because they were likely slaves."

"Your feelings are understandable; how can you address them?"

"You mean besides bitching to you?"

"You can always go to a counselor."

They laughed. They knew they both needed counseling but were too busy. Rose still suffered from PTSD from the horrific attack by cartel gunmen in the Big Bear room weeks after they arrived. The memory of gunfire echoing through the resort, and the screams haunted her dreams. The attack had left scars deeper than she cared to admit. Jackson had long term PTSD from his time in Iraq and Afghanistan; this event only made it worse. But they both coped by focusing on work.

"I could tell Gardner my concerns and hope he considers them when planning the next engagement."

"Jackson, you are the Minister of Defense. Your concerns and feelings aren't the issue, your orders are. Just order Gardner to write up protocols to prevent collateral damage in the future. State what a top priority it is."

Jackson looked at her, realizing once again how much he loved her. She not only supported him, but she also improved him.

"You're right. I forget I'm his boss sometimes. I don't always have the ends justifies the means mindset. There is something else bothering me about what is happening in New Orleans. What can you tell me about Kevin Dillon?"

"Why? Is there a problem?"

"Not sure yet; tell me about him."

"We recruited him for this position. We could spare no one from Omímeya and had to look at County. A typical small-town lawyer and family man. I heard the loss of his wife and children beyond the Circle had devastated him. He was depressed and at loose ends. There's not much demand for lawyers. He's smart, could be a real asset down there."

"He has a slave as a mistress."

"What?!" Rose exclaimed.

"Well, she's not a slave anymore. She was freed with the others when we bought the plantation. He calls her his girlfriend and said he sent in the dating employee form back to Omímeya human resources. He hired a former slave, an older woman, to set up an HR department to make sure similar relationships are consensual and not coerced."

"Do you think she was coerced?"

"No," Jackson sighed. "Evidently, she chased him hard, finally catching him. He was very careful not to do anything until he felt everything was above board."

"I'm not understanding the problem. They are consenting adults. She is an adult, correct?"

"Yes, a former slave, but he is essentially the new plantation owner. They can't possibly have an equal relationship."

"People have unequal relationships all the time. Many of the executives I've known have trophy wives who only wanted them for money and position."

"He is White. She is Black. You don't understand," he said mulishly.

Rose laughed, pointing from her White face to his Black one, and said, "Nope, don't understand."

"It's different in our time."

"Yes, and I hope he marries her. You realize he is going to become a big deal down there. Maybe governor. Can you imagine plantation owners having to bow and kiss the hand of Mrs. Dillon, the former slave? Hope she is smart."

Jackson realized he had lost this argument, but determined, he moved on, recalling the story about the cook and stories about the bribes to officials.

"Honey, I know Omímeya and Changleska are so interconnected, it's hard to distinguish between the two, but Changleska is the government. Omímeya is a business. Portraying wealth is important in business, especially now. These kinds of things are part of his directive. He was given funds for this."

"I didn't know, but what about the bribes?"

"Giving them or taking them?"

"I only heard about him giving them, but crooked people do both."

"Not necessarily. People expect bribes in this era, just as they did in foreign countries during our time. Kevin was given funds specifically for this, with a form and codes. We don't call it bribes but expected remuneration. He must account for every penny. Taking bribes is another matter entirely. We have zero tolerance. If we find out he has taken bribes, he will lose his position. He knows; it's clearly spelled out in his employment contract. Between his salary and bonuses tied to production, he is due to become a wealthy man soon. We want his loyalty to be tied to us. If you hear about him taking bribes, please let me know."

Rose thought, *it's probably nothing, but I'll have Phil keep an eye on him just in case.*

"Don't you think giving bribes is an ethical problem? Don't we want to promote Changleska values of transparency and fairness?"

"Of course. Do you know what we instructed Kevin to say if someone offered him a bribe, even a small one?"

"No, what?"

"I can't accept any gifts for myself or family. My company and country have very strict laws against any gifts or payments to officials or employees. I would lose my position. However, we look favorably on anyone who contributes to our Freedom Assistance League."

Jackson had to laugh. "I wonder what the slaveholders will do?" He added, "The other bad thing I heard about him is that he sends out a lot of memos."

Rose laughed, remembering her inbox filled by previous managers. "By email?"

"No, not set up down there yet. Printed and posted on the wall and read during daily muster."

Rose was curious. "What do they say?"

"No idea. He is your employee. But the private said they were annoying."

"I haven't had time to read his recent reports that came up with *Endeavor*. I'll make the time."

"Evidently, I have been stressing over nothing."

"Not at all. You had valid concerns; we needed to talk about them. And isn't this better than a meeting room?" she said, pointing to his drink, the fire, and their comfy position on the couch.

"You're right, as usual," he said, kissing her gently as they grew closer together.

Chapter Eight
Mary

—◇≫◯≪◇—

MARY WAS GRATEFUL. The First Summit went better than expected. Yesterday was the closing ceremony. The visitors were set to leave on the *Endeavor* tomorrow. Life was returning to normal. Even though it was still stressful, she didn't have to watch her every word.

Spain's hold on New Spain was already tenuous. Changleska's independence threatened to accelerate the collapse of that hold, but only if they played their hand right. Spain still saw this land as its own. The challenge wasn't just claiming sovereignty; it was convincing the world to recognize it before someone else tried to take it by force.

The problem was Changleska claimed the land from the borders of the old United States west of the Mississippi, all the way to the Pacific Ocean. Now called New Spain, it extended beyond the Rocky Mountains to include modern-day Texas, New Mexico, Arizona, and California. Spain even claimed much of the Pacific Northwest, although that was in dispute. The original Louisiana purchase was much smaller than they were asking for. It was a big ask.

Changleska was offering maps to some of the world's most valuable mines in Spanish-controlled lands in South America and the Caribbean as payment. Gold and precious metals that would be worth billions over time. But even including plans for twenty-first-century mining techniques may not be enough. Mary hoped none of the spies would tell them about the gold fields in California and rich mines in Nevada. New Spain technically owned those resources. Spain would ignore Changleska's assertion the land belonged to the Indigenous people. They needed to dissolve Spain's claims to these lands as soon as possible.

Changleska tried to downplay that they came from the future. If they did, they emphasized the butterfly effect, that everything would change, they couldn t predict the future. That did not stop the speculation that what happened before could happen again. It was an open secret that France received fifteen million dollars in gold in 1803, and they wanted payment. They were still willing to give up land in Tuscany. It is unclear whether the events of eight years from now would include Napoleon s rise to power, which might never happen. Revolutionary fervor was at its height; the idea the monarchy would be restored with a despotic emperor might not sit well.

Mary made the most diplomatic progress with the women that were sent as key representatives for Spain and France. Isabella de Villalobos, a noblewoman and advisor to the Spanish court, played a critical role in advocating for Spain's interests, while Henriette Dupont, the French businesswoman who lived in New Orleans, combined her business acumen with revolutionary fervor. Mary couldn't figure her out. She seemed motivated by both personal profit and revolutionary ideals, leaving Mary uncertain of her true priorities. Phil Gallo said she was a spy. Mary considered everyone who came to the summit a spy, she wasn't sure why Henriette was any different. Mary liked both these women. They were fiercely independent and rose to the top in a world dominated by men. Isabella had deftly navigated the intricacies of the Spanish court, leveraging her intelligence and charm to become a trusted advisor on critical matters of state. Henriette built a mercantile empire through shrewd investments and strategic alliances, often outmaneuvering her male competitors in the volatile world of French commerce.

Mary used Rose's suggestion to meet with them during spa visits. Any of the progress made with Spain or France came from suggestions from these women. They had long discussions during saunas, soaking in the hot tub, sipping iced teas, getting facials or manicures. Even though they were both wealthy women, modern spa luxury was new. But neither was so seduced by their surroundings to forget why they came. They had a keen understanding of the political landscape and knew how to sway the different envoys. They both saw Changleska could offer their countries a chance to use 233 years of progress, but would face tremendous obstacles. Isabella's cautious diplomacy and Henriette's probing questions showed how deeply their societies clung to tradition and resisted the unknown, revealing fear of change could outweigh the risks of a future opportunity.

Most promising was the assurance from Sir Edward Havilland, King George's envoy. He could recommend official recognition of Changleska, after negotiations with the Hudson Bay Company and Northwest Fur

Company, who were British companies with political power. It was in their interest to protect trade routes from the growing American influence. Mary was unaware that Britain had already designated all lands west of the Mississippi as Indigenous territory. People often spoke of the American Revolution as being primarily about 'taxation without representation,' but one of the driving factors was the American desire to expand into Indigenous lands, which the British sought to prevent.

Mary wasn't looking forward to her next meeting with Rose. While they'd debrief the summit, the main agenda item was deciding what Omímeya would contribute to Changleska to fulfill promises made at the summit. Assets to secure the lands from Spain, funds to France and America would come from Omímeya. Changleska Coalition was an idea and the nation had little resources of its own. Its money was fiat, based on trust. They had little hard currency.

A consortium of Indian casinos had funded parts of the Omímeya Casino and Resort as a secret, luxury, bug-out shelter. They planned for almost every contingency from small, localized natural disasters, to economic collapse, social unrest, pandemics, even alien invasion, but time travel was not one of them. The resources and expense that had gone into this place was extraordinary. Omímeya had saved many sections of the internet, including Wikipedia and vast databases of incredibly valuable information such as the locations of every valuable mine and every resource in the world. The US Patent Office database, along with those of other countries, was among the many repositories of knowledge they accessed. They delved into databases covering science, medicine, history, and weaponry, seeking any information that could hold potential value. While they couldn t utilize all this information immediately, much of it was preserved for future generations to explore and apply. Using these significant resources, they possess the capacity to effect substantial change, building a more sustainable and environmentally responsible world for future generations.

Mary had to admit that Rose, and Omímeya had been generous. They'd given up some patents for Changleska to sell and had created the new patent office run by Changleska, who would keep the filing fees. Omímeya had even paid the office staff for the next four years. They were paying other government salaries as well, with priority hiring of former Omímeya staff and Lower Brule or Crow Creek tribal members. Previously, Phil Gallo had been the casino director and was high in the Omímeya hierarchy. As the Intelligence Chief of the First Shield Command, he was now a government employee. Omímeya would continue his high salary for five years. He also was a major stockholder in the Omímeya corporation. Independent wealth was probably best for a man with that much power, Mary thought.

The resort leased Changleska 30,000 square feet of their building for office and meeting spaces. They added the significant remodel costs to their loan. The lease payments, which would increase over time, currently didn t offset the loss of income in hotel rooms and conference space. While Changleska paid for health care and social services, they needed loans for anything requiring hard currency. Although various banks offered loans, Omímeya s were the most substantial. Mary knew logically that Omímeya had given a lot, but deep down, she was still resentful. She thought they should give, not loan, more.

One of the first laws passed was a thirty percent tax on all corporate gross income, allowing no loopholes. They prioritized this tax to prevent the accumulation of unchecked corporate power and ensure a steady revenue stream for the new government. Unlike the past systems riddled with tax shelters and exemptions, this straightforward approach aimed to create a more equitable economic foundation. Omímeya faced the largest tax burden. With the size of the loans, it'd be a long time before they would pay taxes.

Today s question concerned the valuable mining databases. Would Omímeya donate the mine data so Changleska could buy the land to become independent? The corporation could open its own mines, pay its thirty percent and accrue even more wealth. Mary knew Rose cared deeply about the future of Changleska, but also knew she felt she had a fiduciary responsibility to the corporation, whose shareholders now included hundreds of employees. Decisions like these were not Rose s alone, but Mary knew the other four members of the board usually went along with Rose s recommendations. Phil was the only board member who understood the new global politics. The others focused on their own areas. Sometimes Mary felt like whatever she and Rose worked out in these meetings would determine the fate of the world. A recent negotiation came to mind, when a single decision to share Changleska s agricultural innovations with France had shifted the balance of their fragile alliance. The stakes were enormous; even a minor misstep could ripple across nations, altering the trajectory of the fledgling country and its place on the world stage.

After Mary briefly reviewed the highlights of the summit negotiations, she acknowledged they were promising Spain and France resources owned by Omímeya.

Rose surprised her by stating, "I'm sure I can convince the board to donate South American gold and silver mine data. Maybe the emerald mines as well."

"Not a loan?" Mary asked, with her eyebrows raised.

"No, Changleska can't have a healthy economy with such an enormous debt. The deficit is already too large."

Sometimes Mary forgot Rose studied economics in college, now more intensely after they arrived.

Rose tapped her tablet, "But only mines for gold, silver, and precious stones. Omímeya will retain ownership of other mining data. We may create partnerships in the future. South and Central America are some of the biggest producers of copper, lithium, nickel, cobalt, bauxite, platinum group metals, and rare earth elements. We need most of these for electronics and other technologies."

"I heard we couldn't recreate electric cars or similar technologies for generations, if ever."

"Maybe, but do you want to sell our grandchildren's future to another world power?"

"I guess not."

They wrapped up the meeting without conflict, but Mary knew it wouldn't always be this easy. Relationships between powerful corporations and governments were fraught with peril, ripe for abuse. Mary wondered how they could navigate these waters, preserving the ideals of their government, protecting the people, the planet, and everything that lives on it, without succumbing to human greed and desire for power.

=..=

Mary had some time after meeting with Rose before her next meeting. She'd postponed her general workload for the summit, resulting in a backlog. Looking over her schedule and task list, she rearranged things. She prioritized drafting key points from the summit for the next Council meeting and reviewing the budget for the California expedition. There was a quote from a book, *Seven Habits of Highly Effective People* by Stephen R. Covey, she found helpful. 'The key is not to prioritize what's on your schedule, but to schedule your priorities.'

She buzzed Travis Hazelhurst, her assistant. "Please have lunch sent up, I'll eat here."

"Of course, Mary. Would you prefer the special or your usual?"

Mary smiled faintly, appreciating his attention to detail. "Just the stew and cornbread, please, Travis. Thanks."

Mary usually avoided eating in her office, enjoying the social exchanges at the resort's restaurant, but today she didn't want to run into any envoys or their staff. She'd said her goodbyes already. Most were probably out shopping. Omímeya arranged for shuttles to make the trading post rounds for them.

She gathered her things to go to a security meeting. She would need to take her own notes, as Travis didn't have a level four security clearance. Few had a level four clearance, which Mary assumed was the highest. What she didn't know was that there was a higher level, limited to the five people who knew the extent of the databases and the full details of the secret storage vaults containing irreplaceable assets.

As she was walking out the door, Travis stopped her. "Wait here, please, for eight minutes."

"What? Why eight minutes? If I leave now, I have five minutes to walk downstairs and walk back up to the meeting."

"Yes, that would get you there on time, but if others are a few minutes later, your arrival won't have the same impact. You're the Chair. Meetings don't start until you arrive. They need to wait for you."

Mary nodded, resigned. Travis took the dignity of her position much more seriously than she did. He'd gotten worse over the last few weeks since the summit. Mary tasked him with meeting the envoys' staff to review etiquette and protocols to learn what was expected to avoid offense. Travis inquired about protocols for royalty, concluding Mary, as head of state, deserved the same treatment.

Mary felt annoyed. Eight minutes was too short to go back to her office and get work done. She hated being unproductive in her workday. After leaving her office and telling Travis she would wait eight minutes, she went down the hall to the other offices, chatting briefly with several staff members. The summit kept Mary so busy she didn't pay enough attention to her staff. She remembered another Stephen R. Covey quote, 'Leaders needed to communicate to people their worth and potential so clearly that they see it in themselves.'

The meeting took place in the First Shield Command (FSC) office, on the third floor of the North wing. They'd recently converted the meeting room from three hotel rooms, creating one long room and converting a bathroom into a mini kitchen. The air smelled faintly of new construction. Some kind of weird insulation covered the walls and the windows. There was a polished wood conference table and chairs, and a large display screen and whiteboard in front. They left all the devices at the door outside the meeting in a Faraday box. Mary thought Phil was paranoid, but that was his job. After the meeting, she realized that his caution may have been justified.

When Mary entered the room, she timed it right. Everyone was present, all rising respectfully when she entered. General Gardner and Oliver Jackson gave her the Changleska military salute of a slight bow of the head with a hand over the heart. She didn't know why Jackson was saluting her; they were both Executive Council members, and he was the Commander-in-Chief. If anything, she should salute him.

She looked around the room. Along with Phil Gallo was Andrea Richter, second in command at FSC, Oliver Jackson, General Jonathan Gardner, and another military officer. Also present was Elliot Gray Owl, Changleska's attorney, as well as Billy Fast Dog, Omímeya's head of security. Rose wasn't there, probably knowing she had enough to do without adding national security to the mix. One surprise was Ken Harris, the Brule County Sheriff. His high security clearance surprised her. Relationships between the county and Changleska were still strained. After a very close election last winter, the Brule County joined Changleska. Citizenship offered free health care and social services, and the county was woefully underfunded. They had sovereignty like tribes, but it was limited. They could collect property taxes and retain ownership of all buildings. Although they had the authority to enact their own laws, they decided, along with the Lower Brule and Crow Creek tribes, to merge their legal and law enforcement systems. The county broadened its services like vital statistics and property records to encompass the entire region. Brule County included the hospital and the towns of Chamberlain and Oacoma and quickly turned into a valuable industrial area. Overall, joining was a smart move, needed to preserve dwindling resources, but a lot of resentment remained with some residents.

Everyone looked at Mary, waiting to begin. "Phil, why don't you facilitate? Let's get started." She sensed a mix of tension and anticipation in the room, the weight of the recent incidents palpable among the group.

"After the incident with John Montgomery selling the phone, we went back and reviewed video footage and stepped-up surveillance. We uncovered eight more incidents where envoys were contacted in person or by message, plus three more technology sales: two cell phones and a Kindle. The data, including locations of all the servers in the area, maps to the armory and outposts, weapon specs, and as much damaging information as you can imagine, filled all three." Phil looked around, getting the shocked looks he expected.

Billy protested. "We locked down the front gate after the Montgomery incident; how did they get in? We are surrounded by the loop of the river."

"Ever hear of a boat?" Phil asked sarcastically.

General Gardner said, "If I knew about the risk of incursions, we could've concentrated the river patrols here."

"I agree. Knowing this earlier, we would've added more security around the perimeter as well," added Billy.

Mary, noting tempers rising, said, "It sounds like increased communication could have helped. Not sure you remember, after 911, the US found critical failures because of lack of cooperation among intelligence and law enforcement agencies. This is why we created the First Shield Command to put all these types of agencies under one roof, but it seems the County, Military and even Omímeya aren't communicating or sharing information. Turf wars are unacceptable. Am I clear?"

Knowing she was right, everyone nodded, but no one was sure how that'd work.

"Past recriminations don't help us with the present problem. Please continue, Mr. Gallo," said Mary.

Phil looked relieved. "Besides the eight contacts we verified, we found another twenty-one people assisting the perpetrators."

Billy asked, "How were these discovered?"

Phil motioned to Andrea, who answered, "Mostly by countless hours of reviewing forum posts and surveillance videos. Routine searches of envoy rooms found the two cell phones. The Kindle was discovered last night by accident." She smiled, "Two *Endeavor* marines engaged in unsanctioned fraternization in the cargo area, knocked over a crate, and revealed the Kindle. They had an alert; they knew it was contraband."

There was a little chuckle. General Gardner said, "We reviewed the port security tapes; someone placed the Kindle there two days ago. We removed the Guard on duty. Under arrest, he awaits a military court-martial. He cooperated, saying someone paid him to look the other way. He thought it was normal tech contraband. People are getting big money for electronic devices, even music players."

"How are people going to charge them without electricity? Extra solar chargers are hard to find. I think we bought most of them for the expeditions," asked Billy.

"No idea. Probably the sellers will lie about how long they will last," answered Gardner.

Elliot Gray Owl asked, "Were there warrants for the surveillance?"

"We don't need warrants for public forum posts. Users of MilNet know data is subject to military review. We also don't need warrants for surveillance video in public areas."

Andrea Richter tapped her screen, and a list of names and biographical details appeared. "I won't go into everything about everyone involved, but these are the highlights. Only three people connected to Clyde Folsom's church group. The rest are average citizens. There are eighteen county residents, two who lived on the rez, two active military, one Sheriff Deputy, two Omímeya staff, one from IT, and the other maintenance. Twenty-six men. Three women. One Native, one Hispanic, the rest White."

A burst of questions, complaints, and accusations erupted. Who was told what and when? Why were they not informed? Were they just suspects or was there proof? People were talking over each other, and everyone was upset. Mary continued writing her notes.

Sheriff Harris said, "What's next? Are we arresting twenty-nine people? Are we going to hang them all for treason? Can we legally do that?"

Everyone looked at Elliot, who said, "We're not ready to make arrests yet. As you know, if we don't have a Changleska law written, then South Dakota law at the time of Big Thunder applies, and South Dakota had capital punishment for treason."

Jackson explained, "We can't hang that many people, not only for moral reasons, but because even hanging a few will only create martyrs. Perceived injustices and martyrs fuel rebellions. Let's not kid ourselves. What we have is a full-on rebellion, the seeds of revolution. This is more than a few of Folsom's cult followers, twenty-nine diverse people living all over the circle. Those are the only ones we've caught so far. We must assume there are more. People will say we killed people who only wanted free speech. How we handle this can either fan the flames or extinguish it."

Harris said, "Free speech doesn't mean crying fire in a crowded theater. It doesn't mean giving enemies of the state tactical information."

Phil stated firmly, "We need to hang more than just the tech sellers, otherwise, no one will take it seriously."

Mary frowned, recognizing his frustration but also the weight of his suggestion. "I understand your concern, Phil, but we need to consider the broader implications of how we proceed."

"This is more than selling devices, it's the data on them. Conspirators helped commit these crimes. From passing messages to IT gathering data, it all leads to the same result. In 1792, people were hanged for less serious crimes. Everyone needs to understand we're not fucking around." Phil snarled.

Mary kept her tone even, but her hands curled slightly on the table's edge, "I know tempers are up, but I still expect professional language." Phil stared at her.

Ken Harris asked, "Elliot, with the new law only giving seven days between arrest and trial, can the prosecution be ready? Twenty-nine people is a lot of evidence."

"We are only prepared for John Montgomery and a few of the others we caught early. Even using county attorneys, it'd be hard to get ready in a week, maybe two or three. This isn't the old world where you arrested a suspect and had months to build a case to prove it. Now you must have solid proof before the arrest," Elliot answered.

Phil said, "We need to get back to the question of what to do with these people. I get we can't hang all of them, but we need to execute quite a few. People need to be aware of how serious this is. A dozen deaths now could save who knows how many lives in the future."

The general said, "I'm not sure if everyone understands how vulnerable we are. While the US doesn't have a large army now, they could call out their militia. If they combined forces with the Spanish or French, we would have real trouble. Even without modern weapons, large caliber muskets and cannonballs do a lot of damage. We're a long way from replacing some types of ammunition and modern weapons."

Jackson pointed out, "Benjamin Talmadge knew about the ammunition issue. Someone ratted us out. If they think they have a chance of taking us by force, any military will jump at the chance to capture our weapons. We need to punish the traitors, but we should come up with alternatives to executing all of them."

Phil said, "We can't exile them east. Even without electronics, they could give away too much information to the enemy."

Jackson answered, "We could send them to the Lakota. Two Elks will leave his winter camp soon. They wouldn't get in trouble chasing buffalo."

Billy said, "The Lakota would kill and mutilate them, not in that order. They don't take kindly to traitors."

"What about sending them off somewhere to homestead on the frontier? The airplane could drop them off with parachutes far away," said Jackson.

Mary, who'd not said much, busy writing notes, interjected, "Exile to the frontier would be a lingering death sentence. The harsh conditions of the Dakotas, with brutal winters and limited resources, make survival nearly impossible without a resilient and cooperative community. Even with supplies, individuals sent alone would face almost certain failure, battling starvation, exposure, and isolation."

Ken Harris said, "For some of the less serious offenses, fines, community service and the vests may be enough of a deterrent. Most of these people have families, many have critical jobs, like mechanics and steamheads."

Phil said, "If you had people running around with vests that say 'traitor' they'd only attract others with the same beliefs. It's like Jackson said, you'd fuel a rebellion."

Andrea said, looking uncertain to contradict her boss, "It's about public perception. The media's still powerful, maybe more so, with less content to consume. Before making any arrests, release to the media that twenty-nine people are under investigation for providing weapons information and server locations. Paint a picture of cannonballs wiping out Interstate Communications or Tribal TeleComm, destroying NewNet, their children's and grandchildren's future. They were providing information to the enemy to invade us. Remind them that South Dakota law still allows capital punishment for treason."

Phil said, "That's a good idea, but we still need to execute most of them."

The meeting devolved into arguments and counterarguments, some raising points, others venting frustration. Mary listened for a while, her pen scratching furiously as she jotted down key points and arguments. She glanced at the clock and noted how time was slipping away.

"Excuse me, could I have your attention?" Mary's firm but calm voice cut through the overlapping conversations. She had to raise her voice a little, wishing she had her gavel. "It is now a little after four pm. The meeting was scheduled to end at four-thirty."

Phil interrupted her, "You're right, the kitchen will need time to get an order up here. Looks like this meeting will last awhile." Everyone looked resigned to a long evening ahead.

Mary said, "You misunderstood. I'm not suggesting we keep going. My intention is to leave on time. I have a proposal."

Everyone looked at her curiously as she spread out her notes. She had taken a highlighter marking passages of comments people said. Before she gave her proposal, she restated each person's concerns, giving credit for everyone's contributions. Within a few minutes, the previously tense room settled with everyone feeling heard and understood. Then she gave a synopsis of the key issues and consequences of different actions.

"Because it will take a week or more to gather all the evidence to assure convictions, I propose we follow Andrea's suggestions and inform the press about the ongoing investigations. This will put the perpetrators on alert, as Phil said, and possibly shake more bad apples out of the tree. Having people talking about this will hopefully generate outrage instead of sympathy. Instead of inspiring rebellion like Jackson was concerned about, it may do the opposite: stoke patriotic fervor. Everyone wants a better future for their children. Rats, traitors, and tech sellers rob our children of having a chance of antibiotics and a better standard of living."

"That's a great line. Can we use it?" said Andrea.

Mary nodded. "If we do it this way, it won't be a surprise when we start making arrests. The delay works for us to build community support. We can fine and sentence those convicted of lesser charges to community service. They can be at home at their important jobs supporting their families but too busy in their off hours with their service job to stir up trouble on the forums. The wearing of vests is proving to be a crime deterrent. Shame often is." Referring to the notes in front of her, "The Restorative Justice Committee has stated fines that are too onerous can be counterproductive, often leading people back to crime."

Elliot said, "That Committee is proposing all fines should be no more than two to six months of someone's usual salary, depending on the crime, the payments should be based on the ability to pay."

Mary nodded again at this and continued, "I'm afraid I agree that those convicted of treason should be executed."

As the words left her lips, a pang of guilt struck her. Her faith as a devout Catholic clashed with the harsh reality of governance. She thought of the sanctity of life, the teachings of forgiveness, and the moral weight of such a decision. Yet, the safety of their community and the future of their children outweighed her personal struggles. She knew this decision would haunt her, but she felt it was necessary to prevent greater harm.

Everyone looked at her, surprised. Mary continued, "We should not execute the conspirators, only those directly involved. Additionally, we must ensure that those who sold the devices were aware of their contents and were not unwitting participants or mules. Public sentiment could be on our side, if we play the media right. If convicted, the appeal will take time, things will calm down, lessening any backlash. This is not about free speech; it's about protecting our children's future."

Then, she summarized everything in a coherent proposal that addressed everyone's concerns and created a sense of collective ownership over the decisions being made, in a concise format for voting.

Everyone sat for a minute, a bit stunned. Jackson saying, "Ladies and Gentlemen, that's why Mary Landrau is the Chair of the Executive Committee. I second the motion."

The proposal passed, and the meeting ended on time. Mary took the shuttle home as usual, looking forward to making dinner for her family. Not that Mary particularly enjoyed cooking or was very good at it. Mary didn't mind her husband never cooked or felt, if not said, a woman's place was in the kitchen. Making dinner for him, her daughter Bridget, and the grandkids grounded her and gave her a sense of normalcy. These small acts of care felt like love.

Chapter Nine
Brings Him Home

BRINGS HIM HOME hated the thunder people. Everyone else in his band of the Oglala tribe, led by Red Eagle, seemed to love them, or at least they loved the gifts they brought. Now Red Eagle had signed a treaty saying they wouldn't take slaves. Even worse, they couldn't raid other tribes without first talking to their council. He understood why they'd made the agreement: a steady supply of corn without risking lives, muskets and the promise of better rifles, and the trade opportunities. He understood, but he didn't like it. Brings Him Home was a warrior, accomplished at seventeen winters old, one of the best riders in the tribe, with many scalps taken. He was the youngest warrior to capture his own musket, although powder and shot were scarce. Taller than most, he was strong and fast. While other young men learned skills of hunting, bow or knife making, he practiced constantly with bow and musket, throwing knives and ropes. In hand-to-hand fighting, he won almost every time. If he lost, he asked the winner to teach him. He questioned older warriors about past raids. Although he listened to his uncle recount many generations of raids and battles, he declined his offer to train him to become a winter count keeper. He had no patience for anything but learning to be a warrior as good as his father.

Brings Him Home's father, a powerful warrior and war chief, died when he was nine winters old. All his life, the desire to emulate his father's skill and success burned within him. He loved hearing stories about his exploits from his uncle and other warriors. His father died after a buffalo trampled him during a hunt. He lived for a few days after, a painful, slow, and ignominious death for such a renowned warrior. He was driven to surpass his father's achievements, dreaming of a glorious death in battle.

Brings Him Home wondered, with Red Eagle's new peace, whether his dreams would ever be fulfilled. There had been talk of following in Two Elks's footsteps. Two Elks made his winter camp permanent, the thunder people helping build a longhouse like tribes in the east used. They built round structures called yurts, but instead of a fire in the middle with a smoke hole at the top, they built clever cooking stoves that used less wood and heated well, venting smoke outside. Many would stay in the permanent camp, mostly women, children, and elders, protected by their Changleskan allies. They built a hide processing center because Changleska women didn't tan hides. With many people to feed, they needed much meat. While many would leave soon to follow the buffalo, those who remained behind would start farming or work at the processing center tanning hides.

As his world transformed, his peers welcomed the changes introduced by the thunder people, but he only wanted to be a warrior like his father. He didn't know how he could achieve his dreams without the raids that honed skills and taught harsh lessons. He loved tamping down his fears going into battle with prayers, the headlong rush of riding into battle, the satisfaction of the final blow of killing the enemy. The smells of fear and blood, and the rush of adrenaline fed something deep inside of him. He delivered death to his enemies; he wanted nothing else and couldn't imagine another life.

Brings Him Home knew the way of the warrior was more than killing enemies. It was also protecting and caring for his community. He knew his father received praise for feeding the elders and otherwise contributing to the community's well-being. At twelve winters old, he received his name, having taken those lessons to heart. A late blizzard caught his band while they were moving to a different camp. A young mother thought her boy of four winters had been strapped into her travois. When they arrived, with a piercing shriek, she realized the child had untied himself and got out. Their day-long journey made it impossible to determine how long he'd been missing. Amidst the blinding snow, everyone quickly set up camp while consoling the grieving young mother. All assumed the child dead. He was certain his father wouldn't have given up and trudged back into the storm. Though he knew the child's survival was improbable, preparing the body for the spirit world would comfort the mother. He brought an extra robe, fire-making materials, and a tanned, oiled hide for cover to wait out the storm. No one was more surprised than he was to find the boy alive. Huddled together with the blizzard swirling around them, they stayed warm enough and slept through the night. By morning, the weather cleared, and they returned to camp. He would never forget the joy of the mother.

=..=

The summons from Red Eagle took Brings Him Home by surprise. When he arrived at Red Eagle's lodge, he saw two men waiting for him. He could immediately identify one as a thunder person despite his buckskins; his hat and boots, combined with a thick, stocky build, gave him away. He looked only a few years older than him. The other man he recognized as Six Feathers, Two Elks's son. They were about the same age and had worked together during the war games called Changleska Field Day or paint wars. They both nodded at him, then they all moved to sit by the fire. Six Feathers brought out a pipe to share smoke.

Brings Him Home loved the big mock battle six days ago where he was pitted against thunder people's weapons and trucks. He had imagined nothing of that magnitude. He'd heard tales of large battles with the wasichu in the Ohio valley, but seeing a battle of thousands was hard to imagine. Wielding a weapon and spraying opponents with paint earned him battle honors. He desired real blood, not paint, but understood the purpose of war games. He listened with the other warriors when Red Eagle and Night Shield, the war chief, discussed tactics and made their battle plan. When Night Shield asked him a question, as he was apt to do in strategy sessions, Brings Him Home answered with a suggestion they ended up using.

Although the Changleska man could speak Lakota, his accent was hard to understand, and Six Feathers aided with translation if needed.

He said, "My name is Ed Tilson. I've heard good things about you. For someone so young, you've brought much honor to your tribe."

Everyone looked expectantly at him to respond. He remained silent.

"I understand you speak Cheyenne?"

He nodded. His mother was Cheyenne, a prize his father returned with after a successful battle with her tribe. She could speak Lakota but only spoke Cheyenne to him and his sister. After his father died, only his mother and younger sister remained; they were close.

"Expeditions are planned to meet with other tribes. We're looking for volunteers to join the California Expedition. We'll go farther than any Lakota has ever been. All the way to the great water we call an ocean."

Brings Him Home thought, *what does that have to do with me?* But he said nothing.

"We'd like you to join us. You're a fluent Cheyenne speaker and a skilled warrior. I saw you on Field Day. Jumping in that truck was impressive. We're going on a peaceful trade mission, not a war party, but we'll be prepared to face hostilities."

Ed brought out a map, laying it on the ground. They looked as he pointed out the route. "Here's where we'll meet the Cheyenne, Arapaho, Shoshone, Goshute, Paiute, Maidu, Miwok, as well as others. The journey will take about two moons. We will winter here." He pointed to California on the map. "Some will stay, others will return this time next year."

Those tribes were unfamiliar to Brings Him Home. He felt intrigued and curious. But he thought, *who would care for my mother and sister for that long?*

Six Feathers added, "We will bring many weapons, including big guns, many trucks and horses, and fifty men and women."

Brings Him Home asked, "If I go with you, will I get a rifle like yours?" He pointed enviously to the one Six Feathers had at his side.

Ed said, "Sorry, we don't have extras; however, as a member of the expedition, you'll have access to the armory. You can train with ours and use them if there is a battle. We'll pay you as a member of our allied forces in the Changleska Guard. When you return, you may have enough to purchase a rifle. As a member of the Guard, you'd qualify to purchase one."

Brings Him Home was doubtful about ever earning enough. When they first arrived, he'd learned about money. It was clever to bring items to one trader and go to another for something else. Saving money for later purchases was possible, unlike bartering. Even for those permitted to purchase a firearm, the cost was exorbitant. He considered going with the expedition, earning enough to buy a rifle. Traveling through so many tribal lands, they would face inevitable conflict, with opportunities for battle. The problem was he didn t want to join the Guard. Considering them enemies, he observed them with a critical eye, scrutinizing their every action, sound, and mannerism. Those he met during the paint war were happy to answer his many questions. Guardians were required to take orders unquestionably, always. He knew why obedience was necessary, but his leaders welcomed questions and even tolerated challenges under certain conditions. He was torn.

Ed still had the map out. "See here," showing a broad swath of land across the map. "This is Oceti Sakowin today, all the tribes speaking Lakota, Dakota, and Nakota. In the old world, the wasichu forced the Lakota off their lands, to only here and here," pointing to small patches of different colors on the map labeled with English words Brings Him Home couldn't read. "The wasichu are many. They'll not come right away, but they'll come, destroying everything in their path. This is why Changleska must unite the tribes. If we fight each other, we won't have the strength for the battle to come."

Brings Him Home sat silently for some moments, thinking. Finally, he said, "I heard much talk of this. The world that you thunder people came from may never be. People talked of this thing called the butterfly, where the smallest flutter changes things. I heard that was the reason for the war games, to show the wasichu the strength of the thunder people and the Lakota, so they would never attack."

"This is true," said Ed. "But the wasichu are greedy. They will never be content to remain on their side of the big river. They may not come tomorrow, but they'll come. The Lakota cannot fight the wasichu alone. They need Changleska's strength to survive."

This angered him. The thunder people always acted like they knew best, dismissing the wisdom of those who had lived on the plains for countless generations. Some might be Lakota in their blood but looked and acted like the wasichu they lived with. How did they know what would happen in the future? He hated their smug arrogance and resented how they told everyone what to do, from what medicine to take to where to shit. He was taught that anger was the wind that blew away reason. The wise thing would be to take time to think about their offer. But he couldn't seem to help himself.

He stood up and simply said, "No," and walked away.

=..=

Within hours, the entire camp heard he had turned down the offer. His mother chided him. She'd heard he could assign some of his wages to her. Although she could only spend his wages at the Changleska trading posts, she could buy glass beads, making fine beadwork for later trade anywhere they went. His uncle would care for her, and his sister didn't need him to stay on her behalf. His friends heard about it, saying they wanted to go. A chance to buy rifles was not to be missed. They were excited about the adventure, talked about seeing new lands, meeting new tribes, perhaps the chance to kill some of them. Trained as warriors, the concept of peace was foreign.

Brings Him Home directed more anger at himself than at anything else. He hated being thought of as young and foolish, but he'd had made an impulsive decision that he now regretted. Accompanied by his two closest friends, One Ear and Little Dog, he went to the Changleska camp to see whether it wasn t too late to join. They figured if Changleska wanted Brings Him Home enough, he might have enough leverage to ask to include his friends.

With all the confidence of youth, the boys assumed they would be welcomed on the expedition, packed all their gear and horses, and left early the next day. The Guard had established a new base where the Field Day had been, only a day's ride from Red Eagle's camp. The roads and some infrastructure were already there, and permanent structures were being built. Because this would be the base for all the expeditions to launch from, large sections for both horses and cattle were being fenced in.

The boys heard the noise and smelled the smoke long before they reached the base. They followed along a fence to reach an opening. Brings Him Home s training taught him to always avoid chokepoints, which made him nervous. He saw two armed riders approaching. They stopped before getting too close to the fence gate. He motioned to the others to flank the riders, which caused one armed man to shout something in English they couldn t understand and wave his rifle about. With a hand motion to the others, the trio proceeded slowly, but the man on the horse kept yelling.

One Ear, who knew the most English, said, "We don't speak English. We are friends."

The man kept yelling and raised his rifle to point at them.

With a quick whistle, One Ear and Little Dog raised their bows, with an undulating war cry. Brings Him Home sped his horse so fast toward the man with the rifle that he froze in shock and got a wild shot off. Brings Him Home rode right up to him, striking him with his coup stick. As he struggled to stay on his agitated horse, Brings Him Home grabbed the rifle right out of his hands. All the commotion spooked the other horse, throwing its rider. The other man lay on the ground cradling his arm, yelling and screaming.

All three boys whooped and hollered. This was great fun. The man with the rifle looked at them with hateful eyes, but One Ear and Little Dog still had bows aimed at him. He obviously knew that despite their youth, they were dangerous. With gestures, they made him get down from his horse. Brings Him Home hopped down, efficiently searching him, removing a knife and a radio, then tied his hands behind his back. They didn't bother tying up the one with the broken arm, not realizing the man on the ground radioed for help. Having encountered radios during paint wars, Little Dog recognized them. At another whistle from Brings Him Home, they secured both men. He held on to the rifle, let One Ear use his musket, and held both men at gunpoint, waiting while they chatted and laughed.

Not long after, they heard the trucks: a big one called a Bear Cat, another called a technical, both bristling with weapons. Angry men and a couple of women all piled out and surrounded them. Brings Him Home raised the rifle over his head in a nonthreatening way, and ordered the other two to drop their weapons and raise their hands.

Brings Him Home shouted, "We don't speak English. They fired on us. I did not kill them, only counted coup," pointing, he said, "This man was wounded when he fell from his horse."

An older White man, dressed as an officer, approached. During the field exercises, Brings Him Home made a point to learn how they structured their forces. He didn't know all the rank insignia yet, but he knew this man was called a major. They waited for a few minutes while a woman with an interpreter patch on her uniform translated.

The major ignored everyone and walked right up to the man still tied up at Brings Him Home's feet. "What the fuck, Jerry? You shot first?"

"They didn't halt or show ID."

"They don't speak English. Did they threaten you before you shot at them?"

"He," pointing at Brings Him Home with fury in his eyes, "rushed at me with his horse, then hit me with his stick. He could've killed me."

"This stick?" he said, gesturing to look closer at the coup stick, but he didn't touch it. "This is a coup stick used to show courage in battle. It would break if used as a club. See this?" pointing at the scalps. "I count seven. This means this boy who looks your sister's age has killed seven men in battle. You are lucky to be alive."

The medics who had been looking at the man with the broken arm put him in a truck and drove away. The major stared at Jerry, still tied up, sitting at Brings Him Home's feet. Clearly, this man was a close relative, a father or uncle, but he didn't ask Brings Him Home to untie him.

With the translator's help, he said, "My name is Major John Dunphy, commanding officer of this base. And who might you be, and why have you come?"

Brings Him Home gave his name and those of the two others, his heart sinking. He worried that if this bound man was the major's son or nephew, they might not be allowed on an expedition. His disappointment surprised him.

He said, "Ed Tilson and Six Feathers came to my camp and asked me to join the California expedition because I speak Cheyenne. My friends wanted to see if there was a place for them as well."

Major Dunphy said, "I see. Looks like he was looking for warriors as well as interpreters. Since you were invited, welcome. Not sure if there is room for your friends, but if they are as skilled as you, we'll use them somewhere. Please untie my son."

That answered that question, thought Brings Him Home. He wondered if he could keep the rifle and the horse. He wasn't sure whether the usual battle rules applied or if this was more of a game. Hanging on to the rifle and the horse, he motioned to One Ear to untie Jerry. Then he purposefully started looking over the saddle, saying calming words to the horse as he put his hands over its withers. The rifle was a well-used but cared-for Savage 110. In the saddlebag were many rounds of .308 Winchester ammunition. His intent was clear; he was looking over his new possessions.

The major said, "Shit, Jerry, you stepped in it now. According to Lakota custom, he won your horse and rifle fair and square. Jackson himself has instructed us to respect all Indigenous customs."

"But dad," Jerry said, alarmed, "I can't lose Cinnamon. I've had him since he was a foal."

The major pulled out his phone, evidently to read the new Uniform Code of Military Justice (UCMJ) rules. Then he said sternly, "Private Dunphy, I find you guilty of discharging your weapon, endangering a civilian who was considering joining our allied forces. In lieu of a fine, you shall relinquish your rifle, horse, and saddle. You can remove any personal possessions from the saddlebags."

The woman translated. Jerry looked like he was going to cry as he went and emptied his saddlebags and whispered to the horse, patting him softly.

Brings Him Home was ecstatic with the rifle and horse but realized that he'd made two enemies today, and one was the base commander. He might not have wanted to show favoritism, but it was his son. The major wouldn't forget.

He thought for a bit and motioned for the interpreter and said to Major Dunphy, "You are a fair leader and a worthy ally. I am grateful for this fine rifle, saddle, and horse. While I have no rifle or saddle like this, I have four horses and don't need a fifth. Major, I give you this horse. You may return him to your son, or not, as you will."

Jerry looked grateful, though his gaze flickered between relief and anger, hinting at a complicated blend of emotions. He even helped take off the saddle of his horse and put it on one of Brings Him Home's spare horses.

Brings Him Home tried not to show how thrilled he was. Of the seven virtues of the Lakota, humility was the one he struggled most with. He shot a glance at the other boys. With a serious look from him, they got the message. After going through the gate, they arrived in the camp a short time later.

=..=

They expanded the paint war practice ground to create what was now called Expedition Base Camp. They left the middle empty for later use. People were tossing around new names, but nothing official stuck yet. Around the perimeter, they were building storage warehouses, erecting large tents, and a large outdoor kitchen with picnic tables, with a line forming outside. The parking lot held numerous trucks, military vehicles, and trailers. Construction was everywhere. Along the wooded area by the small creek were tents, tipis, barracks, and showers.

The boys were directed to the expedition intake tent. All three hobbled their horses and entered. A young woman sat at a table at the front, several other people behind her working on laptop computers. One Ear looked excited. He loved computers, having seen several during the paint war. The woman looked bored and asked their names. One Ear gave his name, but his poor English was apparent. She summoned the interpreter they'd seen earlier, who approached them with a smile.

After checking her laptop, she said, I don t see your names on the list." She pointed to the people behind her. Applications are still being processed. When did you submit your application?"

Brings Him Home said, Ed Tilson invited me. My friends also want to join."

The woman nodded, talked on her radio, then said, You still need to complete applications. It ll take a while because I m the only interpreter on duty. I ll start with you." She pointed to One Ear. Sit here." She brought a chair close to a table.

Pointing to Brings Him Home, she said, Ed wants to speak to you first. He is working on his trailer in the parking lot. He s welding. Shouldn t be hard to spot."

It turned out he was hard to find. The parking lot was very full, but Brings Him Home looked around until he saw someone on a ladder with a face mask and a tool with a flame coming out of the end, sparks flying, welding a frame on top of a four-horse trailer. He watched for a while, not wanting to interrupt but fascinated. He was worried. If he had offended the man by turning him down, he might not be allowed to join. *What would that mean for my friends?* He thought.

Finally, Ed either noticed him or needed a break. He came down the ladder, smiled at Brings Him Home and said, You changed your mind?"

Seeing he wasn't angry, Brings Him Home relaxed. "Yes," he said, not offering further explanation.

"You don't say much. That's smart."

"I brought two friends, both skilled warriors. Little Dog is one of our best hunters."

"Do either speak another language?"

He shook his head no.

"We're almost at capacity. We have enough hunters, but if I can't fit them in for California, the north and southwest expeditions are short. The southwest expedition will be with us part way and then it will split off. I can try to fit them there."

He nodded again.

Ed sighed, You re welcome." He radioed intake and told them to process and accept all three, promising that he d find places for them.

Here is how it works. Until you can learn to speak and read enough English to pass the test, you can t be full Guard members. You can study for the exam on the trip, but other than a bump in pay, there s not much difference between Guards and allied members on expeditions. You ll need to take the oath. As a citizen, you will receive benefits. I forgot, the other benefit to full Guard membership is spousal benefits. Are you married?"

He shook his head no but said, I care for my mother and sister. I heard they could access my pay."

"Yes, that's no problem. Intake can set it up, but your mother will need to come pick up her card. You can get a message to her and invite her and other family members to the departure ceremony. We are leaving in two weeks."

Ed then shook his hand, saying, "Welcome to the California Expedition."

The thunder people's custom of shaking hands was unfamiliar to him, but he knew it sealed agreements.

Brings Him Home returned to the intake tent. When his turn came, the interpreter asked him many questions he found both intrusive and unnecessary. Like, did he have a criminal history? Some questions he didn't know how to answer, like how do you cope with stress? After she defined stress, he told her he'd either throw knives or people, whichever was closer. He found her obvious fear of him amusing.

The new recruits were told where to camp, where to eat, where to put their horses, and, of course, where to shit. The thunder people still annoyed him, and now he was becoming one of them. It was too late for their medical intake. They had to schedule it for the morning after taking their oath. Then they d get their ID with the QR code with their money on it. They were excited to visit the base trading post after being given a signing bonus. They received a list of required and recommended items to purchase, which further annoyed Brings Him Home. He wore neither underwear nor socks, so why did he need to buy six pairs of each? And what were safety pins?

After they got settled in camp, the three of them went over the lists. Brings Him Home was further frustrated by the growing importance of learning English. They were on Lakota land; he didn t know why the thunder people couldn t all learn to speak Lakota instead. The importance of logistics was clear to him. He d helped plan many raids. For a significantly longer journey, he needed to be prepared, which meant understanding these lists. They all split up, going to different campfires with their lists and asking questions. Everyone s helpfulness surprised Brings Him Home. By pointing to the list with a questioning look, he found he could be understood. People pulled out their packs, showing what each item on the list was. Everyone gave tips, arguing, saying what to bring or not bring.

Before going to sleep, they compared notes. One Ear had remembered to ask about prices, so they had a good idea of what to expect. Evidently, the thunder people bought a lot of snacks. They were being fed three meals a day and could hunt, so they wouldn t spend money on snacks. Most of the recommended items, like safety pins and pens, they didn t need. Everyone said to buy long underwear. Footwear was a concern. Their mothers or sisters wouldn t be around to repair or make new moccasins. Boots and socks were expensive. They d return to Red Eagle s camp and give their mothers the message about their pay and the departure ceremony, and would hope their mothers could make moccasins in time. They d need winter moccasins as well. One person suggested they buy small items like knives or beads for trading with the tribes they visited. Everyone said they'd need soap, and since women collected the plants they used instead of soap, they probably should buy some. No one they spoke to had ever been on an expedition, but enough had been on similar trips to give good advice.

Neither of his friends got on the California Expedition, but Little Dog got into the southwest one. They'd be together halfway. All three were sad, close as brothers. They had faced every challenge together; their bond forged in the fires of shared experiences.

The next morning, they took their oath, got their IDs, and reported to the Medical Corps' tent. On the day of Big Thunder, there was a conference at Omímeya with 153 doctors attending. These doctors organized the Medical Corps (MC) serving both civilians and military. Independent, with their own organizational structure, loosely based on military models, Changleska funded it separately. The MC ran training programs and planned a full medical school. They had sent a medical outreach team to Red Eagle's camp when they first arrived to screen for contagious illnesses.

All three boys endured invasive and embarrassing medical examinations. Syphilis had spread among some tribes due to visits of French fur traders and the practice of wife sharing. All three received clean bills of health. The Medical Corps could even improve One Ear s hearing. He had lost most of his ear and some hearing on that side when a musket ball narrowly missed his head. It would only take a few days because many of their elders had passed away when they initially arrived, so they had additional hearing aids.

When Brings Him Home went to the tent marked California, he'd met the commander. He'd thought the commander was Ed Tilson, but surprisingly, Tilson just headed the Advance Crew. Captain Andrew Morrison was a White man in middle years. Andrew Morrison did not speak directly to him; he spoke no Lakota but assigned Six Feathers to orient him.

The California Expedition would start with seventy-eight people, but twenty-five would break off on Paiute lands, near Green River, Utah, heading south to Dinah (Navajo) and Hopi lands. They would bring twenty-four trucks and twenty-eight horses. Six trucks and eight horses would split off to go south. The amount of food and water required for both people and horses was staggering, weighing over four tons. Although they planned to filter water for people and supplement their food supplies through hunting and trade, they recognized the necessity of carrying backup provisions. The combined weight of people and additional gear amounted to two tons. Fuel contributed the most significant weight, as the journey demanded a round-trip supply. Specifically, eighty 55-gallon drums of vegetable oil fuel added another sixteen tons to the load.

Brings Him Home, overwhelmed with the complexity of preparations, and wanted to understand it all. *If this was a peaceful mission of trade, what would a war party look like?* He thought. He had to admit to being impressed. They placed him on the Advance Crew, the guides and scouts who also provided security for the road crews. They would also help the road crew if needed. They d be a few days ahead on horseback. Brings Him Home was happy he did not have to ride in the crowded, stinky trucks most of the time.

Brings Him Home was still uncomfortable with the thunder people but knew this was an opportunity. If he was going to be a warrior as good as his father, he needed to listen and learn; that is what he planned to do.

PART II
Summer
(blokétu)

The elders were wise. They know that man's heart,
away from nature, becomes hard; they knew that
lack of respect for growing, living things soon led
to a lack of respect for humans too.
— Luther Standing Bear (1868–1939),
Sicangu and Oglala Lakota author, educator, and actor

Chapter Ten
Rose

ROSE WAS HUMBLED to witness the Sun Dance as it was 234 years prior to their arrival in this time. It was a profound experience, but she was grateful to be home after being gone for six days. As far as she could remember, she d never spent so much time without electronics. The Indigenous Lakota held their Sun Dance on the summer solstice, unlike the ones she had previously attended in August. The experience was so different she hadn t fully processed it yet. While the ceremony itself differed from the ones from her era, what changed was her spiritual experience. Before she attended only to support Hotah, her husband at the time. Intellectually, she appreciated the ceremony, but it did not touch her heart in the same way. Before, she had felt detached and often distracted, in stark contrast to the deep engagement she experienced now. Then, she would escape to the parking lot to work on her laptop. Being invited to this Sun Dance was an honor, and they had to travel many miles to attend. Fortunately, they could take the *Endeavor* most of the way, and travel the rest of the journey on horseback. The host tribe, a Yankton band related to Two Elks , forbade any motorized transports, electronics, or other trappings of her old world.

Before she met Hotah, she'd felt disconnected from her Lakota heritage, partially because she was only one-quarter and had been raised by her White mother. Her father, a member of the Yankton Lakota tribe, had only lived with her mother for a short time. After they divorced, he returned to the reservation. She rarely visited him, as she lived several hours away in Rapid City. Rose had mixed feelings about her identity, as she felt someone full blood, or raised on the reservation, deserved it more than she did. She hadn t experienced the same level of discrimination and racism faced by her full blood Native peers. Her light hair and eyes offered her protection they didn t have. For example, she recalled how teachers treated her more leniently in school or how she avoided the racial profiling her peers endured. Although she preferred her Lakota heritage to her mixed European, she only started embracing the culture after she had married Hotah and had Kimi. Before Big Thunder, she always felt out of sync with the spiritual practices, although she attended many ceremonies. After Kimi told her about Big Thunder hours before it happened, and she watched her daughter call the thunder for the Wakíŋyaŋ ceremony, she believed in a way she had never had before. She had faith in the master plan of the Creator, and even if she didn t understand it, she knew everything happened for a reason.

Kimi, with surprising wisdom for her age, told her that spirituality was like a garden. It had to be nurtured with prayer, ritual, song, ceremony, and shared with others, or it would wither and die. Rose knew she spent too little time tending to her spiritual garden. Rose realized how much the ceremony gave her a renewed sense of care and intentionality, focusing her mind on planting seeds of prayer and cultivating connections with others. Hotah would dance as well as other friends and family. They were there as supporters. Her children had come early to help with the preparations.

The spiritual power she felt at this Sun Dance differed from her previous experience. This time, it felt as though the prayers resonated within her, amplifying a deep sense of unity and purpose. Rose stood transfixed, her eyes tracing the forms of the dancers as they moved under the relentless sun. The air was thick with the scent of sage and sweat, a pungent incense that clung to her nostrils. She could almost feel the parched earth beneath their feet. The powerful beat of the drums reverberated through the air, creating a rhythm that echoed like a heartbeat. Witnessing their unwavering endurance as they fasted for four days, followed by the ritualistic piercing, she felt a profound awe swell within her.

Rose knew even in her time people had died from heat exhaustion and from the intensity. She knew the United States government had outlawed the ceremony, and it only resurfaced in the 1970s. Rose had heard stories about people healed from diseases that modern medicine would deem incurable. She knew of visions and insights experienced by both dancers and supporters. Witnessing the ceremony, she understood it was not about endurance; it was about sacrifice. The spiritual intensity of the prayers resonated deeply within her, each word a thread weaving into the fabric of her being. As the ceremony unfolded, a radiant light enveloped her, flooding her soul with warmth and a profound sense of connection, as if the very essence of the ritual had become one with her spirit. She felt cocooned in a force that connected her to the Creator, the Sun, and the Earth. It gave her greater insight and the feeling that she was on the right path.

Rose was glad she'd come, even though she was initially reluctant to be so far away. The thought of leaving Omímeya unsettled her; she worried about potential emergencies or decisions being made in her absence. She also recognized how much she relied on constant connectivity, but stepping away felt both daunting and necessary. Jackson s willingness to attend was the only reason she came. She hated camping, being out of touch, not being able to use her phone or computer. NewNet was just a shadow of its past after Big Thunder, with severely limited cell service, yet she still spent nearly all her time on her devices. Getting away was difficult, but she was happy she did.

Jackson looked forward to attending his first Sun Dance. He was curious and eager to witness a tradition so deeply rooted in Lakota spirituality. He hoped to gain a better understanding of the culture that was so important to Rose. They hadn't spent this much time alone together since they met. They had only been lovers for three months but had been friends and colleagues since the day of Big Thunder six months ago. Working side by side during one of the most challenging periods of their lives had given them a deep understanding of each other's strengths and vulnerabilities, which now enriched their relationship. That foundation of friendship and shared work cemented their connection.

Rose's love for him was deep and encompassed her entire being. She couldn't imagine her life without him. Despite knowing he loved her, his reluctance to move in together created emotional distance. Jackson wrestled with his unresolved grief over Denise, the fiancée he had lost behind the Circle, a burden he hadn't fully shared with Rose. This hesitation often left her feeling uncertain about their future, even as she tried to support him through his healing process. Rose had to admit she wanted marriage, a deeply ingrained instinct, a fundamental drive for security. She fought jealousy whenever women flirted with him, which was often. While she trusted Jackson, these moments of insecurity highlighted her deeper desire for commitment and stability in their relationship. He was such an attractive man, with a powerful position as Executive Councilor. She'd thought she would never remarry again. Fulfilled by her work, she thought maybe the occasional boyfriend would come along. Now she had a great boyfriend, but it wasn't enough.

The time Jackson and Rose spent at the Sun Dance deepened their connection. Their conversations about their personal spiritual journeys were more open than they had ever been. While his Christianity remained a part of him, he acknowledged it didn't diminish his reverence for the Red Road. Once they got settled in their camp, Jackson spent a lot of time with the men, and she with the women. When they were together, without the usual distractions of work and electronics, they bonded, sharing laughter over stories of their childhood. Jackson told stories from his past he had rarely spoken of before. The uninterrupted time allowed them quiet moments as they watched the stars and talked about their hopes for Changleska's future.

=..=

Rose returned to a massive backlog of work. She remembered why she never took vacations. The to-do list seemed endless: reviewing reports on resource allocation, managing budgetary shortfalls, and coordinating the logistics for multiple ongoing projects. Each task reminded her of the mounting pressures on Omímeya s limited resources. She was worried about finances. Rose was frustrated everyone expected Omímeya to pay for everything requiring hard currency. She knew she should be happy if the casino consortium stored gold, silver, and precious stones in the underground safe. Although it had been worth twelve million the day before Big Thunder, it was only worth about $120,000 now. Granted, 1792 prices were low, but Omímeya's gold was quickly running out. Their property in New Orleans was costing a fortune with all the improvements. If they were to buy the neighboring plantation, they'd be able to free the slaves that worked there, and income would trickle in. It would be a good investment for the long term, but the present financial situation was still worrisome. The Changleska economy, at least, was thriving. If they could solve the labor shortage, they d have more goods to export. This was only one problem of many. Each problem had competing needs which usually involved money.

Some progress occurred in the negotiations with Spain to recognize Changleskan independence. The delay in communications made it difficult. They hoped their knowledge of gold and silver mines in South America, some technology transfers, and other trade concessions would be enough to convince the Spaniards to sign a treaty giving them New Spain. They worried that Spain, firmly established in California, might stay and exploit the mines themselves. Their spies may already know the locations. When they first arrived, people cut pages out of library books, particularly encyclopedias containing information on mining and metallurgy, or stole entire books on agriculture and engineering. These volumes were critical for recreating lost technologies and skills. Things could have been significantly worse if not for an online forum dedicated to the science fiction novel *1632* by Eric Flint, which alerted people to the potential dangers. This warning led to the relocation of all books containing sensitive information to the secure Omímeya library.

Almost all the expeditions were underway. Changleska provided most of the supplies, trucks, and fuel, so there was little cash outlay for Omímeya. Such a long round trip with so many vehicles uncovered a critical shortage of motor oil. Her first meeting of the day would be to discuss the plan to address it. She would meet with Kyle Ward, head of the resource department, Richard Russo, the Minister of Infrastructure, and Miguel Ruiz, who had recently returned from investigating the oil seep near Shreveport. The oil was on land belonging to the Caddo Confederacy, a union of related tribes, including the Kadohadacho, Natchitoches, Yatasi, and Hasinai. Although decimated by diseases brought by colonization, they still had small thriving villages.

Kyle opened the meeting by saying, "We knew we had to address getting oil sooner or later. This field is close to the surface. Its proximity to the Mississippi River makes it easy to transport."

"You met with tribal members?" Rose asked Miguel.

"Yes and fortunately many of them spoke Spanish. They were familiar with the oil seep, used for medicine, and caulking for their canoes. The tribe gathers it for trade. They appreciated the gifts we took and wanted to trade with us. The oil dudes didn't make a great impression, but the girls loved them," said Miguel.

The 'oil dudes' is what they called the three men that worked for a North Dakota oil company that were in the casino the day of Big Thunder. Two engineers and a geologist. They were high rollers and hard partiers in their thirties. Two of the men had credit cards and bank accounts at local banks, and unlike many guests, they weren't destitute. They all moved into one suite and stayed in the hotel since. They had a reputation for being unruly. Richard got them jobs in the infrastructure department, including working on plans for creating oil refineries. Since arriving, a large part of their work has involved assessing the resources brought with them and what could be replicated with late eighteenth-century materials.

Miguel said, "When they aren't out in the fields, they are buying favors from young girls."

"How young? Did they give consent?" asked Rose in alarm. "Did this cause problems with their fathers or brothers?"

"Too young to be legal in the old world. Not sure here, teenagers. Their fathers brought them forward and gifts were exchanged. I gathered this happens often. A few of the children I saw were obviously mixed blood."

Rose sighed, "It's not for us to judge their culture, but I'd hoped our people would set better examples. What else can you tell us about their village?"

Miguel said, "About fifty people, the bigger village was further south. A collection of circular houses, built of woven reeds and clay, clustered around a central plaza. The nearby fields where they grew corn, beans, squash, and sunflowers were well tended. There was a ceremonial lodge on one side of the plaza. Along the riverbank, there were canoes and drying racks for fish. This was a common trade area, with goods readily available for river traffic."

Richard changed the subject, "Did you bring up selling the land to us? We need oil for our long-term survival."

"They're not eager to deal with us," Miguel admitted. "They've heard stories about the Lakota. Bad ones. Accounts of raids, stealing harvests, killings, taking slaves, the sad thing is that the stories are true, or used to be before we came."

Rose said. "It's complicated enough negotiating land deals with tribes unfamiliar with the concept of selling land. Add the mistrust, and it's a minefield."

"The forums are blowing up over this," Kyle said. "The Gaia Committee wants to pass a law putting restrictions on using oil for almost anything."

"Not sure if they realize," Richard said, "Oil isn't just about engines. There are important industrial uses, chemicals, medicine, agriculture, transportation. There are too many needs we can't ignore. Hemp won't cut it for everything."

"The Gaia Committee is afraid we are going down the dangerous road of dependence on fossil fuels. We saw where that led. They also don't want petrochemicals for fertilizers or pesticides," Rose said mildly.

Richard said with annoyance, "Don't those crazy hippies realize those fertilizers and pesticides can increase food production 60-70%?"

"Yes, but they believe the cost in pollution and loss of soil fertility isn't worth it. In the old world, it only served the profits of agribusiness." answered Rose.

"Okay, what about kerosene and motor oil? You know the primary lubricant and lighting now is whale oil." said Richard.

Kyle said with a wry smile. "Even the Gaia folks recognize that petroleum's better than hunting whales into extinction. The thought of burning whale oil horrifies them. But they're convinced that veggie oil and hemp will eliminate our need for fossil fuels."

"That's because they live in la-la land," said Richard. We can't produce enough veggie oil for our needs, and while hemp is useful, the oil is not suitable for extraction in quantity."

"He has a point," replied Kyle. "We've been trying to find seed corn, no soy at all. Monsanto or other GMO companies bred all seed specifically not to reproduce, requiring farmers to buy their proprietary seed."

Miguel asked, "Is that why they asked me to bring back as much seed corn and sunflowers as possible?"

Kyle said, "Yes, we're trying to develop our own strains, but it takes years."

"Perhaps throttling by the Gaia committee will help in the long term, but we are stuck with fossil fuels for now. Just because a law is proposed doesn t mean the Council will approve it," said Rose.

Kyle added, The fuel committee is working on alternatives, but converting all gas engines to diesel isn t practical. Cars can only use a small percentage of ethanol. Other fuels like methanol or biogas are being discussed, but there are no quick or easy solutions."

"Back to the idea of buying the land outright." Rose shook her head. "The revenue from oil should go to the Caddo."

"The investment to build a refinery, distill kerosene, and process petrochemicals is massive. They'd never be able to afford it without us. We need a return on the investment. Changleska can't recreate much from our old world without oil. We need to buy the land. We can give them a good price." Richard stated.

"Still makes it exploitation," Miguel said bluntly. "No matter how we dress it up, we know the long-term value. They don't."

"We must be careful here. Think about future generations. Are you aware of what happened with the Osage tribe when they discovered oil on their lands?" asked Rose

Richard and Miguel shook their heads no.

"The discovery of oil on their land brought Osage members so much money that they became rich overnight, but then they were exploited and some were even murdered. There was a great book and movie about it, *Killers of the Flower Moon*," said Rose.

"If they sell the land to Changleska, the government will own the oil. We could provide regular funds to the tribe to ensure their protection," said Richard.

"They're not children," protested Miguel. "Changleska may have their best interests at heart now, but it's still a government. The next elected officials might have a different agenda. We shouldn't trust the government, even the one we created."

"He has a point," said Kyle.

After thinking for a bit, Rose said, "We could create a corporation with shares. The Caddo Confederacy would own fifty-one percent and share the burden of operational costs and distribute profits to their tribal members as they see fit. Changleska and Omímeya would get shares based on how much money they put into building the infrastructure to process and transport the oil. The land stays theirs, and we develop the oil together."

Kyle asked. "Is that possible?"

"Yes, it shouldn't be difficult," Rose said. "Otherwise, it would be too hard to balance our needs with protecting their rights. Even with the constitution and the oaths we swore, it's all meaningless if greed takes over down the line."

"You think a corporation avoids that?" Kyle asked.

Rose said, "It's the best chance we have. Structuring it is easy. Paying for it is the hard part."

Miguel said, The Caddo won t understand what a corporation is. The oil dudes surveyed the fields and marked out a place for the refinery. They warned the Caddo that it would be loud, noisy, and stinky. Fortunately, it was miles from the village."

"We can simplify the concept, comparing it to their existing systems of shared resources and trade. We'll need infrastructure, possibly a clinic, given the influx of workers. With enough resources spent in their village, they may welcome us," Rose said. "Is it a suitable location for a communication outpost, Kyle?"

"A little far from New Orleans. Doable if we are successful in making the Starlink parts work."

Rose smiled. She knew the Starlinks were a sore spot for Kyle. When he was the Emergency Preparedness Manager for Omímeya, he bought quite a few of the larger ones, and numerous minis to have Internet or cell service if cell towers went down, like in a normal natural disaster. No one planned for time travel where no satellites came with them when Big Thunder dropped them in 1791. Now they were trying to repurpose the parts for the new radio stations.

Rose said, "I'll work on the corporation. What shall we call it?"

After various suggestions, they decided to call it Unity Petroleum, to symbolize the collaboration between Omímeya, Changleska, and the Caddo.

Rose concluded the meeting by saying, "We have a solid plan. Let's coordinate the *Endeavor*'s next trip and finalize logistics. And Richard," she added sternly, "talk to your oil dudes. Changleska doesn't have a human resources department yet. This is a good reason we need one. Their behavior directly impacts our relationship with the Caddo. It's crucial we set the right example. They're your employees. I'll hold you responsible for their behavior. We don't want to alienate the Caddo."

=..=

A few days later, Rose and Jackson were hanging out on the deck watching the river, a rare moment of peace, when Kimi came out very excited.

"Gift is coming home today." She said.

"Wonderful. When? Did you get a message from the Arikara?" Asked Rose.

"No message, I just know."

Rose nodded no longer surprised her strange daughter knew things before anyone else. Kimi's uncanny ability to sense events before they happened had become a quiet source of awe among those who knew her. While some in the community regarded her gift with reverence, others whispered about it in hushed tones, afraid and unsure. Jackson looked perplexed but said nothing.

Gift had left a month ago to visit the Arikara village and the man named Ciwaku who wanted to make her his second wife. Despite being only sixteen, she had the right to decide for herself, according to the traditions of both the Lakota, where she was raised, and the Arikara, where she was born. That she was still a minor under Changleskan law made the situation difficult, especially for Hotah, her legal adoptive father. Both he and Rose opposed the match. Hotah was furious with Rose that she suggested Gift visit the village. He was worried Ciwaku would refuse to let her return. He thought she was too young, and with the trauma she experienced, not ready to be independent. But Rose knew Gift needed to make her own decision. They needed to trust her to make the right one. If they forbade the match, she might go anyway. Rose told Hotah that Gift was stronger and smarter than he thought. She needed a chance to look at what life would be like with the Arikara before she decided. She'd been stolen from the Arikara when she was nine years old, so if she wanted to return, it should be her right.

Not long after that, Gift returned to the house on Crow Road, where she lived with Hotah and his family, except for occasional weekends at Rose's house. She told him she would stay but would no longer go to school, even online. There was nothing that school would teach her she needed to learn. Gift spent her time when Kimi was in school training with the Lakota warriors and the Neighborhood Watch, learning to shoot. While some in the community admired her dedication and growing skill, others questioned whether such intense preparation was appropriate for someone so young. She practiced with both bow and arrow and throwing knives. She also asked to take martial arts classes.

A month later, Gift approached Rose cautiously. "Rose, could I have some money to buy guns?"

Rose considered her for a moment. "I'll agree to it if you promise to continue your weapons' training," she replied firmly.

Gift's face lit up, but before she could respond, Rose added, "You might not need to buy any, though. I recently discovered something unexpected in the house."

"What do you mean?" Gift asked, curiosity piqued.

"The former general manager left behind a large gun safe," Rose explained, leading Gift to the closet with a hidden panel. "Jackson convinced me to have the locks opened, even though guns make me uncomfortable. Turns out, it's a small armory."

In addition to the rifles and pistols, the safe contained a variety of ammunition, a couple of hunting knives, and a meticulously maintained crossbow, along with several tactical accessories like scopes and holsters.

Gift's eyes widened as Rose revealed the contents of the safe. "You can pick out what you want," Rose said.

Gift nodded eagerly, carefully selecting the weapons. She chose a Ruger American Rifle and a Glock19 pistol, as well as the crossbow, and a holster for the pistol.

Rose watched her, her expression softening. "I'm guessing this is about feeling safe, considering... what happened to you," she said gently.

Gift glanced at Rose, "That's not it. It is more than protecting Kimi. It's like a storm gathering in the distance, unseen but impossible to ignore. Something is coming, and I don't know what it is, but I can feel its weight. I need to be ready for whatever happens."

Later, when Hotah learned of the decision, he sighed deeply but nodded in reluctant understanding. "If it helps her feel safe, then so be it," he said, though his unease was evident.

Gift never talked about her visit to the Arikara, and what happened between her and Ciwaku. Perhaps she felt it was too personal to share, or maybe she worried others would judge her decision-making. Whatever the reason, the silence seemed to protect a part of her experience that she wasn't ready to reveal, leaving Rose to wonder, but she respected her need for privacy.

A few weeks later, they were at home cooking together. Gift mentioned something about Arikara cooking, then Rose felt comfortable asking, "How was it going back to the Arikara? You haven't said much about it."

Gift answered, "Different than I remembered, more peaceful than here. I liked Ciwaku's first wife. The baby was sweet. I could see myself making a home there. I remembered what you said about Luke's father and how he only wanted to use you. Ciwaku was the same. He not only wanted a wife for the usual reasons but wanted me because of my connection to you. Ciwaku assumed it would give him more standing and a better position to trade with others. But that's what most men want, a wife to use. He's no different from any other man. The Lakota have many wives because they need a lot of hides to trade. Many wives are necessary to complete all the work. I came back for a different reason."

"Whatever the reason, we're happy you're home. You don't have to tell me why, but I'll listen."

"During the Wakíŋyaŋ ceremony, the Thunder Beings spoke to me. To hear it clearly, I needed to return to the Arikara to the lands my mother and father walked. There, surrounded by the echoes of their spirits, I could hear what the thunder whispered. After fasting and praying, I understood. My life belongs to Kimímela. She is important, the Thunder Beings speak to her. They lead us forward in a good way. But her path is full of dangers and obstacles. My job is to protect her, guide her when I can. If she falls, I'm afraid for the generations to come."

Rose was stunned. The depth of Gift's selflessness left her in awe, a mixture of pride and sorrow swelling within her. She realized she had underestimated Gift's strength and the weight of her convictions. This revelation transformed how Rose saw her. Gift was no longer only a survivor, but now a guardian with a purpose far greater than herself. She was humbled and confused. She was also afraid for her daughter. What dangers lie ahead that the thunder people felt she needed a protector?

Chapter Eleven
Jamal

JAMAL WAS DISAPPOINTED at his first impression of Boston in 1792. No one looked friendly or happy. The harbor was filthy and stank. The quaint historic buildings he remembered from his visit in the twenty-first century looked grimy and poorly maintained now. After eleven long weeks filled with stops and frustrating delays, the arduous journey finally ended, yet a sense of anticlimactic disappointment washed over him as they arrived.

For Jamal and Nels, arriving in Boston was depressing compared to their arrival in New Orleans. Then again, they arrived on the *Anna Marie*, dressed as normal passengers. They could never pass as locals with their accents and differences in language, but foreigners were common in Boston, one of the biggest ports in North America. At least Jamal wouldn't have to pose as a slave, since Massachusetts had legally banned slavery nine years earlier, although some slaves were reclassified as indentured servants. There were growing free Black communities in Boston, although facing racism and economic inequality managed mutual aid societies, churches, and schools to support their members.

The two men were both happy to get off the ship. Jamal had never been more terrified in his life than during the storm that almost sank the ship. The captain and other passengers seemed to take it in stride as it was nothing too unusual for a gulf voyage in this era. Finally, their mission to combat the horrible institution of slavery was beginning. In addition to supporting the growing abolitionist movements in Boston, he was excited to finally meet Eli Whitney.

Jamal was sad to say goodbye to Dan and Brad after spending so long in close quarters. Before, he never got to know people very well. There were too many distractions, but with nothing to do but talk and play cards, he began sharing things about his life he never had before; they all did. In addition to life stories, they shared complaints about the food, the dirty bathrooms, called heads, and joked about the other passengers. Their shared peril in the storm brought them closer. The *Anna Marie* stopped in Philadelphia to drop them and cargo off last week.

As soon as they debarked the ship, Nels said, "Oh my God, the smell. I thought I was used to it after the ship, but it is bad."

Jamal was too busy breathing through his nose to reply. They both stood on the dock, luggage at their feet, looking a bit disconcerted and lost. Nels left Jamal watching the luggage and speaking to a small boy, asking directions to the inn they planned to stay at. Nels and the boy returned shortly with a teenage boy with a handcart. Jamal was relieved. They had large duffels and backpacks, different looking enough to draw attention, and heavy for a long walk.

The boy, seven or eight years old, mixed race, spoke with a strong, barely understandable accent. "Sirs, did you know the Green Dragon Tavern is where the men met to plot the revolution against the king? Thomas Jefferson and Benjamin Franklin were there."

"No," said Nels, "Tell us about it."

They'd chosen this tavern and inn after reading about it in their history briefing, but Nels didn't want to spoil the kid's excitement in telling the tale.

The little boy, named Benjy, chattered happily about stories of men who were the heroes of the revolution. His friend with the cart adding something now and then. Soon they arrived.

Nels paid them both, by the looks on their faces, overpaid.

Benjy said, "I'll show yous anything you want, I knows Boston good."

"That's it for now. We'll let you know."

"Actually," said Jamal, "we need further advice. Can you meet us here in the morning, not too early?"

"Yes, sirs," they replied and happily ran off. Nels and Jamal looked at each other and smiled, and Nels said, "Cute kid."

As they walked into the tavern, Nels said, "We need to figure out the best way to get to Westborough."

"Not horseback, if we can avoid it." They were both terrible riders. Neither had been on a horse before basic training.

"There may be stagecoaches, or we could rent a private carriage, but we would need a driver. That'll be expensive."

"At least money isn't a problem. Changleska didn't stint."

"We're not sure what will happen or how long it'll take. Let's be smart with the money."

"Yes, dear." Jamal mimicked a nagging wife, a reminder of past arguments. Jamal, raised with money, overspent, while Nels economized.

They laughed, both quickly looked around guiltily, seeing if anyone heard the exchange. They had to be careful. Realizing the mistake, Jamal went back to acting like a servant, struggling to bring their luggage into the tavern, quietly standing in the background while Nels looked around for the innkeeper.

In 1792, you could tell a person's social status by one glance at their attire. The New Orleans tailor had done an excellent job. Nels's travel clothes marked him as a person of substance. It helped that he carried himself with self-assurance and a natural arrogance of any American White man.

Nels approached the innkeeper. "I'd like two rooms, one for myself and one for my valet," nodding at Jamal.

The innkeeper looked them both over, noting that even the 'valet' looked well dressed. "Sorry, sir, we don't have a room for your man here. We have one room open. You'd have to share with this gentleman." He pointed to a large, older man, sitting at a nearby table with an ale in front of him.

"That won't do. I require a private room and a suitable place for my valet. Perhaps you could recommend another establishment."

Jamal knew at this time patrons were expected to share rooms with strangers, even beds, but he wasn't about to. They'd have to find another place to stay.

"Sir, a private room usually is four shillings, five with meals. Perhaps I can ask the other patron to move for some consideration."

"I'll pay ten shillings a night, if you find a suitable place for my valet to sleep, but I require the room be clean, with fresh bedding. My valet will need access to the kitchen, as he will oversee the making of my meals."

The proprietor went over to the large man, who at first shook his head, then agreed.

"A private room is now available. If your valet could sleep in the attic with the other servants, we could accommodate you."

"That'll do," and handed over the money. "We'll sit and have some ale."

"Both of you?" The proprietor asked, appalled. Evidently, sitting with your servant in the common room was not done.

"No, I misspoke," Nels said. "Just me."

"Give me a bit to get your room ready."

"I'll have ale, bread and cheese and any pickled vegetables you have. My valet will eat in the kitchen, but he is to be given the same food as your guests. He is an educated, free man and is to be treated with respect. Is that clear?"

"Yes, sir." The man was obviously not too pleased with this curious sounding guest and his demands, but money talks.

Later, as they followed the innkeeper upstairs, each step made the hallway creak. The man, round-bellied and red-faced, jingled a brass key as he led them to a heavy wooden door. He slid the key into the lock, opening it with a faint grind of metal.

"Here you are," he said, stepping aside. "Good sturdy door. The lock's fine enough for Boston. You'll keep the key. I've one spare, should it go missing."

They exchanged a glance as they stepped inside. The room was plain, with a narrow window and a modest fireplace, but the lock on the door looked like something from a museum exhibit, it was functional, but far from secure.

"We'll ring the supper bell at sundown, give or take. Just head to the common room."

As soon as the innkeeper left, Jamal kneeled by the door and inspected the lock. "This thing's barely more than a suggestion. A butter knife would get through it."

Nels said, "We can't risk leaving the gear unguarded. Not with what we've got."

They had Jamal's laptop, both their phones, smart watches, and their high-end camping gear, everything priceless and irreplaceable. In addition, they carried critical papers containing plans and originals needing reprints.

"Do we trust that guy to not steal our gear?" asked Nels.

"He wouldn't stay in business long robbing his guests. When we leave, we can put thread across the door and see if anyone comes in."

"It'll have to do."

"We should have some luggage made with secret compartments that look like what the locals carry," said Jamal. He was already designing something in his head.

"Doubt if there will be time. If we leave on schedule, I don't want to stay longer than needed. I want to go back home."

Jamal felt the same, wondering when he started thinking of New Orleans as home more than Boulder or Chicago. Later that evening, Jamal was helping Nels get his clothes ready for the next day, while they talked quietly.

Nels said, "I'm so sorry you're treated like this; it pisses me off. I thought Boston would be better."

"It's not as bad as Charleston. Although it enabled me to have conversations with slaves firsthand. Made everything more real. Like the guy in the movie said, 'failure is not an option.'"

Nels asked, Where should we start tomorrow? Straight to Whitney or start on the list?"

They had a long list of shipbuilders, artisans, and merchants to find. Although Changleska sent them lists of needed items and schematics of devices, they had to figure out how to obtain them on their own.

Jamal answered, Whitney. I m worried he ll leave early. That s the priority."

Okay, but we need to start on the ship builders soon too. That ll take time," said Nels.

Fortunately, they'd made an agreement with Captain Harrigan. They deliberated on the risk of trusting him with the shipbuilding schematics, but realized they needed him or someone like him with connections in the shipping industry. Omímeya wanted to commission their own ship to be built using vastly superior modifications. They hoped to use the plans as partial payment, with Omímeya providing the rest in gold.

While Harrigan owned the *Anna Marie*, he owed his investors a considerable debt. The agreement covered profit sharing for any contracts he was to broker. After looking over the improvements the plans showed, the captain realized it would make him a very wealthy man. Changes included innovative rigging techniques, improvements in sail construction, methods for strengthening the hull, better pumps, and improved lightning protection.

Jamal left soon after, not wanting to stay in Nels s room for too long. Earlier, someone had shown him the attic, where he would sleep. He left most of his gear with Nels but drew funny looks as he blew air into his high-end Therm-a-Rest sleeping pad to sleep on the floor. Sadness filled him as he unrolled his sleeping bag, remembering his trip to REI to buy it and choosing one that zipped together with Nels s. Jamal wondered if they would ever zip their bags together again. They managed a few quickies on the ship during the journey. Sailors were much more accepting of homosexuality than the general populace, but you still had to be discreet. With no time to be alone together, it d been a long time since they had truly made love.

=..=

Entering the inn's kitchen the next morning, Jamal ducked under the low beam. The air was thick with the mingled aromas of bread baking, bacon sizzling, and wood smoke. The kitchen seemed a hive of activity. A couple of women hustled about. A boy stoked the fire in the cavernous hearth as its flames licked the base of a heavy iron pot. He noted the surfaces were surprisingly clean and well-kept for such a busy space.

"Can I help ye?" the cook asked, his accent thick, his tone curt as he wiped his hands on a stained apron.

Jamal offered a polite smile, bowing his head slightly. "Good morning. I'm here to ensure Mr. Hansen's breakfast is prepared to his exacting standards."

The cook squinted, his brow furrowing. "Ain't nobody complained about my food before."

"Of course not," Jamal said smoothly. "But Mr. Hansen is particular. I'd be remiss in my duties if I didn't ensure his satisfaction."

The cook huffed but waved a hand toward a tray laden with dishes—fried eggs, crispy bacon, a wedge of cheese, and slices of fresh bread. "There it is. Same as anyone else's."

"No bacon for Mr. Hansen, he doesn't eat meat, it does not agree with him."

"No meat at all? Poor chap."

"I, on the other hand, love meat, especially bacon."

"I was told you were to eat the same as your master."

Jamal despised anyone calling Nels his master and had to remind himself that, at this time, it also meant employer. His gaze lingered briefly on the large iron pot in the hearth, the contents bubbling quietly.

"What's in the pot?" he asked.

"Porridge," the cook replied gruffly. "For the common lot."

Jamal figured if he saw it bubbling, it would be safe. The bread being baked would be fine, eggs, and cheese as well. He saw coffee being ready to be served.

"When you make the coffee, do you boil the water first?"

"Of course, how else would you make coffee, boil it in water?" He answered with disdain.

"I only ask because you know people can get sick from drinking water that has not been boiled at least five minutes."

"Nonsense," the cook replied dismissively.

"Mr. Hansen studies medicine. Many learned people agree."

"What kind of gentlemen studies medicine?"

Jamal remembered in this time, doctors were middle class, often taught through apprenticeship. It wasn't considered a profession suitable for wealthy gentlemen.

"The kind that cares deeply about people."

Jamal removed the bacon from the tray and added a bowl of porridge. Nels had lost weight on the trip and was too thin to start with. His stubborn refusal to eat meat made things difficult. At least there were more choices here, like bread and cheese. Even Jamal had a hard time stomaching ship rations of hardtack and salt pork. They had quickly run out of the rations they had brought with them. Fortunately, rice was available in New Orleans, and Nels mostly ate that. Jamal made up his own plate, set it on the table next to the women.

"I'll be back after I bring Mr. Hansen his tray."

Nels's eyes sparkled as he saw Jamal bringing his tray like a dutiful servant, an untold joke on his lips. Jamal plunked the tray hard on the table.

"If that will be all, sir," he said, "I'll be in the kitchen, and meet you out front shortly."

Upon reaching the tavern's front, they noticed Benjy eagerly waiting. Jamal handed him a hunk of bread and bacon, which, surprisingly, he ate only a little, carefully wrapping the rest in a dirty cloth and tucking it into his shirt.

When he saw Jamal looking, he said, "For my mama, she's poorly."

Jamal looked down at him. "Go ahead and eat, lot of stops today. We'll pay you for the day and give you some food to take to her."

With a cheerful grin, he removed the bundle from his shirt, quickly ate as he waited for them to tell him where they needed to go.

Nels had learned earlier the stagecoach to Westborough would leave the next day for its twice-weekly run. First on their list was to find a printer. That would not be difficult, since Boston was full of them. They used a few different printers to get as many copies made as quickly as possible. That took all morning, then they visited a market, picking up food for the trip tomorrow and some for Benjy to take home. That took all morning, then a market, picking up food for the trip tomorrow, and some for Benjy to take home. They couldn't believe a child that small had to work to feed a sick mother. They guessed, correctly, there was no father in the picture.

After meeting with the printers, they met with some of the leading abolitionists, promising delivery of materials once printed. Nels really connected with the Quakers after they were invited to a meeting. It reminded Nels of Buddhist meditations, but Jamal was bored with the quiet. Quakers were leading the abolitionist movement and listened to what they had been doing and asked how they could help.

After listening to a leading minister talk about how they struggled to bring awareness to the issue, Jamal asked, voice tight. "You really believe you can end this?" He wasn't sure if he was asking the abolitionist or himself.

The older minister nodded. "Truth doth not hurry, but once seen, it may never be unseen."

That's the problem, Jamal thought. Most people refuse to look in the first place. He still saw the dockworkers in New Orleans every time he closed his eyes. Jamal hadn't spoken to them, hadn't helped them, had done nothing except stare like every other outsider who passed by.

Jamal exhaled. "Then let's start opening more eyes."

The next day, they searched for a location suitable for crafting sextants and other marine instruments. They possessed photographs and plans for models more advanced than those commonly available. In landlocked South Dakota during the twenty-first century, they had no actual instruments to use as examples. Starting near the wharf at the chandlers, they looked at instruments for sale. When they asked the clerk about the manufacturer, he fell silent, suspecting they were trying to avoid his commission until Nels clarified they needed an instrument maker to create some new models. The clerk gave them a few names, and they set off.

Benjy earned his pay by guiding them through the confusing streets before finding a workshop qualified to do the work. The artisan looked over the plans, expressing amazement over the color photos.

"You say this works better than what we make already?" The man asked Nels the question, but Jamal answered, surprising the man with the details of the changes, and the rationale why they worked better.

"This is a most intricate undertaking. Each instrument takes considerable time to construct, and you want ten of these new models. Plus, the better chronometers. I couldn't manage it alone. It would take five journeymen and all my apprentices. I must question whether the expense would be justified."

"Not getting lost at sea is worth a fortune to sailors. Any navy would love to get their hands on them."

"Why not bring it to the Navy? I am sure someone would be interested."

Jamal had to think fast. "No, we want to keep this private for now. Eventually, we'll sell to the navy."

They were unwilling to let the small American Navy possess it just yet. They were looking at these instruments as part of their bargaining process with the Spanish and French.

The man looked wary. "I'll see who is available. Leave these with me," pointing to the photos and printouts, "and come back next week."

"No, thank you," Nels said, gathered up the materials and quickly left.

"This is going to be harder than I thought," said Jamal.

"The Chamberlain area was gearing up manufacturing when we left. Why can't they be made there?"

Jamal laughed, Even in our time, we couldn't have produced anything this fine in the US, only in Asia or perhaps Germany. Besides, Changleska is focusing on manufacturing steam and diesel engines, not to mention weapons."

"Vaccines and antibiotics too, I hope," said Nels.

Prior to Big Thunder, Nels jumped around educational interests and only became interested in medicine after he began his medical training with the Changleska Guard. Jamal had never seen him so focused on studying in college. Serving in the clinic in New Orleans had changed him. Motivated by a deep sense of compassion, he was determined to learn everything he could to alleviate suffering. He confessed to Jamal that after his stint in the Guards was complete, he was going to apply to the medical school they were building at Omímeya.

They returned to the Green Dragon Tavern, sending Benjy home thrilled with the food and his pay.

=..=

The next morning, getting up early to meet the stagecoach to Westborough, Jamal thought, *it s finally happening.* He'd endured months of uncomfortable travel, risked his life on a dangerous sea voyage, sacrificed his dignity to pose as a servant, and lived from his new friends, all for this one opportunity. Convincing Eli Whitney not to create the cotton gin would change the economics of slavery enough to make a difference. So much was riding on this meeting. Even if they couldn t persuade him to return to Changleska for a well-paying job, they needed to convince him to not go to Georgia. They didn t plan to tell him about his future invention unless nothing else worked. Jamal knew convincing someone to move away from the colonies and the life he knew would not be easy. If it failed, he was unsure of the next steps. The weight of this burden felt overwhelming as he thought about the suffering future generations would endure if he failed.

Since the stagecoach was crowded, Jamal and another servant rode on top. He perched next to the luggage, holding on to a thin rail. At least the weather was nice. Later, Nels told Jamal that too many people, all smelling bad, crammed inside. Jamal wondered why people bathed so little and no one wore deodorant. He knew herbal deodorants were easy to make. He'd bought some from an herb company near Chamberlain.

After they arrived in Westborough, they found out the Whitney farm was five miles away. With no other way to get there, they walked. Appreciating the fine weather, they saw well-tended farms and people working the fields who gave curious but friendly waves, and they arrived not long before dusk.

"It's getting late," said Nels. We should ve sent another letter. We re not sure he got the first one."

"I shouldn't have been so anxious. With the stagecoach coming twice a week, we could've sent a letter and waited for a reply."

"We're here now. No use fretting."

Following the directions given, they identified the apple orchard, the long driveway, and a white clapboard two-story house set among various outbuildings. Fortunately, they were spared from knocking on the front door when a teenage girl took one look at them and ran into the house.

Two men emerged, one older and one younger, with the look of father and son.

Nels approached them, extending his hand. "Hello, I am Nels Hansen. Sorry for the unannounced visit, but we've come a very long way to speak to young Mr. Whitney. This is Jamal Alston," he said, gesturing.

"You're Jamal Alston?" Eli Whitney asked. His expression was a mix of surprise and unease. Jamal neglected to mention he was Black.

"Yes, sir. I'm the engineer who wrote to you. I sent you plans for some things I've been working on."

"Those were your designs? Not ones you copied?" Eli asked skeptically.

"Yes, sir. All my work. I've brought more for you to look at," Jamal replied.

By this time, two women—one motherly, the other the teenager who had spotted them—appeared on the front porch.

The elder Whitney spoke angrily. "Eli has told us about the job offer you sent. Unbelievable! I understand why the pay is so high. Moving all the way to the wild Indian lands. Ridiculous."

"Things have changed since we wrote the letter," Jamal said. "We're now setting up a manufacturing center in St. Louis."

"Not much better," grumbled Mr. Whitney.

Eli interjected, "Father, let's at least invite them in to talk about it."

They were ushered into the parlor and offered tea. Nels brought out the Changleska story booklet, a letter of introduction written by Captain Harrigan, and a contract for employment. The Whitneys sat in silence as they perused the papers.

Mr. Whitney held up the Changleska story booklet. "This is a fairy tale. People don't just appear from other worlds in a big clap of thunder."

"We had a hard time believing we're here, too," Jamal said. "We brought something to show you to prove our claims, but we'll need a table to set up a small machine."

In the dining room, Jamal set up the laptop and invited the whole family to watch the fifteen-minute video. Created by the Omímeya marketing department, besides the story of their arrival and forming Changleska, it included footage of cars, airplanes, tractors, and shots of Omímeya and Chamberlain. Afterwards, the family sat in stunned silence.

Eli's mother clasped her daughter fearfully and murmured, "Oh my Lord."

Eli erupted. "Father, I must go. This is an extraordinary opportunity. You must believe them now."

His father sighed heavily. "Even if I believe it, it's still a long way to go. We may never see you again." After a pause, he looked at Nels and Jamal, and added, "It's getting late. Might as well stay for dinner. By then, it will be too late to walk back to town. We can offer you a place to sleep in the barn, if that's not too rough for you."

They assured him it'd be fine.

Eli told him he'd talk to his father as he showed them where to sleep in the barn.

Nels said, "I don't see why he needs his father's permission. Isn't he twenty-four years old?"

"Yes, but families differed from our time. I saw the excitement on his face. He'll come."

The next morning, over breakfast with the family, Eli told them he would send a letter in a few days with his reply, as his family still needed to discuss it. Then he looked at Jamal and winked. On the way back, Jamal was so happy he didn't mind riding on top of the coach.

=..=

When they returned to the Green Dragon Tavern the next day, Benjy was waiting anxiously, even though it was late.

"Mr. Hansen, sir, cook told me you were studying doctoring. Could you please look at my mama, she getting sicker, Mrs. Bunders said there was nutting to be done, she be gone soon. Please, yous can help her, I'm sure," he said, snuffling a little.

Nels told Benjy he'd come, saying to Jamal, "No need for both of us to go. Wait in the room. If anyone gives you a hard time, tell them you're guarding our stuff."

A couple of hours later, Nels returned, his shoulders slumped and a heavy sigh escaping his lips. "I thought I saw awful things in the New Orleans clinic, but this was worse than I could imagine. Poor Benjy," He looked like he was going to cry, so Jamal put his arm around him.

He took a breath and continued. "They live in a brothel. That's where Benjy was born. His mother is dying of syphilis. It's very advanced. She and Benjy live outside in a tiny shed. No idea what they do for heat in the winter. The main house was nicer. Benjy took me to the kitchen to ask for hot water. The mother sews for the brothel for their keep, but now she is too sick. She doesn't have very much longer."

"Oh my god, what can we do to help?" said Jamal.

"Nothing for the mother, I'm afraid, but something for Benjy, if you agree. Jamal, it is so terrible I can't believe it," Nels said, choking up.

"Of course we'll help Benjy. You don't have to ask."

"The madam of the brothel, Mrs. Bunders, has only been letting them stay because she wants to sell Benjy to another house, one who specializes in young boys."

"What!??" Jamal practically screamed. "I thought slavery was illegal in Massachusetts."

"It is, but indentured servants are not. They can indenture orphans until age sixteen. His mother asked me to take him because she fears for his life if they send him to that house. I said yes. I should've talked to you first. If you're not willing, we can find another place for him."

"I'm more than willing, but not sure how it'll work. Remember, we're still active duty in the Changleska Guard."

"I thought about it on the way home. Tomorrow I can get the mother to sign custody papers over to me, perhaps both of us. We must find a lawyer, no idea how this works."

"Let's hope we won't need to pay off Mrs. Bunders to keep her quiet. I don't want to give her a cent. As far as the Guard is concerned, as long as Benjy doesn't interfere with our duties, I don't see how it's any of their business. It's not like we're in combat."

The next day, they found a lawyer who told them adoption or legal guardianship was out of the question, Nels was unmarried. He ignored Jamal.

He looked between Jamal and Nels suspiciously, "Why would a gentleman such as yourself want to adopt an eight-year-old mulatto boy?"

Nels answered brusquely, "Because where we come from, we don't sell children to whore houses for depraved men. If we could save more, we would, but he is the one God has put before us."

Jamal thought, *smart Nels, bring God into it.*

The lawyer advised the most expeditious method was to have the mother sign Benjy over as an indentured servant, but they needed to do it before she died, otherwise the madam could do what she wanted. He wrote up the papers, charging extra for the rush, and they left.

Worried, they didn't want to wait until morning, and after some difficulty they found the brothel again. Benjy's mother was still alive, happy to sign the papers, and she asked them to take Benjy with them now. She was afraid that Mrs. Bunders would take him anyway. Benjy packed up his meager possessions. They gave him time to say goodbye and left. The boy was tearful and quieter than they had ever seen him on the walk back to the inn.

Right before they arrived, he said, "My ma said I belongs to yous now, till I'm grown. She said Mr. Nels would teach me to read, and be enough to eat, and warm in the winter. She weren't lying, was she?"

No, they assured him; she was telling the truth.

"And I don't have to suck cock?"

Jamal sputtered in horrified shock. Growing up in a brothel had robbed Benjy of the innocence all children deserved.

Nels kneeled down to him, tears glistening in his eyes. "You're coming with us because your mother loves you very much and wanted to protect you. You'll be safe and cared for and never have to do anything like that ever. But we don't want you to be using those words, okay? Those are grown up words."

Benjy shrugged, satisfied. "Think it's too late for supper?"

They took him to the inn's kitchen, got him bread and cheese. After eating it, he curled up in the corner close to the hearth and quickly fell asleep. They asked Jane, the older Black kitchen worker, for advice, briefly explaining the situation.

She said, "Don't tell Mr. Jones a thing, he won't notice the boy. He can sleep here tonight. I'll get him a blanket. We'll figure out something tomorrow. Poor mite. You good boys. Your mamas be proud of you."

Thinking of his mother, Jamal felt a deep, aching sorrow, a familiar grief squeezing his heart. The crackle of the fire filled the air as he looked down at Benjy's peaceful face, asleep at the hearth; his heart filled with a fierce protectiveness.

Chapter Twelve
Mary

MARY WAS TIRED of being a politician. It wasn t the workload that exhausted her, as she thrived on long hours and difficult decisions. What drained her was the endless political maneuvering, the constant need to balance conflicting agendas. Everyone thought their proposals were priorities, unaware of all the competing projects of equal or greater importance. She had to keep the big picture in mind. Tough choices had to be made daily. Committee Chairs generally had strong personalities, big egos, intelligence, and drive. It didn t matter what the issue was, whether restoring natural gas, creating vaccines, or plastic recycling, every Chair's project had to be top priority. Mary s job often involved placating people who fought over a small resource pie. Changleska was struggling with the lack of engineers, chemists, technicians of all kinds, and general labor. The small number of qualified people worked excessive hours, often on projects outside their training and experience. At least most proposals benefited Changleska. It was rare that someone advocated for a project where they gained personal wealth. Political corruption that existed in the old world had yet to rear its ugly head. It was the outside world that posed the most problems.

The politics of the old world did creep in, despite the new system designed to avoid them. The legislative structure was written in such a short time, leaving many flaws to be fixed. Even with committees instead of a senate or congress, there were problems. At first anyone who could find eighteen people to share their viewpoint could form a committee. This led to more proposed laws than the Council could realistically study and vote on. Without a Changleska law, the laws of the old United States or South Dakota applied, a precedent established in the early days to maintain continuity. This served as a temporary measure, but over time, it transformed many issues such as abortion, LGBTQ rights, or any other law that eighteen or more people sought to change into highly contentious political battles.

In an early Council session, they passed a law limiting the number of formal committees by requiring at least two thousand people to elect the eighteen members. There were complaints that this law lessened the power of the people, while giving committee Chairs more power. Politics was often about compromise, and it was harder when both choices were bad.

At least Mary understood local politics. Where she struggled was the intricacies of global politics. Complicated power dynamics and conflicting interests existed between the different countries. Mary often found herself overwhelmed by the vast amount of information she needed to learn. The long distances and communication delays made accomplishing anything difficult. Correspondence needed to be both clear and nuanced, conveying needed information diplomatically and strategically.

The talks last spring at the summit were bearing fruit. Britain would likely be the first major power to acknowledge Changleska independence. While incentives such as naval technology, advanced mining techniques, and efficient iron smelting methods were persuasive, Mary got the impression that the British mostly wanted to poke the eye of America. There was still ill will between the two countries. The problem with close alignment with Great Britain was the risk of antagonizing the US, a dangerous path they seemed to be heading down. They needed the US for trade. There were too many resources Changleska could not produce. So far, representatives of the US government had been silent. The only word the expeditions sent was that they arrived safely and had appointments for meetings.

France was struggling with its revolution, making communication with its leaders difficult. It was hard to tell who was in charge. France needed to appease the masses. Improvements in agriculture to boost food production and textile manufacturing could help. The problem is the French had heard about the previous timeline where they got fifteen million in cash from the US for the Louisiana Territory. They wanted cash now, not blueprints and plans to feed their people or boost their economy long term. It would take Changleska years to raise that much, even with their knowledge of silver and gold mines.

Fortunately, Spain showed greater interest in Changleska s offer, which included detailed information on the locations of precious metal and gemstone mines in South America, than in France s proposal, which would give Spain Tuscany. One holdup with Spain was religious. The Catholic church was deeply suspicious of Changleska. A papal envoy was being sent, but until there was a ruling from the Pope, the King of Spain wouldn t recognize Changleska. All this would take time, and Mary worried that otherwise, Spain would claim the gold and silver mines in California and Nevada. She wasn t worried about the *Pahá Sápa* or Black Hill mines; they were close enough to be defended by force if necessary. There was already a treaty with the local tribes for Changleska to defend and protect them.

Mary prepared for her upcoming meeting with the Security Council, hoping to strategize effectively about imminent threats. She needed to address the risks posed by both external pressures from countries like France and internal factions influenced by conservative values and the allure of merging with the United States. The stakes were high, and every move required careful consideration and tactical foresight.

The Security Council met in the First Shield Command s secure meeting room. Mary had initially opposed the expense of creating a meeting room to protect against electronic spying because only Changleska possessed the technology. She eventually admitted that Phil Gallo, the FSC director, was right. Between internal threats and stolen tech, they needed a secure meeting room. The Security Council was composed of Oliver Jackson, Kyle Ward, Rose Chasing Hawk, General Jonathan Gardner, Billy Fast Dog, Phil Gallo, and herself. Mary formally opened the meeting in her role as Chair, but she d mostly listen.

Mary formally opened the meeting in her role as Chair, but she'd mostly listen.

The first item on the agenda was the United States. General Gardner began. "It's clear we don't have to worry about imminent invasion. The US is still reeling from the major defeats suffered in the Northwest Indian War."

Kyle asked, "What happened again?"

Mary, adopting a teacherly tone, explained, "In 1787, the US enacted a law claiming vast tracts of Indigenous land as it sought to expand westward. Consequently, the tribes formed a confederation to resist. In two battles, the last one in November, led by Blue Jacket of the Shawnee and Little Turtle of the Miami, resulted in a disastrous defeat for the US, with significant losses. In 1794, in the old world, the US won the third battle and successfully stole the land."

Billy said, "It won't happen now, correct?"

The general answered, "History as we knew it changed. It's doubtful they'll try to invade after witnessing the Changleska military during the field exercises. But it doesn't mean they've given up their expansionist policies. We need to meet with the tribal leaders and offer our support."

Phil said, "This is east of the Mississippi River. We don't have the resources to protect our own borders, much less fight others' battles for them."

"There are good military reasons to fight an enemy far away from your own borders, especially if the war may expand. Historically, wars fought on distant fronts have prevented conflicts from reaching home territories, allowing for strategic positioning and resource control. If we can influence the fight early, we might prevent a larger conflict from reaching our doorstep," Gardner replied.

Mary said, "I heard the general advise to meet with leaders and offer support. That's different from fighting a battle. We can address those questions later. Can we agree to send people to meet with the leadership of the tribes in question? One leader is Tecumseh. He was a powerful voice for unity to protect tribes from the US."

There was agreement and they moved on to the main issue of the meeting: the threat from within.

Phil started the discussion. The faction wanting Changleska to give up its independence and annex with the US is still active. I thought the arrests for illegal tech sales, conspiracy, and treason would dampen the enthusiasm, but they haven't."

People knew the United States had become a world power because of its vast size compared to any other country besides Russia and China. Its size gave it economic dominance, then military strength. Annexation supporters argued that by merging, the US could reclaim its former influence and accelerate technological advancements. It was unclear how they justified taking the land from the Indigenous, when Changleska would enforce tribal sovereignty. Some argued in the forums that with future knowledge, they could make sure the US respected treaties, but most didn t believe it.

"Clyde Folsom is still a problem. A lot of conservative Christians follow him. He is the one pushing annexation. We can't link him definitively to the tech sales or other crimes. Our hands are tied," Phil said.

Rose asked, "It's obviously a problem, but what can we do?"

Billy said, "We've put his followers Phil has identified on a watch list, but some are Omímeya employees. We can limit non-employees' access and watch the others."

"What are your concerns?" asked Rose.

"Sabotage. Assassination. These are all tools of rebellion. These people are fanatics," Phil said bluntly.

The general recounted, "We learned in the Middle East how dangerous religious fanatics can be. This is something we need to address."

Kyle said, "We need to show Changleskan unity. Unfortunately, that means creating an 'us' versus 'them.' People need to take pride in being 'us.' A large shipment of cotton cloth just arrived. We could make a lot of Changleska flags and give them away as prizes. We could start with past and future Gold Star winners."

On the login page of NewNet, along with news links, was Gold Star Weekly, a list of ten people nominated by their workplace, school, committee, or forum for any idea or plan deemed outstanding. It could include improvements in manufacturing, academic achievement, creative or artistic endeavors, even exceptional customer service. The forum that nominated and voted on the weekly winners was very popular. There were no prizes, although some companies offered a bonus; bragging rights seemed enough.

"Great idea," agreed Rose. "Maybe we could make a smaller Gold Star flag to fly with it? People used to have bumper stickers that said, 'My child is an honor student.'"

"What about a national anthem?" Billy proposed. "People get patriotic singing *God Bless America.* We should have something like that."

Kyle's hand tapped the table in excitement. "We could hold an anthem writing contest and let people vote for their favorite. Get everyone involved and invested."

Around the table, heads nodded as murmurs of agreement spread.

Phil protested, "Public unity is all well and good, but what we need is stronger laws against treason. If we hang a few people, fewer will want to join."

Mary said, "Before, we discussed how those kinds of tactics can backfire, creating martyrs instead of deterring dissent. That said, I'm not opposed to stronger laws. Speak to the Law Committee. In the meantime, what are some less extreme things we can do?"

Phil asked, "I need to know from this group how much we can interfere with the forums. We can't do much about Folsom's church or radio show, but we can close the forums that espouse his beliefs."

"Freedom of speech and the right of dissent are in our constitution," said Mary.

"It was in the old US as well, but you are naïve to think that the government didn't throttle speech that ran counter to its agenda. Propaganda is a tool that, in our case, may save lives," Gardner countered.

They spent the rest of the meeting discussing ways to increase surveillance, both the online forums and individuals identified as leaders, such as Folsom. While Phil and the general pushed for stronger measures, others raised concerns about potential backlash. The group ultimately postponed any concrete actions, opting instead to continue gathering intelligence and refining their approach before implementing new policies. First Shield had very few undercover agents. They needed more to gather intelligence and disrupt organizing efforts. They discussed ways to create media campaigns emphasizing the benefits of independence and the risks of US annexation, such as potential loss of sovereignty, erosion of cultural practices, or continued reliance on slave labor. Despite Phil and the general advocating stronger measures, the group failed to agree on further steps and postponed the decision until a future meeting.

After the meeting, Mary and Rose walked together back towards their offices, chatting amiably. They discussed kids and grandkids, and, although unbecoming of powerful leaders, a little office gossip.

Mary asked, "What's the deal with Jennie and Henry? I saw them together at lunch. Are they back together?"

Rose said, "Henry's new job as the Changleskan liaison for the Hudson Bay Company means he needs to live here. He moved into her hotel room. She asked the other day about moving from the single women's floor to the family floor. But there's been no more talk of marriage. Evidently, he can sleep with a Jewish woman, just not marry one."

"He may not realize in our culture, lots of couples either live together for years before marriage or choose not to marry at all. Religious upbringing forms a core part of who a person is. This issue undoubtedly will arise again," said Mary.

"I think the two centuries of cultural differences may become bigger issues than religion, but who are we to judge? I'm blessed to have met Jackson," said Rose.

Mary said, "Being married as long as I have is comforting. I wish everyone could experience the same. Many people jump from relationship to relationship without attempting to resolve problems."

"Not so much anymore. The lack of birth control is changing that," said Rose.

They laughed and parted to go to their separate offices.

=..=

A few weeks later, Mary was preparing for the Executive Council meeting, held on the first Wednesday of the month. The council discussed proposed laws in a private online forum until all issues were resolved before voting. Although they sought consensus, votes were often not unanimous. They were representatives of the people, which was sometimes hard to remember, when public opinion often differed from public good. The public Council meetings were more ceremonial, although in them the Councilors heard from committees and gave their viewpoints for or against proposals, leaving the questions, arguments, and opinions to the Councilors private forum.

Mary scheduled a meeting later today with Theresa Martinez, the Executive Councilor who was Minister of Medicine, about a controversial proposed law. Mary liked Theresa; she was Navajo and Mexican by heritage, but all American in attitude. Before Big Thunder, she was both a medical doctor and a professor of epidemiology at Johns Hopkins University. Mary believed Theresa would be an excellent Chair if she ever resigned or was voted out. Theresa had the academic mindset to look at the big picture, and possessed excellent communication skills, and was absolutely brilliant. It was her idea to create the Medical Corps. Its military type of hierarchy gave the Type A personality doctors a comfortable structure.

The 153 physicians from the medical conference transported with Big Thunder were more than the area needed. Adapting to the eighteenth-century medical environment posed significant challenges for them. Lacking modern equipment, sterilization methods, and many life-saving drugs, they were forced to rely on older techniques and herbal medicine. Some physicians, including Theresa s husband, focused on teaching or establishing the medical school; others worked in clinics they were setting up outside the Circle.

The Medical Corps was a separate entity, not under the jurisdiction of the Council. In the early days when the Council approved its charter, no one, except Theresa, understood the long-term implications. They could bypass the Committees and Council laws with their own rules. The current proposal would curb their independence. Because of the existing South Dakota law, abortion was illegal. It had not changed. A committee with a lot of public support was proposing a law to prosecute doctors who performed abortions under any circumstances, including incest, rape, and the life of the mother. Mary was a pro-life Catholic, but understood the issue was more than abortion. The autonomy of the Corps was at stake.

Theresa and Mary met in Mary's office. Mary had inherited the beautiful top floor office from the former General Manager. With spectacular river views, beautiful art, and well-appointed furnishings, it was a better place to meet, and they settled comfortably.

After the usual pleasantries, Theresa began, "This abortion law is really to curb the power of the Medical Corps. Not sure if it's the intent, but it opens the door."

Mary answered, "It has a lot of public support. The other Councilors are listening. I am sorry to say some are thinking about the next election, not what is best."

"Wasn't extending the terms from four to seven years meant to fix that?"

"It did to a certain extent, but popularity is still important."

"Doctors need the freedom to practice medicine without legal constraints. Independence for the Medical Corps is critical, a point I understand. Patient care needs to take priority. The Corps doesn't ignore bigger social issues. Look at the euthanasia rules. Despite the decisions we made immediately after Big Thunder because of limited advanced medical care and drugs, the principle still works. The patients, families, and doctor make these choices together."

"Arguments are being made about how much power doctors are getting. Abortion is only one issue. There are concerns about mandatory vaccinations and quarantines. A slippery slope keeps getting mentioned," said Mary.

Theresa rolled her eyes, then grew serious. "I'm not surprised that Richard and Duane are in favor of the law. They're both conservative, but Jackson surprised me."

"He has concerns about authoritarianism in any form. You're probably aware most physicians have invested in the pharmaceutical and medical device markets. This will create wealth for generations to come. The

Medical Corps has the potential to create a small group controlling significant wealth and power."

Theresa said, We re looking at other ways to address wealth disparities, including the tax system. Depending on how he votes, the decision may be left up to you. Can you tell me your concerns?"

"Although I'm personally uncomfortable with euthanasia and abortion, that's not my real problem. It's having a powerful organization outside of the Council's laws. We are supposed to represent the will of the people. If people don't like us, they can vote us out of office. The Medical Corps is unelected and will have more power as it grows."

"What are you afraid may happen?"

"Not much now, but in the future. The Medical Corps will choose those who get trained. Advanced knowledge held only by a few is ripe for abuse. You know how hard it was for you as a woman of color in the old world. In this world, it could get worse."

Theresa asserted, "As you know, diversity, equity, and inclusion are core tenets of our charter."

"That's only one concern," said Mary. "I've read enough dystopian novels to worry about a small group of highly educated people with a lot of control. It's not the present, but the future I worry about. Instead of Changleska having executive and judicial forms of government, it will include medical."

Theresa suggested, Instead of the law prosecuting doctors, we could propose the Council reviews the Corps charter every ten years. Perhaps we could establish a system of oversight that reassures the public while still preserving medical independence."

"That would solve the concerns of those fearing the Corps becoming more powerful, but it won't be enough for those who want to punish doctors for having anything whatsoever to do with abortion," said Mary.

Theresa said with resignation, "You're right, but if we can vote this down now, we'll have a few years before we have to be concerned with it again."

"I'm sure Jackson will change his vote if there is a Corps review. That'll give you enough votes, even without me," said Mary with relief.

=..=

Every seat in the Council Chamber was full. The crowd was here for one reason: the medical vote. It reminded Mary of the old world, because so many people focused on the pro-life/pro-choice issue when there were many other critical issues being voted on today. Some were near and dear to Mary s heart, like funding for the creation of adult literacy programs and land grants for former slaves, and critical infrastructure funding, including expansion of the radio towers. Several other important proposed laws could impact everyone s health and safety. But the proposal to prosecute doctors brought everyone out. At least there were no sign-wielding, chanting protesters. The Council Chambers, a solemn place of reverence, didn t allow written signs or even clothing with political slogans. The rest of the Omímeya building, being privately owned, had been designated a no-protest zone. If people wanted to protest, they could do it outside the gatehouse on the road coming into Omímeya; usually only a few people bothered, except today. Clyde Folsom had loaded people on trucks, even chartered Kathy s Bus, and there was a huge crowd of protesters slowing traffic and causing a nuisance.

After the usual opening prayers and songs, they started as usual with short proposals without controversy, getting them out of the way, leaving room for any issues that might be controversial or take longer. Only formal Committee members could speak. Usually only the Committee Chair or sometimes the Vice Chair would speak, but they expected the law to prosecute doctors to bring out all eighteen members. However, each member was limited to two minutes.

Before the final vote, each Council member gave their reason for or against the proposal, usually short. They usually thanked Committee members for their work, then gave their yea or nay for the record, with Mary going last. Today Theresa gave a long, impassioned speech about the importance of medical practitioners having freedom to practice as they saw fit. She gave examples of ways this law could negatively impact patients in all kinds of scenarios. She didn t mention abortion once. Jackson gave his nay vote but mentioned the proposal to review the Medical Corps charter every ten years.

With a deep breath, Mary spoke. "This was a difficult vote, as I believe in the sanctity of life. So do doctors. We must trust them to act in good faith. Oversight belongs to their peers, not the government. However, as a matter of personal faith, I am voting for the proposal. That brings the vote to three for and four against. Nays have it. The law does not pass."

The room erupted in both boos and cheers. Mary banged her gavel for a call for quiet and reminded everyone the Pro-Life Committee could bring the proposal up to vote again in three years.

What they couldn't have guessed is Clyde Folsom took the defeat of the proposal as a call to action, gathering more supporters to his cause. The proposal's opponents were winning hearts, but not everyone's. A few voices grew louder in opposition, especially those loyal to Folsom. There were whispers about the compound hosting nightly prayer circles that sounded more like political rallies. Former supporters were drifting back, drawn by the promise of certainty in uncertain times. Mary didn't underestimate that appeal. When fear and faith walked hand in hand, reason often lost its way.

Mary left the Chamber to meet with her family at the Prairie Abundance restaurant. It had become a family tradition after Council meetings. Mary and her daughter Bridget debated whether her daughters, Cecilia, age eleven, and Amanda, almost ten, were too young to attend Council meetings. Both thought they would learn more there than in school. They talked about issues being voted on, even though some topics like abortion were mature for Amanda. Mary loved these family discussions and was often surprised at the astute questions her granddaughters asked. Even Daniel, normally quiet when it came to politics, participated. No one was sure whether women would have the same opportunities in this new world with all the eighteenth-century influence, but Mary wanted to give the girls the broadest education possible.

Mary gazed at her family as everyone waited in the crowded restaurant and knew what all the stress of politics was about for her—protecting her family and her granddaughters' future.

Chapter Thirteen
Brings Him Home

BRINGS HIM HOME found the California expedition very different from what he expected. To his surprise, he was enjoying the trip, although not all the work involved in cutting trees. He still hated trucks despite their greater speed compared to horses. He now knew what a mile was. The journey of 2,000 miles by horse would take two to three months, with trucks less than a month, even with planned stops. He learned once the road and way stations were complete, follow-up journeys would take weeks.

He was grateful the Advance Crew of six men and two women were traveling ahead of the rest of the group. The rest of the expedition of seventy people was the size of a small village. On the move, it was unlike anything he had ever imagined, with the loaded trucks with people perched on top, or pulling various trailers rumbling along noisily, filling the air with stink and dust. When camped, it was like any village, a cacophony of voices and inevitable frictions and disagreements. Almost all were thunder people; only a handful were Indigenous to this time. Even Six Feathers' wife was a thunder person. She was Lakota, the seventh generation descended from his people, like many of the other expedition members. There were a handful of people from other tribes, including two of the doctors. He heard they would add guides from different tribes as they traveled.

His crew was driven to the first stop, *Čháŋšota* (Smoky Wood), or Pierre on the maps they all carried. He could only bring two of his horses, which had to be coaxed into the four-horse trailer to go to Chansota. He was shocked the trip from base camp only took a little over two hours.

Ed Tilson was driving the truck. This is slow on the dirt roads. It used to take only an hour. I would go often because my girlfriend lived in Pierre," he said with a sad look. This is a better road than we ll use going west, because the road crew started last fall. It even has drainage." He pointed out the ditches on both sides of the road that Brings Him Home had not noticed before.

They d spend the night in Chansota, now a military outpost and a growing village. After settling his horses, he and Little Dog walked around, amazed. Last year, this place was merely a spot along the river where small camps sometimes stayed. The sight of people from many tribes surprised him. Tipis and the round houses favored by the Arikara and Mandan sat side by side with fields of growing crops nearby. Windmills ran pumps bringing river water to crops. He saw several Black families building log houses. He learned they were former slaves given land for farming in designated areas like Chansota. Many people were working to build a school, their combined efforts creating a strong sense of community, visible in the shared smiles and friendly banter echoing amidst the sounds of construction. The familiar red cross of the Medical Corps tent sat next to a building site for a clinic.

They met an older White man, Gordon Wills, a retired mechanic, who taught people how to repair windmills. "We used to throw everything away. Now we fix everything. And I kind of love it," he chuckled, adjusting a repurposed garden hose.

The crew left the truck and trailer for the bigger expedition to collect in a few weeks. Another crew member was joining them, and they'd pick up more pack horses and gear. Heading west from Chansota, the road became prairie after the first few miles. Despite tribal use of various trails, the new route was determined by old world maps to bypass significant obstacles. Periodically, they would stop and place stone road markers. They had to deviate from the maps if there was a river or a body of water. If they couldn't find a way around the river within a day's ride, they needed to locate the shallowest, most manageable spot for the rest of the expedition to build a bridge. They would radio the bridge crew, who would arrive within a day or two.

Whenever the route became wooded, they stopped. The women set up camp, cooked the meals, and cared for the gear and the horses, while the men would start cutting down trees. Brings Him Home was grateful they had limited gas for the chain saw, so only Ed or Tom used it, as they had the most experience. It was loud and obnoxious. Everyone else used manual saws. In thickly wooded areas, all of them, even the women, dug up stumps and cleared brush. He learned to use various tools, and to appreciate work gloves. It was hard, exhausting work, unlike anything he had ever done. Brings Him Home appreciated the days he only had to scout and patrol the perimeter. They would occasionally hunt to supplement the food they brought. He had never eaten so much in his life, but his body seemed to need it with all the extra work he was doing.

Little Dog was complaining after a hard day's work. "It makes no sense for the road to be ten paces wide. You only need room for one truck at a time."

"This road," Ed replied, "will get busy with trucks and locals alike. We need two lanes for trucks to pass each other, to pass horse-drawn wagons or any slow traffic. This road in the old world was four lanes."

Besides scouting for other tribes and scoping out the proposed route, they searched for places to serve as way stations. Specifically, places with clear running water, defensible with good lines of sight, with enough flat space for the entire expedition to park. Brings Him Home enjoyed viewing locations with a warrior's eye, thinking in terms of defense, ambush, and raids. He was told that eventually there'd be a way station every hundred to two hundred miles.

Brings Him Home asked Ed, "Why so many way stations?"

Ed explained, "Mainly to store fuel. We carried all the oil for this trip, but it's bulky and heavy. Fuel stops are more efficient. We'll also cache food and supplies. As the road sees more use, we'll establish trading posts."

Brings Him Home was learning English, although he couldn't read it yet. He knew Whites could be powerful allies or enemies. Understanding their language and writing was crucial.

Their ability to preserve so much on the devices from the old world, as well as the few paper books they brought, fascinated him. He recognized the value because his uncle was a keeper of the Winter Count, spending years memorizing tribal history.

Although Brings Him Home was a warrior with a martial mindset, he'd never seen a military force like the Changleska Guard. There were different rules for allied forces, also called auxiliary forces. Sovereign tribes controlled their own military. He could remain part of the allied force as a scout and work on road building. The pay was less, but the benefits were about the same, with fewer rules to follow.

Little Dog asked him, "Why are you learning to write English? I'm tired when we're done. All I want to do is lie down, but you're with Jody until after dark."

Brings Him Home gave thought to his answer. "During paint wars, I saw how powerful the Guard was. Not just the trucks and guns, but organization was their weapon. Our leaders planned, but still warriors attacked where they wanted or where they saw the opportunity. The Guardians listened to the leaders who could see the entire field of battle and attacked only where they were told. That's why they will win, organization and discipline."

"You are learning to read to pass the test for full Guard membership?"

Brings Him Home nodded, with a determined look.

"But you will have to obey all the silly rules, salute officers, say 'Yes, sir', and wear a uniform."

He nodded again, resigned.

Laughing, Little Dog punched his arm. "You know, this means I may have to join you. I hear the thunder girls like boys in uniforms."

Brings Him Home smiled and went to meet Jody for his nightly lesson. Jody Landreau was older than most of the Guardians he had met. He had been a Lakota language teacher living in Rapid City, visiting his mother in Lower Brule, when Big Thunder occurred. He joined the Guard right away and helped organize the military interpreters. Jody held the rank of lieutenant, but Ed was in command of the unit, even though he was only a sergeant. Jody could speak the three dialects Lakota, Dakota, and Nakota fluently, Spanish, and some French. He asked Brings Him Home questions to answer in Cheyenne to record on his phone. He brought a laptop and several phones, fussing to set up the solar panels at every stop. Jody said that Omímeya had extensive language databases on their servers, but he only brought languages for the tribes on their route. They also practiced *hand sign* the plains sign language used in trade, not only to be used in trade, but for any situation where quiet was desirable. The Guard was integrating it with military hand signals, and American Sign Language to create something they called Quiet Talk.

Learning to read and write in English was harder than he imagined. Speaking English was becoming easier, as Ed insisted everyone speak English all the time, only translating if needed. From a military perspective, he understood how all troops needed to understand orders, both verbal and written.

Allied forces weren't required to attend Dawn Muster, but Brings Him Home found it began his day with a sense of well-being. After his encouragement, Little Dog attended as well.

Tom Chandler, a veteran in the old world, grumbled, "The Guard's new Dawn Muster is soft. The army toughened you up first thing in the morning. No quiet prayers and songs. Instead, we had people yelling while we did calisthenics. Now, yoga stretches and tai chi. This is supposed to get us ready to fight?"

Ed replied defensively, "We changed the routine based on studies. Stretching and balance exercises prevent injuries, shared faith decreases stress, and singing boosts endorphins. The road crew does enough physical activity. If we were at the base, we'd have thirty minutes of aerobics after the warmups."

Brings Him Home was quiet as usual but thought, *Dawn Muster is different, but serves the same purpose as our warrior ceremonies. It creates feelings of unity.*

=..=

Nine days after leaving Chansota, the group arrived at the place the old world called Belle Fourche, a prime area for buffalo and horses. Brings Him Home was familiar with its rich grasslands. The Lakota, as they pushed westwards, fought the Cheyenne and Crow for these lands. They proceeded cautiously, spotting places where roots for foods had been dug up next to rivers and knew an encampment was close, but not knowing which tribe.

Brings Him Home had considered the Crow his enemy his whole life. Feelings of anger and hatred bubbled up in him. Four of the scalps on his pole were Crow. He knew of Lakota warriors the Crow had captured and brutally mutilated. He knew the mission was to make peace, but he wasn't sure he could put away a lifetime of hatred for an idea he wasn't sure he believed in. The ghosts of past battles whispered in his mind, their voices questioning his ability to forgive.

Once they narrowed down the general area of the encampment, they returned to their camp. Their orders were specific about how to make contact. To appear less like a war party, the women, Jody, and Tom were to approach first. Tom was fair, blond, and blue-eyed. They hoped he'd be mistaken for a French fur trader. The rest waited nearby. They would come in weapons blazing if they heard a shot.

As they approached the encampment, a wave of relief washed over Brings Him Home. The style of tipi was Cheyenne, not Crow. The Lakota and the Cheyenne sometimes fought, but also traded, holding each other in cautious reserve. Ed ordered Brings Him Home to accompany the initial group, as he spoke Cheyenne.

He heard a suspicious caw of a crow, looked around, saw no crow, and realized it was a signal. They'd been spotted. Then he noticed a young boy in a tall tree with an arrow pointed right at him. The boy, eleven or twelve winters old, jumped down smiling, mimicked shooting an arrow. Brings Him Home laughed and clutched his heart, giving the boy credit for almost catching him. Inside, he was seething, allowing a child to get the drop on him. Maybe he was getting soft. They all walked towards the camp. Brings Him Home wished he had a pistol not easily seen, like the other four had.

He held his rifle in both hands over his head, saying in Cheyenne, "We are here to trade. I have stories about the thunder people to share."

Cheyenne warriors, more curious than hostile, encircled them immediately, unsettling everyone. As they walked towards the camp, one came up and snatched Tom's farmer-style hat right off his head. Considering Tom's imposing six-foot-four frame, all hard muscle and bone, it took courage.

Before Tom could charge at the man, Jody said, "Hold, they are testing us."

"Translate this. My Cheyenne isn't good enough," Jody said to Brings Him Home, "If you like the hat, we have others to trade, clean ones, without his dirty sweat." Pointing at Tom and making a face, with a hand waving under his nose.

After he translated, everyone laughed, and Tom's hat was given back. The women had changed from their usual jeans and t-shirts to long colorful print dresses, and long beaded earrings, which brought out the Cheyenne women to finger the cloth and chatter.

After they brought everyone to the main part of the camp, several elders and an obvious leader started questioning them. They brought a few gifts of tobacco, knives, and beads. They explained while they couldn't carry much, the others would bring trade goods and gifts of bags of corn.

Brings Him Home didn't like to talk much in his own language, much less to be an interpreter. But between Jody, the few who spoke a little Lakota, and plains sign language, they got the major points across. The Cheyenne had heard of the thunder people, even this far away, but didn't believe the stories.

Ed said, "Seeing is believing. Wait until they see the trucks. It's not our job to convince them to join Changleska, we'll wait for the others."

They found a close spot a little way down the river, large enough for the rest of the expedition, and set up their camp and waited. Soon, people were going back and forth, trading small items, the men having wrestling, archery, or knife-throwing contests. Tom's size and fighting skills required him to be careful not to injure anyone. Brings Him Home won many contests, and when he lost, winners appreciated his habit of asking them for advice. Courtney, Six Feathers' wife, who was studying to be a medic, helped their healers and exchanged knowledge. The Cheyenne admired their camping gear, envied their rifles, and looked over the saddles and horses with interest.

A few women invited Tom to share robes with them. Little Dog and Brings Him Home remembered what the doctor warned them about French traders passing diseases through wife-sharing. The boys said they'd turn down any invitations, not that they got any, being both young and Lakota, but they talked as if they had. Jody later explained condoms to them, mentioning how expensive and difficult to get they were. They speculated on how many condoms Tom had, but didn't ask.

Jody laughed and said, "He is popular because the women think he'll make big, strong babies. I didn't translate, but they don't realize if he uses a condom, they won't get pregnant."

=..=

A week later, the remaining members of the expedition arrived, creating the expected commotion. Brings Him Home admired the organization as they set up. It looked like chaos at first, with the trucks maneuvering in position, tipis and tents being set up, and people running about, shouting instructions. But afterwards, it became a small, well-ordered version of the Guard base camps. Every place they set up looked the same: trucks with weapons pointed outward, strategically covering all directions; latrines, a food truck, medical tent, C&C (command and communication), and supply tents—all arranged in the same layout each time. Tipis and tents stood between the trucks, forming a wide circle that enclosed a large open field, with space for the entire group to gather, to talk, to hold meetings if needed, or simply to play the inevitable game of lacrosse.

After the initial gift-giving, they talked trade. Brings Him Home was the primary interpreter with Jody and a Cheyenne who understood Lakota listening in. The expedition brought many items the Cheyenne wanted, including powder and shot, and discussed the possibilities for rifles in the future. The Cheyenne had many fine horses, but few hides or other trade goods. Rather than trade, Changleska's primary objective was to achieve a formal alliance with the Cheyenne, ideally full membership. They allowed a few days for trading, and for the Cheyenne to watch weapons demonstrations, view videos about Changleska, and build excitement before asking for a meeting with their leadership.

It was warm in the large lodge where they met with the tribal leaders. The tipi provided shade from the hot plains summer sun. A slight breeze entered on the tipi's bottom, which had been raised for the summer, and its door opened. The tipi smelled of tobacco, buffalo from the hides they sat on, and burning sage. After smoking the pipe, they exchanged polite words and waited patiently to begin.

Lieutenant Jack Tilson, Ed's father, was the expedition's second-in-command, a Native who could speak Lakota. He was responsible for establishing relations with other tribes. He began, choosing his words carefully.

"Thank you for allowing me to speak today. We bring more than trade. We bring an offer of peace that will bring strength and protection to the Cheyenne." He paused for translation, and for them to absorb his words. "You've heard how Big Thunder brought people, goods, and knowledge from a different world. You've seen the proof. Many were people like me, the seventh generation of Lakota, who've been subjugated by the wasichu for generations. They stole our land, our children's future, our language, and way of life. The Thunder Beings have given us another chance to protect our people and the Earth from the greed of the wasichu. We call ourselves the Changleska Coalition. Changleska means the sacred hoop, the circle that holds us all. Coalition means sovereign peoples coming together. We wish for you to join our circle, not just as an ally but as a full member."

For a moment, everyone was silent, taking in what had been said. An obvious warrior spoke, "You speak well, but words are only breath unless they carry truth. The Lakota are strong, but they are not our brothers. They have raided our villages, stolen our horses, taken our women and children, and fought us for generations. If we join your hoop, do we stand beside them as brothers, or as slaves?"

Tilson bowed his head in acknowledgment. "I hear your concerns. In the past, you fought the Lakota. But tomorrow you will fight the wasichu. They are many upon many, growing stronger while tribes grow weaker from the diseases they bring." The Cheyenne in the tipi nodded, murmured acknowledgments for his words. "If we do nothing, they'll spread and continue to take and destroy. If we fight each other, we make their conquest easier. Together, we stand strong. Divided, they'll sweep us all away. Changleska offers friendship and trade. The Lakota have agreed to stop their raids. They no longer take slaves. They understand now unity is the only path forward."

An elder spoke, "I have met the wasichu they call French. They trade useful items like metal and muskets we can't make. They often marry our women and become kin. There are very few of them. I don't believe they are a threat."

Tilson answered, "There are different tribes of wasichu. The French are traders, you're correct, with too few to be a threat. Their homeland is across the ocean, the big water that takes moons to cross. It is the Americans who are growing and hungry for land. It may not happen tomorrow, but if you do nothing, your grandchildren will live under their rule."

The men in the tipi all sat in thoughtful silence.

A warrior scoffed, crossing his arms. "Fine words. But words do not stop shots from muskets, or arrows from bows. If we stand with you, who will fight for us when enemies come? Will your thunder people shed blood for the Cheyenne, as we would for our own?"

Tilson met his gaze firmly. "Yes. A threat to you is a threat to all of us. The Changleska Guard is not just Lakota. It's for all who stand within the hoop. We'll train your warriors, share our knowledge, and fight beside you if needed. We don't make promises lightly. Already, we have people of many nations among us—Arikara, Osage, Mandan, Caddo, and people of many other tribes came with us with the Big Thunder, including many Whites who want to do things differently. We hope to add many more tribes on this journey."

He continued, "By joining forces with Changleska, the Cheyenne would be part of a larger, more formidable coalition, improving their chances of achieving lasting peace and security. More than just offering weapons or goods, we offer you access to our knowledge. The kind of knowledge that will transform the lives of your children and shape a better future for generations to come. In Changleska, most babies live until adulthood, and it is rare for mothers to die in childbirth. The Cheyenne will be a sovereign nation with a voice in our council. Your leaders, laws, and warriors would remain under your control. However, this comes at a cost. You must give up your slaves. Changleska believes in freedom for all people."

The warrior said, "I captured my slaves in hard-fought battles. Giving them up seems to be a high price to pay for trade, even for rifles."

"Imagine if you didn't need slaves. We have tools that do the work of five people. If everyone joins, you don't have to worry about your women or children being captured either. We consider slavery anywhere to be wrong." He placed a multi-tool they'd all seen and admired in front of them. "This is only a small thing. A token of what we can share. But knowledge of weapons, of medicine, is the real value of what Changleska offers."

One man stood out, wearing the many talismans of a holy man. His presence commanded respect and silence, as he embodied the connection between the earthly realm and the supernatural forces that guided his people. "The wind changes, the river carves new paths, but the Earth remembers. What will our children say of this choice? Will they thank us for securing their future, or curse us for binding them to a new master?"

Tilson said softly, "The future belongs to those who shape it. If we do nothing, the wasichu will decide for us. But if we stand together, we make our own path. We're not asking you to bow to us. We're asking you to rise with us."

The Cheyenne leaders exchanged glances, weighing the risks and rewards. Finally, the leader nodded.

"We will speak of this with our people. If what you say is true, perhaps it is time for change."

Tilson exhaled slowly, knowing this was the first step.

=..=

Brings Him Home was ordered to stay with the main expedition. He didn't mind because Jody was staying as well. Jody joked he was too old to work as hard as the road crew, even though he was only in his late thirties.

The expedition would remain for another two weeks to let the Advance Crew prepare the roads. After radioing command, they negotiated with the Cheyenne to allow them to make a permanent outpost and way station. It was an ideal location. The concept of buying land differed among Indigenous peoples. Some tribes sold land outright, others believed no one owned the land. Changleska came up with a compromise. Someone could buy the right to use the land, even pass it on to their heirs, as long as they didn't pollute or misuse it. Some lands came with hunting and fishing rights, others did not. This pleased the Cheyenne as they received valuable items with a promise of more, for land they'd move on from in the fall and could return to for hunting. This contested area had been fought over, but the Lakota gave up their claims, and it was uncertain how the Crow would respond. That's why they chose a military outpost instead of a way station with cached supplies. Because the road had been cleared, it'd only take a few days to send reinforcements.

Brings Him Home was thrilled Jody invited him to join Lieutenant Tilson and Captain Andrew Morrison at a meeting to discuss defense strategies for the planned outpost. He contributed his knowledge of the area and Crow tactics. When Brings Him Home found out how much military knowledge was in their books, it motivated him to learn to read. Warfare was in his blood.

A few days later, he was playing lacrosse with some Cheyenne youth, watched by a small audience of women and children, when the new supply trucks came rumbling through the gate and into the open area where the game was underway. Brings Him Home, distracted by the noise, missed his shot just as a child ran out to retrieve the ball and return it to the field. The driver, not expecting to see a child dart in front, slammed on his brakes, and skidded across the dirt. It seemed the truck would hit the child. Just then, a blur of black horse and rider thundered past the truck, a whirlwind of hooves and motion, snatching the child to safety.

Brings Him Home ran over. Someone jumped down from the horse, yelling at him in English. Everything happened so fast he was a bit stunned. His gaze fell on the person whose rapid speech and yelling was incomprehensible, though he clearly heard 'asshole' and other familiar English curses. As he looked down, he realized it was a girl, no, a young White woman with curves clearly seen in tight jeans and a t-shirt. She was small, a foot shorter than his six feet, her blue-green eyes furiously shooting daggers at him, wearing a cowboy hat and boots. He looked, and, suddenly, completely and utterly, he fell in love. With her horse.

The horse, a magnificent black, stood tall and powerful. Its coat gleamed like polished onyx, muscles rippling beneath the surface with every movement. Its intelligent, dark eyes shone with a keen awareness, reflecting the spirit of a creature bred for both beauty and endurance. Most thunder people's horses were a breed called quarter horses. Although bigger and faster than their plains counterparts, they were high maintenance, not used to eating bark and tough prairie grasses. They even had metal shoes. This horse was different, worth whatever extra effort it took. The speed at which the horse moved was astounding.

Ignoring her, he walked around the horse, noticing it was a stallion. He'd heard a prize stallion from a breed called a Morgan was coming on the expedition. The Cheyenne had been trading for stud services. He approached the horse carefully, hand extended, with soothing Lakota words. The horse immediately bared his teeth and stomped. Brings Him Home was sure this horse would bite him or worse if he got closer. But how could this wisp of a girl ride such a horse?

She watched him admiring the horse, softening her tone, and said, "Don't touch him, he bites strangers."

Brings Him Home searched for the right English words, but they all seemed inadequate. "He is beautiful."

The girl smiled, and he realized she was pretty for a White girl, younger than him. It was hard to tell her age, as she was small. She seemed surprised he ignored her and paid more attention to the horse. He didn't comment about her screaming at him, realizing she had been afraid for the child, and he was the nearest outlet.

Looking annoyed at his ignoring her, she further astounded him by clucking softly, and the huge horse bowed down on one knee to allow her to climb up.

Brings Him Home wasn't as good a horse trainer as others in his tribe, but he knew enough to know the difficulty in training stallions, and how long it took to train any horse to kneel.

As he stood and watched her ride off, the driver, who spoke Lakota, said, "Glad it was you she was pissed at, not me. That was a close call. Don't think anyone else could have pulled it off."

Brings Him Home had to ask, "Who is she?"

"Andrea Dunphy, Major Dunphy's daughter. She goes by Andy."

Brings Him Home realized with a sinking feeling that, although her father stayed on the base, her brother, Jerry, was here; he'd seen him in passing. Even though he'd kept his horse, it was clear he was still angry about losing his saddle and rifle.

"Beautiful horse." He still felt his English was inadequate to describe his feelings about the horse.

"She won a few rodeo prizes with him, trick riding and barrel racing. Her mother was a well-known trainer. She was shopping in Pierre and got left behind the Circle. That horse is worth more than my car, hell, probably my house."

Brings Him Home walked away thoughtfully, the lacrosse game forgotten. He had never wanted anything more than he wanted that horse.

Chapter Fourteen
Jackson

JACKSON WAS TROUBLED. As a former soldier, he hated war. As the Minister for Defense, it was his responsibility to oversee weapons development, to review defenses of bases and expeditions, as well as to conduct strategic planning to wage war. He knew defense was not a strategy; it was a reaction. Winning when the stakes were too high to lose would require a proactive approach. People were going to die, not only his people, but the so-called enemy who also fought for what they believed in. There would inevitably be innocents caught in the crossfire, displaced, with their homes and lives destroyed. Jackson wrestled with this reality daily, questioning whether his strategic decisions would minimize collateral damage or merely justify it in the name of survival.

Conflict escalated on many fronts, worsening steadily. The Defense Department received regular communication from the two Guardians sent to Haiti to support the burgeoning slave revolution. They routed messages through the New Orleans radio station. Progress was being made. They contacted Toussaint Louverture, the leader who orchestrated the former colony's independence in the history of the old world. When the Black population became citizens of France, Louverture joined the French army, becoming a leading general who helped France eventually defeat Spanish and British forces in the Caribbean. In 1802, in the old history, Napoleon had gained power and wanted to reinstate slavery. France invited Louverture to parley but arrested him upon his arrival. He died of starvation in prison a year later. Changleska wanted to change that history.

Jackson was proud of the two young Black men who volunteered for this crucial mission to end slavery, not only in Haiti, but all over the Caribbean. Neither was a veteran, nor did they have any skill set other than a fierce determination to end slavery. With Toussaint s help and twenty-first century knowledge, they fought several battles, creating a growing army of escaped slaves. They successfully negotiated with plantation owners to free and pay slaves, and they negotiated trade deals between Changleska and Britain to buy their sugar. They were participating in talks with the United States, but so far, they had made no agreements.

At Oca Landing in New Orleans, they crafted Grown Without Slavery" stamps to be imprinted on eligible products. The growing abolitionist movement was publishing lists of Sugar Without Sin" plantations. The Harvested by Free Hands" movement was expanding. Some merchants embraced the movement, eager to profit from the ethical label, while others resisted, fearing economic repercussions. Consumers who could afford it increasingly sought free sugar," but plantation owners tied to slavery viewed the movement as a direct threat to their way of life.

The Omímeya marketing department was busy writing articles, sending letters, and placing paid ads in newspapers. They knew newspapers were more inclined to publish articles submitted by paid advertisers. Besides health tips, they sent in human interest articles about the accomplishments of Black people, as well as stories about the horrors of slavery.

The Haiti group needed more radios, weapons, and personnel. It was the same for the California expedition, which kept having skirmishes with the Spanish. Other groups might need to fight the Crow. Every new base needed scarce resources. And looming over everything was the new United States, a growing threat due to the support they were getting inside Changleska. Spies were everywhere, illegal tech sales were booming, and the voices for annexation were growing. Indigenous forces had recently defeated the US in a battle during the Northwest Indian War, killing over nine hundred. The United States wanted payback for that humiliating defeat, as well as desiring the lands of the Shawnee, Miami, Lenape, Wyandot, Kickapoo, Potawatomi, and Ottawa. Another confrontation for control of the Ohio valley seemed inevitable. Many, including Gardner, felt that Jackson should send troops to support the tribes.

Charlotte, his assistant, reminded him of his meeting with General Gardner in five minutes to discuss weapons production. Fortunately, many South Dakotans owned guns. There were many hunting lodges and gun shops, as well as a fair number of knowledgeable gun hobbyists in the area. With all the plans in the Omímeya databases, they wouldn't be starting from scratch, but in the ten months since Big Thunder, they still had not come up with enough new weapons. The only ammunition was powder and shot suitable for muskets or cannons.

At the appointed time, he grabbed his coffee and put the phone on speaker to look over the written report as they talked.

Jackson began, I've read the reports. I see we ve got severe bottlenecks with the weapons we can produce, and no modern ammo at all. If we can t scale production, it s going to bite us in the ass."

General Gardner answered with a sigh, "I know. Making bullets isn't the issue, it's the primers and smokeless powder. We don't have the chemistry or the infrastructure to produce them. Without those, reloading spent casings is a dead-end."

"What are our options?"

"Well, the only real lab we've got—Pharmco—was converted from making veterinary to human medications. We can't risk mixing primer chemicals there, not unless you want an explosion that levels half of Chamberlain. So that's out."

"Damn. I was hoping we could at least start small-scale primer production there. What more can you tell me not in the report?"

We've made progress in modifying flintlocks into breech-loaders, as well as some prototype air rifles. It s not ideal, but we can at least start production. We have chemists trying to make percussion caps, but even if they succeed, mass-producing is going to be a challenge. We'd be months away for smaller scale and years for anything major."

Jackson said with resignation, "Basically, we can maintain and ration what we have, but replacing it isn't happening for months, and only small amounts."

"Exactly. We've got to be smart. Black powder we can make, but smokeless powder? Not for a year at least, and then, only limited quantities. We can outsource rifles and pistols and focus on ammunition. We'll also need to get creative with non-gunpowder weapons like crossbows, air rifles, whatever gives us an edge."

Jackson knew from three tours fighting in Iraq and Afghanistan how hard it was to train soldiers to new weapons. "I don't like it, but I don't see another way. We'll have to train people differently. A firefight isn't going to be about who has the best rate of fire anymore, it'll be about who makes their shots count. We can't fight like we're still in the twenty-first century. We need to think like warriors of this time, but with enough of our tech to stay ahead. Let's not forget how well the Lakota did without modern weapons. We need to learn from them."

Gardner ended the call by saying, "We should set up a time to look at the air rifle prototypes. We have plans for the one Lewis and Clark brought on their expedition, made in this era, modernized. It could be an asset. As for ammunition, if anything changes on the chemistry front, you'll be the first to know. But until then, we'd better get used to fighting like it's the 1800s."

Jackson s hopes that there would be ammo or weapons to send to any conflict zones soon faded. He couldn t send personnel either, they had none to spare. Despite a mandatory two-year service for citizens aged eighteen to twenty-five and efforts to expand local militias like the Neighborhood Watch, Changleska remained critically short of trained personnel. An influx of new people from Indigenous tribes, freed slaves, and eighteenth-century settlers and adventurers arrived, but without the ability to read, write, and speak English, they couldn t join the Changleska Guard. They were adding new people as auxiliaries for support staff. It made Jackson uncomfortable to see so many Black faces working in the kitchens, laundry, and cleaning staff. Logically, he knew this freed support staff for administrative roles if they weren t suited for combat. A few of the support staff might even move into combat. This still didn t relieve his concerns they were creating a segregated military. All bases now offered adult literacy programs, which could provide long-term solutions. As much as he hated to think of himself as a role model, the fact that a Black man headed the Changleska military inspired many former slaves to want to join the Guard.

=..=

The next day he had a meeting with members of the various expeditions committees to go over reports in person. All expeditions fit under the responsibility of his defense department, but he had not paid enough attention to the fact that they were inundated with other responsibilities. He had only briefly skimmed the forums and reports and was glad for an in-person meeting to get a better picture. When he arrived at the meeting, everyone stood up respectfully. He sat down and Charlotte brought him coffee from the side table while he looked over the agenda on his tablet. The expeditions had been tasked with recruiting tribes to join Changleska and become formal allies. They were desperately short of troops and the tribes were critical to meet that need.

Expedition committees were not formal lawmaking bodies. Although they could gather the two thousand votes required to propose legislation, more laws were not needed. Their purpose was to organize and support the expeditions from home. The chair, secretary, and treasurer for the five active expeditions were present at the meeting. There was another meeting next month for planned expeditions in the spring.

Jackson looked around the room. "Let's start with California."

"Road building has been slower than expected," said the chair. "There have been some deaths from accidents. Details in the report. We have had problems with tires, not enough spares, not totally unexpected. It is possible we may have to leave a vehicle with a friendly tribe awaiting spares, but the problem is we don't have many spares at home."

Jackson motioned to Charlotte, who looked at her tablet. "Defense has secured a number of tires from the junkyards and gasoline cars that could possibly be used. Please get me the sizes you need. Can't promise anything, but I will see what I can do."

"Thank you," Then he nodded to the secretary who took over reporting.

"So far we have secured an alliance with the Cheyenne, Pawnee, Arapaho, Shoshone, Paiute, and Goshute, including the purchase of land for way stations. Negotiations with the Crow have been slow. They killed a messenger, likely due to mistrust or a past grievance, but we have hopes for the trader we sent in, although we've heard nothing yet. Getting messages is slow. With only one transmitter, they have to be stopped long enough to set the transmitter up with the generator. While the negotiations have been going well, we are going to need a lot of goods to make our new allies happy. I think Angie has the specifics."

The treasurer of the California expedition directed everyone to the online report. Jackson considered the numbers of muskets and gunpowder and felt a tightening in his chest. The demand far exceeded what they could currently supply, and he had no clear solution. It was a sobering reminder that promises made in good faith might soon become liabilities on the ground.

Great job everyone, can you please pass onto the leadership, and this goes for everyone, to be careful what they promise. We may be a year or two away from getting weapons of any kind out to the tribes. Now Southwest, what've you got for us?"

The Chair, an older Hispanic man, took a deep breath before he started his report. They initially made good time, and the Ute agreed to join. They hoped for the Dine, Hopi, Zuni, Pueblo, and Apache, but they are spread over a broad area, haven t yet made any firm commitments. However, they are trading and word is spreading. The expedition had a problem while camped near the four corners area. While they were stopped for a training exercise, a rifle hit two large IBC water containers. Because it was far away, no one noticed that a single shot had passed through both. About five hundred gallons of water was lost, which is a catastrophic loss in a desert region where every gallon counts. The entire expedition was forced to delay and reroute. Fortunately, a friendly Dine tribe offered guidance on desert travel, and led them to water. The expedition gifted the tribe a few highly valued trade items, which were appreciated. Their radio transmitter wasn t powerful, so I'm not sure how much we will hear from them from now on."

The Northern expedition reported next. They had made good progress with most tribes they encountered had heard tales of Changleska and were happy to join. They had gone via rivers and had lost one canoe and three people, two militia members and a translator, but other than that, made good progress. One potential problem was extent the Cree lands went into Canada. It was unclear how much the British would respect the Cree sovereignty. Jackson was glad he didn't have Mary's job.

Jackson was a bit more familiar with the Eastern Expedition's report, as their contacts with Philadelphia and George Washington were critical, and he had followed them more closely. So far, the Americans had refused Changleska an embassy but would accept envoys. A method of communication had been established, although it didn t appear promising. The Boston expedition was recruiting vital artisans and getting needed supplies, including minerals, tools, and muskets. Jackson wished they could produce their own better weapons instead of the Brown Bess flintlock muskets.

The Southeast Expedition had contacted the Waccamaw tribe and were starting an outpost for a radio transmitter. They also met with the Cherokee and other tribes, offering context about future forced removals, broken treaties, and the dangers posed by expanding settler colonialism.

All the expeditions needed money and materials and asked for more troops to be sent. Jackson did not know how he was going to supply all the expeditions so far away when he could not supply projects close to home. They would need another loan from Omímeya. Good thing the boss was his girlfriend.

=..=

His next meeting was with Theresa Martinez, the Minister for Medicine, and Frank Long Feather, the Surgeon General of the Medical Corps, to discuss allotment of drugs. Gardner objected to providing lifesaving drugs to potential enemies, while the Medical Corps was dedicated to serving everyone in need.

Jackson had spent very little time with Frank Long Feather, an older physician attending the medical conference on the day of Big Thunder. His background included working in the Indian Health Service administration for his Shawnee tribe and as a doctor in the First Gulf War. Although he was eminently qualified for his position, he struck Jackson as a poor leader because of his inflexibility. The Medical Corps was his baby, and he didn't like the Executive Council to tell him anything.

They had to use a regular Omímeya meeting room. Jackson's office was not big enough, and the headquarters for both the Guard and the Medical Corps were in Chamberlain. The room's corporate blandness was offset by some beautiful artwork and large windows with river views.

After everyone settled, Frank said, "I know the stocks of human antibiotics are long gone, but we're finding the veterinary ones work just as well. Pharmco had a warehouse full on the day of Big Thunder. Why can't we access those?"

Jackson said, "Most have been distributed. New drugs are coming out. It has been a while since I looked over the reports from Healing Hoop. Last I heard, insulin and penicillin were too difficult to make soon. Theresa, what is the current status on drugs?"

"Aspirin and quinine will be made later; the drugs aren't significantly better than willow and cinchona bark for malaria. Tinctures of the herbs are available at local apothecary shops. Making antibiotics and ether is a better use of our limited laboratory resources. Large quantities of chloramphenicol, for typhoid and meningitis, but tetracycline for respiratory infections, cholera, syphilis, and typhus are in shorter supply. Next, they are working on streptomycin for TB, pneumonia, and wound infections," replied Theresa.

Frank complained, "What large quantities? The New Orleans clinic can't get enough of these drugs, much less the outposts and outreach teams."

"We are holding some in strategic reserve, partially because of the insufficient chloramphenicol supply during last winter's typhoid epidemic, which led to so much loss of life," said Jackson.

"Strategic Reserve?" Frank retorted. "That is another way to say our people are better than yours. Triage doesn't play politics. It's the sickest or those most at risk."

"We lost a doctor last winter to typhoid," Theresa sadly added, "Think of all the lives he could have saved with his knowledge."

Following Big Thunder, tough choices had to be made regarding access to scarce advanced medical resources. Rather than using the old world's traditional medical triage guidelines, which treated the sickest first, the Changleska ethics board decided that medical practitioners must consider the age, health, even the occupation of each patient. Forced to look at the bigger picture, they were now required to swear an oath: I swear by everything I hold sacred to use my knowledge and skills to heal those I can, harm none, and recognize the limitations on whom I can serve, for the greater good of all."

And what about vaccines? I know we ll soon conduct smallpox trials. Tetanus and diphtheria trials will follow shortly. Are you going to limit those, too?" Frank challenged. Jackson responded calmly, although he was annoyed with Frank s tone, CVI (Changleska Vaccine Institute) issues the directives, but you re on the board. Theresa, will they restrict the smallpox vaccine?"

Jackson responded calmly, although he was annoyed with Frank's tone, "CVI (Changleska Vaccine Institute) issues the directives, but you're on the board Theresa, will they restrict the smallpox vaccine?"

"No, it won't be restricted, but there ll be limited quantities to start. We ll likely begin with the Indigenous population, but we just started the smallpox vaccine trial. When it's complete the board will make its recommendation to the Council."

Theresa was an epidemiologist, a disease prevention specialist. Her recommendations would carry weight.

Frank said, "The Medical Corps should make these decisions. This is not politics. CVI should be a private corporation, like Healing Hoop. No government should wholly own vaccines and decide who gets them."

Jackson responded, "The bigger problem is Clyde Folson, a big antivaxxer. He has a huge following. Last week he claimed on his radio show, the new smallpox vaccine has a ten percent fatality rate."

"What?" both Frank and Theresa exclaimed at the same time. Theresa followed up with, "Where's he getting those numbers? The new vaccine's mortality rate is about one in ten thousand, or 0.01 percent. That's already one hundred times higher than the modern smallpox vaccine's fatality rate of one in a million, or 0.0001 percent, but it's still nowhere near one in ten, or 10 percent.

"The funny thing is, people in this era were not too alarmed by a ten percent mortality rate; that meant 90 percent would survive and never get smallpox. It's the ones from our time who are risk averse."

"Will the Council approve Theresa's recommendations for vaccine distributions? This is her field of expertise." Frank asked.

"I expect the Council will listen to Theresa, but I can't promise anything. She is also consulting about the drug distributions, and I know epidemics are a priority."

"We'll see how this plays out, but the Medical Corps needs to have a say in these decisions too." Frank seemed somewhat mollified.

They wrapped up by reviewing the specific medication allocation numbers. It turned out that Frank's concerns about denying potential enemy medications were overblown. There weren't enough drugs to go around for anyone, much less enemies. While Frank's personality annoyed Jackson, he had to admit the Medical Corps was a good idea. Other than their twenty-five percent contribution to their budget, the Defense Department no longer had to worry about medical care. They even handled their own logistics.

=..=

Jackson realized it was Tuesday a few minutes before six pm. He was running late for Rose's Dinner. Right after Big Thunder, Rose had started what turned into a little supper club. Rose didn't like cooking or eating alone and invited a few friends and colleagues to dinner five nights a week at the Red Oaks Restaurant. Omímeya had converted the restaurant from a popular buffet to a basic cafeteria. Food supplies were limited, and costs were high at Red Oaks in the early days after Big Thunder. Rose, with her high salary and few expenses, paid for dinner for a few friends, a number that grew to about a dozen. It became a bit of an elite social club, with people vying for invitations, not for free food, but a chance to rub elbows with leadership. It gradually went down to one day a week. Besides the five or six core regulars, Rose invited a few Omímeya staff she felt were worthy of special recognition. Today, when he arrived a few minutes late, he noticed a woman he remembered from housekeeping along with her husband and two young children, all dressed in their best. He could see what a special occasion it was for their family.

The food at the cafeteria was usually nothing special. In the reserved dining room, catering set up a few special dishes for them. There were tablecloths, beeswax candles, and flower arrangements with wild prairie flowers. Everyone still got their own food, and after the prayer, talked and socialized. The rule was no work talk. Jackson had fond memories of these dinners, as that is when Rose and he really got to know each other.

Seeing Kimi at the dinner surprised him. She usually only came to Rose's house on the weekends, and not always then. He looked around and did not see Gift, her usual shadow.

"It's nice to see you on a Tuesday, Kimímela," Jackson said in his terrible Lakota, knowing she would correct his grammar and pronunciation. It was kind of their thing. "Any special reason you're here midweek?" He immediately felt guilty for asking. She should feel good coming home anytime.

"Community Health Worker training all week. It is one prerequisite for midwifery. Plus, I like it."

Rose said proudly, "She is giving a workshop with Gift on Thursday on local herbs. They're leading a plant walk."

"That's wonderful." Jackson never paid attention to the schedule of workshops Omímeya offered, but he noticed more young women in the lobby since yesterday. He was a man, after all.

After dinner they lingered over tea, most people had left, so they could talk about work. Jackson appreciated Rose's insights, and they'd discuss nothing Kimi shouldn't hear.

He said, "I had a meeting today with Theresa and Frank Long Feather. The smallpox vaccine should be out soon. Frank had concerns that vaccines and drugs could be politicized. He believes the Medical Corps should decide everything."

Rose said, "As long as they listen to Theresa, this is her field after all. I don't see a problem, do you?"

Before Jackson could answer, Kimi surprised him by speaking. "Access to medicine is always political. It was in the old world, and at least for many years, it should be political now."

Jackson and Rose looked at her in surprise, and Jackson motioned her to go on.

"Changleska will offer modern medicine and vaccines that can save thousands, maybe millions of lives. Every government in the world will want access. The price we charge can be no slavery, no stealing Indigenous lands, no limited access to medicines for the poor, and protection for the Earth. Changleska will become the world center for medical innovation, bringing more people and a lot of money. Mom, don't you always say we need great wealth to change the world?"

"I'm not sure it is that simple, sweetie," Rose said.

"It is that simple, mom. We save children's lives. Ask any parent who has ever lost a child what they'd give to prevent it. War is about fighting over resources, but our bullets will run out soon, and so will the resources. Soon we'll be back to the wars of the old world. We must change and take a few uncomfortable steps to keep greed from damaging the Earth again. Thunder Beings brought us here with 153 doctors for a reason. Medicine is our greatest weapon for peace."

Jackson stared at her, a mixture of surprise and awe in his eyes. He thought, *she's only thirteen years old. What is she going to be like at thirty?*

Chapter Fifteen
Gift of Thunder

GIFT OF THUNDER felt the relentless prairie sun beating down on her shoulders as she rode, its heat wrapping around her like a thick blanket. It was always hot in *Waštúŋ Wi*, the Moon When All Things Ripen, or August. While her English was fluent after being here almost a year, she still thought in Lakota. She didn't mind the heat. She was wearing what was called a sun hat, which kept her surprisingly cool. They would need to get to water soon, as her horse *Thaté* (Wind) was getting hot. Just then she saw Bear Runner, the young man from Red Eagle's tribe who'd accompanied them and had been riding ahead to scout, directing them toward a small creek with water and shade.

When they reached the cottonwood trees, Kimi jumped down from her horse. "Finally," she sighed, wiping sweat from her forehead. "I don't think I'll ever get used to riding for this long."

Gift laughed. "You're soft. Used to air conditioning."

"I know, I know," Kimi groaned, fanning herself dramatically. "This will be the longest time I've been away from home. Sure, I miss the air conditioning and my phone. It's a little scary being out of touch, but honestly, I'm glad we've come."

Gift studied her, sensing something unspoken. "You're not afraid?"

Kimi hesitated. "Not of this. But... I had a dream last night. It felt real."

Gift stiffened. "Tell me."

Kimi's gaze flickered. "We were here, but something was wrong. The wind shifted, and I heard the thunder, but there were no clouds."

Gift shivered despite the heat. "You think it means something?"

"I don't know. I have a feeling we should be careful."

Gift nodded. Kimi's instincts were rarely wrong. But she also knew that fear could make people reckless. "Then we watch. We listen."

Kimi gave a firm nod. "We listen."

Gift let the moment settle before nudging her horse forward. "Let's go. Before the sun bakes you like clay."

Kimi rolled her eyes but followed, and together, they rode toward the unknown.

Gift said to her adopted sister, "I'm surprised our father let us go by ourselves; he's usually so protective."

"You just need to know how to phrase things. Going to a buffalo hunt with you and a few expedition members wouldn't have flown. But a camping school trip, that is another thing."

"School? Who is supposed to be the teacher?"

"Little Crow of course."

Little Crow was an older woman from Two Elks' tribe. Earlier in the year, she had been part of the expedition that traveled north to meet with the Assiniboine and Cree tribes, aiming to recruit them to Changleska. Her steady manner and diplomatic skills had helped make the mission a success.

"Does she know she's supposed to be our teacher?"

"She assured dad we'd be safe and learn new things, that was enough. Also, I need practicum hours as a Community Health Worker, and the medic agreed to be my preceptor."

Gift sighed. She wasn't sure whether she would ever learn the dynamics of her new family. Last spring, after seriously considering returning to the Arikara tribe to marry, she decided to remain. It was a big step when she said she would no longer go to school. She was becoming more independent and no longer treated as a child. Hotah, her adopted father, knew she would protect Kimi with her life, and assumed that was one reason they were allowed to go.

=..=

It took two more days to find the Oglala tribe's camp. They missed the buffalo hunt by a day, arriving in time for the butchering and processing. The long, hard, hot, bloody work was normal enough to Gift to be almost soothing. She knew Kimi was struggling. Her movements were slower, her grip on the knife unsteady, and the sweat dripping from her brow betrayed her exhaustion. But she didn't complain, determined to push through. After the butchering was done, and the meat brought back to the camp, they celebrated with a feast, singing and dancing to give thanks. There were many more days of work ahead for the women to further process all the meat into jerky and pemmican.

The sun blazed high over the bustling camp, its golden light casting long, wavering shadows as the scent of drying meat and wood smoke thickened the air. Children, unaffected by the sweltering temperatures, played energetically, mingling with the sounds of laughter and chatter. Gift appreciated how, despite the heat and hard work, there was a sense of unity and purpose in the camp, a shared goal that bound everyone together. She rarely saw that at home in Changleska. Everyone worked hard, but it was on their own projects.

Gift and Kimi, with a few other women, were cutting meat to be smoked. The women complimented the girls for the gifts of new knives, salt, and spices. While officially allied with Changleska and linked to Red Eagle s band, the band had experienced little direct contact prior to this. Several packhorses full of gifts and trade items were warmly received. Gift had brought various items she owned for personal trades. She was having a nice pair of winter moccasins made. Lined with wolf fur, they would be nicer than those she could make for herself.

The women were all laughing and talking as they worked. They made ribald comments and jokes that embarrassed both girls, which, of course, made the older women laugh more and delve into even greater detail.

One asked, "If you are not interested in these men, is there someone at home for you?" After Gift nodded no, she added, "You look the right age for marriage."

An older woman said, "My husband said the other day, we needed a new young wife. Three was not enough if we want enough hides to trade for all the thunder people bring. Maybe you should meet him."

"No, No," another woman said, "he is too old, and I hear he farts so much in the night his name should be Farts a Lot."

Everyone laughed, but Kimi was quiet and thoughtful. Gift knew from previous conversations that Kimi was uncomfortable with polygamy. Until Big Thunder brought them here, she had only known men with only one wife. Ciwaku, the man she had considered marrying, had only one other wife, whom she liked even more than Ciwaku. Growing up, whenever she thought of the family she wanted, it was always one husband and many wives, who would be like sisters to her. She knew she may never marry. She was glad she and Ciwaku shared robes. It took away some of the trauma of her first sexual experience, with its painful violation, replacing it with pleasant and fond memories. It had given her a sense of control over her own experiences. But she was not in any hurry to repeat it. There were too many other things in life to experience. Yet, it also made her wonder whether she would ever seek the same type of companionship again, or if her heart had already settled on a path she wasn't sure she wanted to walk.

Gift spent most of her time with the women, helping with winter food preparations. She also spent time with the young men as they competed in various martial competitions. The young men exchanged astonished glances as Gift's knife struck the target dead center once again. A few muttered grudging compliments, while others grinned, clearly impressed. Gift surprised them when she effectively used karate in wrestling, and performed well in archery. Most of the men still rode better than she did, but she was improving. At one point, Kimi went off with a holy woman to some nearby hills. Gift heard distant rumblings of thunder. Gift paused, her knife hovering over the meat. The sky was impossibly clear, yet the rumble echoed through her bones. She glanced at the others, wondering whether they heard it too. After she returned, Kimi said the holy woman asked her not to speak of what she was learning about the thunder teachings, but she was glad she came.

One evening, Gift and Kimi were walking through the camp, when Kimi heard a slap and a muffled cry. Turning abruptly, she saw a young boy, maybe ten or eleven winters old, being hit by an older woman.

Kimi strode right up to the woman, her voice full of anger. Stop! Whatever he s done is no reason to hit him."

The woman responded, "He's my slave. It's none of your concern what I do to him. I could cut off his finger for what he's done."

A cold weight settled in Gift s chest. The woman s words echoed with memories of the fear and helplessness she had tried to bury. Although she herself hadn t been mutilated, she'd heard others had been.

Kimi's hands clenched into fists, her face burning with fury. She stepped forward, her voice sharp as a blade. "Your leaders have signed the treaty for all the bands. You're part of Changleska now, and slavery of any kind is forbidden. Bands who don't obey will be outcast and cut off from trade."

"I heard something about that," the woman admitted, "but I thought that meant taking new slaves, not ones we already have. I have had this boy for three winters."

Kimi bent down and spoke softly to the boy, who was watching the whole interaction with interest.

"You're no longer a slave. Do you want to stay here, or come with us?"

The boy did not say a word, nodded, and grasped the hand she held out for him.

"Does that mean you wish to leave and come back with us?"

"He does not speak. He is useless. You can take him," the woman said with derision, and walked away.

Gift knew the boy could hear, because he'd come to Kimi when asked, but if he was mute, it was no wonder he was a slave, or perhaps he was mute because he was a slave. She was glad they were taking him home. Disability and survival did not mix, and in small Lakota camps, survival was often balanced on a thin edge.

Gift asked Kimi, "What are we going to do with him? There is plenty of room at Crow Road. He can sleep in the boys' room. Father took me, I'll help."

She answered, "We can figure it out later. Right now, I want to talk to whoever is in charge. Are there more slaves here? Tribes who break the treaty will be sanctioned. They may no longer trade with us. We should take back all our stuff." She went storming off, dragging the boy behind her.

Gift had grown up in a similar tribe and knew Kimi couldn't just barge into the leader's tipi and make demands. Despite her respect as one who spoke to Thunder Beings, she was still a young girl and could not challenge men in such a manner.

"Kimi, stop. They'll not listen to you. Let's go talk to Little Crow. She'll know what to do."

Kimi slowed. They returned to their camp and spoke to Little Crow and a few of the Changleska Guard that had come with them. The Guardians exchanged glances, some nodding in approval, others tightening their jaws. They knew this was progress, but for some, it wasn t enough. They sent a message to the *nacá*, what the Europeans called chief. The Lakota used the term naca for the leader of a smaller band such as this one, although they had many types of leaders. Kimi insisted on coming and brought the boy. They didn t know his name, or what to call him, so Kimi called him sweetie instead.

Naca Good Horn was an older man who listened gravely to Little Crow. Kimi brought the boy forward and pulled his shirt up to show healing bruises from being beaten.

He answered in a serious tone. "We knew some Oglala gave up their slaves. Until you came to us, we had never seen a thunder person, or any of your goods. Not all Oglala speak with the same voice. Why should I listen to Red Eagle? He does not lead my people."

Little Crow said, "You have the goods now. Are you not happy with the muskets, powder, and shot? Cloth, pots, and knives? The gifts of corn and tobacco?"

Good Horn had to admit yes with a nod.

She continued, You received our goods, and our medic shared ways to save many lives. The treaty does not ask for much: no slaves, no raids or war without speaking to our council, to send warriors to learn new ways, and share defense. Is there any part you disagree with?"

"No, I do not disagree. But until I see with my own eyes, these are only words in the wind. Why should I follow Red Eagle? I must do what is right for my people. We have won slaves in battle or traded fairly for them. We need extra hands to prepare food for the winter. Why should we give them up for Red Eagle's words?"

Little Crow said, "With trade, you will have corn and tools to make work easier. Your winters will ease. You no longer need slaves. Since you say Red Eagle's words are not yours, but you signed the treaty."

"A paper with words in a language I did not understand. But I was told about the slaves. You are right, we only have a few. They may go, or, if they remain, we will give them new names and allow them to marry."

Kimi was about to interrupt, but Gift stopped her with a hand on her knee and Kimi instead whispered to Little Crow.

Little Crow consulted for a moment with the other Guard members, then spoke firmly to Good Horn. "You ignored the treaty, even though you knew about not having slaves. Because you are giving up your slaves, and this is our first visit, we will complete the trades we have agreed on. But after today, if we find slaves in your camp, not only will you no longer get thunder people's goods, but no one from the entire Oceti Sakowin will trade with you."

After they left, Kimi said to Little Crow. "He should be punished. It's not like they didn't know."

"And what would you have us do? Take away the trade goods? Fight? We have three warriors and are in their camp. We are on a trade mission. Down the road, others will enforce the treaty, but for now, these kinds of things will happen. This is a good outcome. I will check with the others, but we should leave early, probably tomorrow. And put the word out no more trades."

Kimi kneeled by the boy, still by her side. She placed a reassuring hand on his shoulder, her grip firm yet gentle, as if silently promising him safety. "Sweetie, do you know who all the other slaves are in the camp?"

He nodded and silently led them from one person to another. There were five all together. Two young women chose to stay. They felt at home and had men they had their eye on. Two others, a young man and older woman, were Cheyenne and wished to return. Little Crow gave them two horses they'd traded for, as well as supplies for the journey. They didn t know which tribe the boy was from. He didn t understand Cheyenne or Shoshone. He may have been Crow, but no one knew words to ask him. As far as anyone remembered, he d always been mute.

They headed back the next day. Little Crow took over care of the boy, on whom the name Sweetie stuck.

A few days later, while camped at the river, Little Crow called everyone together. The sun was low, casting golden light on the water, and people gathered quietly, sensing the importance of what she was about to say.

She stood in the center, her hands resting gently on Sweetie's shoulders. Her voice was steady, but there was a tremble beneath it. "My boys are gone," she said. "I have no husband. I have carried that grief a long time. But I still have love to give. No matter how old they are, all men need a mother. Someone who will worry, who will listen, who will remind them who they are. Can I be your mother?"

Sweetie looked up at her, eyes wide, then nodded without speaking. A hush fell over the group. Around them, people nodded in quiet agreement, with more than a few eyes glistening with tears.

=..=

They arrived at the Expedition Base Camp late in the afternoon. For most of the group, it was their final destination, but Gift and Kimi still had a four to five-hour ride home, so they stayed overnight. They settled the horses and dropped their gear in the visitor tent, relieved they didn't have to set up their own. Little Crow told them that everyone had received a dinner invitation from Major Dunphy, the base commander. Jonah, the Guardian who had accompanied them, said it was an honor to be invited to dine with the major instead of just the debriefing expected of all returning missions.

The girls took solar showers and stayed long enough for the water to turn cool. They had both brought dresses and took turns fixing each other's hair. They both looked respectable when it was time to arrive.

Gift asked Kimi, "Why are we invited to have dinner with the major? We weren't part of the mission team. You only wanted to go on a buffalo hunt."

"I know, and we missed the hunt. The major invited us because of politics."

"Politics?"

Kimi patiently explained, We re Rose s daughters. She s the most powerful person in Changleska. Even more than the Executive Councilors. They may get voted out, but mom will always be Omímeya's CEO. It is about money and influence. Jackson oversees his budget, not mom, but she oversees more than the resort. And Jackson is her boyfriend. Everyone will always suck up to us, get used to it."

Gift thought, *suck up to us?*, but got the gist without translation.

The officers' mess was another tent next to the kitchen, but there was a larger building being constructed next to it. After everyone was seated, Major Dunphy arrived exactly on time and everyone stood up before returning to their seats. After a nice dinner full of polite pleasantries, news from their weeks away, and funny anecdotes about the trip, they had their official debriefing. There wasn t much to tell — the trip was uneventful.

The major, unsurprised by the news of the slaves, let out a measured sigh, his expression neutral. "It has come up before," he said, his tone carrying a mix of resignation and mild frustration. "Future enforcement patrols will likely be needed to ensure compliance."

Little Crow brought Sweetie, now looking well-scrubbed and dressed in slightly too-big twenty-first-century clothes. He tugged at the sleeves uncertainly, his fingers brushing over the unfamiliar fabric. His eyes darted around, wary yet curious. The major told Little Crow she should take Sweetie to the Chamberlain hospital for a full evaluation for the muteness, saying maybe nothing could be done, but all possibilities should be investigated.

Kimi surprised everyone by saying, "He has nothing to say. He'll speak when he's ready."

Little Crow gave her a huge smile. As far as she was concerned, Kimi's prescience was better than all the doctors in Chamberlain.

=..=

A few weeks later, they attended a lacrosse game at the high school baseball diamond. While basketball remained the most popular sport, lacrosse was quickly gaining traction. Originating from Eastern Indigenous tribes and played by the Lakota, the twenty-firsters had modernized some rules and shortened the game but kept some traditional rituals. Gambling on the games occurred behind the scenes, with the Omímeya casino taking bets. Because they lacked the capability for live broadcasts, they taped the games to show on big screens later.

Every seat in the stands was filled, spilling over with families and spectators, which created a vibrant and electric atmosphere. The warm summer breeze carried the rich scent of popcorn, mingling with excitement in the air. It was billed as an exhibition match because it wasn t an official high school event since school hadn t started yet. All the same, this game held special significance. Lower Brule faced Chamberlain High, no ordinary rival. They had taken the basketball championship last season, and now, the hope in the crowd was palpable. Lower Brule s team, which had added a few Indigenous Lakota high school students, had the home-court advantage, and everyone was eager to see whether that would tip the scales in their favor.

Gift and Kimi arrived a bit late as they came with the whole family: four adults, two teenagers, three children and one infant, all in one truck. They no longer had motorized transport, relying on horses, but Zitkala's boyfriend, Dylan, owned a truck converted to veggie oil, had been staying with them. Dylan, Zitkala, and the baby in the front seat, the rest all piled in the back of the pickup, Hotah saying he remembered traveling like this as a rez kid, but they made it illegal. It was full circle.

As they approached the stands, Kimi stopped, grabbed Gift's arm, and said, "Wait, there is something wrong." The rest of the family had gone ahead, rushing to find seats. Kimi pulled Gift towards the entrance.

"It's like what happened in the Big Bear room. Something terrible is about to happen, but I don't know what."

Gift remembered with horror when armed cartel gunmen shot automatic weapons randomly into a crowd at the Omímeya's Big Bear meeting room during a political debate. It ended with the death of the shooters but left twenty-nine wounded and eleven dead. Kimi always felt guilty for not having given a warning sooner. She had sensed something ominous but wasn t specific until the moment before the shooting when she shouted, Get down!' and saved her family. A chill ran through her and her pulse hammered in her ears. Her breath caught as memories of the chaos—shouts, blood, the acrid smell of gunfire—came rushing back. She clenched her fists, forcing herself to push the fear aside and focus.

The two girls looked up and saw the rest of the family on the top bleachers. It would be difficult to reach them through the crowds.

Gift said, "Let's find security. They have to believe you."

They looked around and finally found someone in a security t-shirt near the concession stand. Security consisted of volunteers, often parents, whose jobs were to handle rowdy teenagers, or the occasional drunk who sneaked alcohol in. It was harder to sneak alcohol into dry Lower Brule, but not that difficult.

Gift was practically dragging Kimi over, who hesitated for a moment, glancing around nervously as if expecting danger to materialize at any second. Her steps faltered, her breath quickening, but Gift gripped her arm firmly and urged her forward. Neither of them noticed the man dressed oddly in a long coat in this hot weather who was following a distance behind them.

They approached the security guard, a big White man, wearing camo pants and a security t-shirt, armed with both a pistol and a taser.

Gift told Kimi urgently, "Tell him."

Kimi looked hesitant, but said to the man quietly, "There is something wrong. Someone here wants to harm many people."

In alarm, the man looked around. "What happened? What did you see? Does someone have a gun?"

It was a silly question. Lots of people, most in fact, carried pistols, but since the cartel attack, no one carried long guns in public spaces.

Gift said, "This is Kimímela Chasing Hawk. She knew about the cartel attack beforehand and said nothing because she was afraid no one would believe her."

It wasn't exactly true, but it was close enough. The man slowly considered what he knew, and of course, everyone in the Circle knew about Kimímela Chasing Hawk. He didn't know what to believe but chose not to take a chance.

He asked Kimi gently, "Can you tell me anything specific?"

She nodded no, with tears glistening in her eyes. Kimi's stomach twisted. What if she was wrong? What if she caused panic over nothing? But the heavy, suffocating feeling wouldn't leave her.

The man decided, and spoke on his radio, "Keep your eyes peeled for suspicious activity and weapons; we've received a threat."

Just then, Gift caught a flicker of movement, a man shifting his weight, hands buried deep in his coat. The heat bore down on them, making his unseasonable attire stand out even more. A trickle of unease ran down her spine, but there was no time to question it.

The man lifted an M16 automatic rifle from his long coat, screaming, "Thou shalt not suffer a witch to live!" and started to shoot towards Kimi.

In a single, fluid motion, Gift stepped in front of Kimi, reached behind her back, and hurled a knife. The blade struck the man square in the throat, which caused his rifle to jerk upward, sending a spray of bullets wildly into the air. Unaware that she'd been hit, Gift instinctively reached for her sidearm, drew her Glock 19 and began firing repeatedly. Though the man wore a bulletproof vest, the sheer force of the shots sent him staggering backward. Blood poured from his neck. His grip slackened as he gurgled a final breath. The gunfire died with him.

Gift, with blood running down her leg, looked around, relieved to see Kimi and everyone crouched or on the ground looking at her in disbelief. Only when she tried to take a step and her leg buckled did she feel fire burning in her thigh. She had been hit. She staggered a bit and realized she needed to sit down. Gift s breath came in shallow gasps. Her hands trembled, whether from adrenaline or the pain in her leg, she wasn t sure. She had reacted, instinctively, but now, staring at the fallen man, she felt a hollow ache she couldn t name.

Later, at the hospital, Kimi hovered near Gift's bedside, her arms folded tightly across her chest. "If I had said something sooner..." Her voice trailed off.

Gift exhaled, a wry smile playing at her lips. "Then I wouldn't have gotten to practice my aim."

Kimi sat beside Gift's bed, silent for a long moment. "I should have seen more," she whispered. "I should have done more."

Gift squeezed her hand, wincing as she shifted on the bed. "You did enough. We survived. No one died. It was obvious he planned to kill more than you, otherwise why do it there?"

Weeks afterward, now able to walk with crutches, she felt grateful that Kimi s first aid had stopped the bleeding, and the two bullets to her thigh had done no permanent damage. She thought she would rather get shot again than hear from more people what a brave hero she was. It was embarrassing, and now they are talking about creating a civilian medal. However, she was pleased to get praise from her instructors. At Rose s suggestion, and using her funds, she d been taking classes or private lessons in every type of fighting art she could find. Because of the ammunition shortage, this was the first time she had fired the Glock, but the muscle memory of dry firing, plus the skills of archery and knife throwing, had honed her aim.

It turned out the man was one of Clyde Folsom s followers. They hoped Folsom s support would decrease after the incident. Implementing stricter security measures saddened everyone who believed they had escaped the mass shooting fears common in the old world. Many were angry about the loss of freedom that gun control implied.

While she was recovering at Rose's house, Rose came to her room and held her hand, giving it a gentle squeeze. Her eyes shimmered with emotion, and for a moment, she seemed to struggle for words before finally speaking.

"When you told me the Thunder Beings said you were here to protect Kimi, I didn't think they meant it literally. There's nothing I could give you to express my gratitude for the life of my child. But if there is anything in my power to give you, all you need to do is ask."

No one controlled more wealth, more technology, or more secrets than Rose Chasing Hawk. Gift already had everything she needed—comfort, possessions, a fine horse, and all the weapons she had ever imagined. There was nothing else she desired.

Gift shook her head, smiling. "I don't need anything." But deep down, she wondered if one day she might. And if she did, would she know what to ask for?

Chapter Sixteen
Jamal

JAMAL DREADED ANOTHER long sea voyage, although he was eager to finally return home. As he stepped onto the Anna Marie, he couldn't help but reflect on everything that had led to this moment—the months in Boston, the delays, and the unexpected connections they had forged. The weight of those experiences sat heavily on his mind, as the sea breeze promised a fresh start. The journey from New Orleans, originally expected to take three to four weeks, had stretched into seven due to storm damage and necessary repairs. They'd expected to return in May or June, and now it was August. Returning on the *Anna Marie* meant waiting for the completion of the twenty-first century upgrades. They expanded the passenger quarters, and they significantly improved the hull and sails. With the new charts and navigation tools, the ship's upgrades, and the more favorable conditions of the summer season, the voyage should take only two weeks, even with a few days of planned stops.

Benjy's bubbling excitement about the journey was contagious. Jamal and Nels exchanged a smile as they watched him dash up the gangplank, nearly tripping in his eagerness.

"Slow down," Jamal called. "You're not racing the tide."

Benjy skidded to a stop at the top, eyes gleaming. "I wanna get started! Jacob said he'd show me how to tie a bowline today."

Nels chuckled. "So now you listen to Jacob, but not when we tell you to wash up before dinner?"

Benjy scrunched his nose. "That's different. This's important."

Jamal ruffled his hair as he passed. "Sails first, soap later."

Benjy had been aboard the *Anna Marie* plenty of times while the retrofits were being done, tagging along with Jamal, peppering the crew with questions about every lever, rope, and pulley. His curiosity hadn't gone unnoticed. Captain Hartigan had even taken a moment to explain how the wind filled the sails and how they adjusted for speed and direction. Now, instead of riding as a passenger, Benjy was expected to pull his weight.

"You're sure this is a good idea?" Nels murmured as they watched him scamper toward the main deck.

Jamal shrugged. "He needs something to do. He doesn't like to sit still. I have some ideas about how to incorporate math into what he is learning."

A few feet away, Jacob, the ship's boy, a wiry twelve-year-old with sun-bleached hair, waved Benjy over.

"Come on, mate! If you're gonna work, you better learn fast. Cap'n won't abide layabouts."

Benjy straightened up. "I ain't no layabout."

Jacob grinned. "We'll see about that. You've got the look of a dawdler to me. Maybe even a laggard lubber."

Benjy scowled, and Jacob laughed, skipping backward just out of reach.

As Benjy followed him across the deck, already mimicking his movements, Nels let out a small sigh. "I sure hope he realizes what he's gotten himself into."

Jamal exhaled. "That makes two of us."

As Jamal stood on the deck, watching the coastline fade, he thought back to their time in Boston. He was sorry they wouldn t be traveling with Dan Clemons and Brad Walters, the two Guardians who had accompanied them from Changleska. The long and dangerous voyage had forged a bond between them. The *Anna Marie* had dropped Dan and Brad in Philadelphia for their mission to inform George Washington, Thomas Jefferson, and members of Congress about Changleska. They only stayed for a short time; they were couriers, not diplomats. Before they left Philadelphia, they sent a letter to Jamal and Nels, but it was vague. Jamal wondered whether they were worried about the mail being intercepted, perhaps by one fellow passenger who'd asked way too many questions. Jamal wondered what George Washington would think about the movies they sent. Along with *The Changleska Story*, the twenty-minute film made by the Omímeya marketing department, they'd sent *The Crossing* with Jeff Daniels and a few documentaries.

Everything took longer than expected. Jamal and Nels needed to stay in Boston for meetings with shipbuilders to commission their own seafaring vessel, a project that'd take almost two years to complete. Additionally, they sought to recruit shipwrights to relocate to New Orleans to build riverboats, along with other skilled craftsmen, such as watchmakers, fine instrument makers, printers, gunsmiths, and lens makers. Jamal was thrilled they'd successfully recruited Eli Whitney, a brilliant engineer of his time, ensuring he'd no longer invent the cotton gin, which in their history prolonged slavery. They hoped this intervention would make a difference.

"It's not enough," Jamal muttered.

Nels looked up from the ledger he was flipping through. "What isn't?"

"All of it." Jamal rubbed his temples. "Talking to abolitionists, setting up trade deals, recruiting Whitney—it's all good, but it won't break the system fast enough. Even the 'free sugar' plantations don't change the fact that people are still being bought and sold."

Nels sighed. "So, what do we do?"

Jamal met his gaze, resolve hardening in his chest. "We stop waiting for the world to catch up. We start making moves that force them to."

Nels said in alarm, "What? Now you want to join the Haiti revolution? The kind of direct action that takes place in this era is not marches and protests. In Haiti, they are killing people. Is that what you want?"

Jamal looked down. "No, but there must be something faster."

"You are doing a lot; it all takes time."

Beyond acquiring supplies for various artisans, they also needed to purchase key minerals and metal alloys difficult to obtain in Spanish-controlled New Orleans. The sheer volume of materials—iron, brass, copper, lead, tin, and zinc—necessitated chartering an additional cargo ship. They also needed large quantities of sulfur and saltpeter, essential for manufacturing gunpowder. Jamal was relieved he wouldn't be traveling on that ship. They also sought larger quantities of graphite and mica than were available in Boston, while discreetly reaching out to British sources for more. They purchased engineering and surveying books, not because Omímeya lacked the knowledge, but because they needed practical guides suited to the tools available in this era.

Because Jamal and Nels couldn't bring large amounts of gold with them, they secured a letter of credit backed by Omímeya's gold reserves before leaving New Orleans. This enabled them to draw Spanish silver reales and British pounds, the most widely accepted currencies in Boston's bustling trade networks, when the gold they brought ran low. Thanks to Captain Hartigan, they were able to negotiate a merchant credit with a Boston trading firm, leveraging future trade agreements in New Orleans as collateral. This gave them access to larger quantities of metals and minerals needed, as well as charter an additional cargo ship to transport everything. Captain Hartigan was turning into a valuable partner. Jamal and Nels knew they wouldn't have been able to negotiate the complex merchant system without him. None of the internet materials they brought covered any of this. The brief given by Omímeya had long lists of things needed to be done, but not how to do them.

It wasn't as though anything they'd read before arriving had truly prepared them to live in Boston in 1792. The grime, the strange smells, and the wariness in every conversation made it feel nothing like the world they had studied. And nothing prepared them for Benjy, who was becoming the light of both of their lives. Unfortunately, to protect him from being sold to a brothel, they had his mother sign him over as an indentured servant before she died. At first, it was hard to convince him he wasn't a servant. The situation was even more fraught, as they had to fit in with eighteenth-century mores. Under eighteenth century US law, adopting him was out of the question, although, on returning to Changleska, they planned to adopt him legally, thus removing the indenture. They might get away with passing him off as Jamal's brother if no one paid attention to the different accents. They solved most problems by moving. Also, having money helped. Being known as strange rich foreigners helped smooth over many faux pas.

Earlier in Boston, they ended up moving from the tavern to a boarding house, run by Mrs. Thompson, a widow friend of Eli Whitney's family. They paid a premium to move one resident out and have exclusive use of the house for the duration of their stay. Eli moved into one of the rooms so he could start work with Jamal right away. He was a great deal of help in meeting with the various merchants and navigating their new world. Treating Jamal as an equal didn't come easily to Eli, but with their shared love of engineering, his attitude was slowly changing. Even Benjy was growing on him.

Nels took over Benjy's education and promptly decided to find him a school. Fortunately, Boston had several schools for Black students, though none were near the high-end neighborhood where they lived.

"This isn't ideal," Nels muttered, unfolding a large, printed surveyor's map of Boston across the table. The fine lines detailed the city's winding streets, wharves, and neighborhoods, but it wasn't as precise as the maps he was used to. He frowned. "None of these schools are anywhere near us."

Jamal glanced over Nels's shoulder, frowning. "I agree. No way he's walking that far alone every day."

Eli, who had been listening, interjected. "The kid's been looking after himself for years. Didn't he guide you through the city? Seems like he can handle it."

Nels exhaled, tracing a route with his finger. "Just because he's used to fending for himself doesn't mean we let him keep doing it."

Eli shook his head. "The way you treat that boy will lead to trouble."

"Maybe around here, but not where we live," Nels said, adjusting the map. "I'll try to schedule my meetings to take him to and from school."

Just then, Benjy walked in, hesitating at the doorway. He glanced at their faces, his eyes flicking to the map, then back to Nels. They were talking about him. His shoulders tensed.

Nels smiled and reached for a wrapped bundle from a bookseller's shop, handing it over.

"Here, we got this for you. It's *Aesop's Fables*. When you learn to read, you'll like these stories. It's got animals tricking people and each other."

Benjy took it, eyes widening. "This book is for me? My own book?" He turned it over in his hands, carefully flipping through the thin pages with their woodcut drawings.

From the doorway, Mrs. Thompson let out her usual disapproving harrumph, arms crossed. "Another gift? New clothes, new shoes, toys, and now books? You're spoiling the boy. Nothing good will come of it. He needs to know his place."

Benjy shot her a wary look, half-expecting another lecture, but he caught something unexpected, a small, almost hidden smile as she watched him turn the pages.

At least at Mrs. Thompson s, Jamal could drop the valet act, and even later when Benjy had realized he wasn t a servant, he was still helpful around the house. He was sweet and affable; he even softened up the dour Mrs. Thompson. Jamal and Nels still couldn t come out as a couple but they could steal a bit of privacy more often. They tried to be discreet, but they weren t sure whether they were fooling anyone who knew them well. Benjy knew their relationship from the day they met, but he'd grown up in a brothel. Eli and Mrs. Thompson probably didn t want to know. It would have made them uncomfortable, so the couple slept apart.

Right before their departure, they received a letter from Changleska announcing the establishment of a new outpost near Georgetown, South Carolina. It included a radio station with a powerful transmitter. Since the US government had refused to allow an embassy, Changleska needed a location on the east coast to reach London by radio. They set up the outpost on Waccamaw tribal lands. Without official diplomatic recognition, they hoped the United States would respect the tribe's sovereignty. They also set up a small medical clinic. The setting was rural and impoverished, and both the outpost and clinic needed nearly everything. The letter included a long list of supplies and requested additional printed materials.

By the time the letter reached them, the radio station had already been transmitting each night at nine p.m., as shortwave radio waves carried better at night. The letter specified the frequency. They hoped the hand-crank emergency radio and flashlight they had brought would work. They had packed it for the flashlight, not expecting to receive a transmission from so far away.

That night, they were thrilled to hear, "This is 'Voice of Changleska,' broadcasting live from Indigenous sovereign lands."

The broadcast continued with much-needed news, detailing accomplishments such as the freeing of enslaved people and the growing list of Indigenous tribes that had joined Changleska. It was inspiring. Nels said it reminded him of a movie about the Voice of America during the Second World War. He wondered aloud if they would start sending coded messages.

=..=

Four days into the journey, most everyone on the ship got sick. Diarrhea spread through the ship like, well, diarrhea. It was sudden, severe, and contagious enough that Nels diagnosed it as dysentery. More than half the crew was down, and the ship slowed, proceeding languidly through the summer heat. Nels suspected the illness had come in with the fresh food they'd picked up on their stop in Philadelphia. He was sure the cook had been ignoring his instructions on boiling water, cooking food well, and handwashing. Unfortunately, there wasn't much to be done. The disease had to run its course, which often killed the young and the weak. Vegetarian Nels, who was very underweight, still refused to eat meat or drink meat broths, and got weaker and weaker. The most effective herbal remedy used at this time was from the Carapichea ipecacuanha plant. Oddly enough, it is the source of ipecac, which induces vomiting, and can even cause diarrhea in small doses. Nels had ordered some in Boston, although it was hard to obtain. It worked on Jamal and a few of the sailors, but not on Nels or Benjy. The Oral Rehydration Solution helped stave off deadly dehydration for most. Severe cases called for laudanum or opium tincture, a medication so common it was stocked on board. Activated charcoal proved to be the best remedy and helped with the gas and pain, but drinking the slurry was awful.

Jamal got better in a few days, along with most of the crew. Even Eli, who'd been hit hard, recovered. Benjy helped with the cleaning, emptying the chamber pots as most people couldn't even make it to the heads, and sometimes not even to the chamber pots. But then he came down with it as well. He couldn't keep the ipecacuanha tea down, or the black cohosh and slippery elm tea either. The charcoal helped some, but not enough. He was small enough that he grew sicker and sicker.

Nels was so weak he could barely speak. "I don't know the safe dose of laudanum for a child. It would only be a guess based on weight."

Jamal said, "We must do something. He's barely arousable."

"If it doesn't work, we should give him the amoxicillin. There's one dose we were saving as an emergency. This counts."

"But it means there will be nothing for you. You are getting worse, and now there is blood in your stool."

"Benjy gets the dose, promise me. Please, we're not sure it'll work."

The amoxicillin had come from the Pharmco veterinary facility. While the chemical constituents were the same for both human and veterinary drugs, the quality controls differed. They weren't sure it would work as expected. From Changleskan correspondence, they knew other antibiotics were being made, but Boston hadn't received any.

Jamal agreed, thinking the laudanum would work with Nels, along with the charcoal and other herbs, but nothing worked and Nels got progressively worse.

Benjy bounced back quickly enough to stay by Nels's side, offering him sips of the rehydration fluid, and trying to convince him to take sips of beef broth. The ship's crew was too small to have a medic or surgeon, only an older sailor, called a loblolly. He said he had dealt with dysentery many times, and beef tea made from salt beef was the best remedy, especially when there was bloody stool. The salt in the tea probably helped, and the beef could help for anemia if there was bleeding.

Jamal, his voice choked with tears, urged Nels, "Please drink the beef tea. We love you. We need you with us."

Nels murmured, "I've been a vegetarian or vegan since I was fourteen years old. Not killing is part of my spiritual beliefs. I'm sorry, but I can't do it."

Benjy had seen more than enough people die in his brief life, trembled as he reached for Nels's hand, as if holding on could keep him from slipping away.

His small frame tensed with fear. "Please, Mr. Nels," he whispered, his voice cracking. "You must stay. You can't leave me too."

Jamal put his hands on Benjy's shoulders, both feeling helpless with pain.

Benjy said to Nels, "You never eat meat because you don't believe in killing, right?"

Nels nodded weakly.

"If you don't drink this tea, you will kill yourself. Don't make a lick of sense. Please don't die, I needs you."

Finally, Nels agreed and started sipping the tea. He seemed to get better for a day, but that night he slipped into a coma, and did not awaken.

=..=

Grief smothered Jamal like a blanket. It was only because of Benjy that he didn't follow his partner overboard when the sailors gently tossed Nels, sewn into a weighted shroud, into the sea. He could not even summon the strength to object to the Christian prayers said by the captain, though it gnawed at him. Nels had been Buddhist, but Jamal didn't know any Buddhist prayers. Nels had believed in reincarnation. Jamal, raised a Baptist, didn't know whether he did. He had to believe there was something after this life, heaven or a different life. It had to be more than nothingness. He could not bear there to be nothing for Nels, his beautiful, sweet man, who cared deeply about everyone. Jamal's mind replayed Nels's laugh, the way his eyes crinkled when he smiled, the warmth of his touch. Nels was his first love, overpowering and all-encompassing. Jamal knew he would never love like that again. He could not imagine a life without Nels.

Eventually he cried himself out. The first night he'd been so hysterical, the captain ordered him to be dosed with laudanum. It had taken two sailors holding him down to force him to drink it. He still had the bottle next to his bed. It muffled the pain a bit. He hated drugs, had never even smoked weed. Even with his grief he knew he didn't want to become an addict, if for nothing else, for Benjy.

Benjy was handling the loss better than Jamal, even with the recent death of his mother. Perhaps it was easier to handle loss when death came every day in this era, even taking young, previously healthy people. Jamal had known no one that had died. He had a grandfather who died before he was born, but the rest of his family was alive when he came to this century.

Benjy's quiet resilience nudged at Jamal's grief, grounding him to the present. Benjy brought him meals and made him eat. Told him to wash and change his clothes. Part of him felt bad. He knew it was his job to take care of Benjy, not the other way around. But he could not muster the energy to function. Even breathing seemed like a lot of work.

Suddenly it occurred to him that Nels, not himself, was Benjy's legal guardian, the holder of his indentured papers. He wasn't sure whether that mattered under the Changleskan legal system. Also, Nels had been Jamal's protection against being captured and sold as a slave. They both were in danger without Nels. He knew it would be best to stay aboard the ship until they got to New Orleans.

Nels was supposed to go with the crew to deliver the supplies for the Georgetown outpost they named Circle Echo Station. Nels had been excited to see the clinic being built and the people behind the *Voice of the Changleska*. The captain said his crew would go and pass on any messages. Jamal knew he didn't need to go. It was risky to leave the ship, but he felt he owed it to Nels's memory.

Leaving Benjy in the captain's care, Jamal, Faraji, the large African bosun, and two other crew members drove the two wagons the harbormaster had helped them hire. Fully loaded, the wagons rattled across the muddy lane, with supplies lashed tightly under the canvas. The twenty-mile journey from the port consumed the entire day. As dusk approached, Jamal spotted the radio mast on the tallest tree in a thicket of loblolly pines. He wondered if locals knew what it was. Circle Echo Station stood like a quiet sentinel, its slender antenna reaching skyward, carrying the *Voice of Changleska* through the air.

"Looks quiet," Jack, the sailor, muttered beside him, his hand resting near his flintlock pistol.

Too quiet, Jamal thought. A village with a clinic and an outpost should bustle with children running about, people hauling water or weeding gardens, and elders sitting in the shade. Instead, just two Changleska Guards stood near a newly built gate, visibly tense. A half-built wall surrounded what looked like a small village facing the Waccamaw River.

One Guard stepped forward, his rifle slung but his stance rigid. "You're late. We expected these supplies weeks ago."

Jamal shrugged, and they all entered the gate.

"Sorry for the harsh welcome. Everyone's on edge. There's been trouble," the other Guard said. "A group of local assholes came yesterday looking for an escaped slave, and someone was killed. That's where everyone is now, at the burial grounds west of here."

"I understand," Jamal replied. "I'm Private Jamal Alston, and the rest of these guys are *Anna Marie's* crew. Let us know where to unload, and we'll be out of your hair first thing in the morning."

One of the Guards stepped forward, extending a hand. "I'm Sergeant Jeremy Turner, in command of Circle Echo Station. Thank you. We really need these supplies."

Sergeant Turner looked younger than Jamal, maybe nineteen or twenty. He was tall and thin, with long brown hair tied into a ponytail. He wore jeans and a Star Wars T-shirt. Jamal had to smile. Turner looked like any college freshman back in Boulder.

Inside the gates were low, rounded homes made from sapling frames plastered with clay and bark, blending naturally into the riverbank landscape. Scattered among these structures were small log cabins, a standard Medical Corps tent, additional tents, and a larger log building under construction.

As they started unloading, people returned from the funeral to assist. Surprisingly cheerful, they talked and laughed. Though many spoke a mixture of English and trade pidgin, Jamal caught the fluid cadence of the Waccamaw language among the elders. Jamal hoped that with Changleskan influence, the Waccamaw could preserve their language, a living thread connecting them to their ancestors.

The medical staff were thrilled to see the supplies, but yesterday's events had left everyone uneasy. Four members of the Medical Corps and four Guard members staffed Circle Echo Station, all either radio techs or trainees. Everyone, including the medics, took turns on watch and patrol, all armed and weapons qualified.

Jeremy explained their mission was to run the radio station and clinic while maintaining peaceful coexistence with the locals, obeying laws, and keeping a low profile. Despite the difficulty, they needed to recognize that they lived in a slave state and must avoid interference. The radio was critical to Changleska; the relay needed to reach London. They were part of the bigger picture.

"I know our mission is peaceful," Jeremy admitted, "but after yesterday, we need more weapons. What do they say? Peace through superior firepower."

No weapons had been included in their delivered supplies. Jamal realized that with Nels gone, he was now responsible for the ship's cargo. Making an executive decision, he offered to share some of the firearms stored aboard the *Anna Marie*. They had bought as many guns as possible in Boston, packing hundreds in grease. Sparing a box of twenty was feasible if someone would return to the ship and retrieve it.

Later, as they ate smoked catfish, hominy stew, wild greens, and drank sassafras tea, Jeremy recounted the previous day's events.

"Yesterday, late afternoon, six men rode up, weapons drawn, looking for an escaped slave. They'd read in the papers about a new country of mostly Indians and freed slaves. They assumed escapees would seek sanctuary here. We allowed a search, but one elder objected when they pointed guns at him. He raised his spear, and they shot him. The poor guy was probably eighty and could barely stand, let alone throw a spear. Afterward, they left, thankfully. There's a favor you could do for us, but it can wait until morning."

They left at first light, Jeremy and another man, Faraji, accompanied them to bring back the guns, asking Jack to ride his horse so he could sit with Jamal on the wagon.

Jeremy said, "It's cool to have another person from the old world to talk to besides our group. Plus, I hate riding. Even getting a sore butt on these boards is better." And they both laughed.

They rode along, chatting amiably about their lives before Big Thunder. Jamal found he was afraid to mention Nels, as he knew he might start crying. In the old world, if they chose, he and Nels could have legally married, and he would have been a widower, a recognized role for someone who lost a life partner. Here there was no term for him. He knew Jeremy wouldn't care if he was gay, and would sympathize with his loss, but he didn't bring it up. It was still too raw.

About ten miles into the journey, they saw a group of horsemen come out from a thicket.

"Fuck," said Jeremy, "they were waiting for us. They knew the wagons had to come back. Keep cool. They only want to harass us."

A cold dread washed over Jamal as he realized his freedom papers could be thrown out, leaving him vulnerable to being sold. And it was the same with Faraji. If anyone found the "favor", they would all be up shit creek without a paddle.

The favor, whose name was Virgil, crouched in the back of the wagon, under empty crates and tarps. He was the escaped slave the six armed men were seeking. Of course Jamal intended to smuggle him onto the *Anna Marie*. The poor man had endured the top part of his foot being cut off from a previous escape attempt and hobbled slowly with a bad limp. The Changleskans had cleverly broken off the sides of crates and his body was in one part, his head in another. A tarp had been pulled over his head and tucked under a crate. A casual glance at the returning load would reveal nothing unusual, since only the square outlines of crates were visible under tarps. But if anyone were to pull up the tarps, the ruse would be discovered. Jeremy told Jamal, "Whatever you do, don't look them in the eye, and don't show your weapon unless shooting starts."

Shooting starts? I never even fired this gun, thought Jamal.

The men rode right up, peering in the wagon, inspecting the wagon behind it, even examining the packhorse. One said to Jack, presumably because he was White and the oldest. "This all belongs to you?" waving at the wagons, Jamal and Faraji.

Jack, a canny old sailor, responded nonchalantly. "Nope, I'm just a sailor off the *Anna Marie*, but this property," he said waving, "including both wagon and men, all belongs to Mr. Henry Bostrom."

The man's attitude shifted. Henry Bostrom was the harbormaster, a man of considerable wealth and power in Georgetown. He was no one to cross.

"You can go now." And they turned around and rode back towards town.

When the riders were out of sight, Jamal said, "Have to get down, about pissed myself there."

"You're not the only one," laughed Jeremy.

Jamal was thrilled when they returned to the *Anna Marie* and snuck Virgil aboard. After he brought Virgil to Captain Harrigan's cabin, Virgil still looked nervous.

Jamal said, "I know there is no cabin space, but he can sleep in my cabin. I'll still pay his passage full fare, like any other passenger."

Captain Harrigan looked over at Virgil, a young man with an obvious limp. He'd have a hard time keeping his balance on a ship.

"What work did you do before?"

"A field hand, sir, but I'm a hard worker. I'll learn anything."

"We'll bed him down with the crew. He can work in the kitchen for his passage."

"I's grateful sir."

He said to Jamal, "It's only two weeks until New Orleans. It's best to keep him busy. Slavery is an abomination. I'm happy to do my part."

The rest of the voyage went smoothly. Seeing Benjy lifted his spirits. Before he left, Eli had tried seeking his input on engineering projects, but Jamal hadn't found the energy. Now he knew he needed to reengage with life, and started working again, and keeping busy helped. The waves of grief still came over him but were more manageable.

As New Orleans came into sight, the familiar port filled Jamal with sadness. Even Benjy's joy couldn't reach him. As Jamal remembered the times he and Nels had enjoyed here, a profound longing settled into his chest. He wished deeply that Nels was here beside him.

After the pilot led them into the harbor, they sailed up the Mississippi to the Oca Landing dock. The growth in the five months since his departure amazed Jamal as he surveyed the bustling activity surrounding him. Jamal forced himself to focus and take a deep breath. For Benjy's sake, he had to move forward, honoring the life he and Nels had hoped to build. One step at a time.

Chapter Seventeen
Brings Him Home

BRINGS HIM HOME missed his friend, Little Dog. The absence gnawed at him, creating a hollow space. More than friends, they were like brothers. Little Dog was a few years older, but they had grown up together. Little Dog had split off with the southwest expedition last moon. Throughout the first month of the journey, he and Little Dog had experienced everything together, from the quiet intensity of scouting to the hard work of the road crew, to the differences in the main expedition. They'd shared the outsiders' view of the thunder people, whom they often joked about. It was not the same without his friend. Brings Him Home was quiet, unlike Little Dog, who enjoyed talking to people and picked up English quickly. Little Dog engaged with others, while he would stand by listening silently. His father had told him he could learn more by listening than by talking. After his father had passed to the stars, Brings Him Home recalled every lesson his father had taught him, which became part of who he was.

After they'd been on the road for some time, all members of the expedition were officially informed of their primary mission: securing the gold fields and building a fort. Most people had guessed the expedition was about gold and understood why they needed to keep quiet, but it bothered Brings Him Home he hadn't been informed upfront. Securing gold fields was very different from making alliances and bringing more tribes into the Changleska Coalition. He wasn't sure whether he would have come had he known, but having the choice would have been nice. He was enjoying the adventure, although he'd yet to kill anyone.

Brings Him Home enjoyed meeting new tribes and noticing the small differences in how they lived. It was exciting to roll into a camp with the trucks, which sparked both amazement and fear. He enjoyed hearing others talk about the benefits of joining Changleska. Over time, he began to believe it himself. The medics sometimes brought powerful healing to the people they met along the way, and that made him feel proud to be part of it. Sometimes, when the drums began at night and the firelight danced across unfamiliar faces, he felt stirring within. Not every meeting went well. There were villages that kept their distance, or warriors who watched their movements too closely. He was learning to read the silences, too.

Brings Him Home was grateful he was building this first road; the trail others would follow. In front of him, the earth was untamed and free, but behind him, the road was a scar across the land that would forever change it. The road crew created a wide path, cutting trees, the Fresno scrapers leveling the ground, the small bridges taming rivers, and creating way stations in which people will congregate. The thunder people explained how easier travel increased trade, which increased prosperity for all. Brings Him Home understood the reasoning but couldn't help to question all the changes this road would bring. He had watched videos during the expedition depicting a future they hoped would never come to be. This future had the wasichu settlers taking over the land and subjugating the Indigenous people. Their destructiveness spread and threatened the Earth itself. He feared the Changleska could not prevent it, as he knew reality often differed from ideals. He worried he was building a road that would be a path of loss for his people. By helping negotiate with local tribes, and bringing more alliances into Changleska, he wondered whether he was part of the problem or part of the solution. The tribes they contacted would be forever changed by becoming part of Changleska. He feared the future being shaped might not belong to his people at all. Yet, without unity, how could they stand against the forces that would inevitably come? So, he worked hard and built. This first road had taken immense effort and resources, and by the time they arrived, it had cost eleven lives.

The expedition leaders didn't listen to Brings Him Home or Little Dog about bypassing Crow territory, as it would have added too much time to the journey. The leaders wanted the Crow to join Changleska and to make peace with the Lakota. Brings Him Home told them the Crow was an implacable enemy, ruthless and cunning. They may promise peace but wouldn't keep it. The leadership didn't listen and sent a negotiation team ahead with the Cheyenne and Lakota thunder people. They had invited him to stay away. He assumed Six Feathers had told them he'd kill any Crow with the slightest provocation, and truthfully, he was probably right.

The entire expedition camped outside of Crow territory while the negotiation team went ahead with pack horses full of gifts and trade goods. Back at the main camp, they set patrols, but horses and other items kept disappearing. They tightened the perimeter and posted guards around the horses night and day. One evening, screams pierced the night. Brings Him Home knew exactly what it was, a man being tortured and mutilated. After a head count, they realized one Guardian disappeared. He and several others searched, but whenever they thought they were close, the screaming started from another direction. The Crow moved their captive often. This went on for four days. Brings Him Home had seen many similar instances, but the thunder people never had. After throwing up, some vowed revenge on the Crow, but had explicit orders to stay put in a defensive position and let the negotiation team try to bring peace. Tension gripped everyone, as leaders ordered increased patrols and instructed everyone to remain in the camp and stay in groups. Brings Him Home was worried the beautiful stallion would be stolen. Little Dog and Brings Him Home approached the owner, Andy, and Little Dog expressed their concerns and offered to help watch.

Jerry, her brother, scoffed, "We don't need your protection. I'm here and the whole expedition is buttoned up."

Little Dog said, "You need to sleep sometimes, and we know the Crow. He," nodding at Brings Him Home, "admires the horse and doesn't want him taken. If we wanted to, even with your guards, we could steal that horse. If we could get him, so could the Crow."

Andy, the small, feisty owner, said, "Jerry, why not accept their help? Are you still mad? You didn't lose your horse, and it was only your working saddle and rifle. I can't imagine losing Jet. You know I was there from the day he was born." Looking up at him with big eyes, she said, "Pleease."

Jerry looked down at her fondly and agreed. To be closer to Jet s separate enclosure, Brings Him Home and Little Dog moved their camp and rotated shifts, including Jerry. This meant they saw Andy more. Little Dog chatted often with her, laughing over the language barriers. But Brings Him Home kept his distance, only watching the horse. He had Little Dog ask Andy what the name Jet meant. After the explanation, he thought it was a powerful name. This horse was as fast as flight. He had seen videos of airplanes, and once at home he'd seen one overhead although at the time no one knew what it was.

Andy brought a portable paddock for Jet and kept him distant from the other horses except Jerry s gelding, Cinnamon. Brings Him Home brought his and Little Dog s four horses and kept them close to their camp. One early morning, he woke to the sound of distressed whinnying. Jet had broken his paddock down to reach his mare, who'd gone into season earlier than expected. As they approached, they saw the stallion mounting his mare, who was tossing her head but not resisting. Little Dog, who was on watch, was running over and yelling. That woke the others who came and watched. It was too late—the act was complete. Andy fumed; horse breeding is serious business, and horses can be hurt. It was typically done with intention and a price agreed upon; then one party held the mare with ropes while the other, using ropes, guided the stallion.

Andy approached Brings Him Home, shouting angrily. "Why do you have a mare in heat so close? Jet could have been hurt."

He understood more English than he could speak. He carefully crafted his answer. "I would have moved her if I knew. She is a valuable mare, much smaller than your stallion. She and the foal may not survive the birth. I am not sure I would have risked it."

Andy responded defensively, "It wasn't my fault! He broke out!"

They were at an impasse. Andy didn't get a stud fee, but an unplanned breeding that might endanger a mare's life was serious. She owed him. Brings Him Home hadn't planned to breed this mare to Jet, not wanting to risk her, but he also wanted a foal from Jet. He had nothing to trade for a stud fee, but now the act was done, he was ahead. He liked the fact she was in his debt, and not the other way around.

"How do you want to make this right?" he asked slowly, putting her on the spot.

"I don't know. Let me think about it or tell me what you want."

They left it at that. In about a year when the mare gave birth, if she died or was damaged, Andy would owe Brings Him Home. He was happy to wait.

The whole expedition was relieved when the negotiation team returned from the Crow, reporting some success. The Crow would consider joining Changleska, but for now would harass no one going through their territory. Brings Him Home didn't trust the agreement but had no say in the matter. It cost quite a bit in trade goods, promises of muskets, stud services from Jet, and an older Cheyenne as a new husband for a Crow wife to help seal the bonds. The negotiators preferred having a Crow wife to one of the Lakota to seal the peace, as the Cheyenne and Crow already intermarried occasionally. Six Feathers said he was going to stay with the thunder people's custom of only one wife, and both he and Little Dog would rather have a venomous snake in their beds than a Crow wife.

The Guardian the Crow killed was the first death. He wasn't present, but heard about the next three accidental deaths. The first happened after the road crew cut down a big tree, because of wind or a crack they didn't notice, it fell in the opposite direction intended, crushing a man nearby. They radioed Courtney, Six Feathers' wife, the medic. She worked on him, but he died before they reached the main expedition in the truck. A fall from a horse broke another person's neck, killing them. Another man, unfamiliar with flintlocks, had his gun explode in his face. Brings Him Home witnessed the deaths of the seven more, where he could do nothing but helplessly watch. It affected him deeply. Not only were two of the seven women, and another a young boy he'd played lacrosse with, but worst of all, the accident had been caused by a failure of the road that Brings Him Home had helped build.

It occurred while Little Dog was still with them. They were in Crow territory, in what had been called Bighorn, Wyoming. They had finished the road through the mountain a few days before, in most difficult and rocky terrain they had found yet. They'd had to create switchbacks to navigate the mountain passes, with room for only one lane. They'd needed to figure out a warning system for future travelers. Everyone rode their horses up from the base camp to lighten the load for the steep climb. Little Dog and the rest of the road crew were at the top with the horses and could see down the road, getting a clear view of what happened.

Heavy rain had fallen the day before, but the group proceeded because they were behind schedule. At first, the caravan of trucks, all pulling trailers, seemed to navigate the narrow dirt road with its hairpin turns well enough. Everyone went slowly, with a safe distance between each other. He watched in horror as one of the truck's wheels slipped too far onto the shoulder. As the earth beneath the tire gave way, the truck lurched violently, the trailer dragging it further off balance. The driver fought the wheel, but there was no road left to steer onto. It plunged down the steep embankment, rolling once, twice—then more times than could be counted. Unable to see the wreck from where they stood, the crew knew the situation was dire. They heard the frantic long three horn blows signaling -all stop- accident.

Ed Tilson, with the road crew at the top, shouted, "This looks bad, Brings and Dog, you go first with a radio as you are better riders. The rest of you gather tools. We need ropes and pulleys and get medics heading down."

Ed's quick thinking impressed Brings Him Home as he'd felt shocked and unsure of what to do next. He and Little Dog weaved their way slowly and carefully between the parked trucks until they saw people from the other trucks standing and looking down at the fresh wound where the road had collapsed. Rocks and mud were still sloughing away, trickling down the steep embankment. Below, the wreckage lay still and crumpled, half-buried in debris. No movement. No sign of life. His stomach tightened. Little Dog radioed as medics and more people with rescue supplies showed up.

After Ed arrived, he looked down, muttering, "Son of a bitch... I thought the shoulder would hold. The rain softened it too much. We should have waited."

Brings Him Home, accompanied by two experienced climbers who improvised rappelling equipment, volunteered to descend the slope. He followed the others, who secured lines and set anchors. He moved fast, heedless of the mud slicking his hands as he grabbed at the exposed roots for support. By the time they reached the wreck, it was clear there were no survivors. The truck had taken the full brunt of the fall, with the cab crushed beyond recognition, its frame twisted where it had rolled. The trailer had broken loose and wedged against an outcrop of rock, its contents spilled but mostly intact. He didn't need to see the bodies to know they were gone. The silence told him everything.

One man called up to the crew above. "We can't get the truck out—it's done for. Focus on oil barrels first. If we lose those, we're fucked."

They pried open the battered doors, finding supplies scattered inside. The heavy barrels of vegetable oil, their most precious cargo, had miraculously held together. They rolled the barrels one by one to safer ground, where a team above rigged ropes to haul them up. Next, they pulled free crates of food and tools for anything worth salvaging.

As they examined the truck, it became obvious that they needed tools they didn t have to free the bodies from the twisted wreckage. While they salvaged supplies, others discussed what to do about the bodies. They decided to leave the bodies where they were. A future trip would retrieve the bodies with the Jaws of Life' tool from the fire station. After recovering the supplies, people gathered at the roadside and held a short prayer service for the lost. A future salvage team would recover the truck and trailer. The metal and engine were enormously valuable.

After the accident, the group was more subdued and cautious. No one seemed to blame the road crew, except themselves. From that point forward, they took their time, ignoring the pleading from leadership to rush.

=..=

They arrived at their destination much later than planned in *Čaŋwápe Ǧí Wí* (the moon the leaves turn brown), or September. They settled next to what the Miwok tribe called the Mokelumne or Condor River, the old world called the American River, next to what would have been Sacramento. While they had the general area picked out from their maps, they sent scouting teams with their building crew to find the best site for what would become Fort Condor. The site offered access to the river, protection from floods, good high ground, natural sightlines, level ground for buildings, and nearby lands for farming.

After they identified the fort site, a small group was sent to view the surrounding area for defense purposed. Brings Him Home was surprised to see Andy. He was told she was a winning competition shooter who brought her rifles, and they needed her perspective. Ed, Jerry, and some others stood on the small rise, surveying the area for a potential attack. Brings Him Home watched with his usual quiet intensity. The land sloped gently before them.

Andy pointed across the way. "We could put marksman positions along that ridge. Maybe two-man teams staggered out."

Ed, arms crossed, squinted at the ridge. "You're assuming we'll have enough trained shooters to hold a line?"

Jerry, the practical one, chuckled. "Hell, we don't have enough ammo to sustain a real fight. We're sitting on a limited supply."

Andy scoffed, slapping her rifle. "This rifle can hit a man-sized target at 800 yards. If we can train a few solid shooters, we won't need a constant barrage. A few well-placed shots will change a fight before it starts."

Brings Him Home spoke for the first time in his slow, careful English. "Lakota warriors do not fight like you. We do not stand behind a barrier or stand in lines. We move. Strike fast, fade away. You should learn to fight that way."

Andy turned, nodding thoughtfully. "I understand. But we've also got trucks, big guns, and a fixed position to defend. That changes the game."

Brings Him Home tilted his head slightly. "Assume the enemy is aware. They will not attack where you expect. You should train like them, not like the old world's soldiers."

Ed clapped Brings Him Home on the shoulder. "That's why you're here. Help us blend old ways with new ones."

Andy exhaled, shifting gears. "Fine. We'll work on mobile defense. We still need to train people to shoot straight."

Jerry rubbed his jaw, thinking. "How many rounds are you thinking, Andy?"

"A couple hundred for zeroing rifles, another few hundred for training. Maybe a thousand total to get a solid team ready."

Jerry let out a low whistle. "That's a hell of a bite out of what we've got. We don't know when or if we'll get more ammo. You might have the best rifle here, Andy, but once those rounds are gone, it's only a fancy club."

Andy frowned, gripping her *Remington 700* custom-built rifle a little tighter. "So, what, we just let these guys go into a fight without proper training?"

Brings Him Home folded his arms, considering. "Train them differently. Give them bows and knives to learn to perfect their aim first. Use your bullets only when needed."

A silence settled between them. Finally, Andy sighed. "Fine. We'll be selective. I'll pick only six shooters to train. But they train properly."

Brings Him Home asked, "Can I train with this?" pointing to the rifle he got from Jerry. He had so little ammunition he had only shot it once but knew there was compatible ammunition in the armory if it came to a fight. It came with a *Vortex* scope, which he had been trying to get used to.

Ed came to his defense. "Brings is the best shot with a musket I've ever seen. With a modern rifle, he will be unstoppable. He has flawless aim with the bow and knives. He'll be great on your team."

Andy looked up at Brings Him Home with careful consideration. It looked like she wanted to say no, but knew Ed was right. He was a great choice. "Okay, but during training, I'm the boss."

Jerry laughed, "You act like the boss even when you're not training."

Brings Him Home was thrilled that he'd be on the shooting team and have access to ammo to train with. It was even worth putting up with Andy, whom he admired but didn't understand. He couldn't help the small grin tugging at his lips as they walked away.

=..=

Brings Him Home learned a great deal about military fortifications while building Fort Condor. While he knew about situating camps with defense in mind, this was different. Fort Condor was not only a military outpost to protect the goldfields, a winter camp for miners, a trade and diplomatic hub for local Indigenous tribes and Spanish visitors, it would be a permanent home to those who would provide services to the miners. Later, there would be farms surrounding the fort in some of the best agriculture areas in the world.

When complete, the fort had strong outer defenses with a palisade wall, fifteen feet high, made from thick logs, cut from the cottonwood trees along the river. The four corner watchtowers were stocked with rifles, bows, and a large drum as a warning system. There was a deep ditch dug around the perimeter for extra defense against attacks and flooding, and a main double gate with a kill zone between the sections for firing positions.

Brings Him Home was told as one of the original expedition members he was entitled to a mining claim and after paying taxes to the local tribe and Changleska, the gold was his to keep. The crew's eagerness to strike it rich was palpable. He understood why they called it gold fever. He couldn't care less. Wealth had a different meaning for him, but he decided he'd accept the claim and perhaps work it someday.

Everyone had to wait until spring to start mining or even start building their camps. They first had to negotiate with the local tribes, the Miwok, Nisenan, and Maidu, then formalize their entry into Changleska, decide on taxes, and specify which sacred sites were not to be mined. The local tribes welcomed them, having been hunted by the Spanish and forced into slavery to work in their missions. The impact of the diseases brought by the Spanish was devastating, scattering the population into small, isolated tribes, but their culture remained remarkably rich and complex.

Everyone anxiously awaited short-wave radio reports to see if the treaty with Spain had been signed, allowing them to proceed unhindered. If the Spanish knew about the goldfields, the deal may fall through. If they decided to attack, they needed to prepare accordingly. The Spanish at this time had limited forces in the area, none inland, and the hope was the fort would go unnoticed. They were told to keep to a defensive posture, to hide their presence as much as they could. They asked the local tribes to say they got their trade goods from the northern coast, where ships from the Far East brought trade goods. In case those measures failed, Guardians and Brings Him Home scouted with members of the local tribes all the Spanish missions, and camps of rogue Spanish forces, and sat in planning meetings to take control of the missions, likely killing many Spanish. For him, this was the real wealth, not gold, knowledge of how to protect his community and how best to attack the enemy.

There were few unattached women in this first group, and Andy received a lot of male attention. However, her brother Jerry, as her legal guardian, was very protective and found himself in an enviable position. No one interested in Andy wanted to get into an argument with him or get on his bad side. He clarified he was following his father's rules by not allowing Andy to date until she was sixteen. Since their father was also a major in charge of the Expedition Base, everyone behaved.

Brings Him Home didn't understand the thunder people's dating customs, other than it would be another six months before Andy would be available. Andy would have her choice, and many young men hung around her politely and tried to be helpful. Brings Him Home stayed out of it.

Andy was the physical type that attracted men from her century, as she was curvy and busty. Lakota men expected only pregnant or breastfeeding women to have large breasts, and there was a strong taboo against sexual relationships with them. He didn't have the same visceral physical attraction to Andy as he did to slimmer young women. Andy could sense it, and he got the impression it annoyed her. She was used to being the center of male attention.

One afternoon, Andy stopped by him and sighed dramatically, tossing her hair over her shoulder. "You know, Brings, you're the only guy around here who isn't tripping over himself to carry my stuff or bring me water."

Brings Him Home glanced up from sharpening his knife, his expression unreadable. "You do not need me to carry things. You are strong."

Andy narrowed her eyes. "That's not the point."

He shrugged. "What is the point?"

She huffed, crossing her arms. "Never mind."

Brings Him Home considered her for a moment, then returned to his task. "You will have your choice in six moons. I am not one of your choices."

Andy scoffed. "I didn't say you were."

Brings Him Home only nodded. "Good."

Andy muttered under her breath and stalked off.

=..=

The team formed to learn marksmanship evolved and grew to twelve members; it was now called the Guard Special Forces. Sergeant Jack Hall, a Guardian in his late twenties, became the leader. At eighteen, he had joined the Navy, hoping to become a SEAL, but he washed out in his first week. He ended up being trained on radar that had no civilian job equivalent and left after his two-year hitch was up. He had been driving on the freeway when Big Thunder occurred, leaving his new wife and whole family in San Diego. Brings Him Home was thrilled to be part of the Special Forces — not just because it got him out of tree-cutting duty. He was the only Lakota, and he and Andy were the only ones who weren't full Guardians. She and Brings Him Home also taught horsemanship. They learned about all kinds of weapons, flintlocks, and explosives. Brings Him Home taught scouting, archery, Lakota fighting and what they called outdoor survival skills. Other expedition members taught various skills, such as demolition, martial arts, and first aid.

The Indigenous members of the expedition tended to congregate together. They often shared their amusement or confusion about the thunder people's ways. Ed, a Lakota thunder person, sometimes laughed with them. He provided explanations and translation help. As they traveled, he and his father Jack interacted and traded with many other tribes who often joined Changleska. They asked for guides and interpreters to the tribes ahead. Some went partway, and others stayed with the group. By the time they arrived at Fort Condor, they added thirty-four people, including children. Besides Lakota, there were Cheyenne, Arapaho, Pawnee, Shoshone, Goshute, Paiute, and Washoe. The fort invited California tribes to relocate nearby for protection, medical care, and trade. The fort encouraged them to create farming villages, offering agricultural guidance. Although the local tribes learned to farm from the Spanish, they were open to learning more.

Brings Him Home admired the local tribes with their beautiful baskets and shells on their clothing. He understood the new settlement needed farmers, as more people would be arriving. There was even talk of bringing foodstuffs back along the trade route to the Dakotas. Some people talked with longing about all the different food crops that could be grown and brought many seeds. For many of these tribes, previously exploited by the Spanish, prosperity was a new concept. He knew he was witnessing the death of the old ways and the birth of something new. He wondered what the next generation of California tribal people would be like. Could they preserve their culture, or would the thunder people's values and beliefs take over? Would this mixing of all the different tribes that made up the Changleska be a true coalition? In his old life, he had never pondered these matters. His life was simple as a warrior. He'd always expected to live a life just like his parents and grandparents. The future of this new, bigger and more complicated world was uncertain, but he had to admit it was more exciting than he had ever imagined.

PART III
Fall
(ptanyétu)

There can never be peace between nations until there is first
known that true peace which is within the souls of men.
– Black Elk, (1863-1950), Oglala Lakota Holy Man

Chapter Eighteen
Rose

ROSE WAS VEXED. Her nerves were frayed by her entire situation, not only by her most recent meeting, and she could feel her frustration simmering dangerously close to the surface. More than her most recent meeting, it was all of it. People expected too much from Omímeya. Her life had changed in ways she could never have anticipated before Big Thunder's seismic shift through time. How her expertise in hospitality management had morphed overnight into the stewardship of an entire nation was beyond her. She was the behind-the-scenes organizer and financier, a role she was beginning to despise. The constant juggling of budgets, endless meetings over resource allocations, and the pressure to balance diplomacy with hard-nosed leadership left her drained. She was tired of being a number-cruncher, far removed from the dynamic, guest-centered work she once loved. Instead of curating memorable experiences for visitors, she now brokered deals, navigated political landmines, and wrestled with the moral weight of decisions that affected entire communities. It was isolating, relentless, and far removed from anything she had ever envisioned for herself. Rose thought, *how did I get from managing guests' experiences to guiding the fate of Changleska?* The irony wasn't lost on her; what once required ensuring four-star ratings now demanded diplomatic savvy capable of warding off colonization and preserving a culture's very essence.

Changleska needed so much, and all the priorities were competing. As CEO, her job was to look at the big picture. Rose tried handling the overload through delegation, which was more or less effective. Good leadership was supposed to be finding good managers, then letting them do their jobs with minimal oversight. Sometimes that maxim worked better in theory than practice.

Today, her frustration had erupted into what she called "fuel fights" or oil wars—a battle over resources needed to boost veggie oil production, which now powered every diesel vehicle they owned. At the same time, there were increasing demands from the new oil refinery processing petroleum seeps, coupled with efforts to revive natural gas supplies. Petroleum was needed not only for cars but also for many industrial uses, including the production of kerosene.

"Look, we need to decide. Do we channel our resources into veggie oil or into the refinery? Are natural gas pipelines going to take all the steel?" one manager snapped, his voice rising in frustration.

Rose, who had founded Unity Petroleum, a corporation co-owned by the Caddo, the Indigenous residents of the oil-rich land, could scarcely believe the enormity of the task. She marveled at how many skilled workers, tools, spare parts, precious 3-D printer hours, and additional resources were required to yield even a drop of usable petroleum product. Veggie oil was simpler to produce, but scaling up for it posed a formidable challenge because it demanded some of the same resources as the oil refinery.

Another manager interjected, "It's like trying to run three factories on one set of resources!"

Restoring natural gas was a time-sensitive priority, given that so much of the area's heating depended on natural gas and propane. Although they knew the location of the nearest gas wells, drilling safely, storing, and transporting natural gas and its byproducts, such as propane, butane, and ethane, proved to be an immense challenge.

Fortunately, there was a ray of hope. Hutmacher Drilling, a water drilling company, was inside the Circle during Big Thunder, and it had the skills and equipment needed. After some modifications, its systems were up and running.

"At least we can drill now without fearing a catastrophe," Rose remarked, trying to inject a note of relief into the tense meeting.

Meanwhile, the chemists had developed the sulfur-smelling additive, critical for natural gas, which is naturally odorless. Creating safe, pressurized tanks was the latest hurdle, but progress was promising. The steel mills were running, and most of the piping was nearly finished. For the time being, they were recycling cars for steel, though they knew it wouldn't be long before they needed to import ore and set up a Bessemer-type steel mill.

At the meeting, managers finally stopped yelling at each other before turning to Rose for intervention. Everyone had a point. Each department needed similar resources. In the end, they reached a compromise that left no one truly happy, including Rose. She often found herself forced to choose the option that stung the least, a bitter pill to swallow among many bad choices.

She returned to her small office, with its corporate vibe despite the Indigenous art on the walls. She had given up the larger general manager's office to Mary. Rose thought the nicer office, with river views and beautiful furnishings, would better suit the chair of the Executive Committee. But on days like today, she regretted her choice, wishing she could look out her office windows and see the river instead of the triangle. Rose thought seeing the triangle-shaped industrial park with the geothermal plant, warehouses full of supplies, trucks, and shipping containers would give her hope for the future. It didn't. She would prefer a calming river view. She settled for straightening her desk, creating order, which was her way of centering. Her meticulous nature served as both armor and a weapon, her method of control in a role that threatened to spiral into the chaotic unknown.

Jenny, the assistant manager, came in. Her job was to deal with all the hotel and resort issues, to free Rose up for all the other projects.

"We have a problem in the tipi village."

The tipi village was a former tourist attraction offering the experience of sleeping in a real tipi. Now, it housed the visiting Indigenous tribes.

"Now what?"

There had been issues, usually involving alcohol. Alcohol sales were supposed to be limited to the hotel bar, where the staff were well trained not to overserve. But alcohol was easy to buy at the trading posts and bring in. Beer was not a problem, but the rum and homebrew whisky were strong.

"The Cree aren't leaving," Jenny said, her frustration showing.

The tipi village was designed to be temporary. Instead of tourists, it now housed tribal delegations who came to sign the compact and to trade. Because of the cost of rooms, most preferred the tipi village. Omímeya still charged the same for a high-end hotel from this time for rooms but gave delegations a discount. In a few days, the leaders of the tribes who had successfully won the battles of the Northwest Indian wars were arriving.

One was Tecumseh, a leader famous in her century for organizing resistance to American expansionism.

"We can house the Shawnee and other tribal leaders in the hotel. We can comp them rooms, not suites, for the week," said Rose, wondering what the problem was. Jenny was usually pretty good at solving these types of problems herself.

"That's not the real issue. The Cree are building more permanent structures, like wigwams, kind of like tipis but made with wood. They are also expanding outside the village area. There aren't enough bathrooms in that area for so many people."

"Wigwams are temporary, correct?"

"Yes, but they're building them to house more people. They said their families are on the way."

"Now I see the problem. Did you tell them the tipi village space is temporary?"

"Yes, but they want to live close to the center where the Thunder Beings spoke. They visit the 11:11 memorial daily."

"Oh, I get it. They are pilgrims. We'll probably get more. Tell them the land inside the river loop circle is sacred, and very few people can live here."

"They like it here; not sure they want to leave."

"Tell them they can set up at either of the new farm villages, or next to a base, or a land grant if they want to set up a permanent village. The daily shuttle stops at the Chamberlain base. If there are enough of them, we can send a bus instead, once we solve the veggie oil production issues."

"That might work."

"Let them know they don't have to leave the Circle, just Omímeya. Give them another month. Tell them we need space for more pilgrims who may only stay for a few weeks. This will make them feel like they received a special privilege instead of giving them the boot."

Afterward, she and Jenny went over other hotel issues. They finally found places for everyone they had housed over the winter and early spring. Omímeya went back to being a hotel, albeit a short-staffed one. Getting the rooms back to their previous standards wasn't an easy job. Tourists started arriving with the *Endeavor* passenger service and, due to the schedule, stayed for a month. Omímeya hosted the wealthiest guests, largely plantation owners. The casino proved very popular. A few area hotels reopened as lower-cost inns, though most had been converted into apartments.

At first, there had been incidents of ugly racism. The comments made to people of color were worse than casual racial slurs; the old world would never have tolerated them. A law was soon passed fining anyone involved in such incidents. The aggrieved party could report without fear of reprisal. With repeat offenses, fines would increase, or a visitor s pass could be revoked. The mandatory visitor orientation's explanation of the new law significantly reduced incidents. Jackson told Rose about one incident, which she shared with Jenny.

Jackson had been walking through the lobby when a man called out, Hey, boy, bring me another drink and one of those pastries."

He walked closer, looming over the man. "Sir, I believe you are mistaken in several areas. First, this is the lobby. The bar is there," pointing to the bar. "Go there for a drink. The pastries are at the restaurant there," pointing the other direction. "In addition, I'm not a boy but a man. Calling me 'boy' is derogatory and racist."

The man spluttered, momentarily speechless. "Racist" wasn't a term used in the eighteenth century but was defined in the visitor orientation. Signs everywhere listed fines for racist or hate speech. He knew at this moment Jackson had power over him, not only the small fine, but Jackson could ask for his removal from the hotel, and the man knew it.

Jackson looked at him for a moment, letting him squirm, finally letting him off the hook. "Since this is your first visit, I won't report you; however, I would like an apology."

"Mmm, sorry," the man muttered, almost incoherently.

"Apology accepted," Jackson replied, and held out his hand to shake. Jackson was sure the man had never shaken a Black man's hand before. By this time, a small group of people were watching. The man shook, probably in more ways than one.

When Jackson told Rose this story, she asked him if he had told the man who he was. He said no; it was better that the man thought of him as any Black man, not someone important. Rose's heart swelled with admiration for him, but she was also sad that he'd had to experience that.

After Jenny left, Rose returned to work on budgets and to prepare for the next meeting. She wasn t looking forward to it.

=..=

Rose's meeting with the economic committee was looming. She hoped to catch a few minutes with Jackson beforehand. Sometimes they caught each other between meetings, although both rarely had time to lunch together.

Seeing him, catching his eye, smiling at each other, or a touch of hands had been sufficient to lift her up. She entered the meeting room with resignation. Rose had chosen not to be an officer or one of the official fifteen members on the Economic Committee, or any other committee. She was too busy with her CEO duties and worried about potential conflicts of interest. Omímeya was the wealthiest corporation and the biggest employer in the Changleska Coalition. Rose tried to be amused that she now represented the one percent," but it wasn t funny. She felt an uncomfortable mix of irony and guilt, knowing she now stood among the very elite she once criticized. Her contribution to the committee, while unofficial, was crucial.

Most committees were open to anyone who wanted to attend, but only official members and officers voted. Each committee made its own rules on whether they limited speaking time or allowed only observers. Rose was grateful that after the first few meetings, everyone realized how boring and complicated economics was. They had a hard time even getting all the members to attend, much less outsiders. Consequently, they could get a lot done in the rare in-person meetings, usually held only if there was a proposal to bring to the Council for a vote. As with most committee work, the committee conducted its business via the online forum. There was something to be said for in-person meetings, especially for those used to working in corporate settings.

No professional economists were among the roughly 8,000 people transported back in time with them. The absence of economists also made it challenging to forecast the broader impacts of their financial decisions, increasing the risk of economic volatility in the fragile Changleska Coalition.

Most on the committee were bankers or businesspeople like Rose, who had taken economics in college. Rose understood the critical role of a healthy economy in their new country's success and was deeply involved in the committee's work. Rose tried to find the time to study more economics from the resources they had. The few classes she'd taken over a decade ago were not enough.

Because there wasn't a minister for economics, and since the role influenced everything, Adam Diedrich, chair of the Economic Committee, held a great deal of power, much like an Executive Counselor. Rose noticed everyone rose from their seats as he entered the room, unusual for most committee chairs, and addressed him as Mr. Diedrich.

221

Rose was grateful to see the meeting open with a brief prayer. The secularism of the twenty-first century was quickly dissolving in Changleska due to both Native spirituality and the eighteenth-century Christianity that prevailed in this era. It helped Rose, as an affirmation at the beginning of each meeting, to ask the Creator for guidance in the mundane area of money.

Afterward, Adam Diedrich, his voice low and serious, began, "Along with the items posted on the forum agenda, we have three items of a confidential nature. Two of these requests came as loans to my bank, and another to Jerry at Wells Fargo. The reason I wanted the committee's input is that there are broader issues at stake than purely economic ones."

Jerry Caswell, CEO of Wells Fargo, said, grinning, "This is all very exciting. Most of our loans are for making things like safety matches, egg incubators, or washing machines. The banks accept most projects with good business plans. This is different. These are loans for treasure hunting. You go ahead, Mr. Diedrich."

"Many have suggested using twenty-first-century technology to explore famous sites like King Tut s tomb and to locate shipwrecks. We rejected most proposals because they lacked adequate planning; however, two met our criteria. We considered preservation of historical and cultural value in addition to monetary value."

Rose said, I m very aware of the shortage of gold and hard cash. Who knows how long the fiat funds bubble will last? But how much actual gold is in any of these sites? Most of the value is in their history."

Jerry answered, That s true with the proposed loans at Mr. Diedrich s bank, Tut s tomb as well. The Hoxne Hoard had over 14,000 gold, silver, and bronze coins, worth about ten million in 1992 when found. But my loan request is to recover treasure from the lost Spanish galleon *Nuestra Señora de Atocha* off the Florida Keys. It carried 400 tons of gold, silver, and emeralds—one of the most valuable treasure ships ever found."

Another committee member asked, "Won't the Spanish claim it? It was their ship. What are the current salvage laws?"

Jerry answered, "Yes, Spain would claim it, and probably offer a reward. It's their territorial waters. There are private individuals who want to create a salvage company. They would presumably deal with the Spanish."

"Even with the California gold fields, which we have yet to see anything from, we are probably five years away from having any substantial gold in hand," said Adam.

All the bankers slumped. They all feared runs on their banks. Most money was now digital. They kept old US money in circulation at 1792 values. US paper bills were being phased out, with larger denomination bills planned once they had a way to counterfeit-proof them. There had been enough silver and gold to mint a limited supply of one-dollar and fifty-cent denomination coins. Smaller coins presented a problem because nickel and copper were valuable for industrial uses, so they used existing coins for now. If enough people wanted to withdraw their money in gold, the banks would fail. The whole economic fiat system was based on trust, the ephemeral value of the Changleska Coalition. Occasionally, when people moved out of the area, they wanted to cash out in gold; it was a stretch for the bank. All the area banks and Omímeya would cover each other, but if it kept happening, everyone would be in trouble. Gold was coming in from the outside, but not enough. It was a threat hanging over everyone's head.

The hidden vaults of Omímeya contained tens of millions in gold and silver saved by the casino consortium both as an investment and in case of a potential economic collapse. The day they arrived, gold was about two thousand dollars per ounce; however, in 1792, the value of gold was roughly twenty dollars per ounce. While prices were lower in 1792, they weren't seventy percent lower in most cases. Because local banks didn't have gold in their vaults, they hoped to find some in individuals' safe-deposit boxes. There were many unclaimed boxes. The banks gave six months for everyone or their heirs to claim their safe-deposit boxes. But the boxes ended up yielding very little gold or precious gems for circulation.

Jerry said, "Even if we only get a portion of the forty tons of gold from that sunken treasure ship, we need it. Changleska will get its ten percent tax, and the bank and the other investors will profit."

"I'm not clear what you want the economic committee to do. Is there a proposal?" asked Rose.

Adam said, "Not specifically. We are hoping for input from our economic brain trust. Rose, you're more aware of the political situation with the Spanish and the British. Is there any reason anyone can think of why the banks should turn down the loans? The people involved are trying to keep this quiet for obvious reasons. That's why they're attempting to obtain private loans instead of forming public corporations."

Rose snapped, "First off, we don't have any Egyptologists who came with us. Fanboys with books don't count. Any gold or treasure from King

Tut's tomb belongs to Egypt. We wouldn't want anyone coming over here and robbing our ancestors' graves. Omímeya won't contribute and would oppose it for ethical reasons. If the point is to save it from future desecration, someone can reach out to scholars in Egypt."

She looked around the room with a flicker of anger, realizing that everyone present—ten men and two women—was White. No one had considered the implications of grave robbing, and that omission offended even her one-quarter Lakota heritage. A pang of frustration twisted in her chest, not only because of the oversight, but because it pointed to a deeper issue: whose voices were being left out of these conversations?

More thoughtful looks circulated, calming down the ebullient mood of the room.

"As for the Hoxne Hoard and Spanish ship, those projects are more feasible in cooperation with the authorities. We're very close to an agreement with the Spanish, but it might help. The Florida Keys will remain Spanish waters for some time. It's not part of Changleska. I suggest we run this by Mary. I'm not up on all the politics."

Adam asked, "If it's only the Hoxne Hoard, we wouldn't need outside resources. The bank could fund the expedition, provided they receive a letter of approval from the British and an agreement on fund allocation. I would think the coins could remain in the British Museum, as all we want is the actual gold value. Do people think that is a good approach?"

There was more discussion. Some committee members voiced concerns about the political ramifications of treasure hunting in foreign waters, fearing it might strain diplomatic relations with Spain and Egypt. Others argued the potential influx of gold was too valuable to ignore, emphasizing the dire need to stabilize the Changleska economy. No one mentioned the Tut tomb again, and Rose hoped it would be dropped, but it wasn't up to her. The Hoxne Hoard and Spanish ship received everyone's support. This process was going to take some time, not solve the immediate gold problem, but this had been the Economic Committee's most exciting discussion ever. The rest of the meeting was dull and uneventful in comparison.

=..=

Rose texted Jackson to see if he was coming home for dinner. Jackson texted back that he was busy with work and would sleep in his office. Rose tried not to be annoyed. She understood working late, but he insisted on keeping his bedroom in his office suite. Rose knew Jackson loved her; she felt it deep down, but she worried Jackson was emotionally distancing himself. Rose couldn't shake the fear that his choice to keep separate spaces wasn't only about independence, but about protecting himself from getting too close. While she understood the scars left by losing his fiancée beyond the Circle, moments like these made her wonder whether he'd ever fully let her in. But that was the bigger issue. Today, Rose worried because it was Wednesday, one of her son Luke's required days to be home for dinner. Not that Luke and Jackson didn't get along. Their relationship had improved compared to the cop/juvenile delinquent vibe it had at first. They'd bonded over basketball, especially when Jackson started helping coach at the high school over the winter.

This spring, the two had often played basketball at the medical school's recently finished full-size court. While Changleskans were converting a nearly completed 6,000-square-foot golf clubhouse into a medical school building, they'd realized that turning its large asphalt parking lot into a basketball court would be a no-brainer. They'd even made a lacrosse field next door, on the carefully nurtured Kentucky bluegrass golf greenway. They kept the underground sprinkler system in; it was turning into a nice park, along with an extensive medicinal herb garden.

Rose picked up some of Luke's favorite takeout foods from Red Oak. She thought Jackson just wanted to give Luke and herself space. When the three of them were together, she couldn't deny the gravitational pull she felt toward Jackson, and their conversations often unintentionally excluded her son. Luke had just turned sixteen and surprised her with his maturity level. It probably helped that most of his friends were in their twenties. Jackson was better than Rose at getting him involved in conversations.

"How was work?" Rose wished she could have come up with a better question.

"Good."

She tried again. "Are the classrooms done?"

"We finished months ago," he said with exasperation. "We're finishing the dorms now."

"What's next?"

"Most of the guys are finishing up with the other Riverview cabins, but we're held up waiting on materials. Some will move on to other jobs outside Omímeya soon. Mom, are there any projects that'd keep the crews busy here?" Luke asked hopefully.

"It'd be good to keep the crews together. They work well as a team. I'll review what we have going on, but we don't have long left in the outdoor construction season."

"If they don't work inside Omímeya, I can't work after school. I hope you can find something."

Rose hoped so, too. Working with the construction crew was the best thing that had happened to her formerly very troubled teen.

"We'll figure something out. Oh, I got good news. Elliot got the judge to amend your probation to include hunting trips, as long as an adult family member is present."

"Yes!" Luke exclaimed, pumping his fist into the air.

Rose was surprised because Luke had previously hated hunting and camping. Now that he was court-ordered away from video games, he had changed.

"Does this mean I can go with Luis and the guys on the whole two-week trip?"

"Yes, but you'll have to invite Hotah or one of your uncles. It shouldn't be too hard. They are taking a truck, right?"

"Yes, Mateo just bought a diesel truck. He's going to borrow a horse trailer so we can bring horses."

Rose knew that truck would've been expensive. With no need to send money south to their families, the largely Hispanic construction crews were now flush. They lived frugally, with free housing in crowded crew quarters included in their contracts.

"Are there any girls coming?"

"Of course not."

"Why, of course not? I thought you had Penny on construction, and Vicky—they're women on your crews."

"Penny quit. She got married and moved to Chamberlain. And Vicky is an electrician. Sparkies don't hang with us."

"By the way, the girls are having a sleepover with their friends. Do you mind if they use your room when you are gone?"

Luke looked mulish. He didn't want girls in his room, although he was rarely there. It looked like he was trying to say no.

Rose said, "How about this? Before you leave, since you'll pack anyway, you put anything personal in the closet, and I'll have Carmen clean your room before and after."

Luke nodded but didn't look happy. Carmen was their housecleaner and home assistant. Rose had stopped feeling guilty about having personal staff. She didn't have time for housework or running errands, but the kids still had to clean their own rooms.

26

With a funny look on his face, Luke said, "Will Darla be sleeping in my room?"

"I'm sure Darla is coming. No idea where the girls will sleep. Why?" Rose asked, smiling.

"No reason."

Rose smiled again. She'd hints before; now she guessed Luke had a crush. She debated saying anything and realized she might not have another chance.

"Sweetie, I'd been wanting to talk to you about girls."

"No way," Luke said, reddening and raising his voice a little, looking like he was about to bolt.

"No, not about that." She didn't even want to use the word "sex," which they had never discussed—one of her many parental failings. "Not so much about Darla or other girls from our time. It's the girls from this era I wanted to talk to you about."

"Why?"

"People in this time treat those of status and wealth differently. You may not like it, but because of my position and our wealth, you d be a valuable catch and might be approached by girls, even older women, who are interested in what you can give them, not in who you are."

"I know your job pays well, but we're not personally that rich, are we?"

"I've been investing in a lot of companies. It may take years, even decades, but yes, we will be very wealthy."

Luke grinned. "I'll be like a rich earl, and women will be falling over me? I don't see a problem."

"Honey, it's not money, it's culture. A woman of this time has spent her whole life for one purpose: to find a good, preferably rich husband, because she'd had no other choice. Let me ask you, what are Darla's plans when she graduates?"

"She'll be an electrician like her mom and stepdad. She's taking the first test soon and will start her apprenticeship soon. Her mom worked out that she can do her Guard service while doing her electrician training. They're desperate for electricians."

"I bet if you asked every girl in your class, they'd tell you what career they were considering. Girls from this era would say wife and mother. It is more than choices; it is self-worth. Independence is something innate in every woman from our time. There are a lot of mixed marriages happening now, but I imagine it is more difficult than one would expect. I want you to be happy."

"What are you saying? Only date girls from the old world?"

"Relationships are always hard, but when you're from two different cultures, it creates an extra layer of difficulties. Not that love can't overcome them, but similar cultural backgrounds are smooth, and different ones are rougher."

"Like you and Hotah," said Luke with wisdom beyond his years.

Rose felt a sudden pang in her chest. Luke's words cut deeper than he realized. Her relationship with Hotah had been layered with the weight of cultural differences she hadn't fully appreciated until it was too late. Memories of arguments over traditions, values, and their contrasting upbringings resurfaced; conflicts she had once dismissed as minor but she now saw had eroded their foundation.

"Yes," Rose said softly, now needing the conversation to be over. "Hey, Carmen made huckleberry pie."

Later, Rose thought about that conversation and realized there were more to cultural differences in relationships than she might have previously credited. Luke s simple observation brought that ache back, a quiet reminder of how love alone hadn t been enough. And now, with Jackson, she wondered whether similar cultural gaps could hold them back by quietly shaping their dynamic. She had never dated or even known very well any African Americans. She knew Denise, Jackson s fiancée, had been Black. Perhaps his connection with her had felt easier or more natural in ways Rose couldn t fully understand. The thought lingered, unsettling her, as she wondered whether part of Jackson s hesitation to fully commit stemmed from this gap they hadn t addressed.

That night, Rose couldn't sleep. The shadows of the past and the weight of the future pressed in, unrelenting. Across the Circle, storms were gathering. Some were political. Some were personal. Others were born of old wounds finding new ground. She didn't know it yet, but a fire had already been lit in California. And a young Lakota warrior was about to remind the world that Changleska kept its promises.

Chapter Nineteen
Brings Him Home

FORT CONDOR PLANNED a ceremony for the Fall Equinox and the first anniversary of Big Thunder. There were many discussions on how to mark the occasion. Some wanted something solemn to mourn the loss of loved ones and the old world. Others wanted a celebration, recognizing their survival and accomplishments since their arrival. They ended up with a compromise. At 11:11 am, the exact time of Big Thunder, a somber ceremony and prayer service, both Christian and Lakota, took place.

After the prayers concluded, the crowd stood in silence. Then a quiet breath of melody drifted through the stillness. Andy stepped forward, her hands clenched at her sides, and began to sing. Her voice, soft but steady, carried the opening lines of *Circle Unbroken*, the new anthem chosen by vote across the settlements. By the second verse, others joined in. Few knew all the words, but followed along. There were no instruments and no fanfare, only voices rising together into the autumn air. It was the first time the anthem had been sung in Fort Condor. There would be other performances, more polished perhaps, but none more powerful.

Changleska Anthem *Circle Unbroken*
From the rivers wide to the mountains tall,
We stand as one, we will never fall.
Through the storms of time, through the dark of night,
We rise together, walking toward the light.
Big Thunder strengthens the circle,
The circle protects the Earth.
We remember those who walked before,
The songs they sang, the lives they swore.

Now the future's ours to claim,
Not by conquest, not by chains.
From the past we take our stand,
This is our home, this is our land.
No more lost, no more forsaken,
We are free, we are awakened.
By the thunder, by the rain,
We will never bow
Big Thunder strengthens the circle,
The circle protects the Earth.
With our voices, with our hands,
We will heal, we will expand.
This is our home, this is our land

Afterward, they dedicated a memorial wall with photos and written memories in the still under construction dining hall. The first section, dedicated to Big Thunder and the old world, was followed by a section dedicated to the First Journey, which included a map and pictures of those lost in the construction of the first road. A photo of the road crew was also on display. Brings Him Home had seen small photos of himself on people's phones, but this was the first time he had seen one printed out. The Changleskans told him it was an honor as they had little printer ink left. Looking at the photo on the wall made him feel strange. The wall provided space for others who might, in the future, become lost. That evening, they celebrated with a feast, singing, and dancing. The locked alcohol stores were opened, and those who brought private stashes shared. Brings Him Home disliked the taste of alcohol and hated the effect on people but still had an enjoyable time.

That evening, they celebrated with a feast, singing, and dancing. The locked alcohol stores were opened, and those who brought private stashes shared. Brings Him Home disliked the taste of alcohol and hated the effect on people but still had an enjoyable time.

A few days later, Brings Him Home saw the captain and a few others at the river talking. He wandered over, listening, fascinated when he realized they were talking about harnessing the river to create electricity.

Dave, a Guardian from the engineering crew, eyed the river's steady flow. "A Pelton wheel won't cut it here. There's not enough drop. But a Kaplan turbine? That could work."

Captain Morrison asked, "That's the one for low-head, high-flow rivers, right? Adjustable blades?"

Dave nodded. "Exactly. It'll take some engineering, but we could divert part of the river through a controlled channel, set up the turbine, and generate enough power to run the fort and then some. Not enough supplies on site, but Chamberlain has everything we need."

The captain, after a moment's thought, said, "Old world resources are at a premium. There'll be a political fight, but this is our best shot at long-term electricity." Sighing, he asked, "What do you need? The next convoy will leave in a few weeks." They'd sent the trucks back a while ago, and they were expected to return with more people and supplies.

Dave said, "Steel piping, a bigger generator, probably a ton of welding gear. We could retrofit something, but we'll need heavy transport to get it here."

The captain said, "I'll see what I can do. We may have to start small, but hopefully they'll recognize the potential here."

The group wrapped up their discussions and left. Brings Him Home wondered what the Fort would be like with more electricity than the solar panels provided.

Brings Him Home had grown in the four moons since he left home. He had been a little under six feet tall, but he shot up two inches and wondered whether he'd grow even taller. His body, fueled by abundant food, specifically carbohydrates, transformed noticeably. Working road crew, he built up a lot of muscle mass. He would never be as big or bulky as Tom, but he could beat him in their wrestling matches now and then. The problem was: Brings Him Home was outgrowing his clothes. Even the give of deerskin was not enough. Fortunately, it was warm in California. While he often wore only his breechclout, it wasn't a solution. He had very few trade goods left, but with his pay, he could shop at the Fort trading post. He coveted blue jeans and the camo pants worn by the Guardians. When his full membership was complete, he would need to buy some for his uniform. But the prices were too high, so he bought two soft, tanned elk hides and looked for a woman to sew for him.

There was a Pawnee family who had joined them en route. He'd noticed the man's fine clothes, and using English and sign language, Brings Him Home requested that his wife sew two shirts and a pair of pants for him. After they haggled, his wife said although she was busy, her daughter could do it with her supervision. The girl's name was Hisha, which meant light. She was tall and pretty, a few years younger than him. It was unsaid but clear the girl was available for marriage. Brings Him Home enjoyed a respected reputation, regular pay, his own small tipi and two horses, a saddle and a rifle. The family may have wanted a closer tie to Lakota or to him personally.

Brings Him Home liked Hisha after spending a little time with her. Between working on the fort, scout patrols and his evening lessons, he had little free time and rarely saw her. But he didn't want to marry. Instead, he wanted to learn the ways of war, which he knew would take years. Sharing robes with the older women or widows who invited him at home had been enjoyable, but this was different. He found himself in a dilemma. Needing advice, he missed his friend Little Dog. Strangely enough, Andy solved his problem for him.

With only a hundred residents of the fort, gossip was a chief source of entertainment, particularly romance. Soon everyone knew the Pawnee family had more or less offered Hisha, although he had neither expressed interest nor offered a bride price, and speculation percolated.

Andy stopped by his camp one day and said, "I heard you and Hisha are dating and may get married."

He had been drinking tea and almost choked in surprise. "No."

"No, you are not dating Hisha, or no you're not getting married?"

I do not date or plan on marrying for many years. I am returning in the spring." He hoped to attend the Officer Candidate School in Chamberlain that Jody had described.

"Does Hisha know you don't plan on marrying her?"

"I never asked."

"You realized you can't just ahh.." she blushed, "...sleep with her. Her family would expect marriage."

He looked at her in confusion, finally realizing the euphemism, getting so embarrassed he couldn't speak. He just nodded and left, even though they were in his own camp.

Later, he heard Andy had spoken to Hisha's mother, and then people started looking sympathetically at Hisha and giving him dirty looks. As usual, he ignored it all.

=..=

After they'd been there for two moons, Brings Him Home was summoned to the C&C on Captain Morrison's orders. Although construction wasn't complete, the C&C building was functional. The Communication part of the 'C' was in the newly built upstairs, with the computers and radios. Eventually, it would house the new Signal Corps, but there weren't enough of them yet. The Control or Command part of the 'C' held Major Morrison's office, and a few other offices, but the large briefing area took up most of the floor space. He walked through the briefing room to the captain's office. The door was open with a few Guardians standing outside. He approached hesitantly.

"Come in, young man, come in," said Captain Morrison.

Brings Him Home wasn't sure if he should salute, he was a scout, auxiliary force, not a formal Guardian yet, but decided it was respectful, so he placed his right hand over his heart, dipped his head slightly in a small bow, then straightened to attention. "Scout Brings Him Home, reporting as ordered, sir."

The captain looked surprised and pleased with the attention to military protocol. "At ease."

Brings Him Home shifted to the at-ease position, standing with his feet shoulder-width apart and his hands clasped behind his back.

Looking around the crowded office, on the futon which folded into a bed, was a young Miwok girl, looking bruised and battered. A female Guardian was holding her, while another with an open medic bag was finishing up bandaging her. Nearby, looking protective, was a slightly older man with a family resemblance, likely her brother. Several other officers were in the room or the hall.

The room was growing warm and stuffy with all the people. The captain just seemed to notice. He glanced at his watch and said, "Joanie, will you take Shaasss.." he gave up trying to pronounce the girl's name. "The girl to medical for a full workup, get her cleaned up, fed and clothed, and a place in the women's dorm to sleep. She'll be here for a bit until we can get this mess cleaned up."

He looked at his second in command, "Lieutenant Iron Cloud, please take him..." pointing to the man, not even trying to pronounce his name. "...upstairs, get the geek squad to pull up Google Earth and figure out a map, print a copy, take it downstairs and put it on the whiteboard. Also, pull together as much information about the Spanish camp as we have. Schedule an operational planning meeting with all officers and NCOs at 1300."

As they started out the door, the captain waved at the others to leave, pointing to Brings Him Home, "You stay."

Brings Him Home felt the excitement of a coming battle approaching. It was obvious what was going on. The Spanish had been raiding Miwok villages for slaves for the Spanish missions. Now that the Miwok had formally joined Changleska, they were honor-bound to intercede. He wasn't sure if the orders about defense orders still applied, but knew Captain Morrison had a lot of latitude.

The captain looked carefully at Brings Him Home. He had taken a few minutes to both clean himself up and put on some weapons. Most of what he carried consisted of his everyday tools, like knives and the tomahawk. He'd left his rifle, bow and coup stick at his camp but added more knives and his war club. Even without his paint and feathers, he looked like the proud Lakota warrior he was.

The captain looked at his laptop, punching a few things and reading while Brings Him Home tried to patiently wait.

"It says here you are only seventeen years old. Eighteen this winter." The captain knew the Lakota didn't count birthdays the same way. Brings Him Home knew he was born in the late summer. He was actually sixteen, but he said nothing.

Brings Him Home nodded, remembering protocol, and said. "Yes, sir."

"Seven scalps on your pole. Are those men you killed in battle yourself?"

Brings Him Home tried not to sound as offended as he was. "Yes, sir."

"From the reports here, you are an excellent scout, worked hard on the road crew, you're studying to take the guard exam and you're training in the Special Forces, and teaching Lakota warcraft." Smiling, the captain said. I remember you from paint wars. You gave us a bloody nose,"

Brings Him Home wasn't sure whether to reply, so he just nodded.

The captain asked, "Please tell me about your fighting experience. Have you ever led others?"

He took a breath, wondering how much to say, but kept it simple. "I helped defend our camp five times. Three of the scalps on my pole were Crow who attacked us. I've been on twenty-one raids, mostly for horses, and other prizes of war, the last five I led. Our raiding parties were between four and seven warriors."

Captain Morrison digested this information, adding notes on his laptop. He asked, "In our terms, we use kill ratio. How many did you lose versus how many you took out?"

His stoic answer didn't reflect the pain he felt. "In the five raids I led, we were outnumbered, sometimes many times. I lost one and had three wounded to the degree they could no longer fight."

The captain looked thoughtful, then seemed to decide. "Even though you're young, and not a full guard member, I'm going to award you command of a squad. We expect close contact with the enemy. Are you ready for this?"

"Yes, sir," he said, unable to suppress the pride swelling within him, a broad smile spreading across his face.

"Although not a full guard member yet, for this action, you'll be an acting sergeant with all the same responsibilities. Read up on the rules if you're unfamiliar. You'll be leading a squad of eight. Any questions?"

"Can I pick the eight?"

The captain looked impressed. "Yes, within reason, Sargeant Tilson can give you names. Is that it?"

"Yes, sir."

"Okay, get something to eat and be back for the meeting at 1300. He nodded curtly, dismissed."

He gave the Changleska salute. "Yes, sir." Without further hesitation, he turned sharply and left.

Brings Him Home had a little over two hours to prepare for the meeting. He found Ed Tilson in the mess hall. Not wanting to take the time to eat, he grabbed a roll, sat next to Ed, and discussed people for his crew. He wanted the Special Forces guys he'd been training with, but other squads also wanted them, so he only got three. They ended up returning to C&C to look up personnel files. Brings Him Home was surprised by the extent of information on everyone the computers held. After all that, he ended up choosing all people he knew except one. Besides the Special Forces guys, he picked Tom from the road crew and three Indigenous men that had joined along the way. He was unsure of the last man, Harold Rogers, whom everyone called Bones, probably because he was wiry and skinny. In his thirties, he was not in the regular Guard, but had been sworn in as militia, as all were on the expedition. The promise of gold clearly motivated Bones. Brings Him Home remembered conversations he had overheard—his habit of listening had often paid off. Bones talked about being a "biker", whatever that meant, and recounted fights he'd been in, but more importantly, he bragged about picking locks. Brings Him Home didn't know what kind of locks the Spanish might have, but he figured having a lock picker might come in handy. None of the others had ever killed anyone, but he got the impression Bones might have. Brings Him Home didn't have to like his crew members, they only had to be competent and tough.

The meeting started with an examination of a rough area map on the whiteboard. They narrowed down possible camps from those scouted earlier.

Captain Morrison began. "This action will be in three days. We don't want to wait long, as intelligence," he nodded at the Miwok man, "tells us the Spanish move camps every month or so. Scouting parties have been dispatched to confirm the location, although we already know the general vicinity. We expect about twenty-five Spanish, mostly irregulars, often mercenaries. They may be led by cuera (leather armored) cavalry officers from the San Francisco presidio. Their job is to raid Indigenous villages. They kill men, anyone older, and bring girls and young boys to the priests at the missions. It is supposed to be for education and to save their souls, according to Tiswaya here." The captain seemed pleased to pronounce his name right. "They call them neophytes, but it is just another name for slaves. The captives are often raped, including the boys." He gave everyone a moment to absorb this. Then he motioned Tiswaya and the interpreter to come forward. "Please tell us everything you can. Not everyone heard the first time."

Tiswaya came to the front, looking over the dozen assembled, sitting attentively. He spoke fluent Spanish. Through the interpreter, he told his terrible story. The Spanish had captured him when he was eleven years old. His parents had been killed, but his sister had escaped with an aunt. He was sent to the Mission Dolores near the San Francisco presidio. He escaped when he was fourteen. A few weeks ago, while he was on a hunting trip, the Spanish raided his village, killing many and capturing his sister. His sister escaped from the mission six days ago. Running and hiding, it took five days to reach the village. With her brother, they took another day to run all the way here.

Tiswaya, with calm deference, said, "Thank you for stopping these men. They are a pox on our lands, and we welcome Changleska with open arms. Please let me know how we can help."

Captain Morrison spoke confidently. "You're welcome. We would've waited, as we haven't wanted to engage the Spanish while treaty negotiations are ongoing, but we recognize the threat. However, it's important that no word gets out that Changleska forces are involved. Everyone, let's discuss a rescue plan."

The discussion went on for a while, with everyone throwing out planning ideas. The risk of the Spanish seeing Changleska's only drone, or worse, shooting it down, was too great. They considered a night raid but rejected that idea because they had only two sets of night vision goggles. They discussed prisoner treatment and other aspects of the rescue mission. Tiswaya said the Spanish would typically chain captives until there were a few dozen, then move them to the mission. A bounty was paid for each captive, so they tried to take as many as possible at once. The number of captives currently held was unclear. Brings Him Home listened silently, as was his habit. Then the captain asked him directly what he thought.

"There's only one way for word to not get out. We must kill everyone in that camp. Soldiers, cooks, their women. If you had prisoners, at some point you'd need to give them back. Unless they escaped. Either way, to keep a secret like this, all must die."

Lieutenant Iron Cloud said, "That's not our military's way. We show mercy." Brings Him Home knew he had served in the faraway war against desert Indigenous people that they lost. He'd asked many questions about that war from the expedition veterans. From what he heard, they hadn't shown the desert people much mercy.

Captain Morrison said, "Unfortunately, the young acting sergeant here is probably correct. Remember this is 1792. Adaptation to these times is crucial. The bigger picture is we need to achieve peace with the Spanish and we need them to turn over their lands. Remember, this is New Spain, not part of the original Louisiana purchase. We can't endanger the treaty to free prisoners." Looking at Brings Him Home, he said. "If you were in charge of this action, what would you do?"

Brings Him Home said, feeling the weight of every gaze upon him. "I am learning to read. Jody, my teacher, believed Sun Tzu's *Art of War* would hold my interest. Sun Tzu said, 'Let your plans be dark and impenetrable as night, and when you move, fall like a thunderbolt'." Then he looked around and said firmly, "The Spanish aren't prepared for us. They're used to fighting poorly armed people in villages, or men in open battle. We strike when they're most vulnerable, before dawn when they're abed, when their weapons are out of reach, their throats bare to our blades. No warning. Only then will there be no one left to send word of what happened."

The room stirred with uneasy murmurs and the exchange of a few sharp glances. No one objected outright, so Brings Him Home laid out the attack plan with precision. Before first light, his squad would move in first, eliminating the perimeter guards and silently killing as many as possible before the alarm sounded. Knives would be the primary weapons, clean and quiet. Firearms were to be avoided for as long as possible. He suggested consulting the armory officer about crafting a suppressor. During his shooting lessons, they had discussed makeshift designs like wooden baffles or water-filled chambers that could muffle a shot. The alarm would be the first loud shot by either side, then the main force would strike all at once. To save ammo, those skilled in archery would use bows; others would take crossbows, effective at close range with minimal training. At every corner of the camp, long-range snipers would be ready to take out any who attempted to flee. One squad would be dedicated to hunting down and killing anyone who escaped the initial assault. Another squad would free and care for the captives.

Lieutenant Iron Cloud raised his voice a little. "We're not butchers. Killing men in their sleep is simply cowardly." He looked abashed, hoping he didn't just call this young fierce Lakota warrior a coward.

Brings Him Home said calmly, "A Lakota warrior would also see no honor. This isn't a battle risking the enemy killing you. This is a slaughter. There may be no honor in this attack, but there is honor in obeying the order of your commander, who sees the bigger picture. There is honor in protecting our allies, who joined Changleska with promises of protection. If Changleska is to be free from Spain, to become a coalition of tribes united to fight against the wasichu and save our lands, then the treaty with Spain must be signed. Stealth is essential. If we can't kill every Spaniard, and assure that Changleska's role is never found, then we should cancel the mission. We can always rescue the captives in the spring after the treaty is signed."

Everyone, including Captain Morrison, stared at him in shock. Surprised at his English, his understanding of the politics, and the order of battle he proposed. Most had never heard him speak more than three words. The captain thought, *glad he's on our side. Someday, I may be saluting him.*

They revisited the issue if the mission should wait until the treaty was signed. They decided to move ahead. Some were willing to shed blood. The Spanish were not innocent. They all signed up for the Changleska Guard to protect others. The stain on their honor was the price they'd pay. It'd been hard hearing the degradations of the Spanish for months, knowing they had a superior military force, but had to stay hidden, limited to defense. They were ready to fight.

The officers made a few changes but agreed to the plan Brings Him Home proposed. To leave no trace, they'd eliminate all traces of the camp and bury all bodies. If identifying objects or distinctive horses turned up later, it'd be a mystery.

=..=

Three days later, the squad set up camp a few miles away from the Spanish. An hour before first light, Brings Him Home led them in. At first, everything went as planned. He moved silently, slit the throat of one guard, slipped into a tent, and cut the throat of another, then another. A muffled scream broke the silence.

Brings Him Home thought, *I thought I taught them how to kill clean and quiet.*

Another shout rose from deeper in the camp, followed by the dull thud of a body hitting the ground. Then came a soft pop, a suppressed shot, quieter than a flintlock, but still loud enough to carry in the night air. A loud crack filled the air. A flintlock. That was the signal.

Brings Him Home flipped on his radio. "Now. Move in."

The rest of the nearby force headed into the camp, where men shouted, and a woman was heard screaming. Dark figures tumbled from tents, scrambling into gear, reaching for weapons. Everything dissolved into chaos. A dawn light was softly chasing away the lingering shadows of night. Brings Him Home carried a loaned Glock 17. The pistol nestled in the small of his back, but he didn't reach for it. A Spaniard rushed toward him, raising his flintlock. Instinct took over. Brings Him Home whipped his tomahawk forward, aiming for the man's ribs. Metal clanged. The Spaniard staggered but didn't fall. He was wearing a breastplate. The tomahawk dropped uselessly to the dirt.

Brings Him Home barely had time to register his mistake before gripping his war club and sprinting forward. A rifle cracked. The Spaniard's head exploded in a mist of red. His body crumpled like a dropped sack of grain. More gunfire. Everywhere he looked, men collapsed before they could take three steps. He froze. None of his men were firing. This wasn't magic. It was Andy.

She'd built a sniper's nest almost a mile away. He had no idea how she could hit at that distance. Many were headshots. Andy taught him to aim for center mass because headshots were easy to miss. Yet she never did. For the first time, Brings Him Home felt something new. Complete admiration. Andy wasn't just good. She was something else entirely.

Brings Him Home moved through the camp, calmly using the Glock to shoot every wounded man in the head. A faint noise stirred from inside a tent. He turned, shifting the Glock slightly, and pushed back the flap. A woman huddled in the corner, sobbing. Her eyes, wide and dark, fixed on him. Brings Him Home scanned the space. Seeing discarded women's clothing, he knew she wasn't a captive taken in this raid. He shot her, then stepped back out without a second thought.

Lifting his radio, he keyed it on. "Check all the tents. Make sure we got them all."

A crackled voice came from the radio. "We found the captives north by the horses."

Brings Him Home followed the voices, passing the picket line where the horses were tethered. A group of mostly women and children sat huddled, manacled together. Thick chains linked them in rows, long enough to shuffle. The stench told him how far they could move. Not far. Tiswaya came quickly, looking at the group in horror.

Brings Him Home approached him, speaking low. "Yours?"

He nodded toward a woman clutching a child. "My cousin. Others from my village." He swallowed hard, his hands fisted.

He heard an order go out on the radio. "Search all bodies and tents for keys."

Seeing his squad gathering where captives were, he motioned to Bones. Wordlessly, he pointed to the chains.

Bones pulled a small leather roll of tools from his pocket and kneeled beside the first set of manacles. Seeing the captives in the chains, he muttered, "This is fucked up," he muttered, inspecting the captives' locks. "Old-school iron. Shouldn't take long."

One by one, the manacles were opened. Captives rubbed at their raw wrists. Some wept. Others simply stared, too numb to react. Brings Him Home stood, watching the last chain hit the dirt.

The squad assigned to care for the captives arrived, mostly women and medics. They moved swiftly, checking for injuries, distributing food and water. One medic, a stocky woman with sharp eyes, turned to Brings Him Home.

"Check the tents for clothes. Anything clean, preferably."

Brings Him Home glanced at the huddled figures. All the women were naked. His jaw tightened.

He gathered his squad, checking to make sure everyone was okay. One man had been wounded, but not seriously. He sent him to the medics. They all looked shaken. The scent of vomit clung to the air near the bodies. None of them had ever killed before. They needed tasks.

He raised his voice. "You should be proud. We freed the captives, killed the enemy, and didn't lose anyone. If you were Lakota, you'd all receive honors."

Some of them exchanged looks, uncertainty flickering in their expressions. After a beat, a few tentative smiles appeared. Someone gave a high five.

"Tom and Bones, stay here. Mendez and Thompson patrol the perimeter. The rest of you start cleanup. Check with Sergeant Tilson. He's in charge."

Bones hesitated, shifting on his feet. "Brings, err.. I mean sergeant, what about war prizes? Don't we get to keep what we find?"

Brings Him Home studied him. The man's tone was too eager.

"Men you killed with your own hand, you may claim their weapons or anything on their body," He recalled this having been discussed in the meeting. "We'll send the horses and camp salvage to the fort and fairly distribute anything not needed by everyone to the fighters," he said.

Bones said nothing, but his face tightened in dissatisfaction. Brings Him Home didn't care.

Afterward, he went to each of the five men he had killed. He stripped them of weapons and anything useful, then set to work, efficiently and swiftly scalping each one. He tied the scalps to his belt. When he stood, he noticed the eyes on him.

Other Guardians had stopped what they were doing. A few exchanged glances. One of the younger men, Mendez, looked visibly ill. Someone muttered under their breath. Brings Him Home ignored them. Their discomfort wasn't his concern.

A large pit was being dug for the bodies. Nearby, Lieutenant Iron Cloud directed the salvage operation. Brings Him Home started toward the horses, wondering which one he could claim later, when a soft noise from a nearby tree caught his attention. His hand went to the Glock as he approached. Then he saw her.

Andy sat on the ground, her back on a tree, her knees drawn to her chest, shoulders shaking, softly crying. He stood over her for a long moment before lowering himself to sit beside her.

Andy's voice was raw. "I shouldn't have looked. Why did I come?"

Brings Him Home said nothing at first. He let her cry.

When her breathing steadied, he spoke. "You saved my life. You saved my men. Did you see the people you freed?"

She nodded miserably, but her shoulders still shook.

"Fourteen women, seven children," he continued. "They will return to their homes and families. They will grow up free because of you."

Andy let out a long breath. Some of the tension in her face eased, but her hands still gripped her knees.

Brings Him Home had been told about PTSD, the illness of the mind some people got from war. When asked if his people had it, he had answered, "Sometimes warriors return from battle shaken, with bad dreams. They go to the *wičháša wakȟáŋ* (holy man). The inípi and other ceremonies heal them."

Perhaps the Miwok or Ohlone would have a spirit healer. He took her hand, gripping it firmly. She needed to feel strong.

"I've seen no one with your skill. More than saving my life, you alone made this battle a success. No deaths. No serious injuries. Because of you."

Andy still looked haunted, but she listened.

She whispered, "They weren't paper targets. They were people. They had mothers. Sisters. Someone who'll miss them."

Brings Him Home met her gaze. "And what of the mothers and sisters you saved?"

Her breath hitched, but this time, she nodded.

She held his gaze, eyes searching his face. Slowly, her fingers curled around his hand in return for his outreached one.

The silence stretched between them, shifting from heavy to something else. Their gaze met, caught and connected.

She let out a breath and laughed weakly, then inspected him.

"What the fuck, Brings," she muttered. "You took scalps?"

For the first time, he grinned. And they rose and joined the others.

Something changed between them after that day, a connection he thought he would never feel for a thunder girl. A bond usually felt between warriors who fought together, with an undercurrent of something different. Tenuous, fragile, but unmistakably strong.

Chapter Twenty
Mary

—◇◇◯◇◇—

MARY'S FEELINGS RAN from cautious optimism to paralyzing dread. Progress was finally being made on the global political front. The treaty with Spain edged closer every day, but much depended on a separate deal with France. A political house of cards that could collapse at any moment, taking Changleska's survival with it.

She was grateful to the researchers in the online forum, as well as Elliot, Rose, and the rest of the negotiating team. She couldn't have done this alone. Their arrival in this time had triggered a tsunami of a butterfly effect, yet knowledge of the future-that-was had become their greatest weapon. Information was their currency, not only discoveries in science, medicine, industry, and agriculture, but also awareness of historical events that could unfold again.

Leveraging this foreknowledge was key to their possible success, but they couldn't completely control the flow of information. Despite their best efforts, illegal sales of history books, phones, and computers still occurred. Now, rumors of someone in Europe with cell phones and encyclopedias causing chaos had been confirmed. She'll get more details at tomorrow's security meeting. How this would affect their plans, no one knew.

The papal delegation was due to arrive in three days. The stakes couldn t be higher. Spain wanted Rome s blessing before formally relinquishing New Spain. Her parish priest, Father Murphy, had written to every mission and priest he could find, including directly to the Vatican, inviting them to witness the miracle. Father Murphy believed the true wonder wasn t the event itself, but the opportunity the foreknowledge offered to halt the abuses of the past and the decline of the Church in his time. His letters, along with the reports from the priests who visited last spring, could influence the outcome. Pope Pius VI wanted to assess Changleska firsthand before making a final decision on the treaty.

Mary glanced at her briefing notes. Cardinal Ramón de Solís, a seasoned Spanish diplomat tasked with securing Rome s approval, would lead the delegation. Bishop Jean-Baptiste Durand, a Jesuit, had been assigned to evaluate Changleska s stance on Catholicism. The Church wanted a place here, a role in what was New Spain. Mary knew these assurances would make a difference.

Monsignor Edward Fitzpatrick stood out. An Irish cleric fluent in English. That was telling. The Vatican didn't want to rely on Spanish or French interpreters; they wanted direct negotiations with Changleska's leaders. It was both a sign of respect and a reminder that Rome didn't fully trust Spain's version of events.

Mary was looking forward to having lunch with her daughter Bridget. Although Bridget and her two girls lived with her, they had a rule of no work talk at home. Occasional lunches at the Red Oak were her way to catch up on work gossip or talk about things without Daniel or the girls around.

Mary was annoyed because Bridget had arrived ten minutes late without an apology or a text. Mary believed punctuality showed respect, plus her food was getting cold. But she softened quickly, remembering how lucky she was. So many family members, including Bridget's husband, had been left behind the Circle. She continued to mourn the two sons she would never see again. She was lucky to have Bridget.

After they settled in to eat, Bridget asked, "Are you excited about the papal delegation? The hotel staff are all aflutter, wanting everything to be perfect."

"Excited and worried. It must go well. Many things depend on the treaty with Spain."

"I'm proud of you, mom. I can't believe how much you got done since Big Thunder. Starting an entire government in two days seemed impossible. Now that the treaty is in place, we may actually succeed. I can't imagine a US where Indians are not second-class citizens."

Mary replied, "It's not like I did it alone. Besides, most of it was based on the tribal government, the Iroquois Confederacy model, and, as much as we may hate it, the US Constitution and Bill of Rights."

"A year seems like so long ago. Life is now so different," Bridget said, with a hint of sadness.

"It's not so bad. Winter was hard, but things are improving."

"You think we'll get bananas and chocolate again? I swear, I'd kill for a proper candy bar."

"Not anytime soon. South America grows bananas, but transporting them requires refrigeration. Once the paddle steamers are running next year, trade will pick up. Coffee, cocoa, and sugar, will start flowing again."

Bridget sighed, "Everything is so hard to make. Tina's husband said that they're struggling to make decent glass. Half the windows in the new buildings are warped or cloudy."

"Yeah, the industrial processes are coming along, but it'll take time. We lost so much specialized equipment, and some of it we can't replicate yet."

Mary changed the subject. "Did you hear Elliot Gray Owl is getting married?"

"To the White girl who changed her name?" Bridget's tone conveyed a quiet disapproval.

Mary knew the situation troubled people on multiple levels, although few openly acknowledged it. "Yes, she's pregnant, due in the winter. But she changed her name back; said she's keeping her maiden name, too."

"Oh? What was it?"

"Debra Cohen. She returned to her birth name because she's Jewish. She said she felt she needed to embrace her heritage. Jenny mentioned the few Jewish people in the area have been renting a meeting room once a month for a service. They've been discussing ways to influence the future, to prevent pogroms and the Holocaust."

Bridget's eyebrows rose. "Are there many Jewish people here?"

"Jenny said about twenty-five regularly attend. A few lived here, a few were caught by Big Thunder. There's also a small Jewish community in New Orleans, but most live on the East Coast."

Bridget leaned in closer to her mother, lowering her voice. "Speaking of which, did you hear about Jenny and Henry LaChamp?"

"I heard he had some issues with her being Jewish. They broke up but then got back together."

Bridget nodded. "Yes, she requested to move to a suite because Henry moved in and likes finer things. When Hudson Bay Company hired him as their representative here, they didn't intend for him to live in an expensive hotel. They're paying for his stay, but only enough for a modest room in town. Apparently, he kept apologizing to Jenny until she took him back."

Mary shook her head, concern evident in her eyes. "Sounds like trouble brewing. Poor Jenny." Then she thought, *she must've hoped his apologies meant change. But too many women mistake remorse for transformation.*

They'd nearly finished their food when Bridget said, hesitantly, "Mom, I invited you to lunch to talk about something."

"Okay, you can talk to me about anything, sweetie."

"I'll always love Alan. He'll always be the girls' father, but it has been a year, and I'm starting to see someone."

Mary had to admit her first reaction was selfish—not happy for Bridget, who deserved every happiness, but worried that if she remarried, she might move out, and Mary wouldn't get to see the girls every day.

"Who is it? Anyone I know?"

"Yes, Billy."

"Billy Fast Dog?" Mary's surprise was evident. He was a decade older, not particularly attractive, and his job as Security Chief of Omímeya was demanding, with many hours on call.

"He lost his wife behind the Circle, and two college-age daughters. We started talking about that, started hanging out, and now..."

Mary didn't want to ask if they were sleeping together, none of her business.

"Is he Catholic?" This might tell Mary whether they were considering marriage or using birth control.

"No." Bridget answered rather defensively. "Shouldn't matter. Who knows what the Church will look like in this era? Will it go back to the abuses and boarding schools?"

"That's what Father Murphy is trying to prevent. As far as Billy's religion goes, the only reason it matters is it's one less area of potential conflict. It makes it easier, like you and Alan, or me and your dad. I want you to be happy."

"I'm inviting him to dinner on Friday, and he'll meet the girls."

"Looking forward to it." She was lying. She dreaded it, especially what Daniel might say.

=..=

The next day's Security Meeting had the usual participants, Phil, Kyle, Jackson, Billy, with the addition of FSC staffers. Mary eyed Billy with suspicion, although she wasn't sure why. They'd only interacted professionally, but he seemed competent enough. She knew he was Lakota from the Pine Ridge reservation and, unlike her, he'd had grown up speaking Lakota. It was the only non-security-related conversation she'd ever had with him.

Since the briefing materials were comprehensive on the papal delegation, that discussion was brief. There were two main issues of concern on the agenda.

Phil opened with, "We have news at home and in Europe. Even with the additional First Shield staff, we need more analysts. These reports..." waving his tablet, "...reflect a lot of time-consuming, exhaustive work. It's extremely difficult to get timely reports from Europe, with the French Revolution. And at home, we need more work if we are ever going to seek criminal convictions."

"I thought Clyde Folsom was too careful to be convicted?" asked Kyle.

Phil agreed. "That's true in his public statements. He figured or suspected we planted observers in his church. His sermons have toned down. Most tech sellers we've caught seem to be his followers, but that's not actionable proof. We are following money trails. His funds exceed easily explainable amounts. A report indicated that he asked his followers to donate cell phones."

"Why would anyone donate their phone? They still work inside the Circle. Everyone knows we may never make more," Jackson asked.

"Many people have old phones lying around. Anything that can hold data or take photos sells for thousands. Which is a lot of money here and now," Phil responded. "People either donated them outright or got a percentage of sales without the risk of breaking the law."

Kyle said, "I've been working with IT to trace the phones, but no luck so far. They're probably used outside the Circle. We can't trace them away from our cell towers."

Mary asked, "How much damage can old phones do?"

Phil listed off things from his fingers with a superior air. "Maps, military plans, tech specs, books, to name a few. Even very old phones hold a lot of data. More importantly, the more money he raises, the more dangerous he becomes."

Billy said, "If Folsom and his group dislike it so much here, why don't they leave, like the Mormons?"

Everyone laughed. There hadn't been many Mormons in the area before Big Thunder, but a family reunion nearly doubled their numbers. They were a tight-knit group. Being thrown back in time before the birth of their prophet, Brigham Young, forced them into a theological crisis. They adapted by reorganizing, electing new leaders, embracing polygamy, and taking Indigenous wives. Now, they were preparing an expedition to settle in the Salt Lake Valley come spring. As long as they worked with the Shoshone and the Ute, Changleska had no objections and offered logistical support for the journey. Surprisingly, they were gaining converts, and if this continued, the group in Salt Lake could become much larger than in original history.

Mary, trying to keep the meeting focused, asked, "We need an action plan. Does anyone have a concrete proposal on what to do about Folsom?"

Phil leaned forward, his tone sharp. "We need a change of tactics. Relying on patriotism, fines, and public humiliation isn't working. The tech sellers don't care, and we're not stopping the flow of information. We need stronger measures." He paused, adding, "We need to hang someone. At least one."

A ripple of unease passed through the room.

Jackson's expression darkened. "Is supporting annexation treason? Selling tech is one thing, but does it meet our definition?"

Mary shook her head. "Not supporting annexation. That's free speech. But Elliot said selling tech might constitute 'providing aid and comfort to the enemy.' That's the language of the US treason laws from our time. Treason carried the death penalty. Unless we change the law."

Jackson's voice was firm. "Hanging people for treason is a slippery slope. I'm not sure we should start down that road."

Phil's jaw tightened. "I don't think everyone realizes how serious this is." He glanced around the table, voice rising. "Washington and Jefferson have been told the US becomes the greatest power in the world. That power depends on controlling all the ports and waterways, as well as the entire continent full of raw materials. Folsom probably told them about the gold." He exhaled sharply. "And let's not forget, our stance against slavery, and support of Indigenous sovereignty is everything they hate. They'll fight us. And they outnumber us."

Jackson's tone remained measured. "I don't think they can do much militarily. They saw our weapons, and their army is too far away."

Phil shook his head. "They don't need to send an army. They have Clyde Folsom." He met Jackson's gaze. "You should remember, Washington and Jefferson are revolutionaries. They beat the biggest military power in the world. Sabotage will be their weapon." He let the words settle before adding, "A bomb in the server room could destroy our chief advantage."

A stunned silence filled the room before someone let out a sharp breath.

Billy broke the tension. "I want to assure everyone we're taking every precaution. We've increased video surveillance and added biometric locks to all computer areas."

Kyle added, "A lot of the old computers we bought right after Big Thunder have small but functional hard drives. We've been doing triple backups and storing them in a very secure offsite facility."

The tension eased, but only slightly. Knowledge from computers was the lifeblood of Changleska. It needed protection.

Mary tapped the table lightly, bringing attention back. "Is there a concrete proposal?"

Phil sighed. "Not exactly. This was more of an update." He glanced at Mary. "And don't look at me like that. I heard you the first time. Folsom can't have a 'convenient accident.'"

Mary's expression remained unreadable. "Glad we're clear." She shifted her notes. "Unless anyone has something to add, let's move on. Next item, Europe. Phil?"

Phil said, "Let's start with France, since it's short. For those who don't know, Katherine Enberg is now an FSC officer and the head of the Europe desk. Go ahead, Katy."

Mary had never met her in person but 'knew' her from the Foreign Affairs forum. She was an older, large woman, with a radiant smile. She had clearly lost a significant amount of weight recently, with loose skin around her face. The prevalence of obesity had sharply declined since Big Thunder. A retired teacher, she had spent a year in France after college. Known for her sharp intellect and strong research skills, she had made valuable contributions to the forum. Mary was confident she'd be an asset to the FSC.

Katy began. "For those who haven't read my full briefing on France, I'll give you the CliffsNotes." She smiled at the room. "France is in the middle of its revolution, progressing much the same as it did in our history. King Louis XVI is imprisoned. In our timeline, he was executed in January 1793, and his wife, Marie Antoinette, later that year. Rumors of his execution are circulating, but it's doubtful anyone can stop it. However, Marie Antoinette's brother, Francis II, is the Holy Roman Emperor. With this foreknowledge, he may attempt to rescue her, which could alter history."

Jackson asked, "Should we try to help with her rescue, have London offer logistical support, like radios?"

"Politically, no," Katy replied. "The Republic of France is who we need to be working with, not the monarchy. I get it, she's a famous historical figure. And for the record, she never said, 'Let them eat cake.' But there's no question her and Louis XVI's excesses helped fuel the revolution."

She moved on. "The War of the First Coalition is just beginning. Revolutionary France is facing off against a coalition of European monarchies determined to crush the revolution and prevent its spread. In our history, France survived and eventually won, but Napoleon played a crucial role. Right now, he's been sidelined. We're not providing France with military aid, but that doesn't mean they haven't benefited from information leaked from Changleska. Smuggled phones and history books have been mentioned..."

"Napoleon has been sidelined?" Jackson asked.

Phil grinned. "You'd love this, Jackson. It's the greatest example of nonviolent intervention ever. Probably saved hundreds of thousands of lives." He recounted the story with more enthusiasm than usual. "In 1792, Napoleon was only an ambitious artillery officer, not yet one of the greatest generals the world had ever seen. Instead of assassinating him before he came to power, Anna May Worthington came up with a different plan. She assassinated his character."

Mary smiled. Anna May was proving her worth ten times over. She was the wife of Martin Worthington, Changleska's newly recognized Ambassador to Great Britain.

"She started a whisper campaign, spreading rumors in London and during their brief visit to France," Phil continued. "All very subtle, casual conversations with officers' wives, remarks made where servants would overhear. Over the course of a month or so, she planted different stories: that Napoleon got a poor girl pregnant and abandoned her, that he cheated at cards and had serious gambling debts, even that he fled from a battle in disgrace. And then there was the best one, that after an attack, he was so frightened, he shit his pants. That one spread like wildfire." Phil shook his head in admiration. "She quickly realized no one cared if he was cruel to women or children. That was too common to ruin a man's career. But in the French army, courage and reputation as a 'gentleman' mattered. Since he already had his low birth working against him, those rumors stuck. Some heard the stories of how he crowned himself Emperor in our timeline. With so many doubts about his character, he was quietly relieved of command under a flimsy excuse." Phil's grin faded slightly. "He may not be out of the picture yet. Some other country could still hear about his achievements in our history and decide to hire him for their army."

Everyone smiled. Mary thought, *changing history sometimes means breaking a few eggs.* At least we didn't kill anyone.

Phil added, "There's more about the revolution and the key players in your briefing packet. Mary, anything to report on the diplomatic front with France?"

Mary said, "Henriette Dupont, the French businesswoman from Louisiana, has been a capable go-between. We now have a deal outlined. France will cede Tuscany to Spain, as they did in our timeline, in exchange for agricultural and industrial improvements, as well as scientific advancements from us. Our first college-level science and medical courses will start soon, and the French will have guaranteed slots. Hopefully, France will also formally recognize us soon. It's complicated because they're an ally of the US, which considers us an enemy."

Phil changed his tone with the topic. "We've confirmed the source of some of the information leaks in Europe. The first expedition to New Orleans had three people who left here last November. Their mission was to blend in and gather intelligence ahead of the main group, expected a month later. They never arrived. We assumed they all perished. However, bits of twenty-first-century gear kept appearing. Then rumors of cell phones and other leaks of modern knowledge in Europe. This happened months before we established our London embassy. We're not sure what happened to the other two members of the original expedition. We assumed they're dead, but we know that a German man, Karl Bauer, survived. It took a lot of work, but we tracked him on a ship's manifest to Cuba, then from Havana to France. It looks like he arrived in Europe last spring and has been wreaking havoc ever since."

"Do we know what he wants?" Jackson asked.

Phil said, "It's not clear. He left a cousin behind when he left." Looking at his notes, he said, "Leon Bauer. He was very forthcoming about his cousin. He said he was a right-wing nationalist but wasn't violent. Doesn't think he could kill anyone but would take advantage if they died."

Billy said, "Leon Bauer? We hired him right after Big Thunder. I remember vetting him for access to sensitive computer systems. If his cousin wishes us harm, he'll have an inside track."

Phil said, "He didn't seem very close to his cousin, didn't like his politics. The only reason he was with him when Big Thunder caught them was because Karl bought the tour tickets for a girl who stood him up, and they were nonrefundable."

Billy thought, *the difference is a White guy's cousin would help you move. On the rez, your cousin would help you move a body.* What he said aloud, though, was, "Just to be safe, maybe we don't give this cousin the keys to the kingdom. We should transfer him to a less sensitive area."

Phil replied, "Okay, frame it as a promotion with a raise; we don't want him damaging anything on his way out or copying data for his cousin."

Kyle said, "I remember Karl Bauer. He was the only available French speaker we had. I got a bad vibe from him, but there was no reason to keep him from joining. I asked him why he wanted to go, and he said to go home to Germany. We offered him a position as our European contact."

Katy asked, "Did he realize that there was no Germany in 1792? It was all principalities and vassal states under the Holy Roman Emperor."

"I assume he knew his country's history. He had a college degree, a civil servant of some kind," answered Kyle.

Phil continued, "The rumors started in France, where he spread the news about Napoleon. There are stories about a German with a small device that showed photos and movies. He didn't stay in France for long. He was posing as a noble, which wasn't popular. Now we have reports of him in Vienna at the court of Francis II. We're not sure of his agenda, probably money and power. If it involves uniting Germany decades ahead of schedule, that may work in our favor."

"How so?" asked Jackson.

Mary answered this one. "If a united Germany aligns with Britain, it stabilizes Europe. They're all afraid of revolution. A good trade relationship could benefit Changleska. The German states have a lot of raw materials and skilled craftsmen."

Katy interjected, "It would support the monarchies. That is what the Coalition War was about. Monarchies in this time support slavery. They'd oppose Changleska."

"This is very complicated," said Jackson. "Is there anything we can do about Karl Bauer? Maybe we can sic Anna May on him." Everyone laughed.

To get more information, they needed people on the ground. Following the discussion, a proposal to fund a European expedition was approved. There were many trade reasons to go to besides intelligence. Mary pointed out that France might formally recognize them by the time they arrived, therefore, they ought to send a full embassy staff. From there, send an envoy to the court of the Holy Roman Emperor and perhaps meet with Karl and get answers directly.

Everyone left the meeting with more questions than answers, the situation unresolved.

=..=

There was less drama when the papal delegation arrived than with the envoys for the First Summit. With more passengers arriving regularly, the Oacoma port authorities had streamlined their process. Father Murphy and a few other local priests greeted them at the dock and accompanied them to Omímeya. The shuttle driver made the usual detour around Chamberlain to show the buildings, houses, stores, and the hospital. The sight of streetlights and paved roads, with the few cars sharing the road with horses and wagons, surprised them all.

Although the papal delegation had heard stories and even seen pictures, nothing compared to the reality. By the time they pulled up to Omímeya, they were in full culture shock. When the twenty-five delegation members entered the lobby, they looked around with quiet awe. Even Bishop Durand seemed momentarily struck by the uniqueness of Omímeya's architecture. The servants and soldiers stood silently while the Cardinal and Bishop spoke softly to each other. The hotel's senior staff greeted the group and got everyone checked in promptly.

Cardinal de Solís s black robe, trimmed in red, marked his rank clearly, even without the full regalia packed in the luggage behind him. The attendants stayed with the luggage, which included a velvet-wrapped altar chest and a cedar case bearing the cardinal s vestments. His valet remained close, clearly mistrusting the bellman who offered to take the cart to the room.

Cardinal de Solís's black robe, trimmed in red, marked his rank clearly, even without the full regalia packed in the luggage behind him. The attendants stayed with the luggage, including a velvet-wrapped altar chest and a cedar case bearing the cardinal's vestments. His valet remained close, clearly mistrusting the bellman who offered to take the cart to the room.

Mary was surprised by the meticulous attention to detail Rose and Jenny had put into the visit. They gave the Cardinal the best suite, usually reserved for high rollers. The large master bedroom led to a glass-enclosed jacuzzi with a river view. There was another smaller bedroom, a kitchenette, a living room, and two bathrooms. The suite included all the usual amenities, down to little bottles of shampoo and lotion. Rose even stocked the minibar at no charge. A smaller suite was arranged for the bishop, with comfortable rooms for the other priests in their party. The ten soldiers and five servants were placed in shared rooms on another floor. Rose had told Mary earlier she was glad she had resisted pressure to use the high roller suite for emergency housing. It was still in excellent condition, unlike the rooms used during the winter, which had yet to fully recover. Besides actual damage, even normal wear and tear was hard to repair without twenty-first-century materials.

Upon arriving at his suite, while his valet attended to the luggage, Father Murphy inquired, "Will this do, Your Eminence?"

The cardinal responded, "It's very luxurious, more than I had envisioned. Reading Don José de Esquivel's reports had not fully prepared me."

Father Murphy presented the welcome packet to Cardinal de Solís. Drawing from prior correspondence, it contained a detailed agenda for the forthcoming two weeks, outlining meetings, receptions, ceremonies, and tours. Father Murphy assured the Cardinal it could be adjusted easily. Father Murphy added a comprehensive medical evaluation for the senior members of the delegation, emphasizing how early detection and advanced medicine could prolong health and life. The Cardinal reluctantly agreed.

Father Murphy suggested, "Please take some time to settle in, perhaps refresh yourself with a shower or change from your travel attire." When they first arrived, Julian, the Guest Manager, had provided a tour of the suite, demonstrating the use of the bathroom facilities. The cardinal appeared surprised, unaccustomed to the concept of frequent showers. "When you're ready, Your Eminence, please call me using this phone." He indicated the device on the side table next to the suite's couch. "I'll get your call on my phone and will be nearby to escort you to the reception room, where you and the others will meet Mrs. Landrau."

Cardinal de Solís asked, "This woman, Mary Landrau, she truly leads Changleska, elected akin to the American president? And she is Catholic?"

"Yes, Your Eminence. Her title is Chair. She is one of seven Executive Councilors, but she wields considerable authority." He continued, "She is an intelligent and strong woman and has been my parishioner for fifteen years. However, her Catholic faith doesn't overtly influence her political decisions. Changleska, like the United States, maintains a clear separation between church and state."

Reflecting, the Cardinal acknowledged, "There are many differences here, perhaps more than can be bridged, but I shall endeavor to remain open to all I hear and see during my visit." He gestured towards the desktop phone. "So, I can speak to you through this, and you will hear me in another room?"

"Indeed, Your Eminence." Father Murphy produced his mobile phone. He demonstrated how to use the hotel phone, writing his number beside it to call his mobile. "Some phones, like this one, are portable and can communicate across many miles." He added, "They function within the area encompassed by the Circle that was brought back in time. They are working on increasing how far they work, but it will take many years to make any real advancements."

The cardinal's expression grew serious. "Father Murphy, I have read all your letters. Do you truly believe this phenomenon is a miracle from God, free from any malevolent or satanic influences?"

"With all my heart, Your Eminence," Father Murphy affirmed. "This is what we hope to demonstrate during your visit."

The Cardinal quoted from 2 Corinthians, "And no wonder, for Satan himself masquerades as an angel of light." He added, "We shall see what we see, then decide."

Mary was nervous. Meeting a cardinal was a big deal, and so much was riding on this. She knew women leaders were unheard of in this time. She dressed carefully for the initial meeting at the Welcome Reception, saving her elaborate dress and sash of the office for the opening ceremony scheduled for tomorrow. Mary wore a long brown skirt and a simple blouse. She covered her short hair with a colorful scarf and wore her nice jewelry. Hair coverings had evolved from a health prevention measure to avoid lice, to being fashionable, with many popular styles.

It wasn't only the cardinal who concerned her. There was Bishop Durand, the French Jesuit scholar with extensive missionary experience. Missionaries had a history of problematic interactions with Indigenous cultures during this era. The briefing materials provided little information on Monsignor Fitzpatrick, but she hoped his Irish heritage might offer a more favorable perspective. Her greatest concern was Father Ignacio López, a Dominican traditionalist known for defending orthodox practices. Phil's observers had reported him stating that the devil was responsible for Changleska's existence and that his mission was to expose Satan's influence. Conversely, she felt hopeful about Brother Luca Moretti, the Jesuit scientist interested in Changleska's technology and medicine, who intended to report on scientific advances to Rome.

Mary waited in her office until she received a text from Rose saying the full delegation had arrived and was drinking wine and beginning to sample the hors d'oeuvres offered by the circulating servers.

Upon her entrance, the seated Changleskans rose, and many gave the little Changleska salute, a head nod with hand on heart. She approached Cardinal de Solís, who wore a scarlet cassock, matching short cape, and a large gold cross. His red *zucchetto* (skullcap) completed the ensemble. Mary knelt and kissed his ring. "Welcome to the Changleska Coalition, Your Eminence."

Cardinal de Solís extended his hand graciously. "Thank you, Madame Chair. It is an honor to be here." After a few moments, "Madame Chair, I am intrigued by the governance structure of Changleska. A female leader is quite...unconventional."

Mary smiled, choosing her words carefully. "Indeed, Your Eminence. Changleska strives to embody principles of equality and meritocracy, values we hold dear."

The cardinal's gaze was thoughtful. "Such ideals are admirable, though they present challenges to tradition."

"We believe," Mary replied, "that our diversity makes us strong." She thought, *that may be a well-worn cliché in my time, but that doesn't make it less true.*

"A perspective worth considering. I look forward to learning more during my stay."

Mary inclined her head respectfully. "We are eager to share our ways with you, Your Eminence, and to learn from your wisdom as well."

Their conversation continued, delving into topics of governance, faith, and the blending of tradition with progress, each seeking to understand the other's world. Afterwards, Mary thought it went well, despite the glaring from Father López. The scheduled tours would not only highlight what twenty-first-century knowledge could bring, but they would visit the school set up at Two Elks Camp by Father White Bear, the Lakota priest who headed the museum and school that blended Lakota tradition with Catholic teachings. Mary began to hope. Maybe this would work after all.

Chapter Twenty-One
Rose

ROSE SAW THE LIGHT at the end of Omímeya's financial tunnel. Spreadsheets were her happy place. Even when filled with red, they didn't stress her out, as long as everything was in place and added up correctly. She could examine deficits and devise plans to address them. Preparing reports for tomorrow's board meeting, Rose made short- and long-term projections and reviewed the investments made in over eighty small businesses and corporations. Two had promising futures. The Healing Hoop Pharmaceutical Company was already turning a small profit, which was reinvested into research and development. It would be years before Omímeya would see dividends, but they didn't need more funding. Unity Petroleum was currently a money sinkhole. Returns might not come for a decade, but they would be substantial once the business became fully operational. Many of the businesses to which Omímeya had provided start-up funds, in which it held a twenty-five percent stake, were beginning to pay off. Making twenty-first-century products with eighteenth-century resources wasn't easy, but there was a ready market. Between St. Louis and New Orleans, everything those companies produced sold as fast as they could make it. Items like fountain pens, metal safety razors, coffee percolators, matches, barometers, washing machines, and treadle sewing machines were incredibly popular. The biggest challenges were gearing up production and overcoming labor shortages, but these new enterprises were making money hand over fist.

Sales of items they brought with them, either stored in their warehouse or bought by Kyle during the first days after Big Thunder, brought in a quick infusion of cash. However, once those items were gone, they were gone. Currently, their biggest source of income came from any of the trading posts in which they owned a percentage. Most of the money came from furs. There was a ready market, and Indigenous people were flocking to Changleska to bring their furs. The trading posts offered fair payment, with any unused funds added to ID cards that could be used anywhere in Changleska. They had set strict limits on beaver fur, understanding that, in their own history, the overharvesting of beavers during the fur trade era had led to ecological imbalances, including altered waterways and the decline of wetland habitats.

Omímeya owned only one farm in the area before Big Thunder but purchased more afterward, and sales of agricultural products were becoming a reliable source of income. The transition from farming that relied on pesticides and chemical fertilizers to regenerative farming was difficult. Lowered production resulted, and they might never achieve the same yields the old world had, but the yields they had were much higher than anything from this time.

Even the hotel was emerging from the red. Last winter, the board had discussed converting Omímeya into a government office building with apartments, as the number of paying hotel guests had dwindled so much since Big Thunder. All the new recent guests prompted them to abandon those plans. The First Summit last spring and the papal delegation that left the previous week provided a welcome influx of cash. Omímeya was even attracting tourists. The Reign of Terror in France caused wealthy nobles to flee in droves. Some went to Europe, a few to Canada or to the French colonies in the Caribbean where they owned plantations. Tales of Omímeya s beauty, luxury, and technological wonders drew those who could afford it. Some came to the resort for medical care, though most of those stayed at the less expensive inns near the hospital.

After reviewing the numerous zeros in the projections for the next five to ten years, Rose realized Omímeya would soon become not only the wealthiest corporation in Changleska, but potentially one of the biggest in the world. Although the new law limited her salary to no more than five times the lowest-paid employee's salary, bonuses were profit-based, and she'd soon be one of the wealthiest women in the world, excluding royalty. Rose wasn't sure how she felt about this. She believed many of the old world's problems stemmed from wealth disparities. The most affluent one percent were often directly responsible for environmental degradation and social injustices, all in the name of profits. Now she was becoming a member of the class she had spent her life despising. After Big Thunder, she was grateful that the billionaires who were part of the casino consortiums had funded all the improvements and supplies at Omímeya. The Lower Brule Reservation was small, and without that funding, the casino would've been tiny. Having all the resources to prepare for every possible doomsday scenario had saved their lives and given them the means to stand up to the eighteenth-century world. Those resources would help them create a future different from her old one. Rose wondered whether she was up to the task of utilizing all this wealth to do great things. Or would she get sucked into the delusions of the ultrarich and become self-serving? Still, all the wealth in the world didn't excuse her from the daily grind.

Even with fewer guests, Rose still had hotel issues to manage. Jenny was a big help, along with Linda Gagnon, Rose's administrative assistant, but there was still plenty to do. Jenny was new to hospitality, originally hired as the event coordinator.

At their regular weekly meeting, Rose noticed Jenny looked tired and wan. Rose no longer paid attention to human resource guidelines about keeping professional distance from subordinates. She asked, "Is everything okay? I know Henry moved in. How's that going?"

"It's an adjustment," Jenny smiled. "Can't wear pants anymore. He wants to choose my clothes now."

Rose didn't like the way Jenny laughed it off with, "Just a man of his time." *Controlling a woman's wardrobe was hardly harmless*, she thought.

She asked gently, "And how's the religion issue going?"

Softly, Jenny answered, "I want to go to temple with the new group that's meeting. I wasn't religious before, but since Big Thunder, spirituality feels more real. But Henry wouldn't like it."

Rose had known many women in abusive relationships, including her own mother. This had all the signs: his controlling behavior, her excuses. But she wasn't sure what she could or should do.

"If you ever want to talk about it," Rose said, "I'm here. Not just as your boss, but I hope also as your friend."

"Thank you. Now, about that laundry issue..."

=..=

The following day, the Omímeya Board of Directors convened for their monthly meeting. Present were Rose, Phil, Kyle, Billy, and Facilities Manager Wayne Becker. Typically, Wayne remained quiet during these sessions, focusing on maintaining the geothermal plant and facility operations without twenty-first-century materials. Today, however, he had items on the agenda.

"I've finally caught up enough to assess our long-term energy needs," Wayne began. "After discussions with Rich and the infrastructure team, we've identified an opportunity. Historically, Nikola Tesla's work wasn't fully utilized, but we can change that."

"What are you proposing?" Kyle asked.

"Tesla designed a bladeless turbine using smooth discs to harness energy from fluids like steam," Wayne explained. "With our geothermal resources, integrating such a turbine could efficiently convert steam into electricity, potentially boosting our energy output."

"You're suggesting we use this turbine to improve power generation?" Kyle inquired.

"Exactly," Wayne confirmed. "Its simple design and capability to handle geothermal steam make it a promising addition. Rich says the dam will last another couple of decades. With our growth inside the loop, like the medical school, campus, and all the new buildings, we'll need more energy soon."

"It can't be that easy," Phil interjected.

"While the Tesla turbine has potential," Wayne acknowledged, "its efficiency in large-scale applications hasn't always matched traditional turbines. However, with modern materials and design improvements, it could be valuable for our energy infrastructure."

"Do you have a cost estimate?" Rose asked. "If it's labor or materials we have, fine, but anything requiring hard currency is problematic."

"For the electric conversion," Wayne replied, "it won't need many external resources but will put a big dent in our 3D printer stock."

"For plastics," Kyle added, "we're working on polylactic acid (PLA), a biodegradable polymer from fermented plant starches like corn or sugar pulp, but it's likely a year or two away. Metal printer stock is more complicated."

"On the topic of Tesla," Wayne continued, "we could explore his concept of wireless energy transmission to power our outposts along the Mississippi."

"Wireless energy? How would that work for us?" Kyle queried.

"Tesla envisioned transmitting power without wires, using methods like resonant inductive coupling," Wayne explained. "Implementing such a system could allow us to deliver electricity to remote locations without laying extensive infrastructure."

"Why is that better?" Phil asked.

"It reduces our reliance on physical cables, conserving copper and steel," Wayne responded. "They're also vulnerable to storm damage or sabotage. It also allows rapid deployment of power to new or mobile units without constructing traditional power lines."

"Are there any security concerns?" Phil inquired.

"There's a slight risk over wired systems," Wayne admitted. "Someone could theoretically intercept transmissions if they had not been properly secured. We'd need an encryption system for protection."

"I want to see your protection plan before I sign off," Phil stated, "but the other Tesla project for the geothermal plant seems doable."

"I need a budget, including the amount of hard currency required," Rose added.

"Understood," Wayne replied. "I'll bring back details for next month's meeting."

"Speaking of hard currency deficits," Billy interjected, "when can we start getting gold or other metals from the mines we sent expeditions for?"

"At least a year," Rose sighed. "There's another idea. Our historical knowledge shows gold will soon be discovered in northern Georgia, near Cherokee settlements. This discovery will lead to an influx of settlers and increased pressure on Cherokee lands. If we were to inform the Cherokee leadership about this and the Trail of Tears, they could secure resources to strengthen their position against forced relocation."

"Sounds more like a Changleska project than one for Omímeya," Phil observed. "How does it help us?"

"Because it's in the US, Changleska must consider political implications," Rose explained. "Omímeya, as a private corporation, could partner with the Cherokee, where they extract the gold, and we could get a percentage for providing information and mining plans. It would cost us virtually nothing. This could provide Omímeya with gold while empowering the Cherokee to use their land's resources before it's stolen, and they are thrown off."

Billy remarked, "Won't finding gold increase settlers' hatred toward the Indians?"

"Yes, there's a risk," Rose conceded, "if our involvement becomes known. We must be discreet. Also, we'd need to spread cash around to avoid trouble."

"Do you think this could prevent the Trail of Tears?" Billy asked hopefully.

"I don't know," Rose admitted, "but if the Cherokee have resources, it'll help. If people receive warnings, changes can happen. Elliot sent copies of broken treaties with the first expedition. It's the same with us. In fact, changing history to protect Indigenous sovereignty is core to Changleska."

=..=

Rose wanted to do more things with her kids, but finding the time was hard. She wished for more quality moments, instead of constantly feeling rushed. The girls were home this weekend, so she took them to Chamberlain to shop for clothes and shoes. The girls were growing fast, and Rose wanted a few new things. Last month, she'd tried a spa day with the girls, but that didn't go well—none of them were the spa type. Hopefully, shopping would go better. Afterward, they planned to visit the new pizza place in Chamberlain. With homegrown tomatoes, Italian spices, and locally produced mozzarella finally available, everyone was eager for pizza after going without for so long. She'd even bring some back for Luke and Jackson.

Before Big Thunder, shopping had meant trips to Walmart or Target in Pierre or Sioux Falls. Now, stores like Family Dollar thrived by buying and selling used clothes and household items. Bomgaars, previously the area's largest farm and ranch supplier, expanded their clothing section by stocking locally produced garments besides the usual ranch items.

The new law allowed any business owner who lived outside the Circle ninety days in which to file for ownership and form a corporation with employee shares and a viable business plan. After one year, the business had to be self-sustaining, or its ownership would revert to Changleska. Over a year later, most businesses still operated, pivoting to specialty goods or small-scale manufacturing. Larger businesses became trading posts, but few restaurants remained. With no large central stores, shopping required multiple stops. Rose now understood why she rarely shopped; it was too time-consuming. She couldn t fathom why people found this enjoyable, although it felt different knowing she could afford anything they wanted. Still, prices for new items were eye-watering.

A couple more stops were necessary. They needed bras and underwear, items difficult to find and expensive. They also planned to visit a shop specializing in moccasins and shoes. At Bomgaars, each bought several pairs of sturdy, locally made indigo hemp culottes. These wide, calf-length garments were becoming fashionable, allowing freedom of movement for riding and work while fitting the modesty mores of the era. Rose appreciated their wide cuts and adjustable drawstring waistbands, ideal for her weight fluctuations and the girls' growth. She also bought Carhartt work pants for Luke and Jackson, carefully choosing sizes from the measurements she'd brought. These new Carhartts closely resembled those from her original time, made of canvas dyed yellow-brown, complete with loops and pockets. They had recently entered the market at premium prices.

When they arrived at Kent's Trading Post, a former Family Dollar, they saw it had hitching posts installed in the parking lot. Horses, wagons, bicycles, and various motorized rigs were parked, some looking distinctly Mad Max-like. Beside them, a harried mother was getting her baby strapped into the car seat in front of a horse-drawn wagon, loading her purchases in the back, and trying to keep her four-year-old little girl from running off.

Suddenly, the child darted toward them, and the mother yelled anxiously, "Alyssa, get back here right now!"

Both Gift and Kimi walked toward the girl, Kimi grabbing her hand and returning her to her grateful mother. But she abruptly stopped, grasping Alyssa s hand tightly as a distant rumble of thunder echoed, despite there being only a few clouds in the sky. Rose felt a shift in the air, a prickling sensation. Kimi looked stricken. She helped get the little girl loaded up. After quietly speaking to the girl s mother, who looked perturbed and angry at her words, Kimi returned to the car, visibly upset, and refused to discuss the incident. A gloomy pall settled over them for the remainder of the trip. They enjoyed the pizza, though Rose missed white flour. Today s flour was not as finely ground, and since chemical bleaching produced white flour, it was the best they were likely to get.

The next day, the girls were in their room beading. One of the local shops specialized in beads. They had glass seed beads recently imported from Bohemia, and they bought a nice collection in vibrant colors. Rose was in the kitchen, looking through the cupboards, wondering whether she should cook or have someone at Red Oak drive down a food order. They didn't normally deliver food. *Sometimes it's great to be the boss.* Just then, everyone's phone let off a loud alarm-type ring. Rose picked up her phone and saw an Amber Alert. She hadn't seen one since before Big Thunder.

Kimi walked into the kitchen with her phone, a stricken and horrified expression evident on her face. "It's her! It's her!" she gasped through tears. Gift trailed behind, looking troubled.

"It's who?" Rose asked, suspicion arising as she looked at the photo on the phone.

"The little girl who ran over from the wagon yesterday. Her name was Alyssa."

"This is awful. It says here she disappeared yesterday, probably in a wooded area near her house. Is this something you felt a warning about?"

"Yes. I saw her fall into a deep hole. Not exactly saw, but felt. I didn't know where or when. I tried to warn her mom, and told her to watch her, to be careful around holes, but she didn't believe me. I should have done more," Kimi wailed, shoulders shaking. Gift put an arm around her but didn't speak right away.

"It's not like I choose when it happens," Kimi said, frustrated. "It's strongest with storms or when someone's in danger, but sometimes it's just noise."

Gift nodded. "Maybe it's like weather too. The pressure builds, then something cracks open."

Kimi was quiet. "I've started tracking the days, the feelings, the weather. Trying to make sense of it." She didn't say it out loud, but sometimes she felt like thunder watched her back.

Rose didn't know whether the girl was still alive, but Kimi's urgency left no room for hesitation. Even if it was too late, the family deserved answers.

"I'm calling Jackson," Rose told the girls. "He has police connections; he'll know what's happening."

Jackson had spent the weekend sleeping in his office suite, as he often did when the girls were home. When Rose called and explained the situation, he responded without hesitation, "I'll be right there."

When Jackson walked in a short time later, he approached Kimi, who was curled up on the couch with Gift, her face tear-streaked, staring at her phone.

"Sweetie," Jackson said gently, "we're going to find Alyssa. I understand you can help. This is a good thing."

"But I should have done more. Why do I get warnings if they don't help?"

"They helped when you prevented all those deaths at the game last summer."

"But Gift got shot."

"She saved your life. I don't doubt your messages come from God. Let's listen and figure this out, okay?"

Rose was surprised by Jackson openly referencing his religious beliefs. She knew he had been raised Baptist, though he had attended the Sundance ceremony with her, viewing it more culturally than spiritually.

Jackson continued, "I talked to Kenneth Harris, the sheriff, on the way here. Alyssa was missing all day yesterday before being reported. She lives on the same property as her grandmother and walks between the two houses regularly. Her parents thought she was at grandma's, and grandma thought she was at home. They didn't realize she was missing until almost dark."

"Why wasn't the Amber Alert sent earlier?" asked Rose.

"It didn't occur to anyone. There aren't many houses nearby, and they assumed she was lost in the woods rather than abducted. People don't carry their phones like before, and no one knew if the Amber Alert software even worked."

"But Kyle used the Emergency Alert system right after Big Thunder."

"Once someone thought of it and contacted Kyle, the alert went out immediately. It was mainly to recruit more volunteers for the search at first light. A smaller group had been searching throughout today."

"The girls and I can go. We can go now."

"The sheriff doesn't want more people lost. The farm is on the circle's edge, a heavily wooded and wild area. They already have many volunteers and drones out searching. We can join at first light, but for now, we can try something else."

Jackson opened his laptop on the kitchen table, booting up Google Earth—the full software program unavailable to the public—and zoomed into the area. He motioned Kimi over. Jackson called the sheriff, explained their approach, and asked about search progress. The sheriff seemed skeptical about Kimi's insight but was willing to try anything. Jackson pointed to their current search area on the map.

"They're looking in the wrong place," Kimi exclaimed.

"Where should they look?" Jackson asked.

"Northwest. They need to find a big tree struck by lightning. She's in a hole at the bottom of that tree. There aren't any trees on this map, Jackson. She's in a wooded area."

"This Google map was made before Big Thunder. Nearly two hundred years changed the landscape; trees were cleared for farming, waterways altered. The map is close, but not exact."

"Will the sheriff change direction?"

After a brief, heated exchange, Jackson turned back to Kimi. "They're using a grid search protocol. Your area is outside the grid, but the sheriff agreed to send a small group to check. You can help tomorrow."

"But tomorrow will be too late," Kimi said, tears streaming again.

About an hour later, after dark had fully settled, everyone's spirits were low. Volunteers would soon head home. Then Jackson's phone rang.

"It's Harris, relaying from radios—the cell service is spotty. The team sees a larger tree with smaller ones around it. Does it sound right, Kimi?"

She closed eyes. "Is there a creek nearby?"

The message was relayed. "Yes, there is. Can you tell us more?"

"No, just the hole. She's in a hole." Kimi clenched her fists, her expression hopeful.

Minutes passed like hours before another call came.

"They found her! She's alive, barely, but alive. She fell into a four-foot hole. It had leaves and pine needles which helped keep her warm."

The room erupted with screams, cheers, and tears.

"You did it," Gift said.

"No, the Thunder Beings did it," Kimi smiled, but only for a moment. Deep down, she still felt it. The shadow was pressing closer. The real danger hadn't revealed itself yet.

Chapter Twenty-Two
Jamal

JAMAL STILL FELT the pain and loss of Nels every day, but in the two months since his return to New Orleans, the pain was receding bit by bit. Responsibility and hard work helped, but he longed for the old days when he could escape his feelings by watching movies and playing video games. So many people depended on him now, not only Benjy or even his crew, but everyone who relied on his engineering projects, whose success or failure often hinged on his decisions.

He vividly recalled the first day of his return. As the captain handled the ship and cargo, Jamal went to report. He needed directions, as the C&C had moved from a tent to a brick building clearly still under construction, though the bottom floor was functional.

Jamal approached the office he'd been directed to, thinking, *I hope I remember all the military protocol.*

He approached the officer behind the desk, came to attention, gave the Changleska salute, saying, "Private Jamal Alston reporting from the Boston Expedition, sir."

He immediately noticed the rank bars Lieutenant Mateo Rodriguez had been promoted to captain. Jamal remembered him as a combat engineer who had been at a Chamberlain National Guard training during Big Thunder. His entire family had left behind the Circle. Jamal had worked closely with him on *Endeavor*'s maiden voyage, helping to wrestle many steam engine issues.

Captain Rodriguez looked up from his laptop. "I've read your reports, or at least some of them. Outstanding work. Where is Nels Hanson, the medic?"

"Died of dysentery aboard the ship about a month ago."

"I'm very sorry to hear that. I know you were close." It was all Jamal could do to keep from crying.

"First stop is IT. They're still in the big house until the upstairs here is finished. You can sync with NewNet and upload your reports to MilNet. Then, check in with medical. Tomorrow, after I've read your full reports, we'll meet again to debrief. Do you need anything right away?"

"Yes, sir," Jamal replied hesitantly, unsure how his request was going to be received, but plowed ahead. "Nels and I rescued an orphan boy named Benjy, eight years old, from being sold into a brothel. I'd like to adopt him. I know I'm young, active duty, and single, but I can manage him alongside my duties."

Captain Rodriguez smiled warmly. "Lots of adopting orphans happening around here lately. We have the paperwork down. You'll need to make an appointment with MFRS, and they'll help get you squared away." Seeing Jamal's puzzled expression at the acronym, he explained, "That's Military Family Readiness System."

"There's one more thing," the captain continued. "We desperately need more officers. It says here," he glanced at his laptop, "you've been active duty for ten months now and were in your second year in college studying engineering when caught by Big Thunder."

"Yes, sir."

"We need more engineers. To lead projects, you need rank. Everyone's getting promoted faster than usual. With the online training, you could be an officer in four months. Interested?"

Jamal hesitated. He had slightly over a year left of his required service commitment and didn't need the military to become an engineer; a job at Omímeya awaited him. The idea of holding rank felt strange. He hadn't grown up with this kind of structure. His father used to say real leadership wasn't about titles, it was about showing up. But maybe that's what this moment was. Showing up, again and again, until the world changed.

Recognizing his hesitation, the captain pressed on: "We're doing important work here, especially combating slavery at Oca Landing. Also, as an officer with a family, you qualify for better housing."

Taking a deep breath, Jamal decided. "Yes, sir, I'll sign up to become an officer."

He remembered walking around Oca Landing that first day, amazed how much it had changed in eight months. Construction was everywhere. Omímeya had bought several neighboring properties, leaving the original one hundred acres of Oca Landing for the military base, Changleska administrative offices, and the Medical Corps clinic and headquarters. The Big House still housed IT, but Kevin Dillon, the General Manager hired by Omímeya, was building a large mansion on the neighboring property. Although people discussed him as a potential governor, his responsibilities managing Omímeya's extensive business interests might create a conflict of interest. Who the new governor might be when the treaty was signed was a source of intense speculation.

Jamal bid farewell to Eli Whitney on that first day. *Endeavor* was docked with room for him and a couple of gunsmiths they brought from Boston. They were going to the St. Louis area, to Niokaska where the new rifle manufacturing plant had been constructed. On the westbound journey, Eli and Jamal had worked on new rifle designs with the gunsmiths. Since there could be no communication with Changleska, they thought it would be interesting to see how the new rifle models might differ. Despite spending a lot of time together, Jamal and Eli had acted more like colleagues than friends. Jamal wasn't sure whether he'd made Eli uncomfortable because he was Black, or gay, or both, but he was happy that his mission had been successful, and that Eli was on his way. Stopping the cotton gin from being invented would disrupt the economics of slavery. They had reached an agreement with Eli that after a few years, he could patent the cotton gin and avoid being ripped off, as he'd been in his original timeline. Only plantations that didn't employ slaves could purchase a cotton gin.

Jamal qualified for family housing. Even though he hadn t completed the training, he was assigned officer quarters. He lucked out, as one unit was just finished right before he arrived. The small two-story townhouse featured a combined living room and kitchen downstairs and two small bedrooms upstairs. To Jamal s surprise, it had running water, a flush toilet, and a shower—unimaginable luxury after months aboard ship and in eighteenth-century Boston. He was told the solar-heated shower was usually lukewarm, but the communal bathhouse could provide hotter wood-fired showers and baths. The townhouse was so new he had to wait to move in until the paint dried; still, a few finishing touches needed to be done. Small, wavy-glass panes, set in a decorative pattern, formed the downstairs windows, but these windows couldn t be opened. They were on the waiting list for large clear panes for the upstairs, to be made by a recently opened glass factory. In the meantime, the empty frames had mosquito netting and wooden shutters. It was wired for future electrical service. Securing more electricity would be one of his engineering projects.

Currently, power from the Kaplan turbine went only to shops. The Big House and C&C relied on noisy generators and solar power banks.

Jamal found the MFRS office helpful. Most people called it Family Services. There was a lot of paperwork, including getting letters of recommendation from two people, one of which was Captain Rodriguez, another from a friend, Joe Dunning, the Sergeant from his original unit.

The paperwork asked for Benjy's surname, but Benjy said he didn't have one. Jamal suggested, "How does Benjamin Hansen Alston sound?"

Benjy's eyes widened. "But I'm still Benjy, right?"

"Of course," Jamal reassured him.

When they had the home visit, he was glad to be in officer housing where Benjy had his own room. A staff member interviewed Benjy without him being present.

At the last meeting, when the woman said she saw no reason the judge wouldn't approve the adoption, Jamal couldn't help a shout of joy, pumping his fist up. "Yes!" He picked up Benjy and swung him around, saying, "Now I'll be your dad, legally. The adoption will go through!"

"I never had a dad before. Yous can be my dad now?"

"Yes, but say you, not yous," Jamal couldn't help correcting him. "No more calling me Mr. Jamal, call me dad."

"Really?"

"Really."

Family Services said it would take a few weeks to process the application and get an appointment with a judge. They filed the paperwork in both New Orleans and the Brule County courthouse, making Jamal Benjy's legal parent anywhere in Changleska.

Secretly, Jamal imagined Benjy as his and Nels' biological child. Benjy's startling blue eyes reminded Jamal of Nels, while his dark curls and coffee au lait skin made him look a bit like Jamal. He was a striking child. Jamal was certain Benjy would grow into a beautiful man, just like Nels.

There was a school right there, and Benjy fit right in. Jamal loved the diversity of the students, freed slaves, children of the Guard, and employees. They didn't have enough teachers or space for anyone outside of those residing or working at Oca Landing, but the long-term goal was to train more teachers to have schools throughout the city.

Jamal was happy with his decision to become an officer. Now he was Second Lieutenant Alston, a 12A engineer officer. He completed the online Basic Officer Training Course in half the expected time. As Jamal settled into his new role and life at Oca Landing, responsibilities quickly piled up.

The pain of losing Nels never vanished completely, but he was beginning to feel hopeful. He'd made the right choices, and each day affirmed his new life as Lieutenant Alston, engineer and father.

=..=

It was a fine late October day, the humid heat of summer finally dissipating. Jamal wasn't sure if he would ever get used to the heat. He was raised in Chicago, went to college in Colorado, and was transported back in time to South Dakota. Whenever he'd visited the South with his family, there'd was always air conditioning. Despite the heat, he loved New Orleans. The area known as the French Quarter in his time had grown under Changleskan influence, with a busy open-air market, various shops, food stalls, and restaurants. One of the Guards was a New Orleans jazz fan and an amateur musician. Starting with playing music from his phone, other musicians joined in, and a new sound started developing. With more African and Caribbean influences, the new music was similar, but different. The sounds played all over the streets added to the vibrancy of the area.

The significant risks of malaria and yellow fever, during the warm season, still classified New Orleans as a hardship post eligible for hazard pay. There wasn't a vaccine, but they could mitigate the risks significantly. Jamal was happy to read on the bulletin board today that there had been no yellow fever that season. All the mosquito control methods seemed to be working. He still worried about Benjy getting sick. He considered moving to Chamberlain to be closer to the hospital, but he loved New Orleans and now considered it his home.

Although as an officer he was not supposed to socialize with enlisted, Jamal still spent time with his old friends when they could get away with it, like Dan Clemons from the trip to Boston and Joe Dunning from boot camp. They had long talks about Changleska, their old world versus the new one they were helping create.

One early evening, they sat in Jamal's backyard drinking beer. Joe said, "You know who's the real unsung hero of Changleska is?"

He paused to let the rhetorical question hang in the air.

"Kyle Ward."

"Who?" asked Jamal.

"Before Big Thunder, he was hired as the Emergency Preparedness Manager for Omímeya. Now he's the Resource Director. He's the reason we have radios, most of the tech we're using, and all those databases we're selling plans from."

"I never heard of him."

"Not surprised. Unless you work at Omímeya, you wouldn't know him. He's what you'd call a prepper on steroids. The casino consortium gave him a massive budget, and like a kid in a candy store, he stocked up on everything he could think of for any possible emergency. Not expecting time travel, I'm sure, but floods, earthquakes, EMPs, social unrest—he planned for all of it."

"You're right. Unsung hero. His foresight might be what saves us all."

They sat in silence for a moment, each imagining what it would have been like if they'd been dropped into 1791 unprepared. No radios, no tools, no guides, and no computer databases on how to do anything. It would not have been pretty.

Rumor was the Spanish would sign the treaty any day now. Some of the Spanish left, but many stayed, same with the French. Plantations that used slave labor still existed, although almost all now were on the east side of the Mississippi outside the city. Conflicts still arose, and incidents of vandalism. Any violent attacks resulted in such a disproportionate response; they stopped occurring. The word was out, 'don't fuck with Changleskans.' Many saw the writing on the wall and sold their plantations and moved to other places in the US friendlier to slave ownership. Suspicion of Changleska had diminished. People loved the new inventions flooding the markets, like safety pins and pencils with erasers. With treadle sewing machines, clothing was becoming less expensive. Agricultural output increased, at least among the places that used Changleskan recommendations. The Medical Corps were opening new clinics, training more people, and saving lives every day. In a little over a year, the world changed, and New Orleans was young and diverse enough to embrace change and thrive. The rest of the world, not so much.

=..=

Jamal had a long walk to the brickmaking and concrete workshop. He went to review their process and identify potential improvements. It was at the neighboring property, about three miles away from where he was. He probably should have canoed, but disliked water travel. In addition, he did not care for horses, so feet it was. He could smell the smoke from the kiln long before he arrived. The new kiln was bigger than he'd imagined, with smaller ones scattered about and clay pits dug along the river. The scent of fired clay and lime dust hung in the air. Several men were stacking bricks near a drying rack, and a small lime slaking pit bubbled nearby. Jamal looked in satisfaction at the sweat-slicked shirtless Black men, mostly former slaves, hard at work. Jamal knew that every man there was now free and received a decent wage. Most had probably contributed to the Freedom Assistance League fund to free even more enslaved people.

An older man with hands like gnarled roots was overseeing the crew, checking brick alignment with a practiced eye. "That one's not square. Start again," he barked, and noticed Jamal approaching. "You're the engineer the captain sent?" extending a hand. "Isaac. Been laying brick since before most of these boys were born."

Beside him, a younger man with brown curls, worn boots, and a smudge of soot across one cheek, looked up from a wheelbarrow of crushed materials.

"Francisco," he said with a nod. "We're trying something different from Portland cement."

Isaac said, "New but old. The Romans did this nearly two thousand years ago, but I hear you Changleskans have rediscovered the method after its formula had been lost. It's supposed to set underwater, even for wet foundations, but we don't have volcanoes around here, so I'm not sure why you're bothering."

Jamal knelt beside the wheelbarrow and sifted a bit of the powder through his fingers.

"This brick dust might work. You've got the ratio right?"

"Still testing," Francisco said. "About three parts brick dust to one part lime, but we're adjusting. The kiln temperature doesn't need to be as high as for Portland cement, closer to 900°C, which makes it easier on fuel, too."

Isaac added, "You never could get that kiln to go that high reliably. I heard you need to use that new oil coming from Caddo lands for it to work. I know about your Portland cement, another idea that is supposed to be better than brick."

"Portland cement is waterproof and solid, but its long-term use is polluting, since the kiln needs oil to run that high. You've considered other alternatives?" Jamal asked. "The databases have information about green cements. Did you read the materials we sent over?"

Francisco nodded. "We looked at fly ash and slag, but no coal means no fly ash. We must import volcanic pozzolana from the islands, so we're using crushed brick dust."

Jamal nodded thoughtfully. "Good approach. Let's also start collecting wood ash and experimenting with other natural pozzolans. Even partial substitutions can help reduce environmental impact."

Isaac chuckled. "Always the newfangled ideas with you engineers. My bricks don't crumble in the rain."

Francisco said, "With cement you can build taller and stronger. Bridges, very tall buildings, like they had in the future. Bricks won't cut it."

Jamal offered, "Roman cement works better for lining water pipes and cisterns. It has mild antimicrobial properties. We might combine it with terracotta for pipes, but we'll need faster production methods if we want to expand sewers and running water beyond Oca Landing."

After Jamal looked over their entire operation, he began thinking about how to improve the brick molds, maybe by using a foot-pedal press. The current method was slow and inefficient, involving a lot of stooping and manual labor. He'd check the patent database, see what designs were available, and come up with some recommendations later. One useful thing about the database was that it often included inventions that were never widely used, either because they were ahead of their time or because they were eventually replaced by something more practical. Sometimes, those forgotten interim steps were exactly what they needed, using the resources they had on hand. Reproducing twenty-first-century technology was difficult, but nineteenth- or twentieth-century solutions were often more achievable.

Afterward, he started walking home, thinking he should learn to use a canoe. Living on the river was how people got around. But the walk gave him space to think, and today, designs for better brickmaking filled his thoughts. He liked knowing he was making a difference.

A soft buzz in his pocket pulled Jamal's attention. He glanced at the mesh phone clipped to his belt. No towers, no satellites, just the small, silent hum of the cell network they'd built themselves. The mesh system had been expanded steadily, linking the few goTenna units they brought from the Circle with new repeaters built across the city. It wasn't the internet, no voice yet, but it was enough to send secure text messages across New Orleans and up the river.

The next day, he went back to his usual project: trying to get electricity not only for Oca Landing but also for the surrounding farms, workshops, and industrial areas belonging to Changleska or Omímeya.

His "office" was still a large tent next to the engineering building under construction. The tent walls didn't muffle the noise, so he often had to shout to be heard. He wore headphones while working to help him concentrate, though he worried his phone or Bluetooth headset would die.

It would happen sooner or later. Finite technology that couldn't be reproduced.

With the tent doors all open, there was plenty of light, but the construction dust still blew in and settled across his schematics. It was annoying. He had a meeting with Captain Rodriguez to go over what he'd come up with so far and to finalize plans. When they worked together, they were just two engineers, but the captain still insisted on using ranks instead of first names. He'd been military before Big Thunder, and the new Changleska Guard informality bugged him. They stood in front of the big table that took up most of the tent, pointing at sections of schematics and flipping through pages of notes.

Jamal said, "When I first started, I hoped we could power a city with Tesla towers and zero-point energy. I watched a movie about Tesla and Edison. It made Tesla look like a genius whose ideas got buried because Edison had more money. But now I find out his ideas weren't as solid as I thought."

Captain Rodriguez replied, "Not entirely. I'm sure we can integrate some of his concepts later. But for now, water turbines, steam engines, maybe solar thermal if we get lucky."

"It would've been nice to have lightning towers zapping power across the sky," Jamal said wistfully.

"At least you read up before you tried anything. I heard Omímeya built a prototype Tesla-style tower. Rumor is, you could light a bulb if you stood close to the coil and didn't mind a few nosebleeds. You'd need a dozen towers and a miracle to get more than a couple of kilowatts out of the thing."

"Too bad it was a bust," Jamal said. "I liked the idea. But we don't have the luxury to play with theories. I've already wasted too much time on it."

"We've got to stay with what we can build today, fix with hand tools, and count on to power a neighborhood. A whole city is still a long way off."

"We're building lead-acid batteries like it's 1880," Jamal added. "Too bad lithium mining's not practical. I read the Gaia Committee isn't approving lithium mines because they are too damaging to watersheds."

Rodriguez shook his head. "It's hard to rebuild technology under the Council's seven-generation rule. Everything must be safe for our grandchildren's grandkids. I get it. We don't want to repeat the old world problems, but sometimes I wish we had a few quick fixes."

"Looks like we're stuck with duct tape and elbow grease," Jamal said, only a little frustrated.

"You did good, looking into Tesla power," Rodriguez said. "Knowing what doesn't work is half the battle in figuring out what does."

Jamal smiled. Compliments from Captain Rodriguez were rare.

=..=

News of the many problems among some freed slaves surprised Jamal. He had assumed that once free, given good jobs and opportunities, everything would be all bread and roses. But it was not. He'd heard the complaints. Some freedpeople were listless, others defiant. More than a few had been caught stealing or refusing work. Some turned to drink or crime. A few men had already begun pimping, preying on the vulnerabilities of women who thought they had no better options. Streetwalking increased, though some women found work in brothels, where the Medical Corps could at least offer basic health screening. All the problems were growing. Freedom, Jamal was learning, didn't come with a manual. And it certainly didn't erase the scars, fears, or habits of captivity.

"Did you think it would all be parades and hymns?" his friend Dan Clemons asked him once, not unkindly.

He hadn't, but he hadn't expected how deeply the wounds ran, either. Or how quickly some people who claimed to be abolitionists began whispering about 'those people' becoming a problem.

Jamal had spent sleepless nights turning it over in his mind. You couldn't just free people, drop them into a foreign system, expect them to know how to navigate it, and blame them when they stumbled. No one had ever allowed them to handle their own money, sign a document, or offer an opinion in a meeting.

In times like these, he missed the robust antislavery online forums available in South Dakota. They had updates synched every few weeks, but it wasn't the same. The smaller group of the Freedom Assistance League at Oca Landing was swamped, freeing slaves and finding them jobs. Dealing with people who didn't want to work was not in their remit. After much discussion, a Freedpeople's Council was proposed. The freedpeople themselves would elect the Council's members, who would serve as both a bridge and a shield. Offering more help than the League offered, helping newly liberated individuals understand their rights and responsibilities, and giving them a voice in shaping policies that affected their lives. This would provide a place to raise concerns, organize mutual aid, mediate disputes, and preserve dignity under scrutiny. Unlike the Freedom Assistance League, it wasn't a charity; it was empowerment.

Now the Council was forming. Slowly, awkwardly, and beautifully. Elders among the freedpeople were stepping into leadership roles. Women taking part gave strong opinions that were listened to. Young men who'd once been field hands now stood as spokesmen. Of course, not everything went smoothly. Some still fell into crime, or refused help out of pride, or struggled with rage that couldn't find a target. But wasn't it true of every community? Freedom didn't mean perfection. It meant choices, and consequences, and the right to shape one's own path.

Jamal wished he had more time for these issues, but his engineering projects and Benjy left him with very little free time. But he knew these were problems that needed to be fixed now, so they wouldn't become entrenched social issues that would impact Benjy when he was grown. He wanted a world for Benjy where freedom and dignity weren't a privilege but a birthright. If Changleska meant anything at all, it had to begin there.

=..=

When Jamal was growing up, his parents were always active in his school despite how much they worked. Jamal tried to do the same with Benjy. Seventy children from preschool to high school age had enrolled in Oca Landing school. Older students most often served in apprenticeships. Those who could read studied "online," not exactly online without access to NewNet but using only a localized Wi-Fi signal from the Big House. Teaching modules downloaded from Khan Academy provided excellent education, including for adult learners. The school grouped students differently than by the grades Jamal was used to. They were grouped by ability, as many older students were not literate.

All the teachers were locals who used eighteenth-century teaching methods, such as rote memorization, oral recitation, and strict classroom discipline, with little focus on critical thinking or student-centered learning. Some practices, like corporal punishment, were stopped right away, but other outmoded attitudes had crept in. Modern concepts of boosting a child's self-esteem by using praise instead of criticism were unheard of in this era. Jamal shared his frustration with a few other twenty-first-century parents; however, most children were from this time, and their parents were delighted that their offspring received any education at all. They couldn't understand why paddling children was no longer allowed. At home, parents often swatted their kids to keep them in line.

Benjy was bright. Because of all the earlier help Jamal and Nels gave him, he was already reading, which put him in a group of older children. Jamal was unaware there was a problem, as Benjy never let other people diminish his cheerful disposition. He was picking Benjy up one afternoon, chatting with another parent, Cathy Anders, as the children were playing, and he heard the teasing from an older boy.

"Brothel boy, brothel boy, your mama was a whore, died of pox, then you sold cheap." Other boys chiming in, "Brothel boy, brothel boy."

Benjy looked stricken. Fists clenched, steeled himself, and replied with sharp defiance, "Yeah, my mama was a whore, but your daddy was the one who poxed her. Your daddy killed my mama 'cuz he can't keep his cock in his pants. He probably got the pox buggering sailors, or maybe sheep or goats."

Although horrified, Jamal had to admit Benjy had a great comeback. He hoped the trauma of growing up in a brothel was behind him—evidently not so much. But what bothered him was: who was this boy, and how did he know about Benjy's past? It's not like he ever discussed it with anyone, including teachers.

Jamal strode over to the exchange, as it looked like it might come to blows. His approach surprised the other boy, maybe eleven or twelve, with reddish hair, and lots of freckles.

"You, yes, you. What's your name?"

"Dan Gurney," he sputtered.

Benjy piped up, "Say, sir, don't you see his rank?" Oca Landing was a military base, and even children could read rank.

Jamal asked firmly, "And what are your parents' names, and where do they work?"

The boy now looked frightened. "Kevin and Ann Gurney, sir. My dad works in Steamworks and my mom works in Family Services."

That's where the little shit got the info, thought Jamal.

"Go home now. This isn't over," Jamal told him. Then took Benjy by the hand and went back to the schoolroom.

Miss Laurent was an attractive quadroon woman in her thirties. As someone with one-quarter Black ancestry, local society didn't permit her to teach except as a governess. She came from a wealthy family and was well-educated, but it was hard for her to marry because of her racial background, even in relatively progressive New Orleans. She liked her job, thought she was good at it, but couldn't fathom twenty-first-century parents, and Jamal Alston was one of the worst. Never had she seen a parent who hovered so much, much less a Negro man. She sighed when she saw him coming, Benjy in tow.

"What seems to be the problem?" she asked, trying to be pleasant.

"Daniel Gurney and other boys calling Benjy brothel boy, and worse."

"Is that all? Boys will be boys."

It was all Jamal could do to not yell at her, but he settled for rolling his eyes.

"Benjy," she said to him, standing beside Jamal. "Just say to the boys, 'Sticks and stones may break my bones, but names will never harm me.' Was that it, Lieutenant Alston?" she asked, smiling.

"In my time, we took bullying seriously. It was even grounds for suspension or expulsion."

Miss Laurent could never understand education from their old world, although she had access to a Kindle with many books on education.

"I'll speak to Daniel."

"Thank you."

The next day, Jamal made an appointment with Martha Tucker, the head of MFRS or Family Services. She was a civilian, middle-aged, a social worker with years of experience. The Guard didn't have enough people to staff all the positions needed and often placed civilians in noncombat roles. Jamal remembered her from Benjy's adoption; she seemed competent and caring.

"Lieutenant Alston, how can I help you today?" she asked warmly.

"I am very concerned about a breach of confidentiality that occurred with the adoption records of my son, Benjamin."

"Oh my, that does sound serious. We have strict rules on confidentiality."

"You should." First, Jamal told her what he overheard but didn't give Benjy's response. He pulled out his phone, reading the rules off MilNet on MFRS confidentiality, including consequences when disregarded.

"I promise I will investigate."

"No investigation is necessary. I heard the exchange myself, along with Mrs. Anders. The only question is what you are going to do with Mrs. Gurney. If she was in the Guard, she could face court martial."

"We are very short-staffed, especially with people from the old world. They have a perspective the locals don't. There must be an alternative you'd find acceptable."

"No," said Jamal harshly. "My child was harmed because your employee broke the law. You investigate all you want, but this will be addressed. I'd hate to see Captain Rodriguez dragged into this mess."

"No, you're right. We'll handle it ourselves. Give me a day or two, and I'll get back to you." Martha knew Alston was very close to the captain, both engineers, as close to friends as those of different ranks could be. She hated to lose Ann. What had Ann been thinking?

It turned out Ann hadn't been intentionally malicious, only careless, gossiping within earshot of her son. They didn't fire her but quietly reassigned her from Family Services to Logistics. Still, she carried a grudge and made sure everyone knew who was to blame. That resentment trickled down to her son, causing Benjy more trouble at school, though he never let Jamal see it.

Benjy loved Jamal fiercely. He never imagined life could be this good. Tolerating stupid boys and enduring taunts was a small price to pay. Those kids had no idea how lucky they were. There was promise in his future now, and he wasn't about to jeopardize it. Not for anything. Not if it might disappoint Jamal.

Chapter Twenty-Three
Mary

THE QUIET FAITH Mary held in the treaty's progress was cracking. Don Manuel de Godoy, the Plenipotentiary of the Spanish Crown with the authority to sign the treaty, had been at Omímeya for the last three weeks, finalizing the treaty terms and language. With the Circle Echo relay near Georgetown, the radio could reach London, and with fast couriers to Spain, they could consult with the Spanish king. Mary believed the signing was imminent, because all issues were resolved and no points remained for discussion, but de Godoy's repeated delays frustrated her, leaving her wondering why.

News of another skirmish at Fort Condor, where Spanish soldiers died, further unnerved her. The California Expedition had arrived months ago, building a fort and preparing to mine the gold fields. If Spain found out about the goldfields, it was unlikely they would give up California or Nevada, where there were more mines. They would likely keep the entire West Coast. Not only would that be a blow to the coalition of tribes Changleska was building, but Mary really wanted orange juice again.

The only hope was to sign the treaty before the Spanish heard about the group in California, but that was becoming more unlikely. Fort Condor had been given orders to maintain a low profile until the treaty was signed. However, with the military skirmishes, they would likely receive reports soon, and with them might come word that mining had begun.

Any delay risked the agreement they made feel tenuous. All this was on her mind when she sat down at a banquet with de Godoy and his entourage, as well as a few of the Executive Councilors and their spouses. Jackson had invited Rose, who didn't usually attend diplomatic meetings. When de Godoy mentioned he was going back to Spain soon, not wanting to risk a winter crossing, and would return in the spring to sign the treaty,

Mary nearly lost it. She knew what a risk waiting was; they had days or weeks at the most, not months.

She couldn't help it; she snapped. "Ambassador de Godoy, you must want to be back in your own bed very much to put your personal desires above your country's needs. We've already reached an agreement. We only need to sign it."

There was a gasp around the table. She had given a grave insult. A man might have been challenged to a duel who said the same thing. While Mary had learned from being faculty at a community college and chair of a small tribe to be diplomatic, she had never learned diplomacy and made a terrible error. Showing her frustration and insulting her guest, she might have thrown away the treaty at that very moment. But Rose, both to Mary's relief and annoyance at needing rescue, intervened.

"Ambassador de Godoy, I share Mrs. Landrau's frustration, but I'm sure she didn't mean to disparage your patriotism. Would you like to know why I'm frustrated with the delays?"

Of course, he had to nod affirmatively, keeping diplomatically quiet, probably still processing the insult.

"Money," Rose said simply.

"Money?" de Godoy questioned.

"Yes, each day the treaty is delayed causes Omímeya to lose money. While Spain also loses, Changleska loses the most." Then she took a casual bite of her food, chewing carefully, giving everyone a moment. "Omímeya has many small businesses which want to do business with Spain, and we know banks are waiting for the treaty to be signed before loaning funds. But that's not the main issue. Changleska has a big problem with the delay. Do you want to know why?"

"Please enlighten us, madam," de Godoy answered tersely.

"Because small businesses and people waiting for loans are people with little money who want to get rich. They are impatient, but like all people without riches, they are used to waiting. You know who isn't used to waiting?" This time, she didn't wait for a response. "The rich. Wealthy people are used to getting what they want when they want it. Changleska will not release the patents for our inventions to Spain and France until the treaty is signed. The banks won't release funds or make money from the interests from those loans. That means all the people who are going to make millions are waiting, and they have made their unhappiness known to Mrs. Landrau."

de Godoy seemed to calm down.

Rose continued, "I'm not sure if you have ever experienced disappointing a wealthy patron, but when they are upset, it is easy to pass on that frustration, even if it is not deserved."

Mary said contritely, "I hope you will accept my most sincere apologies. My tone and words were inexcusable."

He was put in the position of having to accept the apology.

Mary set aside her pride to act the part of a helpless woman. "Mrs. Chasing Hawk is correct. I'm being constantly harassed by powerful men asking why I can't get this treaty signed. I need your help. A delay will make things worse for me, and there is nothing for you to gain. Please reconsider leaving before you sign. We could set up a signing ceremony within a day or two, and you could still return before the storm season."

Perhaps driven by a man's need to be a rescuer, he acquiesced with a condescending sigh. In fact, wealthy interests weren't pressuring Mary. It'd been understandable; politics and money usually go hand in hand. The pressure came from the risks of what was happening in California being discovered.

They finally had a firm agreement for the treaty to be signed right away, thanks only to Spain's slow communication and Rose Chasing Hawk's intervention.

Mary could hardly believe it. Only a little over a year after Big Thunder, a tribe of reservation Indians and small towns had joined and created their own country, incorporating Indigenous sovereignty. They successfully bypassed the French and got the Spanish to sign over New Spain— everything west of the Mississippi River to the Pacific Ocean. The new border had less land than the original United States, with most of southern Texas, southern New Mexico and Arizona staying with Mexico, but they hung on to California as far south as San Diego. They now had a different future. But even more unbelievably, they had paid without gold. Instead, both France and Spain received valuable mine locations, technology transfers with major advances in science, medicine, agriculture, and industry. The US missed out on what would have been the Louisiana Purchase, losing the valuable port of New Orleans and the United States' future place as the world's superpower. Changleska created not only a rival, but an enemy, one with whom they shared a continent with.

They scheduled the signing ceremony for four days later, set to begin at 11:11 a.m. on November 11th, to mirror the exact time Big Thunder had struck on the fall equinox. The timing would mark the birth of their nation with numbers that added up to four, a sacred number in the Lakota tradition. Some called 11/11 an angel number and spoke of cosmic meaning. Mary dismissed that as superstition, but even she felt the weight of the moment.

Getting everything ready in four days for the formal signing ceremony and celebration afterwards would've been nearly impossible without all prior planning. The next day, she had a meeting with Billy Fast Dog to discuss security. Meeting him professionally was a bit awkward since he started dating her daughter. If things continued the way things were looking, they would be family, so she'd best get used to it.

Travis showed Billy in right on time. He stood uncertainly for a moment, nodded his head respectfully, saying, "Mrs. Landrau."

"Mary, in private, please."

He smiled briefly, then grew serious. "We have some real security issues. I've been reviewing everything with Jenny and Rose, but there're things we'll need confirmation from you for."

"Like?"

"Signing the treaty in the Council Chambers isn t a problem. We ve reserved 400 seats for vetted ticket holders, including diplomatic parties, visiting Europeans, Council members' families, and Committee chairs. Security will scan tickets when they come to the doors. The problem is with this Independence Ball you are holding. If it's open to the public it will invite trouble. We need to take the threats from Clyde Folsom's followers seriously. Much of his movement focuses on annexation. After we gain independence, and it s clear we ll never be part of the US, Folsom will lose supporters. It s likely they ll try to delay or disrupt the proceedings any way possible."

"What could they do?"

"Violence, bombs, or calling in bomb threats. Protestors could fill the ballroom."

"And you'd propose what?"

"That day, we should limit access to the Ball and the entire Omímeya grounds to ticket holders. Lines will be long at the checkpoint, but maybe we can open another line. Free tickets will still be open to anyone, but ordered online first-come, first-served."

"That would alleviate our overcrowding concerns, since the Big Bear room only holds 2,000, but I'm not clear how it would mitigate the security risks."

"Anyone would need a NewNet account to get a ticket. As far as IT knows, all accounts are still traceable. No one has hacked and created fake accounts. If people know they'll get caught, it reduces crime."

Mary asked, "This isn't everything. You and Rose could've done this without me. What do you need me to sign off on?"

"We shouldn't allow weapons. Make the entire event a weapon free zone."

"People will freak out. Everyone equates freedom with gun rights. We can't celebrate our independence and tell folks they can't bring their guns. Plus, are you going to search 2,500 people?"

"We have metal detecting wands from concerts. They haven't been used since Big Thunder. We're not taking anyone's right to carry away, only the right to carry to the Independence Ball."

"I'm not sure. How big of a risk is there?"

"If I were a fanatic wanting to stop the treaty being signed, I'd shoot the ambassador and probably you. Spain would probably withdraw."

"If I permitted this, how'd you go about it?"

"No weapons rules were common at concerts and public events in the old world. State clearly: no weapons allowed, there will be checks at the door. When they sign up for their tickets, they check a box saying they agree to no weapons."

"All weapons are too broad. Almost everyone carries a knife these days. The Spanish would be offended if they couldn't wear their swords. Make it no firearms instead."

Billy smiled. "I can live with that."

"Do we have time to pull this off? It's only three days away."

"The website is ready. Give the word and it will be live in minutes."

"You were pretty sure I'd agree?"

"Not much of a choice."

Mary nodded with resignation, and they parted.

=..=

The morning of the treaty signing broke cloudy and cold. A whisper of winter hinted at snow, which came early in the Dakotas. Mary was running behind; she not only had to dress in her ceremonial Council clothes but also had to get the rest of the family ready and out the door. They still arrived well over an hour early, but it was still nerve-wracking.

The Council Chamber had been transformed with bunting, banners, and commemorative art. The scents of sweetgrass and burning sage mingled with the faint tang of beeswax polish. Instead of the usual maps, the large wall screen displayed both nations' coat of arms in equal size. A deep red velvet cloth covered the table where the committee members usually sat, with the sacred pipe and Spanish silver crucifix side by side. In the middle was the document that would change the course of history: Articles of Peace, Recognition, and the Cession of New Spain. On two large parchments, inscribed in elegant calligraphy in both English and Spanish, the treaty sat, each copy bearing the same seals, signatures, and the solemn weight of history.

After the prayers and songs, a hush fell over the gathered audience. Mary stepped forward. She spoke clearly into the microphone, her words simultaneously airing live on the radio, appearing on the building's internal video screens, and being saved for future use.

"Today, we write not only words upon parchment, but hope into the future. May this treaty bind not only nations, but generations. Let it be a promise, not just of peace, but of partnership. Not just of recognition, but of responsibility. What we sign today must live beyond politics. It must live in how we treat one another, how we share this earth, and how we protect those who come after us."

She presented Ambassador de Godoy with a gold fountain pen made for this occasion, engraved with his name and the date. Later, she would send a similar pen to Charles IV, the King of Spain.

Don Manuel de Godoy, resplendent in a red velvet coat trimmed with gold lace, replied in accented but excellent English, "The Crown of Spain, in recognizing the sovereignty of Changleska and in ceding this land with honor, seeks peace, mutual prosperity, and a lasting friendship between our peoples."

They stood in front of the table, pausing for pictures before signing. A woman who looked very pregnant came forward with a large camera hanging from her neck. The other photographers politely gave her room. Then, she dropped the camera and raised a knife.

"Knife!" someone shouted, and Charles Archambault, a large man from the security staff, rushed forward, putting himself between her and the ambassador.

The woman was shouting, "This will end in blood, it will end in bloodshed!"

Charles tried to wrestle the knife away from her, but she wasn't aiming at the ambassador. She was trying to stab her own stomach. As he reached for her, the knife came down toward the top of her belly. A faint popping sound was heard, and blood splattered everywhere. Mostly over Charles, but some blood hit the treaty parchment, the ambassador and Mary. It smelled strong, clearly old animal blood.

Within moments, the woman was restrained and hauled off, while everyone stood in shock.

De Godoy burst out, "*¡Dios mío! ¡Por Dios y por el honor de España, esto es una afrenta!*" (My God! By God and the honor of Spain, this is an affront!)

Mary said loudly, "It's just a protester with paint or blood. Is everyone okay?" She received shaky nods from those nearby.

"I am so sorry, Ambassador de Godoy. Are you hurt? Oh no, there's blood on your beautiful coat. Don't worry, the Omímeya laundry can work miracles," she added.

Oops, miracles may not be the best word, Mary thought.

They took a break to clean everything up and to calm the upset nobles with reassurances and wine. The Spanish had extra copies of the unsigned treaty, as was normal. Accidents like spilled inkwells were not uncommon. The ambassador offered to exchange both, but Mary decided she wanted to keep the one with the lightest blood spatter as everything was perfectly readable. It added historical flare.

Afterwards, the actual signing felt anticlimactic. The Independence Ball went off smoothly, with celebrations not only at Omímeya, but across the area. People gathered in high school gyms, attended block parties, and packed into the bars. Fireworks were displayed and there was no small amount of drinking into the wee hours. It was a rare moment of joy and unity, etched into memory as the day their new nation took its first official step. That was the true miracle. Independence had been won, but treaties were only the beginning. The day-to-day building of a nation would be the true challenge ahead.

=..=

A week later, Mary was still happy, feeling such a weight off her shoulders. She could devote some time to education projects that were long neglected. She'd left most of those duties to Dr. Jessica Tooley, who was both the Chair of the Education Committee and president of the community college. However, education was supposed to be under her purview, and she hadn't done enough.

She was meeting with Travis, dictating email responses, and discussing priorities. Travis, looking over his tablet, said, "We should probably answer this lieutenant at Oca Landing about the teacher situation. He's emailed three times."

"What lieutenant? And what's the issue?"

"Lieutenant Jamal Alston has a son in the Oca Landing school, staffed by local teachers. He objects to the curriculum, the teaching methods, about everything. I'll flag it in your inbox if you want to read the details."

"It doesn't matter. We don't have teachers to send. We train them as fast as we can, but it takes at least two years to train a teacher. Many of the kids at Oca Landing are from this time. The teachers probably only seem bad to twenty-firsters."

"His complaints are not only about the teaching methods, but about the teachers' evidently ignoring bullying, promoting sexism, and that sort of thing."

"Alston, Alston, why does that name sound familiar?" mused Mary.

"He was the one who went to Boston, got us connected with ship builders, and brought back Eli Whitney."

"Now I remember, he's an engineer. Isn't he too young to have a child in primary school?"

"Adopted an orphan in Boston."

Mary nodded. "When I was teaching younger grades years ago, the most demanding parents were adoptive parents. Honestly, hated them, couldn't do anything right for their precious babies."

"Should I tell him now the treaty is signed, you'll have more time to finding more teachers?"

"No, it's none of his business how much time I spend doing anything. I don't think he's aware of how few twenty-firsters are left for anything, let alone for teacher training. Big Thunder brought a little over 8,000 people. We lost about 500 in the first few months because of a lack of critical medicines. Around 500 are between the ages of eighteen and twenty-five and still in their two years of national service. About 1,200 are elders or disabled; almost all the rest are working critical jobs. We don't have anyone to train or send, and we won't for years."

"Okay, I'll try to let him down gently. Would you like me to schedule a meeting with Dr. Tooley? Maybe you could brainstorm some ideas to speed up teacher training."

"Great idea." Mary brightened. "I'd love to see her."

Later that day, Mary met at the First Shield offices to discuss the protestor incident and the situation in Europe.

After arriving in the secure meeting room, she looked around; other than Phil and Jackson, she hardly knew anyone. Most were FSC officers, largely older women.

Phil began as soon as everyone settled. "I sent the report about Helen Corson, our blood-spilling protestor, to the rest of the Security Council. We also have a report from the Europe desk."

"You have more information than you sent yesterday?" asked Mary.

"Mostly the same. Corson slipped by our screening. She came in posing as a photographer, with a real film camera. As she seemed to be a pregnant woman, no one gave her a closer look. She's not a big follower of Folsom, not a member of his church. Church members didn t receive tickets. But you could say she got radicalized online. Followed conspiracy theories on the forums. She had been on mental health meds; without them, she couldn t work and attends the Daily Harmony Center."

There were a few of these centers, mostly in converted nursing homes. Some lived there full-time, others came during the day. They offered a peaceful space with shared purpose, structured activities, gentle work, and meals, with staff trained in mental health.

"So, nothing is going to happen to her?"

"What do you suggest?" asked Phil snidely.

Mary felt stupid for asking. She was angry at the woman, but it could've been worse, and she was mentally ill. There wasn't anything else they could do.

"No, you're right. I suppose you already limited her NewNet access."

"Yes, but new forums pop up all the time. Monitoring her will take staff time we don't have. But I don't see a choice. One of Folsom's forums that got by us was called 'Bison Tongue Pickling Recipes'. We only found it because one of our officers wanted the recipes."

Jackson said, "I've had pickled tongue. It's not bad."

"Okay," said Phil, "I think everyone knows Katherine Enberg, head of the Europe desk. Katy, why don't you fill everyone in? New information came in with last night's transmission from London."

Usually a cheerful woman, she looked serious. "We have found our mystery German tourist, Karl Bauer. He never changed his name. Anna Worthington found him after asking in France."

"How does she do that, anyway?"

"By speaking mostly with women. She asked about a distant cousin from the Germanies, visiting France, as she heard he came upon some hard times and wanted to reconnect him with family."

"She's highly effective, isn't she?" said Jackson.

"You have no idea," said Phil. "I've asked her to write us up a training manual."

Katy continued, "Karl was in France for a month or two. Not sure if he met Napoleon. He went to Austria, meeting with Francis II, who'd just succeeded his father, Leopold II, who died unexpectedly this last March. Not sure how he got into the Habsburg Court; it is very difficult without connections. But Francis II is twenty-four and likely open to new things like the wonders of the twenty-first century. We'd been hearing rumors of someone close to the emperor with a phone, showing pictures and revealing things from our history."

"But nothing is the same anymore," Mary said. "Napoleon has been sidelined; the French Revolution has been softened somewhat. Marie Antoinette was saved. History is very different now."

"The War of the First Coalition was started to preserve the monarchy in general and the Habsburg Dynasty in particular. It was also a reaction to the spread of revolutionary ideology. The French recently declared war on Austria about this same time in our history. But without Napoleon, who knows what will happen? While the French have some of our advanced knowledge, like avoiding disease in war, which killed more soldiers than guns, Austria may have the same information. London shares medical knowledge with everyone, so that may not matter. We don't know if Karl Bauer has weapons data on his devices. And we don't know what happened to Napoleon. He's dropped off the map."

Jackson asked, "If France is now our ally, does that mean we want them to win against Austria?"

"It's complicated," said Katy. "The French Revolutionary Wars under Napoleon devastated Europe. The Habsburg Empire was on its last legs, as it tried holding on to places like Italy. With foreknowledge, they could give independence to their vassal states, consolidate, and create a new Germany many years early. As an ally, Germany could be a stable force in Europe, and with our influence, we could even prevent both world wars."

"But, there is always a but." said Mary.

"It depends on Bauer. He could be a force for good or evil. And we must find Napoleon." Phil answered.

"What is your recommendation?" asked Jackson.

"We need more information, and that means more intelligence officers. We have no one in Europe, and Anna May is mostly in London. I have a plan to recruit more, but we need funds, a lot of funds."

"I wondered why I was invited to this meeting," said Jackson with a smile.

"I'll bite," said Mary. "What's the plan?"

"A cadre of young attractive women fluent in French. There are many from good families, made destitute from the revolution. A few men too, and a couple of toughs as well. But mostly women. We may rig some kind of radio connection between France and London."

"Can you trust them?" asked Jackson.

"Revolutionaries overran their country, and many lost their homes or family members. Plus, we'll pay them well. I always trust money," said Phil, grinning.

Jackson said, "No matter which side we support, we need more information. Sun Tzu said, 'Know your enemy, win your war.' I support this. Intelligence can save lives."

"Get us a budget, and I'll likely approve it, but don't go overboard," said Mary.

Later that night, after spending time with her family, as she lay in bed with her husband Daniel, talking quietly about their day, as was their habit.

"I saw Billy today. I'm not sure how to deal with him. Do you think it is serious with Bridget?"

"I'm sure it is. Last time he was at dinner, he just about asked for her hand."

"What? Bridget hasn't said anything."

"I don't think he's proposed yet; he was just letting me know."

"What did he say?"

"He said his daughters had been of marrying age when his family was left behind the Circle, and if a man was serious, he would want to know about the man's background and finances. Then he proceeded to tell me about his."

"That's old school, but I guess he's not much younger than us."

"A lot younger."

Daniel seemed a bit offended. "We are not that old, he is forty-seven. He made a point to say that he owns fifteen acres off Highway 17 with a three-bedroom house. He rented it out after Big Thunder and lives in the hotel because it's convenient. He's from the Pine Ridge reservation. Both parents were alcoholics, so he never drinks. His grandmother, very traditional, raised him, and he's spoken Lakota his whole life. He enlisted in the Army right after high school and served as an MP in Germany during peacetime. Afterward, he started working security at Indian casinos and worked his way up to Omímeya. He's been there since before they opened. He is a member of the board."

"I forgot about that. They don't make a big deal about the board, but you know what it means, don't you?"

"No, what?"

"He's rich, soon to become very rich. Board members get a percentage of profits, and Omímeya is on track to become one of the biggest corporations on the continent, someday maybe even the world. That means our baby girl will essentially marrying into royalty. Our grandkids will be ultra wealthy."

Daniel chuckled. "There are worse things."

"I know. But poor man, losing his wife and two daughters. I'm grateful I have you and Bridget, but I sure miss Jeff and John."

They reached for each other, cuddled close, sharing the grief for their two lost grown sons, and the grandchildren they'd never see. Not dead, but never to be seen or touched again—the loss felt the same. *Death alone did not measure grief, but absence, which could be just as hollowing*, she thought.

Chapter Twenty-Four
Jackson

JACKSON ALWAYS LOVED the first big snow of the season. It was the first of December, still technically fall. Although there had been little flurries, none stuck. There was something magical about the first big snowfall, casting a spell that transformed the world into a pristine landscape blanketed in white. The first winter snow in Jackson's childhood Chicago neighborhood brought the excitement of snowball fights, snowmen, and snow forts. Coming inside afterward for hot chocolate created some of his best childhood memories.

Today, he was at Oacoma Training Grounds, the site of the newly established Guard base, as the existing National Guard Armory was too small for training and housing all the new troops. Jackson was there for the ceremony for the sixth graduating class of the Changleska Guards. With sixty-one members, this cohort was the largest class yet.

Initially, local Indigenous warriors had dropped out in droves. It wasn't the physical demands; they were in superb condition. Nor was it culture shock, different food, intense study, or language immersion. The problem was deeper and took time to understand. Military boot camps from his time were designed to break down individuality, which could be dehumanizing, then to build them back up with the group as their support system. Indigenous warriors already had their oyáte, or tribe. They hated being cursed at, belittled for minor mistakes, or forced to perform tasks they didn't understand the rationale for. So, they simply left.

Integrating Indigenous tribes into the Changleska Guard was critical. Despite their twenty-first-century weapons, they'd lose any major battle due to sheer numbers, as contemporary armies consisted of tens of thousands. They needed more trained troops to be effective. When tribes joined the Changleska Coalition, they maintained sovereignty, including command of their own forces, designated as allied forces, sometimes functioning as scouts. However, tribes desiring advanced weapons or benefits from Changleskan military training had to send people to learn English and complete Guard training. A condition of joining Changleska was a mandatory two-year National Service for all young adults, whether training with the Guard or within their own systems. Those trained at the base would eventually train others in their tribal lands at home.

General Gardner had already transformed the Guard's military structure, merging best practices from his beloved American military with Changleskan ideals and eighteenth-century realities. Changes were ongoing, from updating the Uniform Code of Military Justice, new salutes, and terminology, to incorporating elements from his National Guard unit, particularly a focus on defense and engineering. The new Guard would prioritize building rather than destruction. Training to manage civilian unrest without casualties had already proven valuable during Clyde Folsom's large protests. The Guard's disciplined presence and riot gear served as effective deterrents. Combating the disastrous drop out rates, were another challenge.

Using exit interviews, Gardner identified reasons recruits left and implemented changes accordingly. Now, every recruit began training with the inípi ceremony, which emphasized transformation and renewal. Recruits who excelled in areas such as horsemanship or archery would teach others. An instructor-cadet rank was created to recognize them.

Boot camp instructors were all older veterans, including some from the Vietnam era. Spending time figuring out what worked and didn't work from their own training, they collaboratively developed a better training model.

Two Elks had thought he was being clever, sending only women to be trained, and other leaders followed suit. But Gardner loved it. Women soldiers were unheard of in this time. If the Indigenous sent their women, in time perhaps others would too.

Looking at the new graduating class, Jackson saw many women, freed Black men, a few Indigenous men, and only a handful of those from his time. Most young people who had come with Big Thunder had already completed training. Those in this cohort were seventeen- and eighteen-year-olds who had just became eligible. Most were Lower Brule or Crow Creek, but there were some Hispanic, and a few Whites from the

Chamberlain or the surrounding area. Jackson was pleased to see such diversity.

Snow crunched under boots and moccasins as the recruits stood in formation, steam rising from their breath into the cold December air beneath a pale sun. After the prayers and singing, General Gardner's voice resonated from the stage: "Today, you join the shield that protects the Circle. You come from many walks of life. Some were brought by Big Thunder, some freed from cruelty, and others live on the lands of your ancestors and are part of it. Today, you stand as equals." He went on, speaking about specific instructors and sharing anecdotes from the training.

Jackson, wrapped in a heavy wool coat with his sash of office over it, stepped forward. "This isn't the end," he declared. "It's the beginning. You've earned your place, not through training, but by your choice to defend, to serve, to rise. By becoming a member of the Changleska Guard, you've chosen to stand for something greater than yourself: the circle that binds us in purpose, in protection, in unity. From this day forward, your fellow Guard members are your family, your tribe, your oyate. Together, you carry the shield of our people. Together, you will stand the line, hold the ground, and guard what matters most."

He raised his hand. "What do we guard?" he asked, prompting the call and response they all knew.

The answer came back with the power of sixty-one voices: "The Circle. The Circle protects the Earth."

Then the training officers delivered their speeches, and Jackson handed out ribbons to honor graduates, and awards for academic excellence, rifle and bow marksmanship, horsemanship, and drill. One by one, they all came forward and got pinned. Among them was one recruit whose journey had already begun to stand out, a young, recently freed Black man.

"Private Elijah Walker—report!"

Elijah Walker stepped forward; shoulders squared beneath his crisp indigo jacket. Eight weeks earlier, he hadn't held a weapon, stood tall, or felt a sense of belonging. He had flinched at loud voices, expecting orders, ownership, or indifference. Now, he was Changleska Guard.

Elijah's boots left dark prints in the snow as he saluted. Jackson pinned ribbons for leadership and rifle marksmanship to his jacket and quietly said, "Good job, son. You'll make us proud."

After the final salute, Jackson nodded, dismissing the formation. Elijah spotted movement at the crowd's edge, excited, he saw his family was there.

His sister ran forward, throwing her arms around him. "You did it, Elijah!"

He looked at his ribbons and at the snow-covered fields beyond. "I did," he whispered. "And I'm not done yet."

=..=

After the ceremony and lunch, Jackson had a face-to-face meeting with General Gardner and his aides. Most of their meetings had taken place by phone, or Gardner had come to him, since Jackson was technically Gardner s commanding officer. He hadn t visited the National Guard Armory in a while and was surprised by all the changes. They had taken over an entire block across the street, converting seven houses into administrative offices and weapons research and development facilities.

General Gardner launched into the meeting with brisk urgency, his tone clipped and businesslike. "The United States is pissed Spain that signed the treaty. No big surprise there, but according to First Shield Command, Jefferson is having conniptions and looking into military options to take New Orleans. They want the port."

"No one in this time fights in the winter, correct? We've time to prepare?" Jackson asked.

"Probably. But Jefferson's calling up the militia in the warmer southern areas and has started training camps there. They've gotten hold of some of our training materials. Our advantages could be shrinking."

"Fucking Clyde Folsom! Now the treaty's signed, do you think he'll stop his traitorous activities?"

"He's still dangerous. He only wanted annexation because the Americans promised he'd become governor."

"I remember the first day after Big Thunder, he thought since he was the only member of the South Dakota State Senate present, he should be governor. Many people agreed."

"Yes, we had multiple meetings about that. Back then, he even tried convincing me to put my command under President Washington. That's when I realized just how dangerous he could be. When he failed to become governor, he set his sights on your job, then lost the election by a landslide. His ambitions extend far beyond just being a religious leader. He wants political power. With another election six years away, and the treaty signed, I'm worried about what he'll do next."

"What can he do? Other than spew hate."

"Don't underestimate hate. The tool of authoritarian dictators is to create division and fear of the 'other.' The whole 'us and them' mentality. For Hitler it was the Jews, for modern leaders it was immigrants. Clyde is setting himself up to lead a coup."

"I'm not sure what we can do. He has a right to free speech, and he's been careful to distance himself from tech sellers." Jackson added, with frustration evident in his voice.

"According to FSC, many of the sales were for money, not politics. The tech bleeding will continue if there's money involved. Now, you, Councilor, could propose a political solution, like harsher punishments."

"Phil thinks we should hang a couple of tech sellers."

"Might work," Gardner said thoughtfully.

"Slippery slope. We should reserve executions for the worst of the worst."

"Do you think you're influenced by our old world's flawed judicial system? I know they executed mostly poor people of color."

"Perhaps. But execution doesn't sit well with me. There must be a better way."

"Different times call for different solutions."

"There's not much we can do now. I'm sure you're doing all you can to secure vital data. And I can tell you, at Omímeya, even I need a pass to access IT. They've got it locked down three ways from Sunday."

"I'm sending most of this graduating class to Oca Landing. I wanted to send them to Haiti, but New Orleans has become a priority. We need more soldiers. Once some have experience, we can send them and some training officers to the more distant tribes to recruit and train—but that's a long-term solution."

"Aren't we getting a lot of freed slaves wanting to join?"

"Yes, but even easing the literacy requirements, we have training problems. Not having enough people who can read English well enough is going to bite us in the ass sooner or later."

"Do you have any proposals?"

"Nope. Hoping you did." Gardner said, smiling at Jackson.

Gardner changed the subject. "You know the Northwest war will heat up this spring too. We gave advice to Tecumseh and the other tribal leaders, and promised some resources, but if the Americans are coming for New Orleans, we need to prioritize that."

"Losing the Ohio valley will be an enormous blow to the tribes. After the Americans settle there, they'll want to come west. We'll be next."

"I know, but hard choices have to be made."

They looked unhappy. Jackson said, "What can you tell me about our new Navy? I've been reading the reports. I'm impressed. This could save our asses in New Orleans come spring."

"Lieutenant Parker, why don't you brief Councilor Jackson?" said Gardner. "Parker oversees the Navy. We'll need to promote him soon. The old National Guard never had admirals, but perhaps the Changleska Guard will."

Lieutenant Parker was a solidly built, blond, blue-eyed man in his early forties, with a steady demeanor.

"Were you in the Navy before Big Thunder?" Jackson asked.

"No, Army. After my twenty, I was starting to enjoy retirement when caught by Big Thunder and reactivated. I did some sailing, mostly on the river or a lakes. I was the only one in the Guard who knew anything about boats. But I didn't know a damn thing about eighteenth-century sailing. But I'm learning."

Everyone laughed. Making do was what they did.

Parker started his debrief. "Our Navy started with the seizure of the pirate ship."

"I remember from last spring."

"Yes, sir," Parker continued. When we got that ship, General Gardner realized the potential and brought me in. Sailing and fighting using these ships is very specialized, and requires years, even a lifetime, of training. We didn t have it. We tried hiring people, but let me just say, it was bad, very bad. Men who will go with an unknown captain and a new crew, even with regular pay, but no chance of a rich payout, are the dregs of seaman."

"Rich payout?"

"Piracy or privateering when you are capturing ships during war and claim them as prizes. They split the money based on rank."

"Okay." Jackson knew little about naval practices, even from his own time.

"We solved the problem by finding British officers. They recruited better sailors. We paid above average and got a good crew. The ship was renamed the *Spirit Wind*. We improved it, equipped it with better cannons and some weapons from our time. *Spirit Wind* went on a piracy patrol in the

Caribbean and captured three more ships, plus a lot of fine cargo. We set up a prize court using the British naval model, and we're training more crew every day."

"Any problems with how your captains from this era run their crews?" Jackson asked.

"Yes," Parker answered firmly. "No one from our time would ever serve on these ships. The conditions are horrible. Flogging is the least of it."

Gardner murmured his agreement.

"We're slowly making changes. There are waiting lists for our crews. Our ships are the fastest and best armed in the area. Leadership is good, food is great, and punishments are now more reasonable. Unfortunately, we didn't bring any naval training manuals, unlike army ones. Recreating a new Navy to Changleska standards is a big job."

"Omímeya, with all its money, couldn't or didn't want to hack military or CIA databases. Phil complains about reinventing training manuals." Jackson said, smiling, "I think he uses spy novels."

Gardner added, "Since the treaty, we've gotten word the British Navy will now help us train, find officers, and build ships."

"Not out of the goodness of their hearts, I presume."

"No," Gardner replied. "They have disputes with the Americans over Canadian borders, not to mention they're still sore about losing the war. Irritating Americans is a bonus. But they will also get better ship plans, navigational tools, sea charts, and cash for shipbuilding. And we solve a problem for them."

"Which is?" Jackson asked.

"They have too many officers and not enough ships. The British Navy puts officers on half pay and keeps them ashore until a position opens, sometimes for months or years."

"In our history, France declared war on Britain around this time. No one's sure what'll happen now. But it looks possible."

"All the more reason to get more ships and build up the Navy," Parker said.

Jackson had been a politician long enough to recognize a plea for more funding. He didn't answer, wondering whether the Navy expansion was worth the scarce resources, or whether they should conserve for the conflicts already brewing inland.

"What's happening with the ships being built, the one in Boston, and the riverboats in New Orleans?"

Gardner answered that one. "The steam riverboats are on track. A smaller cargo barge just launched, and more are close behind. The big passenger steamboats are still a way off. But there's a problem with the Boston ship."

"I haven't heard anything."

"Just got the news. When we contracted to have a ship built in Boston, we partially paid for it with plans for improvements like advanced hull design, reinforced rigging structures, and updated armament placements. The ship would have been one of the best sea-faring ships anywhere."

"What happened?"

"At the time the ship was contracted, we'd no idea how adversarial our relationship with the Americans would be. We just got word. After the treaty was signed, they declared Changleska an enemy, and the government seized the ship under construction with all its blueprints."

"Shit."

"Yeah," Gardner replied. "This means they have access to one of our primary advantages. We may need to bypass the whole lot and move straight to steam. Although I understand building ocean-going steamships is much more difficult than river steamboats."

"Steamworks is making significant progress. I hear good things. They even have steam trucks."

Gardner consulted his laptop. "Moving on, you wanted a debrief about Haiti?"

"I've heard a few things. James Reynald and Lucas Sullivan sent requests for funding and more weapons."

Gardner sighed. "They're bypassing the chain of command coming to you, but I understand. Haiti's heating up fast. Reports are Toussaint Louverture, the leader of the Haitian rebellion, has built up an army, which is growing faster than anyone expected. They've organized training camps, started standardizing weapons, even using some of our field tactics."

"That soon? I thought it would take longer to build a proper command structure."

"Would've, if they didn't have foreknowledge and our advisors. They've got a quarter of the northern plantations in open rebellion. Word is spreading, and the planters are terrified."

"That's going to ripple through every slave port in the Caribbean."

Gardner nodded, added more quietly, "Our advisors also stopped a bloodbath. They said a few massacres had occurred before they got there, with whole plantation families killed. But our guys convinced Louverture to rein it in. Being known as a revolutionary is one thing, being known as a ruthless killer of women and children is another."

"That's no small thing. In our time, the whole world was against them."

"Exactly. And now? They're talking about building a republic with real structure, trade routes, education. If this keeps up, Haiti won't just be free, it'll be a beacon. The 'Sugar Without Sin' campaign is growing, and the boycotts are starting to work. We're already buying their sugar from plantations they freed at a slightly higher price. That's been a good incentive for plantations to move from using slaves to paying workers."

"Working conditions is a whole other issue, but we'll start with freeing as many as possible. Hopefully killing as few people as we can along the way."

=..=

After the meeting was done, Jackson just wanted to go home. He realized that home for him no longer meant a room in the hotel but Rose s place. Rose was his home. He probably should bite the bullet and finally move in and stop pretending he still needed space. At first, it was her kids that held him back. But he had gotten used to them, and they weren t around that much, anyway. A new administrative building s construction was underway, and his office would be located there once it was finished. Then he d no longer have an excuse not to move in. He had always been afraid to commit. That was probably why at age thirty-eight he'd never married. If he was being honest, in the past he hadn't wanted to limit himself to having sex with only one woman for the rest of his life, but maybe because he was getting older, or because of his love for Rose, it was no longer the reason. Jackson still grieved for Denise, but time helped the pain fade. He often wondered what Denise and the rest of his family thought when he had disappeared. Whether the old world still existed was a subject for much discussion in the Circle, but like most people, he chose to believe it did. The alternative was too awful to contemplate.

Because he rarely came to Chamberlain, he decided he should do some shopping. He was driving the Omímeya electric work truck. They tried to limit the use of all electric vehicles. Replacement parts might be nonexistent in the foreseeable future. He needed socks. Hand-knit wool socks were readily available, but they were too hot when he worked out. Cotton athletic socks were expensive and hard to find. After visiting Bomgaars and another trading post and not finding any, he picked up a few other things and was heading out. Then he saw people clogging the street, some carrying signs. He opened the window to ask someone what was going on and he heard yelling in the distance. He got as close as he could, found a place to park, and could see a small crowd ahead. Some kind of protest was going on.

The crowds were growing, with yelling and name-calling going back and forth. They were all in front of a small tattoo shop, one of the few openly queer-owned businesses in town, which was known to locals as a safe and welcoming space. The crowd held signs declaring God Hates Sin," "Protect Our Values," and other hateful slogans targeting LGBTQ+ people. None of the counter-protesters had signs but seemed to be random people joining in to harass the original protestors. Jackson noticed many on their phones, probably calling their friends.

Jackson recognized an ugly mob when he saw one. The tense energy could shift from protest to violence quickly. Some people leaned forward like they were waiting for someone to throw the first punch. He'd seen that look in crowds before.

He stopped and called Gardner, "There's a protest on the corner of North Main and Mott, and..."

Gardner interrupted, "I know. We're on our way, gotta go." And hung up on him.

Jackson pushed his way through the crowds right up to the front door of the shop. He didn't know how many people recognized he was their Executive Councilor, but they recognized a big Black man with the attitude of a cop and made way.

There was a tough-looking woman with very short hair, wearing men's clothes and a shotgun over her arm, blocking the front door. She wasn't pointing the weapon at anyone, but her meaning was clear: stand back. Her jaw was set, shoulders squared, and her eyes scanned the crowd with a hardened intensity that made even the boldest step back.

For a moment, Jackson looked over at the seething crowd and heard angry shouts filling the air. He wasn't sure when the Guard troops would arrive, but feared it might not be soon enough.

Standing at the front of the crowd, he raised his voice. "Listen up everyone. Can I have your attention, please?" Surprisingly, people quieted, not everyone, but enough. "It looks like what is going on is a peaceful protest, but it doesn't look like it will stay peaceful for long."

"If these assholes wanted peace, they'd leave everyone alone to live their own lives. These women aren't hurting anyone!" someone in the crowd shouted.

A sign holder shouted back. "The Bible says they are sinners; they shouldn't be running a business. Everyone knows it's owned by lesbians."

Jackson lifted his hands for quiet. "No matter what we may think about these people's views," he said, pointing at the sign holders. "They have a right to express them. Does anyone think we should deny free speech rights?"

"Free speech does not include hate speech. Even the law agrees."

Jackson knew they were right. The eighteenth century had no shortage of cruelty, but it lacked the kinds of legal protections they had now. Changleska had enacted new laws fining people for racist and hate speech. He looked over the signs; they approached the line but didn't quite cross it.

"Good point, but it doesn't mean it's okay to yell and cause a ruckus. It doesn't help your cause." After looking around, he said, "The law protects the right to protest, not the right to block entrances. Everyone who is against the tattoo shop on this side." He pointed to one side of the sidewalk, away from the door. "Everyone who supports the owners of the tattoo shop on this side." He pointed to the other side. The two groups separated, but not without grumbling.

Just then a truck pulled up honking to get people out of the way, and dozens of Guards in full riot gear hopped out.

Gardner walked up to Jackson, gave a quick glance to the woman with the shotgun, and said, Looks like you ve been doing some politicking, Councilor." He nodded toward the watching crowd.

"And now I'm done, all yours now." And he left, hearing the crowd start up a chant. *Your hate has no place here.*

The other side promptly started singing, *Onward Christian Soldiers.*

He just wanted to go home.

Chapter Twenty-Five
Gift of Thunder

GIFT WAS WARM all over. Even her back, which was usually the first to feel the cold, stayed comfortable. And she wasn't even bundled up in the thick sweaters she'd worn last winter. At the house on Crow Road, where she lived most of the time with Hotah, her adopted father, crews had finally reconnected the natural gas pipelines after Big Thunder had cut them off. With operational gas, they were making propane now. Before the propane system started working, she hadn't understood what the fuss was all about. The big old farmhouse had a wood stove and a couple of small space heaters. She was warm with sweaters, especially by the fire, unlike in a tipi on the cold winter nights when you had to go outside to make water. But everyone was so excited to have the gas working again. Inside the house, she couldn't even tell it would be officially winter in a few weeks. It was even warm first thing in the morning. You couldn't even see your breath.

She was sitting at the table after dinner holding her baby sister, Anpa, now ten months old, while Kimi and her little cousins, Ethan and Evan, were doing homework. Even though she no longer went to school, she recognized the need for education. She wanted to pass the test to join the Guard, which she could enlist in at seventeen with parental permission. She wasn t sure how she d feel about being separated from Kimi, but she knew she had to learn what the Guard could teach her. Gift found that by helping the boys with their homework, she learned more than when she herself went to school. When she had to explain something to them, she had to understand it first. Now she desired to learn more, her reading had improved. She was even learning math and other subjects. One of her weapons instructors had shown her his collection of books on warfare, saying to learn strategy and tactics she should read about other battles.

She liked the practical skills better, but she was just starting a long learning journey. Last summer, she d used those skills when a man tried to assassinate Kimi, but she d been shot herself, so obviously she still had much to learn.

She knew she was lucky that Rose's generosity paid for private lessons and tutors from anyone in the area with skills to teach her, but that wasn't the same as actual combat. At least, that's what every instructor told her. After returning from the Arikara, the desire to protect Kimi and serve her new country drew her to the path of a warrior. While she'd heard of women warriors, she didn't know any growing up and always expected she would be a wife and mother. Gift knew few women who joined the Guard stayed in combat roles. Everyone had to go through boot camp, but afterward, most women chose jobs in medical, communication, or other support services. Gift wondered whether women tended to nurture rather than kill or simply disliked the company of competitive boys. She had learned the word 'macho' translated to Lakota men, too. Some had more bravado than sense. The time she spent with boys showed her that. Their antics amused her. Another term she learned, testosterone poisoning, like macho, applied sometimes. Because she was small, flat-chested, and didn't meet typical standards of attractiveness, boys treated her like a friend, which was fine with her. She saw how girls they considered attractive weren't respected for their abilities like she was. But sometimes she wished for the attention of young men and fondly recalled her intimate moments with Ciwaku. She missed the special attention.

While she spent some time helping with the baby at home, most weekends she spent training. One of her instructors was an older White guy, Gary Hutchinson, who lived near Reliance. He was a gunsmith and prepper who studied military history. Because of the distance, Rose arranged for her to do weekend classes. After some discussions, they developed a more organized program and expanded it to four days. Rose paid for several other young relatives to join. Gary called it Reliance Military Academy, as the teenagers were all within a year or two of joining the Guard. While informal, the academy followed a loosely structured curriculum focused on practical skills, physical training, and strategic thinking. They camped out in a big tent on his property. Gary taught most of the classes, but other instructors came in occasionally. They mostly learned weapons and fighting skills, but in the evenings, they watched war films and discussed tactics and strategy.

She was the only girl besides the three boys, all her cousins, whom she didn't know well before this. One boy, Matt, had dropped out of school and wouldn't be old enough to join the Guard for two more years. He showed little interest in anything besides video games and partying. His family hoped these classes might turn him around, or guns might catch his interest. What they really wanted was for Matt to get an apprenticeship in Mike's gun shop. It was a long shot, as gunsmith apprenticeships were in high demand, but with Rose's financial backing, anything was possible. Logan was a hunter with a good grasp of wilderness skills, and he was open to learning from Gift or any of the Indigenous people willing to teach him. He wanted to be a scout. He and Gary pored over maps and picked out imaginary battle sites. Jordon, serious and studious, had a goal of being an officer in the Guard. The online Officer Candidate School was only open so far to existing military or those with a college degree, but Jordon hoped this would be a first step in that direction.

At home Gift was helping Evan with a math problem when Kimi put down her pencil, looking troubled. She shook her head and sat quietly for a moment as Gift watched her questioningly. She suddenly got up and walked out the front door. Gift followed, sensing something was wrong, grabbing a blanket off the couch to wrap up herself and the baby. She saw Kimi walking towards the snow-covered field on the side of the house, she heard it—a low growl of thunder vibrating in the distance. Thunder never came in this season, but now its powerful rumbling was closing in, and Kimi was standing in the cold, without a jacket, listening.

Then the baby let out a sharp cry, jolting Kimi, who looked around and said, "It's bad—really, really bad. We must stop it, or the entire Circle could fall." She rushed back to the house, yelling for Hotah as she entered.

Hotah came running down the stairs after hearing her panicked cries.

"There's an attack. Right now, we have to go," she shouted.

"What? Where?" he asked, not questioning how she knew something not reported on the radio he'd been listening to upstairs.

"I don't know who or how many," she answered, frustrated. "At Omímeya, but we have to go now!" she said with urgency.

"Let's see if we can take Dylan's truck," Hotah said.

"Bring guns," Kimi called out.

"How many?"

"All of them."

Hotah stopped, looked at her, and asked, "Is this trouble only at Omímeya? Will Nicole and the rest of the family be safe here?"

"Yes, yes, here's safe. The danger is at Omímeya, but we have to go now."

Gift unlocked the closet in the front hall and pulled out one large duffle bag, put it over her shoulder, and dragged two large, wheeled suitcases full of weapons and put them in the back of Dylan's truck. Between her weapon instructors' recommendations and Rose's generosity, Gift probably had the best private arsenal around. She even had Tannerite, a legal explosive. She'd been taught it was better to have something you don't need than need something you don't have.

As they got into the truck, Gift heard Kimi finishing a call with Rose, knowing she'd talk to Jackson, who wasn't with her. As they drove away, he told the girls, "You two call the cousins, split the list. I'll call the uncles. Gift, do you have your phone?"

She nodded. She hated the phone and had to be reminded to bring it with her. Gift never understood why people needed to reach her anytime they wanted. She only wanted to talk to people standing in front of her.

Dylan said quietly to Hotah in the front seat, with the girls in the crew cab behind, "Are you sure you want to call out all the relatives to show up armed at the casino? If there's real trouble, the militia will be called up."

"Don't want to wait. Kimi has never been wrong about a warning yet. I'm not about to take a chance. Oh no, speaking of the militia, I forgot the radio they gave us; it's set to the militia command frequency. It's still in the charger in the garage."

"Don't worry, I have four in my bags," said Gift, showing the girls heard every word from the back seat.

As they drove down the dark, snowy roads as quickly as was safe, everyone made calls and talked on their phones. Gift suggested they all meet at Dave's Trading Post, on Little Bend Road, the entrance road to Omímeya. A couple of miles away from Omímeya, with a big parking lot with clear lines of sight in all directions. Hotah realized that all the tactical training lessons Gift was getting were paying off. He didn't think of the defensibility of their meeting place. His army career had been many years ago and consisted of working construction in the green zone in Bagdad, but he should've known not to approach a possible firefight without reconnaissance.

Kimi got another call from Rose. She said she knew what the warning was about. There'd been a huge explosion at the gunpowder factory near Shelby, far away from everything but close enough to still have power and water. They assumed causalities, but hoped there were not many, as the last shift had gone home. She tried to soothe Kimi, telling her the crisis was over.

"No, no, it's not over. It hasn't begun yet. It's at Omímeya, I know it is. We're on the way, meeting relatives at Dave's Trading Post. Talk soon." Kimi hung up, told Hotah about the explosion, and said, "What if no one believes me and thinks the danger is over?"

"We believe you," said Gift, comforting Kimi with her hand on her shoulder. "When the cartel gunman made the coup attempt last year, didn't they create a diversion, so all the police were on the other side of the Circle?"

"That's right," said Hotah. "It's probably a diversion. I'll text Rose."

As they drove towards Omímeya, traffic appeared when they turned onto Highway 3, taillights in front and headlights in back. It took everyone a minute to realize the problem. Hardly anyone drove anymore. Even veggie oil fuel was expensive, and no one drove at night in the snow if it could be helped. A breakdown could be deadly. Cell service was unreliable in rural areas, and there were no more AAA or Highway Patrol.

Hotah looked back at the girls. "Call back the cousins. Find out if anyone is driving Highway 3 right now."

"It's not—it's them. I feel the menace in the trucks," Kimi said with alarm.

"Should I slow down or speed up?" asked Dylan nervously.

"Slow down and see if they pass," said Gift. "We don't want to risk an accident, and we'll have to wait for everyone to arrive, anyway."

"Good thinking," said Hotah.

Things got scarier when they saw the truck, a big four-by-four crew cab pickup, used by work crews. As it passed, they could see besides the four in the front, six men in the back bed, bundled up, only their heads with dark caps showing.

"Shit, fuck, shitty fuck," said Dylan, earning a dirty look from Hotah who didn't approve of cursing in front of kids, even if it was justified or inventive.

"Do you have Jackson's number?" Hotah asked Kimi. "Let's not go through Rose. Call him and tell him what we saw."

But neither he nor Gift could get through. All the lines were busy. The cell service couldn't handle very many calls. They both texted Jackson and Rose, as well as a few others, to let them know this was a genuine threat, not a warning. They hoped the messages would go through.

When they reached the parking lot, a few relatives were already there. Everyone stood in the cold parking lot, comparing notes. They'd come from different directions and had seen vehicles on the road. A truck pulled up, and Lou White Mountain jumped out, looking surprisingly jovial given the circumstances. Accompanying him was a couple of Hotah's relatives. Lou was an older man with thinning hair but still had a long braid in the back. He was the current Chair of the Lower Brule tribe, the commander of the new marine corps, and the head of the local militia.

Hotah shook his hand in greeting. "Does this mean the militias have been called up?"

"Not yet," Lou responded. "I just heard about this party and decided to crash it. Your uncle Henry needed a ride," nodding toward the older man who was stepping out of Lou's truck.

Lou was quickly brought up to speed. He'd attempted to text Jackson, Gardner, or anyone else in his chain of command, but the lines remained clogged. Voice calls weren't going through, and text messages queued without being sent.

Lou raised his voice, catching everyone's attention amid the chatter and attempts at phone calls. "Listen up everyone. Because we can't reach command, I'm calling up the militia on my authority. Those of you already here, good job." A nervous ripple of laughter ran through the group. "We'll take only a few minutes to figure out what's going on. Standing out here not only makes us targets, but it's damn cold. Jerry, pound on Dave's door and get him to open up so we can go inside. And you two," he pointed at a couple of men, "you're on first watch outside."

Dave, the trading post owner who lived upstairs, had heard vehicles approaching after hours and was already dressed, shotgun in hand, when Jerry knocked on his door. Dave was also militia, as was every able-bodied adult within the Circle.

Everyone quickly filed inside, grateful to escape the cold. Gift retrieved the radios from the truck and joined Matt and Jordon, who had just arrived. The excitement on their faces showed they didn't grasp the severity of the situation, that they would soon face armed attackers.

"I heard from Logan," Jordon reported. "He's coming with a few others on horseback. They're only a few miles out, so they should be here soon."

Overhearing this, Lou spoke loudly enough for everyone to hear clearly. "We'll wait briefly for the others and the horses. All vehicles are approaching via Little Bend Road. That road will soon be blocked. The Omímeya checkpoint has only one guard on duty and four at the post. The gate might slow intruders, but it won't stop them, and the checkpoint will quickly be overwhelmed."

"What's the point of waiting?" someone called out.

"We have a plan. That's why we need horses. We'll use the riding path parallel to the road to reach the gate. It's unlikely anyone would risk crossing the river at night this time of year, so our focus will be on the entrance gate."

Lou approached Kimi, Gift and the boys standing by her side. "Thank you for your warning. A little extra time can make a big difference. Is there anything else you can tell me? Anything else you sense, even if you aren't certain?"

Kimi closed her eyes and took a deep breath. Softly, her expression filled with sorrow, she replied, "Many people will die. They have many guns. They want to take over. I'm sorry, that's all I know."

"That helps," Lou said reassuringly, turning to Gift. "I heard you came prepared. These are your friends from the class Gary Hutchison is running?"

"Yes, sir," Jordon replied with pride in his tone, "the Reliance Military Academy."

Lou laughed gently, "Four students?"

Matt bristled, defensive. "We've gotta start somewhere."

Lou raised his hands in a conciliatory gesture. "Okay then. Cadets, you can help us with the plan." All four straightened proudly, even Matt, as they realized they'd never been called cadets before. Lou motioned them to join him at a large table now cleared of merchandise, where others gathered around examining maps and battle plans from binders Lou pulled from his backpack.

"You," Lou pointed at Gift, "are in charge of communication. Set up over there." He indicated the checkout counter where a whiteboard listed prices. "Erase that board. Write frequencies and key data as it comes in. Use the landline to reach Mr. Jackson or anyone at Omímeya." He handed Gift a binder labeled 'Communication.' "Inside are militia call-up instructions with phone trees. Remind everyone to use landlines. Make sure everyone has their radios turned on and to the militia frequency. Start monitoring that channel."

After the girls went over to the counter, Kimi said, "I'll do the board. You make calls," knowing Gift's handwriting was practically illegible.

Gift was annoyed, realizing she'd been assigned to communication because she was one of the few females present and, being small, was often mistaken for being younger. She knew she was better armed, more skilled at shooting than most present, and likely among the few who had killed before. Still, she recognized the importance of following orders and saw it as an opportunity to keep Kimi close and safe.

Lou had dispatched scouts to Little Bend Road. They radioed back, reporting several trucks parked along the road about a mile from the gate, apparently awaiting reinforcements. Meanwhile, Kimi wiped the board clean, and the girls began calling and texting people listed on the militia call-up sheet, confirming their arrival and times, recording details on the board. Lou organized teams to fortify the gate, using foot or horse patrols to avoid detection by the vehicles lining the road.

Addressing the group, Lou announced grimly, "They've counted five vehicles so far—forty to sixty armed men. But we'll easily outnumber them once reinforcements arrive."

Dylan said, "I can't believe that asshole Clyde Folson has so many people willing to fight for him. Most people are happy with independence. They've moved on, annexation is no longer an issue to rally around."

Hotah added sharply, "He's power-hungry, aligning himself with the Americans to advance his own ambitions. He thinks he can remake the new US into a Christian conservative America. He probably thinks he needs the old US borders to establish global dominance with himself at the top. All his preaching and radio shows have gained him plenty of followers, a lot more than anyone likes to admit. He lost the annexation fight, so he's trying to take over by force."

"We don't know for sure who's involved," Lou responded, his voice firm. "In another ten minutes, we'll have hundreds of armed militia here. These pricks, whoever they are, will be so outnumbered we'll kick their asses from here to kingdom come."

"Hooah!" shouted several veterans in agreement.

Gift finally reached Jackson on the landline, quickly updating him, but their connection abruptly ended as the line went dead. Simultaneously, cell phone service vanished mid-call and mid-text, though the phones themselves remained powered. Frustrated users jabbed at their screens, confused and angered at the sudden blackout.

Gift raised her voice above the confused chatter. "Mr. White Mountain, I was speaking with Jackson on the landline and the phone cut off." Others quickly echoed similar complaints about their cell phones.

"They must've hit the communication hub in Chamberlain," Lou said, his tone sharp. "With the explosion at the gunpowder plant, this is clearly a coordinated attack. Don't assume we're only facing sixty fighters."

Lou swiftly issued orders, his voice calm but intense. "We can't wait. Those with trucks load up as many fighters as possible. Head up the road, get as close as you can, then have everyone jump out, half flank and attack the trucks. The others hit the horse trail. Either hold the gate or reach the main building. You two," he gestured decisively at a pair of men who had just arrived, his tone leaving no room for hesitation, "block the road here," he pointed firmly at the map, "and set up a checkpoint. Let our people through but stop anyone escaping. I'll send latecomers your way."

As the group hurried toward the door, Lou called after them, "One more thing. Only young, fit guys in the trucks. There might be a two-mile run ahead."

Gift saw Matt and Jordon exchange a knowing smile. Logan was in charge of the horses, but Matt and Jordon would join the others in the trucks. Gift knew all four of them, herself included, were excellent runners, regularly running two miles as part of their training. Watching them leave, she felt a wistful pang, wishing she was going with them. Her cousins were going into their first battle without her. Filled with a little anxiety mixed with pride, silently praying they'd all come back safely, completely unaware one would not return.

Soon the crowded room emptied, leaving Gift and Kimi to update the board as new information arrived. Gift anxiously wondered if the fighting had already started, or if they'd be able to hear gunfire from this distance. Moments later, a rumbling noise filled the air as multiple vehicles pulled into the parking lot. Looking out the window, they saw a snowplow and several massive road crew trucks, followed by a smaller truck with men in the back with guns.

Gift asked Lou, "How do they know this is our staging area?"

"You're right. Just driving by, it probably looks like a bunch of cars and horses in a parking lot," Lou said, concern etching his forehead.

Kimi burst out, "The radios! They must be listening. They found the frequency."

"They're not exactly secret," Lou replied, frustration creeping into his voice. "Every militia member has one, and that's basically every household. Change the frequency for command and field units. That's the best we can do for now."

Just then, trucks drove straight into the lot, pulling ominously close to the door.

"Get down!" Lou shouted urgently as automatic gunfire erupted outside. Gift hit the floor hard, bringing Kimi with her, adrenaline surging, her ears ringing from the deafening noise. As shattered glass and debris rained around her, she saw Lou, his face grim and resolute, with blood dripping on his shirt, and she realized in that instant their defenses had failed and the battle was at their doorstep. She looked for Kimi, wanting to use her body to shield her from the hail of bullets, but Kimi was gone. Glancing back, she noticed the rear door closing. She had left. Gift needed to keep firing at the attackers in front of her, but she also needed to protect Kimi. Then she heard it: thunder, growing louder and louder.

Chapter Twenty-Six
Rose

ROSE WAS CURLED up on her couch, in her favorite sweatpants and a top she'd had forever, enjoying the cozy familiarity of home. She was scrolling through her tablet, trying to decide if she should read the historical fiction novel about Marie Antoinette she had been putting off or watch a movie. She was disappointed Jackson wasn't coming over tonight; he was working late. With no looming crises for the first time in weeks, she was trying to savor the rare quiet evening, a welcome contrast to the nonstop stress and heavy decisions that usually consumed her days.

There was good news. With many new people coming to the area to work, even European tourists trickled in. Most were French, but there were Hessians from the Germanies and a wave of Americans. Most stayed in the cheaper motels, which now served food, called themselves inns, and catered to people from this time. But four wealthy Americans had taken rooms at the resort.

Rose heard her phone ring from the other room. She reluctantly got up and reached it before it stopped ringing. It was Kimi, but Rose wasn't concerned, thinking it was a routine call.

"Mom," she said, sounding distraught, "something bad is going to happen, worse than anything. Call Jackson and get everyone ready."

Rose said calmly, "It's okay, sweetie, I'm listening. Can you tell me more? Anything specific?"

"No, nothing specific, you know, it's not how this works. Just feelings. All I know is we need lots of guns, and everyone needs to get to Omímeya, right away, there's not much time."

"Alright, I'll call Jackson as soon as we get off the phone. Are you at home?"

"No, we're in Dylan's truck on our way to Omímeya, we're bringing guns, and Dad is calling the relatives."

Rose sighed in frustration, a flicker of fear prickling beneath her exasperation. *What was Hotah thinking, bringing their fourteen-year-old daughter into a situation needing guns?*

"Don't worry, Gift is with me, with all the guns you bought her. You know they took up half of the back of Dylan's truck?" Kimi said, exaggerating.

"And that is supposed to have me worry less?" Rose said with amusement. "I'll call you back after I talk to Jackson, or he may want to talk to you directly."

"Okay, later, love you."

"Love you too."

Rose called Jackson, but he seemed uncertain about what to do. He said, "We have nothing in the written plans about warnings from Thunder Beings. I'm not sure what we're supposed to do here."

"Take her seriously," Rose snapped. "She's never given a false warning. And she lives with the guilt of not having given a warning when the cartel gunmen killed all those people in the Big Bear room."

"I'm thinking," said Jackson placatingly. "I'll call Billy, and we can put together a plan. Just in case there is trouble, or we need to call a 'wildcat', you stay put."

"I won't stay put. I'll see you soon," and abruptly hung up.

Wildcat was the code name for the secret-service-like lockdown of all Executive Councilors and key Omímeya personnel in case of another attempted coup. Rose didn't think this counted, but she didn't want to be stuck at the house if anything was going on. The plan was her neighbor Theresa Martinez, the Executive Councilor, her husband, and two teenagers would shelter at her house because of its safe room. Fortunately, their roommates, Shawn Caris, another Executive Council member, and his husband, had moved out not too long ago. Rose didn't want to be stuck in the safe room with five people, let alone seven.

Rose dressed quickly back into work clothes, foregoing fixing her hair and makeup, grabbed her beaded lanyard with her ID, and headed out. She put her earpiece in and started making calls.

She reached Jenny, who said, "I couldn't find my ID and decided not to waste any more time looking. Fortunately, Terry was working late and let me in."

Staff IDs also worked as keys for secure areas. Rose didn't give a second thought to Jenny's lost ID. It'd turn up.

Jenny added, "We set up command in the admin meeting room. I ordered coffee and snacks. Communication is right next door."

"Sounds good."

"What's going on, Rose? Billy called a code yellow and said it wasn't a drill."

"I'll tell you later, I just pulled up and need to find Jackson." Rose didn't want to justify Kimi's warning to yet another person after several frustrating conversations with others.

"He's not here yet, probably still in his office."

Rose went to her office instead of trying to chase him down, as his office was on the other side of the building and hers was next to the room they'd use for command. Sooner or later, he'd show up.

She picked up her in-house radio from the charger, slipped it into her pocket, and went to the meeting room. She saw Billy and several other staff members pulling out binders and reviewing tablets, all looking confused.

"Any word from Kimi?" Billy asked when she arrived.

"Can't get through. Too many people making calls overload the system. Texts should get through soon. I'm not sure what to do either."

Billy looked at Rose with understanding. What could they do about a warning of an unknown threat heard by thunder that only her child heard?

"I've issued a yellow alert. Kyle sent it out already. People are coming in or sheltering in place."

Rose was grateful. It was exactly the right call. Billy was good at his job.

Just then, Jackson arrived with Phil on his heels.

"Something is definitely going on," Phil said. "It looks like someone stole at least three trucks, maybe more from the road maintenance yard."

"And this is related how?" asked Jackson.

"That's what we're trying to piece together. It may be related to all the Americans coming in," answered Phil in a terse tone. His and Jackson's relationship could be prickly, like his and Rose's.

"We've been monitoring the Americans. So far, they have done nothing untoward." He turned to Billy. "Are the ones staying here still in their rooms?"

Billy called on his in-house radio downstairs to the security office to check the cameras. "They all left twenty minutes ago, and several of them had trunks."

A staffer from communications came in and passed on the report about the explosion at the gunpowder factory near Shelby. It appeared casualties would be limited, but the entire complex had exploded.

Jackson was visibly upset. "At this time of night, this was no accident. Our weapon-making abilities are being targeted. This must have been what the warning from Kimi was. Losing that factory is a tremendous blow."

Rose stepped aside to call Kimi, who repeated over and over that was not it; the threat was Omímeya itself. Then she got a text from Hotah saying it was a diversion.

As Rose came back to the conversation, Phil was saying, "Of course, it was a diversion. The trucks, the Americans, it's all related. This is a puzzle; we just have to put together all the pieces. Billy, you were saying something about trunks. Are those the ones with weapons?"

This surprised Rose, as she had never heard of it. "We had American guests with weapons?"

"You can't allow everyone else to carry, but not Americans. They had them hidden in their luggage, but we found them when we searched. All rifles, all flintlocks, not much of a threat," said Billy.

"Unless they've been adding to their arsenal since we searched their rooms. Billy, have someone go over video footage since their arrival and see if they got any suspicious packages," Phil said forcefully.

Phil addressed the room. "Think people, anything else strange or out of the ordinary? You never know when a piece of the puzzle will fall into place."

"Hessians," Rose said suddenly. "There's a small group of them staying in Chamberlain. They were mercenaries in the Revolutionary War." She was grateful reading historical fiction had proven useful for something.

"That's important," said Phil, waving at a staffer. "Make a list for the board: factory explosion, stolen trucks, Hessians, Americans with guns. Anything else?"

One communication staffer raised her hand. "We had some radios go missing a few days ago."

"What!?" Both Jackson and Phil shouted. Radios were critical military tech and were supposed to be kept secure.

"I wasn't on duty, Andy Martin was. Nothing was reported. I just happened to check the inventory list. They were the older GMRS. They don't have a very good range."

"The range is far enough," said Jackson tightly. "And where is Mr. Martin now?"

"He got the alert and should be here, but he called in sick yesterday, so he might stay home. Andy is loyal. He'd never betray Changleska." The woman defending her colleague was practically in tears.

"Add that to the board," said Phil. "It's only looking like one thing."

"I agree," said Jackson. "An organized coup attempt. We knew they'd try, but we thought not until spring."

"Good thing we got a warning from Kimi. Every little bit of time will help," said Rose.

Jackson nodded in agreement, and others around the room followed suit, others exchanging uneasy glances. The room was tense, as the reality of what they faced sinking in.

Phil remained silent, obviously upset because, as head of First Shield Command, he should have foreseen this. Heads would roll at the FSC. But he couldn't do everything. He was even more irked that it was Rose's daughter who warned everyone. Why couldn't it have been anyone else's kid?

Both Jackson and Rose got the text simultaneously and learned about a truck filled with men heading towards Omímeya. They added this to the board. Jackson and Billy huddled over the table, studying maps and plans. Billy had already sent security to the gate, and they'd locked down the entire building.

Billy said, "We should move to orange alert." He looked over at Rose, since as she was the CEO, ultimately it was her call.

Rose nodded, and soon everyone heard a tone on their phones, and most everyone looked, even though they knew what it would say. Militia to their posts, everyone else sheltering in place as if there were an active shooter. Rose hoped Luke, a message runner at the medical school clinic, would go to his post. She understood why he didn t want to go to the safe room, but still she worried.

Communications from Lou White Mountain had come in. He'd called out his district's militia, some three hundred members, and he'd passed the word about the five trucks parked on the road, about a mile away, who were obviously waiting for more arrivals or a signal of some kind. Jackson headed to the radio room to see if he could speak to Lou directly, as well as Gardner.

As he left the meeting room, he overheard Phil yelling at Billy about not being able to find the Americans on the video cameras. Jackson had spoken to Gardner briefly earlier, but without a lot of information, it was hard to know what to do, except putting everyone on alert. Since word of the explosion came in, everyone knew that an attack was imminent, but no one was sure where or by whom. Jackson filled Gardner in on the recently discovered information, but Gardner was hesitant about calling out the full militia without a specific target. He would send troops to Omímeya and divert the people heading toward Shelby to them. Gardner didn't want to expand the Orange Alert to the full Circle, which would send alerts to all phones and broadcast radio announcements. He expressed concerns that the alert might warn the enemy, or trigger-happy militia might shoot innocents. But Jackson overruled him, which he rarely did. Gardner was seeing through the lens of a former National Guard officer. Jackson, on the other hand, carried the perspective of an Executive Councilor tasked with protecting the entire Circle.

Kimi had reached Jackson from the landline at Dave's Trading Post. As he was talking to her and just asked her to bring Lou to the phone, the call dropped. He redialed, but it didn't go through. He picked up a landline phone to call, but the line was also dead. Jackson looked around. The communication staff was confirming over the radio, every cell phone, landline, and NewNet was down.

"Oh shit, that's the signal to attack," he said out loud to no one in particular. Radio chatter filled the room. He wasn't sure anyone heard him.

He interrupted one tech, "Get me General Gardner back." At least they had a dedicated line for the military. There was no trouble getting through.

"You were right, sir," Gardner said. He rarely called Jackson sir anymore, even if he was commander-in-chief.

"If we would have waited a few minutes longer, no one would have gotten the Orange Alert, and very few people would be listening to the radio. When we go to Red Alert, it will have to be radio only, unless the phones come back."

"When do you think we should send out the Red?" Jackson wanted to let him decide and give him a little dignity back.

"As soon as we hear the first shots, which could be any minute." Gardner was outlining to Jackson next steps in the plan, when he saw Rose enter the crowded communication room, obviously trying to get his attention. She'd have a good reason to come looking for him. But she looked around, saw he was talking to Gardner, pointed to the meeting room, and headed back.

He wrapped up as quickly as he could, said he'd call back soon, and went to see what news Rose had. He knew it wouldn't be good.

Rose told him she'd received a call from Theresa Martinez. She'd taken her family to Rose's place as planned. They hadn't wanted to go straight to the safe room and were hanging out in the basement while their teenage boys watched the monitors from the security system in the safe room. They saw a truck park at their house next door, and several armed men broke the door down. Immediately, they went to the safe room. Theresa was on the phone to Rose when the phones cut out. Rose wasn't sure when they would hear from her again. They would have to wait until this was all over. But it was a very safe room. Good thing there was a toilet in there.

Jackson and Rose debated whether the wildcat plan was enough, Executive Councilors were being targeted. Because the phones were cut, they didn't know if the armed men had invaded Rose's house as well. Although Rose wasn t a political target, everyone knew Jackson frequently stayed overnight at her house.

Jackson caught her look. "I'm perfectly safe here. Didn't you tell me that the admin floor is locked down, even without the alert? There's no way to get in here without an ID from someone with clearance."

"Oh no, Jenny's ID?!" Rose cried out, telling Jackson, "Jenny lost her ID right before this all got started. She has a level three security clearance, that's access to the weapons lockers, everything. Where's Phil and Billy? We need to shut down her card."

Someone said they'd gone to the casino floor to examine video footage, hoping to identify the Americans. She called Billy on the in-house radio to tell him what happened, but he said the missing ID had to be shut down at Information Technology, which would cause another delay. In the background, Phil cursed Jenny for not reporting it sooner. Rose knew things were bad. Then a gunshot rang out, followed by a scream, just fifty feet away in the reception room.

"Everyone down!" yelled Jackson. "Who else has a weapon?" A couple of staffers hesitantly raised their hands. He pointed to one woman. "You guard the door. Don't let anyone in."

Then he headed towards reception. I can t let you do that, sir," a military aide said, while blocking the door, not allowing Jackson to leave. He was obviously enacting the wildcat protocol. This young man s duty was to protect Jackson; he'd take a bullet for him. There was no way he d let him go towards a firefight. He and Jackson stared at each other. Jackson understood the rationale. He was both the Executive Councilor and Commander-In-Chief; losing him would be devastating. But he couldn t just hide in this room while people were shooting staff right outside the door.

He was considering his options, like punching this poor kid in the nose, when another shot cracked through the air. Jackson guessed it was a .44. Then another shot followed from the same weapon, and then a shot from the earlier gun, probably a flintlock. He was still thinking about pushing the kid out of the way when someone shouted from just outside the meeting room,

"They're down, shooters are down, but Doris is hit. Hit bad!"

They all ran to the reception room. They saw the bodies of two men dressed like wealthy men from the colonies. On the floor was a woman trying to bunch up her own apron to put pressure on the big hole in Doris Stewart's abdomen.

Rose gasped in horror and ran over. Doris had been an administrative assistant at Omímeya for years. She was a Crow Creek tribal member, auntie to many. She remained at the main reception desk despite an offer of a promotion to work solely for Rose. *Why did she come in? She should have stayed home,* thought Rose, but she knew Doris loved being in the thick of things. She probably came in when she saw the alert. Doris was still alive, but it was obvious by the amount of blood she didn't have long. She was grimacing in pain. She looked at Rose and gave her a small nod which seemed to say, "I did my duty." Then she expired quietly, with a last shuddering breath.

Rose didn't care who saw her. She broke into loud sobs. Only a handful of people understood Doris's importance to Rose; Rose herself likely didn't realize it until then. Doris was the mother figure she never had, always reminding Rose to eat, teasing her about Jackson, and showing she cared by asking questions about the kids. She'd been working in the administration office when Rose moved upstairs from her job as Guest Manager. Doris gave her the rundown on all the important players in any corporate office. Rose's first few years were tough, but Doris made the road easier. Rose couldn't imagine the office without her.

Jackson looked around and saw a .44 Remington pistol lying next to Doris's motionless hand. He was confused. Doris was an older, sweet grandmotherly type, not the type to pack a .44. It made little sense.

"Anyone see what happened?" Jackson asked the group of people now crowding into the reception area.

"I was in the hall when it happened," one tech said. "Someone let these two guys in, left, and this one," he indicated a man who was missing most of his head and lay in a puddle of blood on the floor, "came in the door and shot Jacob without saying a word." The tech then pointed to a young man behind the reception desk who was also missing a good chunk of his head. "Doris walked in right before them but was behind the door going to the coat rack. She just reached into her purse, pulled out her gun, and shot the guy. The other man turned to her, but they must have shot at each other at the same time."

The second man on the floor had a visible hole in his chest. Jackson noted for the first time that Doris still had her coat on. By the door, a large purse had been dropped. Although Jackson had never worked in homicide, his police training enabled him to visualize and understand the scene as described.

Rose was sitting on the floor with Doris s head in her lap, crying uncontrollably. Jackson didn t know what to do. He d never seen Rose lose her composure. Even during the cartel attack, with so many killed, even when she was shot in the head—granted, it was a graze—she remained calm. Jackson couldn t remember if he ever saw Rose cry. The sight of her unraveling now struck him with unexpected force, a stark reminder of how much she had carried in silence as both a leader and a mother. With every fiber of his being, he wanted to go to her, to comfort her. But he was in charge. The gate was under attack and at least two gunmen were still at large. As much as he wanted to be, Jackson couldn t be there for Rose. He looked around and saw Linda Gagnon, Rose s administrative assistant, a competent older woman, standing against the wall, tears streaming down her face.

Jackson went up to Linda and said, "Please take care of Rose, get her to her office, clean her up, get her coffee, and let her know I'll be with her as soon as I can."

Linda nodded. She went over to Rose, covered with blood, sitting on the floor with a very still Doris, and leaned over, saying, "I know, honey, it's horrible, but there's nothing we can do here. Let's go into your office, and we can get poor Doris covered up." She directed someone to look for blankets or sheets to cover Doris and the other bodies. She helped the still crying Rose get up off the floor and guided her to her office. Linda was glad Rose kept a change of clothes in there.

Jackson looked around the reception room. Almost everyone was there, some crying, most in shock. "Attention everyone, I know this is terrible, but we have jobs to do. Communication, we need you back to your posts. Someone secure this door, both inside and outside. The rest of you have jobs. We're still under attack; that's your priority. We'll deal with the rest of this later."

He returned to the command center. He looked at the screen where a tech had been transcribing the radio traffic. The report was current, but it missed a few minutes. Everything was happening so fast. Using the communication channel on a speaker, he followed the battle as it unfolded.

Last year, after the cartel attack, they installed a gatehouse at Omímeya. This gatehouse included a guard post where people presented IDs and a sturdy metal gate that could be closed if necessary. There was a small barracks on the other side that housed four guards with rotating shifts. The post wasn t heavily armed; its primary purpose was to screen people. The only way to access Omímeya besides using the road and the gatehouse would be to cross the river, a chokepoint that today worked in their favor.

About fifty militia had mustered downstairs in a meeting room, awaiting orders. After conferring with Gardner, Jackson took command. Gardner had his hands full in Chamberlain, trying to take back control of Interstate Communications to get the phones and NewNet back up. The short range radios Omímeya used were too far away for Gardner to hear.

Jackson had never directed so many forces. He'd retired from the Army as a sergeant. He'd helped Gardner design the Officer Candidate School's online program and earned the rank of Colonel in the reserves but still felt unprepared for the level of command required today.

He went downstairs to address the militia directly. They were mostly Omímeya employees who lived inside the loop. Many were women, and most looked frightened. Most likely, the only time they'd ever held a weapon was during training. He assigned a few to the entrances to supplement the security forces, but sent most to the gate. He had them travel in vehicles not only for speed, but for cover. Most crammed into the shuttle buses and could hear gunfire as they approached.

Jackson listened to the radio reports on his headset as he ran up the four flights of stairs to get back to the command center. He was happy to see security stationed at the stairway entrances as he was waved through.

He learned from the command center board he d missed something during his ten minutes of going downstairs and listening to only one channel. Lou White Mountain was under attack at the trading post. He berated himself for the mistake, thinking he needed to address the troops before battle, like a WWII general. He could have sent the order from here.

Much had happened in his absence. A big work truck sped up to knock down the gate, then the Guard shot the driver as he got close, but the truck swerved into the security booth, pinning the Guard, possibly fatally.

Several other trucks still approached. On the drive up, the militia had shot some men riding in the backs of the trucks, wounding or killing them. They returned fire. Bodies of men and horses lay scattered along the two miles of road between their initial parking spot and the gatehouse. Fewer than half the men in the trucks made it to the gate. As the Omímeya militia approached in the trucks and shuttle buses, the remaining men, still attacking, looked around, realized how badly they were outnumbered, and surrendered.

Jackson, listening to the channel Lou was on, heard what sounded like explosions. It was hard not to ask what was going on. Obviously, they were fighting for their lives.

He looked up, and Rose, in changed clothes, with a puffy red face, came in to listen. She asked, "is that where Kimi and Gift are?"

Jackson walked over and put his arm around her shoulders and led her to a seat. "Here, you can watch the board and listen to the reports. This way, you'll know as soon as I do."

Gift's voice came over the radio, reporting clearly and concisely. She sounded young, but understandable in her Lakota accent. A group of trucks drove to the front, and the men jumped out and started firing. Gift radioed still arriving militia, and they attacked from the rear. The two forces wiped out the attackers.

Jackson asked, so Rose could hear, "You and Kimi are okay?"

"Yes, we're fine, but Lou and several others are wounded."

"We found the other Americans," a tech came in and said. "They're holed up in IT with hostages. It took us a while to get the message because no one was checking their phones because everyone thought the phones were down."

"They're not?" Rose asked, becoming more aware and capable, knowing the girls were safe.

"Only the outside lines are out. Omímeya Wi-Fi wasn't affected, it's internal."

"They're trying to get into the main server room, but Henry LaChamp is there with an ID card, which isn't letting him in, its biometric. Obviously, they didn't expect that and took hostages. They're demanding to talk to Mrs. Chasing Hawk."

"I should go down there. It's better to talk face-to-face," said Rose, surprisingly calm.

"It's an unnecessary risk. You can talk over the radio."

"I'm not sure what to say," Rose said.

"I've taken hostage negotiations training. Let's see if they'll talk to me."

The tech connected him to the right channel on the in-house radio. "This is Councilor Oliver Jackson. Am I talking to the person in charge?"

"This is Henry LaChamp. I don't want to talk to you. I asked to speak to Rose. She has men talking for her all the time, but they all do what she says. All women from your time use men like puppets."

Jackson almost laughed; he wasn't entirely wrong.

"Why don't you tell me what you want, and we can go from there? We've met, and Henry, you seem like a reasonable man."

"Put Rose on."

Jackson shrugged, then said on the radio, "All right, they are getting her. It'll take a minute."

Without Henry hearing, he told Rose, "Use active listening skills, use his name, and try to create empathy and rapport. Not sure how that's going to go. He seems to have an issue with women. Don't back him into a corner. If they know the battles are all lost outside, if they surrender, they'll likely hang. Don't give them an excuse to kill or cause damage."

Rose disregarded most of this advice when she flicked on the radio and said harshly, "What do you want, Henry?"

"I want the hard drives. I know there are daily backups."

"Not practical. The data is on cloud servers in another location."

"Yes, at Interstate Communications. We already have control of that facility."

Rose didn't know whether it was still true.

"Okay, if you have it; why do you need the hard drives?"

Rose heard someone speaking in the background, someone with an accent from her time. "Patents aren't in the cloud, and lots of other critical data."

Rose didn't know who the traitor was and was getting angrier. Jackson looked at her and took an exaggerated deep breath, encouraging her to do the same.

"Henry, it looks like you're in a situation you didn't plan for. Why don't you and I figure out a way out of this where no one gets hurt?"

A tech waved at Jackson to get his attention. He made a 'keep him talking' motion to Rose, who did so, asking Henry questions. He ranted more about women from her time, how they were all liars and whores. It was hard for her to listen without comment.

Jackson switched channels and Billy said, "They're in the main IT section. We have them on video, but windows surround the room, and they're not bulletproof. A couple of my guys are excellent shots. We could shoot them all right through the glass."

"Are they all armed?"

"As far as we can tell, only the Americans. That fucker Andy Martin is helping them. Do I have the go-ahead?"

Jackson thought for a moment. He had been a police officer longer than he had been commander-in-chief. But this was different. This was war. The rules were gone, replaced by hard choices and a weight he'd never imagined carrying. It went against everything he believed in to just shoot suspects without giving them a chance to give up. But today, he had no compassion, and his sense of justice about protecting his new country took precedence.

"Yes, but shoot only the armed ones. Make sure you do both at once, so there's no chance for them to shoot a hostage."

"The other two may have weapons we can't see."

"Stage two other marksmen to get a bead in case they raise a weapon. Do you have four down there?"

"Yes, if one is me."

Through the radio, Jackson and Rose heard the gunshots. Then the good news: the hostages are safe. Andy Martin and Henry LaChamp surrendered, knowing they would probably hang. Rose said nothing, but her clenched jaw spoke volumes. The price of the day had already settled like ash in her lungs.

The Battle of Omímeya was layered in complexity, with many moving parts. Between espionage, thunder, and bloodshed, it'd take time to unravel what truly happened. But clearly, this had been an organized, well-funded operation months in the making.

Later, during the debrief, General Gardner concluded, "This attack relied on local support. Mercenaries did the killing, but locals paved the way."

Jackson's brow furrowed. "Clyde Folsom?"

"We're looking into that angle. The timing lines up with his last broadcast, full of fire and fury. Someone found this on one body," passing around a pamphlet in an evidence bag. Folsom's sermons. Handwritten notes in the margins.

Rose took it, flipping through the pages. Scripture. Revolutionary slogans. A crude sketch of the Circle emblem, crossed out in red.

"They weren't just paid to kill us," she whispered. "They believed it."

"I thought he'd pivoted away from annexation. I thought he had toned down."

"Folsom was just a player," Gardner said quietly. "George Washington conducted the orchestra. It was organized by men who had already fought one revolution. And if this was the opening move, the war for the future has only begun."

Rose felt overwhelmed and helpless. Having a powerful enemy from outside while fighting the internal threats felt like too much. That helplessness settled like a stone in her chest. So many had died, so many relatives, so many teenagers, her nephews, they had their entire lives ahead of them, and Doris, poor Doris.

For one long moment, she let the grief pass through her without resisting it. Then she inhaled, slow and deep, and rose to her feet.

There was still work to do.

Part IV
Winter
(waníyetu)

You might as well stand and fight because if you run,
you will only die tired.
— Vine Deloria Jr. (1933–2005),
Standing Rock Lakota author and activist

Chapter Twenty-Seven
Mary

MARY WAS STILL FEELING the effects of the Battle of Omímeya, well over a month since it happened. Winter solstice and Christmas celebrations were muted this year, with funerals, honor ceremonies, special masses, and people gathering to share grief. It was a poor substitute.

She didn't experience the trauma and horror others did, only guilt about being spared. She'd spent the battle locked in her little safe room in her backyard. Calling it a safe room was a stretch. They'd converted their little tool shed, insulated it to be bulletproof, equipped it with a security camera, a radio, a cot, a chair, and a chemical toilet she fortunately didn't need to use.

Being a public-facing leader came with additional expectations, especially with the outside world. One of those was using an honor guard at public functions. The wildcat protocol deployed a rotating group of six young men who acted like the old world Secret Service. They'd been close enough to protect her when the alerts first came in. As the Chair of the Executive Council, Mary was more fortunate than others.

Her next-door neighbor, Carla Two Bulls, had lost her husband after Big Thunder because of lack of medications and had two empty bedrooms. Social Security and pensions no longer existed. Although she qualified for Elder Assistance, Carla wanted to cook her own meals and stay in her home. Not that the Living Wisdom Centers were bad—she had friends who enjoyed them, particularly after they added daycare centers. She ate some meals there, but she couldn't afford to stay in her home without help.

When Mary found out, she mentioned some of her honor guards were looking for rooms closer to her to avoid the commute. It worked out well for two young men to move in. They reminded Carla of the sons she lost beyond the Circle, and she enjoyed cooking for them. She even did their laundry. They helped in the yard, fixed things around the house, and contributed to the bills. It was a good arrangement for everyone.

Barely twenty, Ryan White Mountain was tall and rawboned, still growing into the promise of his frame. He felt he had a lot to prove. His father, a tribal chair, had been a Marine—or as he liked to say, always a Marine. Other Guard members tended to look down on the honor guard, who stood post without combat duties. His father reminded him that Marine embassy guards once played a critical role, often overlooked. He had even helped Ryan redesign the honor guard uniform.

As a kid, Ryan stood in front of the mirror wearing his father's old jacket, sleeves too long, chest puffed with pride. His father gave it to him the day he graduated from basic. Now it hung in his closet, a quiet reminder of the respect he still hoped to earn. At his first Guard training, someone called him "poster boy," and the name stuck. It lit a fire in him to prove he wasn't just there for appearances.

There was talk of standardizing Guard uniforms, but it hadn't happened yet. Pants could be jeans, buckskins, or hemp Carhartts. Utility uniforms were camo, usually hunting patterns made before Big Thunder. Boots or moccasins varied, but everyone wore large black neckerchiefs for their many practical uses. Military uniforms of this era were ornate, and the honor guard uniform matched the style: a long indigo coat with piping in the four direction colors, brass buttons, and epaulettes. Paired with black dress trousers and polished shoes, it set them apart, especially indoors, where they usually served. Ryan took pride in the uniform. As a corporal, he tried to uphold high standards. Like most of his unit, he never thought they would see real action.

Although they weren't in the building, everyone received Omímeya's Yellow Alert when it came in. Ryan and the other Guard came straight to Mary's house. To be safe, they began enacting some of the wildcat protocol even before it was called. They sent Bridget and the girls to a neighbor. Ryan called other members of the unit, but some lived miles away and might take a while to arrive.

While they waited anxiously for word, everyone sat around Mary's table, with her husband Daniel and Ryan listening to the radio, trying to figure out what was going on. Ryan sent the other Guard to patrol the street in front of the house. When the Orange Alert came, they called wildcat.

Daniel refused to go into the safe room with Mary, insisting on sitting on the back porch in front of it with a shotgun. When two more unit members arrived, Ryan stationed one in the house and sent the other to join the patrol. He got on the roof with his Savage 110 Tactical rifle.

Two armed men, dressed like those from this century, rode up the street and tied up their horses a few houses down. The patrol saw them and radioed Ryan, who said to let them pass. As they approached Mary's front door, they pulled out weapons, and Ryan shot them in the head, one after the other. They were both excellent shots. His father would be proud.

They made Mary stay in the safe room for a couple of hours until they got the all-clear from Omímeya. Mary wasn't happy, as the entire battle, including the hostage situation in IT, only took a little over an hour, but it took a while to figure out what was going on. She felt trapped in the small space as those hours passed slowly. Mary sat rigid on the cot, hands clenched in her lap, her thoughts spiraling through worst-case scenarios. She imagined Daniel shot or the kids, Omímeya overrun, the government dismantled. The waiting was its own kind of torment, helplessness pressing against her chest until she struggled to breathe. Then she heard what sounded like far away explosions. She didn't understand. Most of the big guns were in Chamberlain. She didn't find out what she'd heard until after it was over.

She knew she shouldn't complain, considering what happened to the other Executive Councilors. Theresa Martinez waited it out in Rose's safe room. Shawn Caris refused to go to his makeshift safe room, a closet in the RV Clubhouse. Instead, he went with his husband to his militia station, the clinic at the medical school, to await casualties. He told the Guard if they wanted to keep him safe, they could come with him. He would hide by putting on a pair of scrubs, grabbing a clipboard, and doing intakes. As the wounded arrived, he did just that. Later, Shawn and his husband watched a security video of two men kicking down the door to the fifth wheel where he lived. They assumed the two men who shot poor Doris at the admin offices had been looking for Jackson. The other Executive Councilor Jerome Brown, Minister of Agriculture, lived in an isolated area with many others, and no one had even tried to take him out.

It was different for Richard Russo, Minister of Infrastructure. He was at home with his wife, playing bridge with a colleague and his wife. Card games, including bridge, had seen a dramatic upswing in popularity since last winter. No one had their phones on them. They didn't hear the Yellow Alert. When the Orange Alert came in and the wildcat was called, there wasn't time for the Guard assigned to him to arrive from six miles away. Two men approached the unlocked door, entered, saw four people playing cards, and, unsure which one was Richard, shot both men. As they entered, Richard's wife, Evelyn, stood up—possibly in greeting—which blocked one shot that passed through her. The man walked around the table, and saw Evelyn clearly dead and Richard bleeding profusely from a stomach wound, a lethal wound in the eighteenth century. The other man was missing part of his head. Considering their job done, the shooters calmly walked away, leaving the other woman screaming in their wake. She soon collected herself, being a nurse with trauma experience. Richard had a well-stocked first aid kit with QuickClot, and she was able to stop the bleeding. The phones were down, so she and a neighbor drove him to the hospital. Because the bullet passed through his wife first, it did less damage. Richard refused to let anyone say he was lucky or that Evelyn would have been happy to give her life for him. He felt he should have died for her.

Mary was worried about Richard. Once, she visited him in the hospital, but their conversation was stilted and full of unspoken sorrow. She'd sent messages, unsure whether her presence would comfort or make things worse. She saw in his eyes the haunted look of someone caught between grief and guilt, a look she recognized from the mirror.

What happened to Duane Nelson, the Minister of Communication, was another sad but similar story. Two men just walked up to his house in Chamberlain. There wasn't time for the Guard to arrive after the wildcat was called. They broke down the door, found Duane listening to the radio in his den, shot him, and walked out. His adult son came downstairs with a shotgun, and they killed him as well.

More than once, Mary wondered why she had been spared and others had not. That question lingered like smoke, impossible to grasp or wave away.

She and Ryan grew closer after this and talked about how to increase protection services for other Executive Councilors. Mary wasn't sure where her gratitude that her family was safe ended and her guilt began, but she knew it wouldn't go away overnight.

The Battle of Omímeya was the most devastating event in Changleska's young history. Thirty-seven dead and fifty-three wounded among young, healthy people seemed worse than the hundreds who died after Big Thunder without the right medical care. The enemy losses of seventy-eight dead and twenty-nine wounded did not justify their own. While the area had seen loss of life from fires, industrial accidents, and even the eleven dead from the cartel attack, this was far worse. The Chasing Hawk family suffered the largest blow, with fourteen dead and nine wounded. Mary felt terrible for Rose. Her ex-husband, Hotah, was among the wounded, but she lost many relatives. Although they were exes, Mary knew she was still close to the Chasing Hawk family, attending family gatherings, all the weddings and funerals. Mary also knew Rose quietly supported family members financially as needed.

And poor Kimi, while it was her warning that saved so many lives, it was her own family that went out first. Her father, in the rez way, saw danger coming and called his relatives, and they came. They didn't wait for the militia to be called out, the police or the Guard. They became the tip of the spear and paid the ultimate price. Riding their horses or running on foot up the path parallel to the road where five trucks of seventy men with guns waited, they opened fire, and were fired upon in return; however, the attackers had the protection of their trucks, but they had no cover. Mary had spoken little to Rose; she had been busy with the aftermath, including many funerals, but she assumed Kimi would be devastated that her warning had caused so many family deaths. She'd heard Gift was close to the cousins she attended classes with. One sixteen-year-old boy, Jordan Chasing Hawk, single-handedly killed nine men, and even though he was wounded, he'd pulled three other wounded to safety, including his cousin Matt, before succumbing to blood loss from his own wound. He received the Circle Medal of Honor posthumously at the ceremony held last week.

Despite being three miles away in a soundproof shed, Mary could still hear the thunder booming. She thought they were big guns; they were so loud. If she could hear those explosive claps there, they must have been extremely loud at the trading post where the attack occurred. That Kimi could call down the thunder in December on command was hard enough to believe, but to do it in a way to aid the battle was unimaginable. Mary had to examine her own strong Catholic faith against the spirituality of the Lakota, to come to a place of realizing there was no conflict. She even discussed it with Father Murphy. They discussed miracles and saints, knowing that if it was called God, Wakhan Thanka, or Great Spirit, it was all the same. These events should increase her faith, not question it.

Every day since the attack, she sat in her little prayer corner in her room and lit a candle and prayed for the Chasing Hawk family. She believed God held them in his hands.

=..=

Because of the large attendance, they held the meeting in a different room than usual. Many people cared about the fate of the prisoners captured during the Battle of Omímeya, currently held in the Brule County Jail. The room was full of key officials, justice committee chairs, and representatives from the Guard and First Shield Command. Everyone with a stake in justice had shown up. Mary knew from experience how difficult it was for a group of this size to reach an agreement with so many competing viewpoints and agendas. But like eating an elephant, the only way to do it was one bite at a time. She took a deep breath and began at precisely nine am.

"Good morning everyone," she said. "There is a lot of material to go over, and many opinions on what we should do. We've already received an emergency extension requiring those charged with a crime to appear before a judge within seven working days. There'll be no further extensions. The purpose of this group is to come to an agreement on recommendations to give to the judge about what we think should be done with the prisoners. Please remember we are an advisory body. The judge may or may not follow our recommendations."

"Then why give it?" Ed Robinson, the politician, asked.

"Precedence," Elliot answered before Mary said anything. "If you've been reading the forums, many people have proposed innovative solutions, as well as very strict measures. How we respond affects more than these prisoners, but those in the future. While the judges may rule in some cases differently than we recommend, it's highly unlikely they will ignore everything we recommend. Ideally, we represent the will of the people."

Mary said, with a little sharpness in her tone, "We don't have time for interruptions or crosstalk. This meeting runs until noon. We'll come up with recommendations during this time. We created an entire country in two days. This should be doable in three hours." There was a nervous chuckle around the room. "If the recommendations we vote on need fine-tuning, or wordsmithing, after lunch we'll have this meeting room until four pm. But the overall proposal must be voted on by noon. Is that clear?"

Everyone nodded. Those who worked with Mary before knew she ran her meetings like a tight ship. "I hope everyone has come prepared by reading the forums which have been very active. We lack the time to review what's been posted, but each of you will have a chance to briefly advocate for your proposals. Remember your time to comment and disagree with other's proposals was online before this meeting, not now.

However, for security reasons, not all the information about all the prisoners was online, so I'll ask Phil to give us a briefing."

Phil had his aide post a slide on the screen and began. "As of today, there are 126 prisoners in custody. Most of the attackers at the front gate at Omímeya died. Some were involved in the takedown of the Interstate Communication building, either letting them in, or Leon Bauer, who hacked the software to shut down the phones. He was angry about his transfer from Omímeya, knowing it was because of his cousin and no fault of his own. Others sold tech, passed messages, provided intel about the Councilors, or acted as lookouts. We are still searching for perpetrators of the attacks on the homes of the Executive Councilors. We believe there are six still at large. The investigators checked the video and photos against the bodies at the attack sites and the prisoners. We know from interviews, the men were told to join the attack forces if practical, otherwise, to leave the area. General Gardner, can you elaborate?"

General Jonathan Gardner looked older and more tired than most had ever seen him. He said, "Since day one, we've been looking diligently. Likely, they're heading south, but winter and frozen rivers will impede their progress. Our patrol boats stopped every rivercraft, both north and south. They probably aren't hiding anywhere nearby, unless they have something very isolated and well-stocked for the winter. We have the Guard in both St. Louis and New Orleans scouring everywhere. They'll turn up. With the large reward offered, if nothing else, someone will turn them in."

Phil continued, "Of the 126 prisoners, 124 are men. The only two women are spouses. Thirty-four are Changleskan citizens, and nine are legal residents waiting for their two years. Twenty-seven are Americans, with fifty-six of various nationalities, mostly French, Spanish, but quite a few Hessians, and a handful of other Europeans. They all seemed to be mercenaries. Many of the Americans fought in the Revolutionary War, which is very telling. Today, we must decide whether to classify these men as prisoners of war. General?"

Gardner explained. "The rules of warfare at this time were very regimented and strictly followed. If one side were to fail to follow the rules of honor, the consequences could be grave."

Robinson was seen to almost interrupt with a "so what?", but a look from Mary shushed him.

Gardner addressed the unasked comment: "Sooner or later, every conflict turns to peace. But if a nation breaks the rules of war, peace becomes nearly impossible. Remember Carthage? Right, you don't, because they don't exist anymore." A silence fell over the room, with people nodding. "The question of whether to consider these men prisoners of war is valid. There's no declared state of war between the United States of America and the Changleska Coalition. However, after this, that may change. The US has seized our intellectual property and our ship under construction in Boston, ambushed supply trains in Georgetown, and other places to steal tech. None of the captured Americans have admitted who hired them. Most shifted blame to the French, perhaps hoping to sow confusion or exploit longstanding rivalries between colonial powers. There's no Geneva Convention at this time, but there were expectations about prisoners of war—one being they were not to be executed out of hand. In our time, we would have called them terrorists. I will leave it to this body," he said, waving his hand around the room, "to determine which. I will follow the law."

When this issue was brought up in the online forum, it had garnered little discussion. People looked around and realized the first hard decision was coming up.

Mary stated, "We must provide a formal recommendation to the judges. Either we classify them as prisoners of war, to be treated according to the standards of this time, or we charge them as terrorists, which may warrant the death penalty. Let's take five minutes to consider the merits and consequences of each approach, followed by a vote." She pointedly looked at her watch.

Jackson said, "My understanding is they frequently paroled mercenary POWs on the grounds they were following orders. Unlike now, parole was a word of honor not to fight again. This era takes honor seriously. Ships would transport them back to their homelands. But even in these times, killing civilians was unacceptable. Executing eighty-six men for terrorism seems extreme."

Many people vehemently objected to setting them free. The discussion went round and round: hanging all of them, branding them in the face with an M for murderer (not uncommon at this time), sending them to the Indigenous Lakota, keeping them in prison, and various other suggestions.

With no clear answers in the allotted time, Mary said, "General Gardner, I know you usually prefer to remain neutral in these discussions, but how about a suggestion? You know more than any of us the broader implications of this."

The general smiled. "My personal unofficial recommendation is to press them into the British Navy. The Brits are desperate for sailors. They press men all the time, which is a source of tension between the countries involved. Occasionally, the country gets them back, but it often takes years. And from what I understand from our own budding navy, serving on an eighteenth-century sailing ship is worse than any prison sentence we could devise. We'd get rid of the problem without hanging them and put it in the favor column with the Brits."

With a sigh of relief, a proposal to press them in the British Navy was voted on and passed, although some still held out for executing the lot.

Mary allowed a five-minute P&T break, then they resumed with Phil's report.

He presented a new slide on the screen. "Of the Changleskan citizens and legal residents, thirty-six are White, four Hispanic, and three Native. We did extensive interviews with everyone." Everyone knew that meant interrogation, but most hoped that Changleskan values would preclude torture. "That was one reason we asked for the extension on the seven-day rule. We wanted accomplices besides those we caught outright. We didn't include known associates, or people we suspect, only what we could prove in a court of law."

Elliot interrupted again but knew Mary well enough to get away with it. "I worked with Phil and his FSC officers to make sure the evidence was solid, and the convictions would hold, with what was at stake." Everyone knew that treason carried the death penalty.

Phil went on. "The most common reason given was money. A few held personal grudges, like Henry LaChamp and Leon Bauer. Sixteen were active supporters of Clyde Folsom, but only one was a regular church member. The rest followed his radio show and online presence. We believe with his help, the United States organized and funded the attack. It is obvious, but we've yet to find a clear chain of evidence."

Mary said, "Looks like the next decision is what to do with this group. I propose we lump the nine legal residents with the citizens. That'll make it easier. LaChamp is in this group."

Everyone agreed, and Mary said, "I don't think we can offer these people up to the Brits for their press gangs. It's a dangerous precedent to set for Changleska citizens. These cases seem to prove treason beyond a reasonable doubt, but some are not so clear-cut. Should the woman who didn't report her husband hang? Or the nineteen-year-old who said he gave the security code to the road maintenance yard for someone to draw obscenities on the trucks? Are all these cases the same? I suggest we spend a little time on generalities, then go to specific cases."

There was a lot of discussion. The Chairs of the various committees gave the reasons for their proposals. Some advocated alternative punishments for all the accused; some wanted all of them to hang, arguing that treason was treason, and if they didn't set an example, where would it end?

Working through specific cases, they created two groups: one of those people whose direct actions had caused death, such as Henry LaChamp, who'd been seen opening the door for whoever'd killed the receptionist and Doris; and another group comprising those who actively aided and abetted the enemy, like Andy Martin. This included anyone directly selling technology or weapons or giving access to secure areas like Interstate Communication. The other group consisted of family members who knew but didn t report, or stupid people like the kid from road maintenance, people who passed on information they may or may not have known the damaging content of, and a few others who acted as middlemen for sales.

Fourteen people were in the group whose actions led to deaths. The vote regarding them went by an easy majority to recommend to the judge the death penalty. Now they had to decide what to do with the other thirty-one.

Kenneth Harris, whose job as Brule County Sheriff included overseeing the County Jail, said, "As I said in the forum, keeping prisoners long-term in the jail is not viable. We are very short-staffed, and it's expensive. Although the government is reimbursing the County, it doesn't cover everything. In the old world, prisons were being outsourced to private companies, who made a profit by using inmates as a labor force for pennies on the dollar."

Ed Robinson added, "He's right about the reimbursement—it doesn't cover everything, and you know the county has a huge budgetary shortfall. Eventually, some of the county businesses will be profitable, but many are years away."

After Big Thunder, there developed a deep divide between the county and the two reservations. Many in the county wanted to annex with the US and wanted nothing to do with the new country of Changleska. The months after Big Thunder were turbulent and divisive. Brule, Buffalo, and Lyman Counties merged for financial reasons, but after a county-wide referendum, the combined County joined Changleska. However, they retained sovereignty, like the tribes. They collected taxes from county residents, had their own budgets, and their largest asset was property. They bought patents and started small manufacturing businesses, which would hopefully make them more self-sufficient. County independence was a big deal to many people. Others thought the County was wasting resources and should merge completely with Changleska.

People moved on to discuss alternatives to incarceration. There was an animated discussion of punishment for various offenses. Someone said the kid who gave the road maintenance security code should get probation and be required to wear "stupid" on his work vest.

Phil said, "Either that kid is very stupid, or very smart. It was a good excuse."

Someone asked Billy because he was on the Omímeya board, "Hey Billy, did Kyle bring back a lie detector machine with all the other stuff they brought along?"

"No," Billy answered, "but I heard there is a holy woman in Red Eagle's tribe that can always tell if someone is lying."

"Maybe we should bring her in," someone replied, half-serious.

Elliot said, "Everyone should consider the specific charges of the two women. They're not only charged because they didn't rat their husbands out. If that were the case, we would have charged more women. We shouldn't create a police state that forces people to inform on their families. In both these cases, the women passed on messages, arranged payments, and were fully involved. They met the standards for criminal conspiracy."

Further discussion of various cases occurred, but the County Sheriff's stance was a surprise.

Kenneth said, "I read through the Criminal Justice Reform Committee forum on what to do with the prisoners, and honestly, I think it's an excellent solution. Plus, it will get them all out of our hair."

What started as a plan to create a penal colony had evolved into the creation of a farming community, designed not only as a practical solution for incarceration but also as an experiment in restorative justice. The model emphasized labor, rehabilitation, and reintegration, echoing traditional Indigenous values of communal responsibility and healing. A little less than half of the residents would be prisoners. The Committee pointed out that isolating a group of criminals or political prisoners only reinforces negative behaviors. Rehabilitation happens when people want to join society and make a positive contribution. They recommended judges could exile prisoners to the colony for five to twenty years, depending on the offense to the colony.

Near Ponca lands, formally Nebraska, many miles of unclaimed territory held some of the best corn-growing land in the world. The Ponca were farmers, far more peaceful than the Lakota, and didn't claim broad swaths of land like the buffalo-hunting tribes. They cultivated corn, beans, and squash in fixed fields along river valleys, following a more stable and seasonal way of life. The Ponca had joined Changleska recently, and people expected them to welcome neighbors who could bring trade, medicine, and education to their isolated area. By recruiting settlers and granting them land, this plan would enable former prisoners to bring their families and help build a larger community. The goal was to have 150 people in the first group. The first town in the area would be called New Start.

Some argued this wasn't enough punishment. Others pointed out that life on an isolated settlement would be harsh at first, with no electricity or any of the conveniences people from our time were used to like movies or NewNet. It might be a long wait before trade routes brought items like sugar and coffee.

Jackson said, "I'm not sure if our new constitution forbids cruel and unusual punishment or not, but sentencing people to years without coffee seems harsh enough," eliciting a ripple of relieved laughter around the room.

Mary said, "It's almost noon. Can we make a proposal to start a colony near the Ponca lands and propose the judge sentence people from five to twenty years depending on the offense? After lunch, we can dial down details of the plan until four."

The proposal passed by a larger margin than Mary would've suspected.

She ended the meeting with, "Great job, everyone. This was not easy. I also want to acknowledge the Criminal Justice Committee. They have worked tirelessly on this plan."

The Chair said, "Not only us, but we had help from the Agriculture and Social Justice Committees."

Later, when she was in bed with Daniel, cuddling and talking about her day, she said, "I'm pleased with the solution we came up with. Sometimes I wonder about what'll happen to this country we've created, but on days like today, we come up with innovative and fair solutions. It gives me hope for the future."

Daniel said, drawing her closer, "That's because they have you steering the ship. You underestimate the role you play. Someday they will call you 'Mother of Changleska' and make statues of you."

"If I get a statue, you should get one too. I couldn't do much without you by my side."

He kissed her forehead. "I'd like that. Be by your side forever."

Chapter Twenty-Eight
Brings Him Home

HE MISSED WINTER. Brings Him Home couldn't believe it was *Wióthehika Wí* (the Sun Is Scarce Moon), also called January. The sun wasn't scarce at Fort Condor; it rained more often and was a little cool, but was rarely cold. He felt his body was out of touch with the rhythms of the earth. Winter was the stone that sharpened the senses to make one strong. He felt the loss of the snow on the prairie as a missing piece of his soul. Preparing for and surviving the winter made Lakota resilient and, therefore, strong.

Brings Him Home thought the Lakota tribe was more powerful than any other he'd met so far on the long journey. His mother's people, the Cheyenne, were close. He'd heard stories about the Apache and Comanche who had great warriors and won many battles against the Whites in the old world but he'd never met them. His friend Little Dog, who'd split off with the Southwest Expedition, might have gotten a chance. He missed him as well as his friend One Ear, and his other friends back home. His tribe's young warriors spent all their time together, from the time they left their mother's lodges, living and training together. Their play was riding, shooting arrows, tomahawks and knives, practicing all the skills needed for war. They started raiding young, being watched by warriors only a few years older. Shared danger formed bonds stronger than those between brothers. Their absence left a void that even his new friends here couldn't fill.

It's not that he didn't like California. He was learning new things, enjoyed meeting new tribes, and spending time with Andy. His feelings towards Andy confounded him. He admired her skill with horses and shooting. He was drawn to her like a bear to honey, but if he got too close, he feared he might catch a few stings. In another month, she would turn sixteen and be old enough to 'date,' according to the rules of her brother and her father. She was used to receiving a lot of attention from men, and seemed disappointed he didn't join her throng of male admirers. She flirted with a few right in front of him, presumably to make him jealous. He studiously ignored it, but inside he was seething, confused by his own reaction. He didn't want to get married yet. Curious about dating rules, he inquired, finding them changed significantly from the old world's expectations. The dating period was shorter, and marriage earlier, as they could no longer prevent pregnancy the way they used to. He knew women of his tribe used herbs, such as juniper berries and sage, but he knew they didn't always work.

His friendship with Andy's brother, Jerry, surprised him. Jerry initially hated him for taking his rifle and saddle when Brings Him Home counted coup on him the first day they met. Although he could've also lost his horse, he was more resentful than grateful at first. They ended up spending a lot of time together between Guard duties and camping right next door to each other. Jerry told him a lot about thunder people, and Brings Him Home taught him the ways of a Lakota warrior.

At Fort Condor, life was both different and strangely like his village at home. Children played, women gossiped, food was prepared, and clothes mended. While the work was different, like home, it seemed endless and never done. With all the different tribes now here, Whites, Hispanics, people from this time and the world of the future, Fort Condor became a vibrant tapestry of humanity working toward the same goals. Brings Him Home was feeling, for the first time, he was a Changleskan. This was his new country he would be a part of building. It differed from his oyate, his tribe that followed Red Eagle, of the Oglala band. That would always be his home, his heart, but it was now a piece of what was becoming the greater whole.

He was both angered and saddened to hear about the Battle of Omímeya. The Fort held a small ceremony to recognize the losses and the bravery, and to offer gratitude for the victory. He wished he could learn more details about the battle itself, but the radio reports only covered the basics. The enemy he would fight as a full Guard member, and hopefully an officer, was now before him. Stories he heard spoke of the Americans and their settlers who colonized and decimated his tribe in their future. He felt proud to be a part of this new nation, knowing Changleska was created to stop Indigenous genocide and to protect the earth.

Brings Him Home usually spent his evenings in the library, which was temporarily housed in the C&C until the Community Center was finished. There were few physical books, but three e-readers were available on the premises for those who didn t own their own. There were three comfortable chairs, but Brings Him Home preferred the floor. He d become a better reader, enjoying the materials assigned by Jody, whom he only met with weekly now. Jody recommended books like biographies of war leaders, or other war books, but also directed him to books about the Native American experience in his timeline to further his understanding of what life had been like before Big Thunder.

He finished dinner and was on his way to the library when he ran into Jerry coming out of the Claims & Assay office, where miners brought in gold to be weighed and tested for purity. Changleska purchased the gold and credited the value to people s identification cards, which were accepted throughout the fort. Some folks held on to a few nuggets or flakes for trade outside the fort or to feel the weight of gold in hand, but since there were few places around here where they could spend gold, most sold it. The expedition had hauled in a large safe from Chamberlain for gold storage. The next outgoing convoy would carry back the gold Changleska had purchased.

Returning supply wagons would bring back merchandise for the miners to buy. Many placed their orders ahead of time. Before the treaty was signed, only surface panning had been allowed. Once the resource sharing agreement with the tribes and the treaty with the Spanish were finalized, the mining increased. Miners began building sluice boxes, rockers, and other low-impact equipment for separating gold from gravel. Now, the fort felt nearly deserted, with miners off at their claims, despite the colder weather in the surrounding mountains.

Jerry was very excited. "Brings, come out to the bar with me. I'm celebrating our first big find. I'm buying."

Brings Him Home wavered. He didn't like the bar because it wasn't fun to hang out with people drinking when you didn't drink. But he wanted to hear Jerry's news. He'd been gone for weeks at his claim, about fifty miles away.

"I should study."

"You can study any time, not every day I'll be buying. The bar has french fries now the new potato crop has come in."

That clinched it. He loved french fries. He'd just eaten dinner, but he was a teenage boy, he could always eat more.

Jerry was so excited he could barely contain himself. "I cleared two hundred twenty dollars in three weeks, sold most, but I'm keeping this beauty," he said, pulling out a small but respectable-sized nugget. "I heard Sam found over five hundred worth in the first two weeks. You should start working your claim."

Brings Him Home never understood the gold fever that took over the fort lately, but now he got it. That was a lot of money for a short time, over three times the wages he could earn in the same period. There were things he wanted to buy but couldn't afford. Next month, he'll take the test, complete his enlistment, and his pay will increase. He'd wanted to buy a pistol, but they were expensive. When he returned home, he'd want to buy presents for his mother and sister. He needed more money.

"With everyone mining, I've had to do extra patrol and post shifts."

"Talk to the captain. You're eligible for three weeks of mining leave, same as anyone else. They're making scheduling changes to address this, anyway. I'm finished building my equipment. You can have my plans. They cost fifteen dollars, but I'm done with them, so you might as well use them. Your claim is close to mine and Andy's, right?"

"Yes, about five miles away," he confirmed.

He received the claim for being part of the First Expedition. He'd heard the bigger gold strikes only happened early on. It made sense for him to work the mine over the winter and bring back as much cash as he could in the spring.

"Okay, thanks for the plans. I'll talk to the captain. When are you going back?"

"I have to work for a week, but when I go back, I'm bringing Andy with me. You should come with us since we're close. That would give you a chance to gather all your supplies. A lot of things are getting harder to find and more expensive every day, so you should jump right on it. This is the opportunity of a lifetime. You don't want to miss it."

The prospect of a trip with Andy was both thrilling and terrifying.

=..=

The trip would have taken him and Jerry two days with their packhorses, but it took four with Andy and the ridiculous amount of stuff she insisted on bringing. She wanted to bring a wagon, but there were no roads in the mountains. When Brings Him Home firmly told her he wouldn't build a road for her, she actually pouted. The extra horses, heavily burdened, slowed them down. Andy insisted she wasn't living in a mining camp without a comfortable place to sleep, clean clothes, and decent cooking pots. She even brought a portable solar shower, saying she wasn't about to wash up in a cold creek. Jerry teased her about all the things she'd tried to pack into the camper atop the pickup truck that pulled the horse trailer they came on the Expedition in. They had to leave a lot behind, but she still brought plenty.

On the fourth day, they camped just before dark about two miles from Brings Him Home's claim, at a spot where the path that led to Jerry and Andy's claim forked off. They'd mixed the loads on the horses for efficient weight distribution. In the morning, they could split everything up in the light. Andy wanted to ride up and see Brings Him Home's claim. Not wanting to leave the horses and gear unattended, Jerry offered to stay in the camp to watch them for a few hours.

"Don't do anything Dad wouldn't approve of," he told Andy as they left. Andy gave him the finger without turning around. Jerry got used to the idea of his sister courting Brings Him Home, but it didn't mean he wouldn't tease her about it.

They entered the little valley where his claim was located, map in hand. A small creek flowed down from the mountain. Strangely, they found tracks from both horses and people. Further upstream, hammering echoed through the trees.

"Let me see the map. This must not be your claim," Andy said. Without a word, he handed it to her.

"No, this is correct. It's here. I thought you had never been here before."

He nodded. They both looked at each other. *Claim jumper.*

He motioned for Andy to grab her rifle, pointed upward for her to climb and find a vantage point. After giving her a few minutes, he moved slowly upstream, following the creek toward the sound of hammering.

The discovery appalled him. Someone had dug directly into the creek bed, disrupting the flow and clouding the water. The once-clear current now ran murky brown, thick with silt. A heavy foul odor rose from the churned sediment, like decay stirred from deep below.

There were strict rules about placer mining, designed specifically to protect the watershed. Clearly, someone ignored those rules. Torn-up banks, sediment pouring into the stream, scattered trash, and half-built equipment littered the area.

He was furious when he got close to the claim jumper. Freshly cut trees surrounded the man, who was pounding posts into the ground, trying to anchor them.

He raised his tomahawk to throw and split the man's skull when he heard Andy shout above him on the ridge. "Brings, no, don't kill him. You need to bring him to the captain for trial."

He wasn't sure why a trial was necessary, but he would let the man live a little longer. Maybe a quick death was too good for him. The man turned, and he realized who it was, Bones. He'd been on his crew for the raid on the Spanish, the biker who could pick locks.

Andy made her way down, keeping her rifle trained on Bones and telling Brings Him Home all the reasons he needed to keep this piece of shit alive. *Killing a trespasser wasn't murder, despite what Andy said*, he thought.

Bones looked unnerved to see him. "Brings, buddy, I'm surprised to see you. I'd heard you weren't going to work your claim. I've found a few ounces by now, but there's good color, we'll get more, and I'll give you your share."

"My share of my own gold you stole?" he asked, hiding the fury he felt inside.

Andy arrived and asked, "Why aren't you working your own claim?"

"Well, err..., I went in on a big group claim with three others, to share the expenses coming out and setting up, with more tools, and the ability to build bigger rigs. I guess none of us looked at the rules too closely and there was a lot we couldn't do, and we had a falling out. So, I came here. I heard Brings didn't want to mine gold, beneath his Lakota honor or something. Figured it wouldn't hurt anything to work it for him. I'd given him his share if he wanted it. I'm happy to partner in any way that's fair, but I've been here a month working my ass off."

Brings Him Home didn't say a word. Considerably bigger and stronger than Bones, he walked over, picked him up, and dragged him to the post. From a pile of tools, he swiftly grabbed some rope and tied him in place. He squatted on his haunches, not saying a word. He took out his knife, a stone from his pouch, and started slowly sharpening his knife.

"What are you going to do, Brings? You're not going to scalp him, are you?" Andy asked with a panic in her voice.

Bones was looking anxious. Brings Him Home just kept sharpening. "No, not going to scalp him. Sometimes we made bets on how long a man could live without his skin."

Both Andy and Bones looked horrified.

"Bones, you didn't only jump my claim and steal from me, but something much worse. You desecrated the water. We say *Mní Wičhóni*—water is life—and you have damaged that life. Not only our food and medicine depend on that water, but fish, birds, bugs, and animals need clean, flowing water for life. I don't see a reason to give you a clean, easy death. For you have not given the lands below this stream a clean, easy death."

By this time, Andy was almost hysterical. "You can't do this. It's not civilized."

"Who said I'm civilized? It's not civilized to destroy the water." Frustrated, he walked away, upset and needing to think.

He realized he'd made a mistake listening to Andy. He should have taken Bones out with the tomahawk. But once he tied him to the post, Bones had become his prisoner. He had read the Guard's rules about prisoner treatment. If he gave Bones the slow, painful death he wanted to inflict, that act might cost him his enlistment.

He might have gotten away with it as a member of the allied forces. Lakota and Changleska values were still undergoing cultural adjustments, some might say. But did he want to throw away everything he'd worked for—his dream of becoming a Guard officer, of leading battles?

He could return to his tribe and become a war leader in a few years, carrying with him all the knowledge he'd gained here. He wanted vengeance deep in his core. Not for the trespass, he'd never been here before and had no attachment to the place. Not even for the stolen gold. No, for the desecration of the water.

Brings Him Home remembered his father's advice: never make big decisions in haste. The words echoed now, urging him to pause before doing something he couldn't take back.

Needing time to think, he said to Andy, "Take Jet back to camp, stay there, and send Jerry back."

"He better be alive and unharmed when Jerry gets here."

Saying nothing, he stood up, looking at her as she climbed on her horse and rode away.

Walking around didn't calm him, just deepened his anger. The entire camp was a mess. He squatted next to Bones, took out his other knife, and started sharpening it.

His silence was more frightening than threats. Bones twitched, eyes darting between the knife and Brings Him Home's face, sweat gathering at his temples despite the cool air. "Brings, hey, I'll tell you where the gold is. I know I said two ounces before, but there are maybe eight, one nugget bigger than my thumbnail. There's a hole dug at the base of the tree next to my tent. There's a flat rock over it. It's yours. You benefit from all my work."

He said nothing. Bones kept babbling, making promises, then turned to threats.

Finally, Brings Him Home said, "I was told there's a fine art to skinning someone and keeping them alive. It's easy to go too far, nick a blood vessel, go too deep. Here's the important part for you: don't move. The slightest movement and things go from bad to worse."

He took his knife and slowly started cutting through the jeans Bones wore. Terrified, Bones urinated on himself, bringing a smile to Brings Him Home's face. Slowly and carefully, he kept cutting until even the stinking wet jeans lay in long strips around him. Then he started on the shirt. Bones froze, expecting the pain to start at any moment. But it never did. When he was done, Bones sat tied to the pole, naked, with his clothes in neat ribbons all around him. Brings Him Home walked away, leaving him sobbing.

When Jerry arrived, saw Bones tied naked to the post and said, "What the fuck, Brings?"

He stood in front of Jerry, came to stiff attention, saluted, and said formally, "Sergeant Dunphy, I'm releasing my prisoner Harold Rogers, known as Bones, to your custody. Charged with trespassing and theft. He should be sent back to the fort for trial."

"Shit, Brings. I guess it's better than skinning the poor bastard. Andy told me. She is quite upset, by the way. Why is he naked?"

"I was deciding."

Shaking his head, Jerry said, "Go look for clothes for him. I'm not taking him naked. This will take four or five days round trip. You owe me. The captain better grant me an extension on my leave for this, or I'll be even more pissed. As for this piece of shit," he kicked Bones, still tied to the post, "Since he's the first claim jumper, they'll need to make an example of him.

We don't have a jail, but I'm sure they'll come up with something that deters others."

Brings Him Home found some dirty clothes in the tent, dug up the gold to send back with Jerry as evidence, and Jerry led Bones to the creek, let him wash, and gave him some water. After Bones was dressed, they tied his hands in front of him, sat him on a stump, and Jerry walked around with his phone, taking pictures for evidence.

"Andy told me he trashed the place, but I didn't believe it was this bad. No wonder you're pissed," Jerry said, disgusted.

Bones walked tied behind Jerry's horse with a long rope. They returned to the camp. Jerry didn't want to leave Andy alone at their claim, and he didn't want her to accompany Brings and Bones alone on the four-day trip. Telling her this did not go well.

"I'm not returning to the fort with you. I just got here. Not sure why you're worried about me being by myself."

"Now we know there's one claim jumper, there may be another. Plus, there are bears and wild animals."

"Then let me go with Brings. I can help him clean up the mess this asshole left."

The asshole in question was sitting nearby with his hands tied in front of him and his feet tied like a hobble.

Jerry reluctantly agreed, still simmering with frustration, and left to get some distance before dark. Bones rode one of the pack horses, hands tied in front, following Jerry with a lead rope. Jerry wondered why he bothered. If Bones escaped, it might solve the problem for everyone. There was no place to go. He didn't see Bones living with a tribe, and he didn't speak Spanish.

Andy and Brings Him Home spoke little the first few days she was there. She set up her tent and helped him clean up the mess Bones left behind. She made better meals, using the food and spices she brought and her own cooking pots. The shared labor, and the rhythm of two people moving together with a purpose, chipped away at the wall between them. He wasn't sure when exactly the mood shifted, maybe when she smiled at him over the campfire, or when she brushed his hand as they passed tools back and forth, but something changed. He'd looked forward to her presence, to her quiet competence, and the way she never asked him to talk when he didn't want to.

That first evening, as she was cooking, she said, "We've made good progress cleaning up. Pretty soon, you won't be able to tell Bones was ever here. At least you got some gold out of the deal."

He looked at her, surprised—and yet not surprised—she didn't understand. White people never understood the relationship his people had with the land and the water.

He tried to explain. "It wasn't the mess that angered me. It was what he did to the water."

"The water?"

"We have a relationship with it. Water has its own spirit. It speaks to us, cares for us. And we need to care for it in return. I don't know the word in English."

"Reciprocity."

"Yes. Reciprocity. Sharing. Caring for each other. When the water is fouled, everything it touches is damaged. And water touches everything. Water is life."

The next day, they were trying to release some logs from a makeshift dam when they both slipped, landing in the water. Cold and sputtering, they looked at each other and burst into laughter. Coming out of the creek, both soaking wet, they looked at each other, their eyes reaching into their hearts, igniting something deep within. She stepped closer. He reached for her just as she reached for him, and in that shared moment, desire flooded faster than the water flowing by. He leaned in, and she met him halfway. Their lips met, soft at first, hungry and searching. Her fingers curled into the back of his shirt. His hands found her waist, her ribs, the curve of her back. Their bodies pressed together, soaked clothes sticking to skin. He could feel her breasts against him; she could feel his hardness. The kiss deepening, moments stretching timelessly, and the world narrowed down to breath, skin, and need.

As the kiss ended, he reached for her clothes to remove them; she moved to help, then she froze.

She put her hand over his, stopping him, and said, "No, we can't. We both promised."

His breath was ragged, his hands trembling with restraint. Brings Him Home remembered the solemn promise Jerry made them both give before leaving. They'd promised they wouldn't do exactly what they were trying to do. Jerry had said he was leaving the honor of his sister in Brings' hands, reminding him of his own sister back home.

He let out a long, frustrated breath. He didn't argue. Didn't plead. He simply turned and walked away, putting distance between them. Enough distance to get some privacy to take the problem in hand.

Later that night, the fire crackled low. Andy had long since retreated to her tent, leaving him alone with his thoughts and the quiet. Coyotes called in the distance. The wind whispered through the cottonwoods. The smell of damp earth and pine clung to him, grounding him.

He sat on the ground, knees pulled up, arms around them, staring at the last embers. His body still remembered the heat of her, the ache of restraint, but his heart felt something stranger. Not only longing and frustration, but something older. He'd kept his promise. And that mattered.

He remembered his father, lessons passed down not in words, but in how a man carried himself. Of what it meant to lead, to guard, to wait. Not everything he wanted was meant to be taken. Some things had to be earned. And some things had to wait until the snow melted.

He'd return home in the spring, but not with Andy. He'd already made up his mind. She was a warrior in her own right, and she had work here to finish. He saw it in her eyes when she spoke of California, in the way she moved through this place like it already belonged to her. He wouldn't take her from that. Wouldn't ask her to choose. And maybe, someday, they would find their way back to each other.

He stood, dusted his hands on his pants, and looked to the north, where the ridgeline cut black against the stars. The sky was sharp with winter light, the air cool. The world felt quiet. Settled.

Brings Him Home would work this claim, finding gold in a way that worked with the water, not against it. He was grateful for the value these gold rocks that were gifted by Mother Earth could bring him. He thought of the presents he would bring his mother and sister; how happy he would be to see them after so long. Finishing his Guard training was something he looked forward to. He knew he wasn't ready to marry, to have a woman in his life who would draw time and focus away from the lessons he still needed to learn, because he knew deep down, his path was that of a warrior, and a war was coming, one that could destroy everything and everyone he loved. It would take all his time, all his discipline, and all the teachings available to him to become the warrior he needed to be.

Losing this war, losing Changleska, might mean losing the earth itself. Not in his lifetime, but in the seventh generation—just as the Whites had in that other world—poisoning the water, stripping the forests, and burning the soil until even their own descendants could no longer ignore the cost. He was a warrior for the Earth. That was the path he must follow and not let anything or anyone get in his way.

Chapter Twenty-Nine
Gift of Thunder

GIFT WAS WORRIED about Kimímela. Her grief and sorrow were understandable, even her guilt to a lesser extent, but three months after the Battle of Omímeya, it hadn't abated. If anything, Kimi was even more depressed. She'd stopped going to school, even for the midwifery studies she loved, and spent a lot of time in bed. She rarely left their room. In the depths of winter, riding and collecting herbs were difficult, but that season was perfect for visiting, having friends spend the night, playing cards or board games, and working on crafts. None of these interested her.

Because she alerted others to the dangers of the forthcoming attack, nineteen members of her family had died, including three cousins around her age with whom she grew up and was close, and a beloved uncle. Hotah, her father, suffered a wound to his right arm, leaving him permanently impaired. Formerly a carpenter, he was now trying to figure out what else he could do to support his family. The consequences of her warning and her family's arriving first were a devastating blow from which the entire family might never recover.

Gift talked to Hotah, and he shared her concerns, although he was in a bad way himself, having lost two uncles, a brother, and three nephews and sustained a life-changing injury. They decided to send both girls to help his sister-in-law. His brother had lived next door to their father on a small horse farm, which had grown a great deal since Big Thunder as the demand for horses grew. They now had thirty horses, which proved too much for his widow, Donna, who had not only lost her husband but also three sons. Donna didn't think she could keep up with the operation, but the middle of the winter was not the time to sell horses. Fortunately, the community stepped in, everyone grateful for the Chasing Hawk family's sacrifice, and there was often a volunteer, or a friend of the family around.

At least spending time with the horses kept them busy, and their shared grief provided some solace. Kimi was close to her grandfather, Joseph. Previously an active man in his sixties, he seemed to have aged a decade since the attack. He tried to console Kimi that her warning had saved many lives, possibly the entirety of Changleska, but it was still hard for her to hear.

Joseph told Gift that Kimi had a wound of the soul and that the Creator and the thunder would heal her, but she had to be in a place to listen and receive the help. He suggested she go to Three Stars, the holy woman at Two Elks' camp for a Yuwipi healing ceremony, which differed somewhat from the ones from his time. This sacred ceremony involved tightly binding and placing a person in complete darkness to call upon spirits for guidance, healing, or protection. Participants offer prayers, sing special songs, and may witness powerful spiritual manifestations. The ceremony emphasizes humility, sacrifice, and connection with the Spirit World.

Gift had mixed feelings about returning to Two Elks' camp, where she had been taken as a slave when captured at nine winters old. She served in Two Elks' lodge. He ignored her, his wife Many Horses bullied and mistreated her. His other wife, Black Rabbit, was kind or mean, depending on her mood. She barely remembered her life before with the Arikara, but Two Elks' tribe was the only home she knew before Big Thunder. While she had bad memories of her time there, there were also plenty of good ones. She had friends and people she still cared about there.

One reason Lakota at this time was the most powerful tribe in North America was their ability to adapt and change. Two Elks in the way of all good Lakota leaders, adapted when he recognized that Big Thunder brought significant changes to their world. They could try to ignore the changes, keep to the traditional old ways and hide, or embrace them in ways to benefit the people. With the marriage of his son, Six Feathers, to a woman from their time, they became kin, and one extended tribe.

To keep his tribe strong, Two Elks still took his best warriors and hunters out each spring to roam the plains, hunting buffalo and living off the land the way their ancestors did. However, many women, elders, and young children remained in winter camp, which had turned into a growing village outside of the Circle. It was named *Wanáhča* for the snowberry that grew nearby. It had been originally twenty miles south of Chamberlain, but Changleska negotiated to extend the borders of the Circle by ten miles, now forty miles from the center point at Omímeya. Now the village was less than ten miles from Oacoma, which had become a growing port and industrial area.

Wanahca had become a center for the processing of hides, both from their own hunters and from across the Circle. Modern factory processes supplemented traditional tanning techniques, producing high-quality hides with less labor. This was making Two Elks' tribe increasingly wealthy, since they had many women skilled in the craft. But the village smelled terrible. Urine collected from the composting toilets' diverters was stored in tanning vats. The solid waste went to the saltpeter beds, which would take years to produce enough nitrate to combine with sulfur and charcoal for gunpowder. It was an awful job that had to be done.

It wasn't easy to travel in the winter, with snowplows only clearing a few main roads for school buses and emergency vehicles. The forty-five-mile journey used to take an hour by car, but on horseback in winter, they'd cover it in stages over three days.

Joseph, Kimi, and Gift started at the horse ranch and rode to their home on Crow Road. Those fifteen miles took all day. After spending the night, Hotah planned to join them, and the group was set to visit an aunt's house in Chamberlain. They'd spend the night there, then leave early the next morning for the village with another relative who planned to join them.

Rose couldn't get away, and Gift wondered if Kimi was relieved. The two didn't always get along, in the mother/teenage daughter kind of way. Gift didn't understand it. Her own mother was only a distant memory and she wished had a relationship with her own mother. Still, Rose sent a 4x4 full of gifts for Three Stars and the people of Wanahca to the house. There were so many gifts they had to hitch a sled to carry everything. Gift was grateful.

They d be showing up unannounced, of course. No one in the village had a phone or radio, though there was talk of bringing in a landline by the summer. After the battle of Omímeya, Two Eagles offered to have a radio there so they could call for more warriors if needed. Changleska could spare radios, but not solar panels. Hopefully, the village would get electricity in the coming year.

A few hours away from the village, Kimi reined in her mare. An owl sat on the broken fencepost, with its broad wings folded and its eyes resembling frost-bitten moons.   It sees us," she murmured.

Gift shifted uneasily in the saddle, but nodded. Everyone knew what owls meant. They didn't always signify death or a warning; the spirits might have been listening, but the implication was always serious.

A warm welcome and an invitation to stay in the new log longhouse greeted them upon their arrival at the village. The functional, yet artistic large building based on adapted designs from other tribes served as both a community meeting hall and living space for a few people, mostly elders. Most people lived in tipis, yurts, or in the little dome houses made from hemp, with new mass heater stoves that were efficient and warm.

As they unloaded their personal gear and got their sleeping areas set up, Gift saw many people she knew, all of whom seemed happy to see her. While she was sure people knew about the Battle of Omímeya, they may not have realized the personal nature of the visitors' loss until they saw all six family members family with their hair shorn off in mourning. Out of politeness, no one said anything, but they were kind and understanding.

Three Stars lived in her own tipi just outside the village, and someone had sent her word of the visitors' arrival. When she arrived, they unloaded the gifts, and everyone enthusiastically received them, especially the coffee and other foodstuffs unavailable in midwinter.

When Gift lived with Two Elks, she learned a great deal about herbs from Three Stars who never treated her like a slave. Three Stars smiled at Gift and sat down next to the family, who were seated on the floor by the big wood stove, drinking tea.

Three Stars said to Gift, "You have brought your new sister here for healing, but it seems like many in your family are also in need."

Gift nodded, knowing she was correct.

Three Stars said, "It will take a few days to prepare the Yuwipi Ceremony for Kimímela, but everyone who takes part will also benefit."

She saw Hotah's arm still in a sling and asked Gift what herbs she had used. Gift showed her the salve she and Kimi had made with yarrow, buffalo berry, comfrey, wintergreen, and cannabis. Comfrey didn't grow wild in the Dakotas, but she explained how valuable it was for bone healing and said she would bring starts in the spring to grow it in the village. Wintergreen also didn't grow in the area, but the oil was readily available. It contained methyl salicylate, the same active compound found in aspirin. The cannabis, she added, helped with both pain and inflammation. The plants brought back from their timeline by the illegal growers had proven to be a valuable medicinal crop as their strains were much stronger than those in this time, and highly prized by local apothecaries.

On the second day they were there, Joseph and Hotah were conferring with Two Eagles at his lodge, along with a few of the older men. The aunties were all cooking, Gift and Kimi were shucking and grinding corn with young women. Children ran about, babies lay quiet in cradleboards, and toddlers nursed at their mothers' sides. It was restful in an active way. Not being surrounded by others grieving was a welcome relief.

One woman, Cloud Heart, was very pregnant. She kept getting up, moving around, going outside to make water, sitting down to shuck some corn, then getting back up. Kimi asked if her time was approaching soon.

She said, "Anytime now, it's my first, don't know exactly." The women who had babies all asked her questions and agreed she was in early labor and would give birth within a day or two.

Gift saw some interest and light return to Kimi's eyes for the first time since the attack. Ever since her sister's birth, she had been interested in midwifery and had attended a couple of births.

The village didn't have a midwife, only a few experienced women. Three Stars would come with prayers and herbs if needed. The Medical Corps came in the warmer months for periodic clinics, but this time of year, the tribe was on their own.

Kimi said quietly to Gift, "I hope everything goes well. I don't know enough to help. If there's a problem... in the snow, they can't get her to the hospital. It's fifteen miles away."

Gift assured her everything would be fine, not to worry. Lakota women had been giving birth without hospitals forever. But in truth, she and many of the women were worried. Cloud Heart's husband was a big man, and she was a small woman.

All that day, they ground corn while Cloud Heart walked and sat, walked and sat again. Later, they ate a big celebratory meal with as many people in the village as they could crowd into the longhouse. It wasn't until much later, when most had gone home to sleep in their own beds, that's when her heavy breathing began. It was clear she was in active labor.

Gift was invited to be present along with Kimi, and she felt honored. The space was very small, one of the new circular hemp tiny houses, but it was cozy and close to the longhouse, so they could come and go easily. Cloud Heart's husband checked on her periodically, often shooed away by the women who surrounded her with love and comfort. The women knew of Kimi's interest in midwifery and showed her how to apply counterpressure to the back to relieve pain, along with other helpful techniques. Kimi made her cups of prairie rose and wild ginger tea and encouraged her to sip buffalo broth made from jerky.

Late that night, as she tried to sleep, Kimi confided to Gift. "Our midwives listen to the baby's heartbeat to make sure everything is going well. They can tell by listening whether the baby is in trouble ahead of time, then there's plenty of time to go to the hospital if needed. She's been in labor all day. If there is a problem, I'm not sure how they would know. I'm worried."

"Don't be," Gift assured her. "Sometimes it takes a long time. Every baby is different. Trust the process."

By morning, the labor was still going strong, but Cloud Heart was clearly exhausted. Kimi had taken turns with the other women—rubbing her back, breathing with her, helping her through the pain. She never cried or complained, accepting each wave of contraction with quiet fortitude. Between contractions, she would lie down and try to rest, though nearly impossible.

When one woman expressed concern about how little energy she had and questioned if she'd have the strength to push, Kimi remembered they had brought coffee and sugar. A strong cup of black coffee with sugar revived Cloud Heart, and the labor picked up.

The contractions were steady now, each one pulling a low breath from Cloud Heart as she leaned forward, gripping the edge of the blanket. Gift sat close, watching her hands clench and release, her face tightening with each wave. When Cloud Heart whispered that she needed the outhouse, the older women shared a look and shook their heads softly. That pressure meant the baby was coming.

Gift stepped out to find her husband. He stood near the door, shoulders hunched against the cold, eyes fixed on the ground. Some men stayed away, saying birth belonged to the women. But this was their first child, and he hadn't gone far. He didn't speak when she touched his arm, but he looked at her with a quiet ache in his eyes. He was waiting to be needed.

With Cloud Heart's sister holding one side, her husband supporting her from behind, and Kimi on the other, she squatted and pushed. It took some time, long, hard, exhausting work. Offering encouragement and praise, the women reminded her of her strength.

The woman seated in front between Cloud Heart's legs said, "I feel it." She reached forward to support her bottom as the head emerged, and moments later, a baby boy slid out—blue and still.

Immediately, the women sprang into action. The baby, still attached to the placenta and receiving some oxygen, was quickly rubbed and dried. They turned his head downward to drain the fluids, gently tapped his back, and blew on his face.

He gasped. Took a breath. Cried.

Everyone else did too.

Afterward, when the placenta was delivered, they cleaned Cloud Heart, fed her, and let her rest, and they returned to the longhouse.

Kimi confided to Gift, "I was worried about seeing that owl on the way in. When the baby came out so blue, I thought it was a sign. I'm so glad it wasn't."

Gift said softly, "Every birth teaches something. This one taught you not to let fear speak too loudly."

A few days later, they held the Yuwipi Healing Ceremony for Kimi. Attending the birth seemed to have begun her healing, as she engaged more with others. The ceremony was beautiful and powerful, stirring something deep within everyone who attended. There was a moment in the dark, with the singing, when the energy itself seemed to bring light.

Afterward, Three Stars told Joseph, "There is no greater pain than losing a child. It will be with you always. Embrace it. It is now a part of who you are. You serve as a spiritual leader. The connection you have with the Creator must be the foundation your life rests on. Pray and hold ceremonies often. This is what will bring you the strength to continue to serve in a good way."

To Hotah she said, "You grieve your brother and your family, and you question whether you did the right thing, calling them into danger. But think of who you are, and who your family becomes, when you choose courage over comfort. No path of honor is free from sacrifice. You made the right choice."

She handed Gift a čhaŋwá (badger) skull for her medicine bundle, saying, "You have shown yourself a powerful warrior. In our way, chanwa is a healer and a protector. It moves close to the earth, quiet and unseen. When danger comes, it defends what matters with everything it has. You are like that. Steady, strong, and unstoppable when the people need you."

To Kimi, she gave a small deerskin pouch decorated with porcupine quills and gently hung it around her neck. "This is the first of many small medicines to go into your medicine bag." She handed her a small round stone. "You carry a heavy burden from the Thunder Beings. Like an enormous boulder, it is too hard for you to carry alone. But you are not alone. This little stone is to remind you that all burdens shared become smaller. The burden and pain will never go away, just become easier to carry."

That night, Kimi sat alone for a time, outside the longhouse, the cold biting at her cheeks. She turned the small stone over in her hand, feeling its weight both real and symbolic. The words of Three Stars echoed in her chest: *You are not alone.*

For too long, her visions had felt like a curse, something too big, too painful, too strange to hold. But now, for the first time, she wondered if they might also be medicine. Not something to fear, but something to learn.

She tucked the stone into the deerskin pouch at her chest and looked up at the stars. The burden was still there, but knowing she no longer carried it alone made it seem lighter.

On the journey home, Kimi was quiet but, instead of being withdrawn, she was introspective and able to move forward now with less pain. She and Gift even joked and laughed a bit as they shared anecdotes from the visit.

=..=

A few weeks later, Kimi was almost back to her old self, returning to her studies. School was mostly online because of the snow, and she wasn't ready to go back to in-person classes.

Kimi and Gift were in the kitchen, with Kimi studying and Gift cooking, when Evan came downstairs with Gift's phone.

"It keeps ringing. Why don't you carry it?"

"Why should I, if you bring it to me?" she teased him.

It was Rose. She sounded annoyed. "I've been trying to reach you. You should pick up."

Gift didn't give an excuse; Rose knew she hated phones.

"Remember, I talked to you about the endowment I'm giving to the Reliance Military Academy in Jordan's name? I'm negotiating with Gary's neighbor to buy the adjoining property, and I want to pick you up and look at it with me."

"I'm not sure why you need me."

"I don't need you. I want you. Since you'll be going in the spring, you should participate in the process. It's not about the property. I'll be having some face-to-face discussions with Gary you should be a part of."

"Kimímela won't want to come."

"I didn't think so, but ask her whether the weather will hold for a few hours. I don't want to get caught in a storm. Unless I hear there is a storm, I'll pick you up in an hour." And Rose hung up.

I don't remember saying I would go. This must be what having a mother is like, thought Gift.

She was glad she went. It was nice seeing Mr. Hutchinson again; they hadn't spoken since the funeral. Rose, Jackson, and General Gardner had spoken extensively about the need for a two to three years military preparatory academy for ages fourteen to eighteen. General Gardner had even found a couple of people to help them set it up. It would be a boarding school, with an emphasis on education, including math and engineering, in addition to military training.

The property next door to Hutchinson's was thirty acres, no longer farmed. The couple living there was older; their grown children had married but still lived in the area. They would sell the property with the proviso that they could remain in the house until they needed to move closer to town for health reasons. The plan was for them to take part-time jobs at the academy, she in the kitchen, he as groundskeeper. A win-win arrangement. They had sold nearly all the items from the old world they could part with, and the money wouldn't last much longer.

Rose and Gift walked around in the cold and snow, looking over the property, discussing the placement of buildings, and wrapping up a few last-minute details on the proposed sale.

Back at the Hutchinsons', Rose and Gift went over some documents and contracts drawn up by Rose's attorney. But Gary had issues. He was independently minded, with little trust in authority and even less faith in anything that resembled government. He saw Changleska as another extension of government, bound to overreach, if not now, someday. They haggled and argued over several clauses, especially one allowing him to be fired.

"Listen here," he said angrily, "this is my program, my baby. You want the power to take it away?"

Rose answered, "The only reason this exists is because I wanted a teacher for Gift, and you refused to train a Lakota girl. I had to add and pay for her cousins before you agreed."

Gary looked embarrassed and didn't meet Gift's eyes.

I didn't know that Gift thought.

"Now, if we can't come to an agreement, there are other locations, and other directors we could hire, at this salary." Rose said, tapping her finger on the amount specified in the contract.

At that point, Gary's wife, Melissa, stepped in. "I think we're close to an agreement here. I know, Rose, you want it here in Reliance to honor poor Jordan. Another location and director wouldn't be the same. And Gary, maybe you'd prefer the contract to specify what counts as a fireable offense. Like theft or abuse, not political differences, right?"

They went back and forth, finally reaching an agreement.

This is the kind of battle Rose fights all the time, Gift thought. She had a bit more respect for the work Rose normally did.

It felt good to get out of the house. They even stopped in Chamberlain and ate at a restaurant that had recently reopened.

When they got back to the house, they saw Kimi standing out in the field by herself. They heard the low growl of thunder as they got out of the car.

"Oh no, not again," Rose said, running toward her.

Kimi held out a hand to stop them. She stood with her eyes closed, feet planted firmly in the snow, her now-short hair stirring in the breeze. She raised her hands, and thunder rolled in again and again in short bursts. Suddenly, it stopped. Kimi turned and walked toward them.

"Yes, it's another warning. But this time I asked, over and over, until I got more information. This will help. I know this time it will help. If only they will listen."

"What... what will happen?" Rose asked, dread in her voice.

"New Orleans. The Americans are coming. A lot of them. In a month, on the full moon."

Chapter Thirty
Jamal

JAMAL HAD FINALLY solved the Kaplan wheel's energy problem. After a month of long nights and false starts, the new setup extended power across most of Oca Landing, enough to keep the base running and light his own house. It felt like a quiet victory, though he knew the real storm was coming.

It was early February, two months since the Battle of Omímeya had forced a shift in strategic priorities. The Americans' determination to eliminate Changleska came as a surprise. Combined with opposition from Southern plantation owners, Changleska now faced an implacable enemy with greater manpower, deeper resources, and far more wartime experience in this era. Only nine years since the Americans had they defeated a militarily superior British Empire, they were still a force to be reckoned with.

He'd been working mostly alone. Captain Rodriguez, his usual partner on engineering projects, had been promoted to Colonel. Jamal shifted focus after the attack, throwing himself into planning with a single-minded urgency. The order had come down, prepare for war, to prioritize defense and make battle plans.

The question of Oca Landing's defensibility arose because they had built it as a hub with military capacity, a base, not a fort. Now the treaty was signed, Spain was abandoning several purpose-built forts, including Fort St. Charles, a large riverfront installation strategically placed to guard access to the city from the Mississippi River, and some argued the Changleska should shift its forces into those hardened positions.

The strongest option seemed to be to use Fort St. Charles, but the place was a logistical nightmare. Retrofitting would take months they didn't have. They'd already poured a year of hard work into building Oca Landing's infrastructure, defenses, and identity. No one wanted to give that up. Not for an old, crumbling Spanish fortress, even if the walls were thick, and it had a strategic location.

Jamal, Colonel Rodriguez, and another engineer were about to head to Fort St. Charles for an inspection. Although the treaty allowed six months for the handover, the Spanish were leaving early, with the ceremony scheduled for the next week.

The structural engineer joining them surprised Jamal with his expertise. He was a French émigré, a Sorbonne graduate whose classical training included knowledge of defensive architecture. He'd already worked with Omímeya on multiple building projects and, to Jamal's quiet appreciation, seemed to know more about early modern fort design than anyone else on the team.

The gates groaned as they pushed through them, hinges complaining against salt and time. An abandoned and empty feeling already pervaded the place. The Spanish soldier who showed them around seemed embarrassed by the fort's condition. Jamal scanned the walls, measuring with his eyes. The wooden ramparts looked sturdy; they might still hold.

Running his fingers along a seam in the masonry, the French engineer walked slowly. "This section is older," he said, his accent soft but crisp. "French palisade foundation. The Spanish never completed the reinforcement plans here. They'd intended to add a second tier of defense."

"And didn't," Rodriguez said flatly.

"History is full of unfinished walls."

They stepped into the main barracks. The air was close and damp. Mildew curled in the corners. A broken lantern hung by a rusted chain and swayed slightly in the draft. Jamal shook his head, knowing there was no time to make this place habitable.

The French engineer mentioned a sealed tunnel that may once have opened to the river. They didn't have time to explore it, but Jamal made a note to revisit the idea later.

Rodriguez argued for holding Fort St. Charles, citing its elevated position and control of the river. Jamal disagreed, saying it wasn't worth the effort of rebuilding. In the end, they compromised: a scout post, flood traps, and eyes on the east bank. They'd put their primary efforts into fortifying Oca Landing.

Jamal rushed home after returning to Oca Landing. Cathy Anders, his neighbor, and a twenty-first-century parent herself had been watching Benjy. She was one of the few people who understood why he didn't want to leave a nearly nine-year-old alone, even one like Benjy, who had grown up fending for himself, caring for his sick mother, and running errands on the streets of Boston.

She looked after Benjy often, and her two boys visited his house frequently. Truth be told, she did more of the childcare than Jamal did.

Inside, Benjy looked up from the table, where he and one of Cathy's boys were building something with scavenged parts.

"Hey," Jamal said, ruffling his hair. "Did you have a good time?"

"Yeah," Benjy said. "We built a catapult. I didn't break anything."

"That's a win." Jamal smiled and glanced toward the door. "I need to figure out something nice to do for Cathy. She helps us out a lot."

"You could say thank you."

Jamal laughed. "I meant something better than that."

"Cookies?"

"Now you're thinking."

That evening, he brought Benjy to the new officers' mess for dinner. He'd done it once or twice before when working late, and the cooks had always been nice about it. With only eighteen officers permanently stationed at Oca Landing, Jamal didn't like how they couldn't eat with the enlisted, but in officer training they emphasized how fraternization could create problems.

There were a lot of rules in the military that seemed more tradition than logic. While the new Changleska Guard had thrown out some outdated ideas, they'd added others to match the customs of this era: more formality, stricter codes. Officer training included a class on etiquette now. There was talk of adding ballroom dancing. Some parts of military life he enjoyed. Others drove him nuts.

When they returned to their small townhouse, Jamal was pleased to see that Janie had been there to clean. He'd hesitated to employ her at first, as having a formerly enslaved woman work as a domestic stirred a mix of guilt and discomfort, but when Cathy told him Janie was available part-time and needed the work, he got over it. Jamal had grown up with domestic help and was a bit of a neat freak. He hadn't realized how hard it would be to keep things clean with a child in the house. The laundry was the worst.

Even with the new hand crank wash machines, it took a lot of time. There was no way he could keep up.

He was thinking about giving Janie a few more hours, having her pick up groceries and cook as well. It looked like things were going to be busier than usual.

When he'd first moved in, the place seemed large. He had been living in tents, ship staterooms, inns, and rooming houses for over a year. Now, after a few months, it seemed small for him and Benjy. There was no room for a home office, and he often needed space to lay out schematics and plans. He had Benjy come to work with him after school, and he set him up a little desk in the temporary engineering office, which was a tent. But Benjy wanted to play outside with the other kids in the fourplex that served as the officers quarters, a squat and square building with a shared yard where kids often played.

Jamal thought about buying his own place. He had left his car in South Dakota. He'd driven it to the permaculture gathering when Big Thunder sent him and Nels to 1791. A self-charging Lexus hybrid that got over forty miles a gallon, the car had been in storage with his and Nels s other possessions. They'd shipped everything else to him in New Orleans, but without good roads or gasoline there, sending the car made no sense. Someone interested in buying it had contacted him, as it was worth a small fortune now.

He would rather buy or build a house in town, having no desire to farm, but if he wanted running water and flush toilets, he needed a big enough piece of property for a septic system. Sewers in New Orleans were years away. However, if he bought a small plantation, the slaves often came with it. Even after freeing them, he still had the responsibility of giving them jobs, improving their housing, and providing education. The idea of owning a human being even for minutes while he signed papers was an anathema. He thought rural life might be better for Benjy and had a hard time knowing what to do. In the end, he hung on to the car. As more gasoline came from the Caddo plant, it would become even more valuable.

=..=

Jamal was at a briefing with other officers getting some unwanted news. The war was coming to their doorstep, and soon. There was a warning from Kimímela Chasing Hawk, who, so far, had never been wrong. Jamal didn't know what to think about prophetic visions from young girls who heard the thunder speak. It was as if logic itself was being challenged, and he had always relied heavily on tangible evidence rather than mysticism, but here he was, transported back in time 233 years, so who was he to judge?

The military's serious response to the warning surprised him. It helped that intelligence backed it. They'd suspected this was coming, but not this soon, and having a specific date of the full moon was helpful. But they assumed they had months to prepare, not a month. The Americans aimed to attack in the winter, as the frozen river would restrict the number of troops and equipment Changleska could send south. During the field day exercises, the military vehicles demonstrated their power to the Americans. There was no way they would want to face them in combat.

A young lieutenant, Terry Jensen, from the Signal Corps, had been seconded to Intelligence and led the discussion. She began nervously, "We can no longer send radio messages in the clear. Too many radios capable of receiving shortwave signals have been sold or stolen. We're accelerating telegraph repeater stations to minimize reliance on shortwave. Six outposts are up, but we'll need double that."

Jamal asked, "Don't they need tall towers with specialized equipment? How could too many of those go missing?"

Jensen answered, "You only need specialized equipment for transmitting. Any emergency-type radio can listen to broadcasts. Almost every household had at least a small one. Many are solar or crank-powered. Also, any ham radio, even handheld ones, can listen in. We don't differentiate between ham, shortwave, and commercial frequencies, as we only use a few. It wouldn't be hard for anyone with a radio to listen in."

Rodriguez added, "Unfortunately, we can't encrypt military channels. We use too many different types of radios. We can use codes, but it's a time-consuming process, limiting their effectiveness. One of our chief advantages for warfare in this time was rapid communication. That ability is now compromised. We don't know exactly how much they can hear, but we know they can."

Jensen continued, "We recently discovered the extent of American surveillance. Interviews with prisoners captured at the Battle of Omímeya revealed they've been monitoring our communications since the visitors from the First Summit returned. They have many spies in the Chamberlain area, St. Louis, and New Orleans sending reports. With the Circle Echo relay station in Georgetown, they can hear us clearly on the East Coast."

Rodriguez said, "Please remember to practice radio discipline during your exercises. You all have the new radio codes on your phones. We'll update them before the battle. Make sure your noncommissioned officers have them. Some will need printed copies since not everyone has phones. Texting should work for those who have phones, but don't rely on it. The mesh network reliability can vary. Lieutenant Alston, please review the measures you've been working on."

Jamal laid out maps and plans on the table, outlining both defensive and offensive positions. The Mississippi River was designated as the primary barrier and chokepoint. Artillery batteries and fortified barges were placed at key stretches. The Navy had orders to deploy patrol boats and one armed vessel to maintain control of the waterway. Fort St. Charles was being prepared to hold several hundred militia recruits, most of them freed slaves, currently digging earthworks, defensive canals, and flood traps around the perimeter.

Rodriguez provided a weapons update. "The Liège factory in Belgium came through, although it might be the last shipment we get; the war's tightening over there," he said, tapping the manifest. "We received 120 Mark 1 Eagle rifles, sixty revolvers, five standard rifles, and five of the new sniper rifle they are calling Thundersticks. Sharpshooter units get first pick. Those things are accurate past four hundred yards if you know what you're doing."

Jensen added, "Our intelligence suggests between three to four thousand enemy, mostly militia, all armed with flintlocks. Combining this shipment with the 140 new rifles from England last month and the 275 flintlocks from Hudson's Bay Company last year gives us only 575 weapons. Far too few. We expect more from Chamberlain, but it's unclear how much they will strip defenses from there if New Orleans falls."

Jamal asked, "But won't our new weapons be what you military folks call force multipliers?"

Rodriguez laughed, "Alston, remember you're military, not just an engineer. And yes, with trained hands, the Mark 1 Eagle has a rate of fire two to three times higher than flintlocks and works in wet conditions. And we have mortars and field artillery, and a few prototype rockets."

Jamal hesitated, knowing little about weapons since his engineering projects and Benjy occupied most of his time, but still asked, "How many mortars?"

"Fifteen of out of the new foundry. Even better news: using simplified casting and our adapted machining techniques, they can produce replacement ammo for many mortars we brought from our time. About double that for the field artillery. Some arrived last week; others are on the way downriver now."

Jamal asked, "Is all the ammo in the new settlement of Niokaska near St. Louis? Aren't we putting all our eggs in one basket?"

Rodriguez looked surprised at the astute question from the usually engineering-focused young lieutenant.

"Yes, but security for the primers and percussion caps is vital. If the rifle specifications are stolen, or captured rifles are reverse-engineered, they're useless without those percussion caps."

"Couldn't the Americans reverse-engineer the ammo?"

"Even if they captured a few rounds, reproducing the primer chemistry would be nearly impossible without the right laboratories or expertise. That's why site security is so important. If the chemistry secrets leak, even to allies, we'll lose an enormous advantage. Eventually, we'll build another facility, but right now we don't have enough qualified chemists for two sites. Since this facility only produces ammunition, we can limit personnel."

The Niokaska Foundry specialized in producing percussion caps, mortars, and ammunition. Heavily fortified and isolated from the growing city, it was staffed primarily by freedmen and their families who lived on-site under the protection of the Changleska Guard. Their loyalty was fierce, fueled by good wages, a shared vision of freedom, and the knowledge that the work they did helped secure the future of their people.

Rodriguez tapped his coffee cup. "You're right, only one facility holds all our eggs. Luckily, we don't have to worry about air attacks. The place is isolated, heavily fortified against ground assault."

"If the factory's up and running, why the shortages?"

"The team at Niokaska cracked the chemistry faster than expected, but we still can't scale it up. Every cap's made by hand with extreme care." He shook his head. "Flatboats are bringing ammo down from the factory now, but it's slow work. Until we get more people trained, the shortage will continue."

"If the factory is up and running, why the shortages?"

"The team at St. Louis cracked the chemistry faster than expected, but we still can't scale it up. Every cap is made by hand with extreme care."

They finished the briefing by reviewing additional weaponry and discussing methods to enhance militia training. Most new citizens joining the militia had full-time jobs and were only available on Sundays. Each

Sunday, they conducted militia training preceded by an optional church service, which helped those who hesitated to work on the Lord's Day. Unfortunately, there wasn't enough time to provide adequate training for the required number of fighters they needed against the Americans. Because Changleska did not have enough people to send to be full-time Guards in New Orleans, they relied on the militia.

While more troops arrived every day from South Dakota, their there weren't enough. Changleska had been converting the cargo steam barges for passengers and modifying the ones built for animals to accommodate the Lakota horses. Lakota warriors wanted to fight, but insisted on bringing their specially trained horses. Getting these horses to New Orleans presented another logistical challenge because of the distance involved, the usual two-week barge journey taking an extra week to allow the horses time to stop and get exercise. Ice in the river could bring additional delays.

After the briefing, Rodriguez asked Jamal to come to his office.

"Sir," Jamal said, snapping to attention and saluting upon entering, sensing from Rodriguez's tone formality was needed.

"Alston, I know your plate is full with engineering projects and supervising work crews, but I must assign you additional responsibilities. As a military officer in wartime, you will now command a platoon comprising four squads, forty men. You'll begin working with them immediately. The platoon will combine regular Guard troops with militia."

Jamal was surprised, though he realized he shouldn't be. He still saw himself as an engineer, someone who oversaw work crews and logistics. He thought, *leading troops in battle? Shooting people? That's not who I am.* The idea hit hard, and he was sure it showed on his face.

Rodriguez spoke sympathetically. "You'll do fine. Rely on your sergeants and trust your judgment. Dismissed."

As Jamal walked away, reality struck him. He could die in battle. Even scarier was thinking about what would happen to Benjy. He had no contingency plan. Who would care for Benjy if something happened to him in battle? Would the boy return to a life of uncertainty, or worse? The thought of leaving him unprotected was unbearable. Jamal needed a solid plan, urgently. He realized Cathy Anders would probably take Benjy. He needed to ask her and get the required paperwork in order. One more thing to do.

The following morning, Jamal met his platoon for their first muster. The platoon consisted mostly of freed Black militia members and some regular Guard soldiers, including Natives, Hispanics, and a few Whites. All four units were mostly all-male. Although plenty of women served in other military capacities, only a few were in combat roles; they served predominantly in support positions. Jamal wondered briefly about the experiences of those few women in predominantly male combat units.

After the treaty signing, people flocked to the newly opened Citizen Centers to swear their oaths and get their identification, so they'd become eligible for benefits, such as healthcare and access to free meals for children. Citizenship also required everyone between the ages of eighteen and twenty-five to commit to two years in the Changleska Guard. And every able-bodied adult had to join the militia. Despite assigning most women to support roles and granting maternity exemptions, the inclusion of women in combat positions was still shocking for those from this time. Free health care alone wasn't enough to motivate young, healthy people to become citizens in significant numbers. Many were waiting to see what would happen with this new country or deciding they didn't want to join and fight Americans. New Orleans hadn't yet implemented full-scale militia or Neighborhood Watch programs, but the St. Louis area had begun them with its growing numbers of new Changleska citizens.

The platoon's forty men stood in neat rows, organized into four squads of ten. They wore the newly issued uniforms made from durable hemp cloth, tie-dyed green and brown for camouflage. Jamal smiled slightly, imagining how much his era's hippies would've appreciated these uniforms.

He was pleased to see Joe Dunning, his friend and sergeant from basic training, now promoted to platoon sergeant and serving as his second-in-command. Joe had participated in several skirmishes, including the raid in which they'd captured a pirate ship, and he had more combat experience than nearly anyone else in the Guard.

Dunning approached him crisply. "Sir, troops ready for your inspection."

Jamal noticed immediately the clear distinction in armaments; the militia carried flintlocks, while the Guard troops held the newly issued Mark 1 Eagles. Given the limited supply of Eagles, this division made sense, but Jamal speculated about coordination issues which might arise during combat.

Nearby, Elijah Walker, now a corporal, led a small squad through a standard drill, demonstrating efficiency and precision. Elijah's commands were confident and sharp, his movements deliberate as he guided his squad through loading and firing exercises. Watching Elijah in this role, Jamal felt reassured—the promotion had clearly been well-earned, and the young corporal showed promise of becoming a strong leader.

=..=

General Jonathan Gardner arrived at Fort St. Charles at first light, stood on the highest rampart, his steely eyes already scanning with binoculars. Jamal hurried to meet him. Colonel Rodriguez standing next to him with a couple of aides.

The General's voice was calm. "Lieutenant Alston, report."

Jamal squared his shoulders, fighting down nerves. "All flood traps along the perimeter are ready, sir. We've reinforced the levees near the west and east gates. If the attackers breach the outer defenses, the fields will flood, trapping them and slowing their advance. All we need is your command."

"Good work," Gardner said, eyes shifting toward the approaching dawn.

Colonel Rodriguez nodded to Jamal. "Cover the northern wall. But if they have inside knowledge, they might try the south."

Gardner's eyes narrowed. "Inside information?"

Rodriguez hesitated, glancing at Jamal. "The Americans have spent freely on spies. Someone might've leaked our defenses."

Jamal swallowed hard. Betrayal was poison, corroding trust. "We're ready, General."

Suddenly, explosions of gunpowder and musket fire erupted beyond the northern gate. Jamal heard, but couldn't see, the mortars tearing into the enemy lines.

A captain appeared, breathless, his uniform dirtied from scrambling up the stairs. "General, the scouts report they're moving in three columns: north, south, and center. If they breach simultaneously..."

Gardner interrupted sharply. "Then we must ensure they don't. Alston, you'll trigger the flood channels on my mark. Rodriguez, gather your sharpshooters; slow the center advance. Have Baker take the south and Dunning the North."

Rodriguez saluted and vanished swiftly. Gardner turned back to Alston, laying a firm hand on his shoulder. "This is your plan, Lieutenant. Make it count."

Joe Dunning positioned men along the vulnerable northern edge, his stance resolute despite the overwhelming odds. Jamal saw him calmly directing musket volleys. Elijah Walker stood beside him, sharp eyes spotting enemy movements, firing with cool precision.

"Hold the line!" Joe roared, his voice a steady anchor amidst the chaos.

The men held, but not for long. A mass of firepower soon overwhelmed them, forcing a retreat behind the heavy fort walls. They reached the inner wall just as Rodriguez and reinforcements arrived, driving the attackers back and sealing the breach.

Suddenly, a shout of alarm rose. Gasping, a messenger stumbled forward, shouting, "The drone shows the northern levee gate's been sabotaged!"

A chill crawled up Jamal's spine. Betrayal.

"Dunning," Jamal called on the radio, risking it being heard. "Secure the gate. I'll reroute the water." Then he ran down the stairs toward the floodgate lever.

Without hesitation, Joe sprinted toward the compromised levee, rallying a handful of men behind him. Elijah drew his line tighter, understanding the pressure building against the fort.

"Trigger the floodgates—mark!" Gardner's order over the radio cut sharply through Jamal's focus. Out of breath from running, hands trembling with adrenaline, Jamal threw the main floodgate lever. A rumble, low and powerful, reverberated beneath their feet as river water surged, reshaped by the trenches and levees his crew had furiously dug over the last month.

The enemy's northern advance, now dangerously close, stalled in sudden confusion as water flooded around them, cutting off retreat and dividing their ranks. But near the sabotaged gate, Joe Dunning fought fiercely, desperately attempting repairs while enemies closed in.

"Cover him!" Elijah Walker roared, sending volleys of musket fire into the approaching foes. But the enemy pressed on relentlessly.

Amid the chaos, Joe locked eyes briefly with Jamal, a silent understanding passing between them. Determinedly, Joe hurled himself against the failing gate, wrenching it shut with his full strength. Gunfire cracked. A single cry cut through the noise. Joe slumped against the gate, which now held fast, secured by his final effort.

"No!" Jamal shouted, fists clenched, grief and rage mingling. He stood frozen for a heartbeat, the shock like ice in his veins.

Elijah rallied the northern defenses, driving back wave after wave of attackers. Jamal, heart pounding, directed secondary water channels, isolating enemy forces. Rodriguez's sharpshooters thinned the central column, sending enemy morale plummeting.

Hunting and competition shooting had been major sports in the area of South Dakota transported by Big Thunder. A cadre of those sharpshooters had been deployed with orders to target officers. Distinctive helmets identified officers of this time, and the rule against saluting in combat had not yet been established. Except for the cavalry, only the officers rode horses, making them easy to spot.

At dawn, the enemy retreated, broken and disorganized without their officers. Gardner exhaled slowly, evidently exhausted.

We held," Lieutenant Alston whispered with a mix of raw grief and quiet pride.

Gardner nodded solemnly. "For now. But this isn't over. Today, we have a victory, thanks to you and those who gave everything. Remember all of them, Lieutenant Alston. We owe them our victory today."

That evening, they returned to Oca Landing after mopping up at Fort St. Charles. Although they'd won this battle, the reality of how outnumbered they were tempered their happiness.

As Caddo scouts confirmed mass movement near the northern edges of New Orleans, General Gardner reconvened the command team, with Jamal listening intently. As he explained it, the earlier assault had been a diversion to soften up the defenses. Real danger now loomed eastward near Tremé, where abandoned plantation fields stretched between the river and Bayou St. John. It would be a perfect staging ground.

"Drones and scouts confirm they've moved three thousand men there," Rodriguez said grimly, laying out a crude map. "Cavalry, field artillery, and musket infantry. We'll be lucky to hold them for an hour."

A rider arrived under cover of darkness. It was a Spanish officer in a travel-worn cloak. Gardner stood as he dismounted.

"Comandante Ortega," Gardner said. "This is unexpected."

"I was ordered to remain neutral," Ortega replied quietly. "But I cannot. They plan to strike at Oca Landing from three sides at dawn. They've used the old Marigny and Tremé plantations for cover. If you hold this outpost dear, prepare now."

He saluted Gardner, turned and rode off into the mist.

The room erupted with activity. Ortega s warning changed their offense plan which would have brought the fight to the enemy. They hadn t sent the drone to all sides, and they'd heard no word from the scouts, which meant they were probably dead. With that many troops attacking from three sides, defense was the only option. The command team worked late into the night, knowing the danger would come at dawn.

As the first gray light crept over the cane fields, drums and hooves echoed across the levees. They hoped for rain to render the enemy's flintlocks unreliable, but it looked clear and cool. Jamal stood atop the outer barricade of Oca Landing, staring into the rising dust. Shapes emerged; ranks of infantry and cavalry, banners unfurling in the breeze. Cannon barrels glinted at the tree line.

"Positions!" Rodriguez shouted from the west barricade.

And like a wind from the trees, they came.

Two dozen Lakota warriors thundered into view on horseback, led by Swift Bear, their braids whipping in the wind. They rode hard across the enemy's exposed flank, striking supply carts, scattering their formations, firing shots and loosing arrows and war cries as they vanished into smoke and cane. It was a hit-and-run masterpiece, but although it was enough to stall the assault s timing, it could not stall the wave itself.

The main army advanced. Artillery roared. The front barricade cracked. The southern levee exploded in a ball of fire and water. Smoke, screams, dust, and the smell of gunpowder filled the air. Changleska defenders returned fire, but the enemy's numbers were overwhelming.

Jamal raced to the west barricade as cannonballs slammed into the front gate. Gardner's voice carried above the chaos: "Hold this ground!"

Elijah Walker reappeared from the smoke, eyes wide. "They've breached the east trench! We're flanked!"

And he saw it.

A second column of enemy soldiers, slipping behind the main attack, emerged from the rear marshes. Someone who knew the land too well guided them; they weren't the only ones with Indigenous scouts.

Jamal climbed higher up the gate platform, scanning the field.

Thousands of enemy troops were massing beyond the cane breaks. There were thousands of infantry, hundreds of cavalry, and many cannons. The ground trembled.

The deafening roar of mortars and artillery fire from their side was overpowering. A thick haze of smoke made it difficult to see. From his vantage point, he saw the Oca troops' firing position was too exposed. Once the enemy stopped and set up their cannons, they would aim them there. He didn't know if they realized the danger, as he had a better view of the battlefield. He radioed a warning and received a curt response. They'd move when they could. Jamal knew that meant they would fight to the death. There was no place to move to.

"We're outnumbered," he murmured. "God help us. We're outnumbered five to one."

And still more troops kept coming.

Chapter Thirty-One
Jackson

JACKSON HEEDED WARNINGS. Growing up in the projects of Chicago, he'd learned that staying safe meant listening to warnings. He'd seen it too many times. Trouble spread around certain people like a cloud; recognizing it and staying away could save your freedom or your life. In the military, warnings came as intelligence, shared experiences with other soldiers, and situational awareness. When he was a cop, if you paid attention, there were warning signs in all kinds of situations. Hearing from Rose about Kimi's warning only cemented what he already knew from other sources. But having a specific time and place? That was different, and important. Especially since he now trusted her visions implicitly.

After the Battle of Omímeya, the command team knew a major offensive was coming. Feints, diversions, and sabotage were all tools an enemy would use to probe defenses before a major attack. What they had wrong was assuming the Americans wouldn't move until spring. People never fought wars in winter during this era, and the Dakotas' winds were brutal. They never expected so many of their own citizens to turn on them. The enemy's hiring of mercenaries to move here weeks, even months, in advance to take jobs and attempt to fit in was unexpected. He had to admit; that was a brilliant move no one had seen coming.

As the Minister of Defense, he should've known. With 20/20 hindsight, all the warning signs were there. He couldn't change the past. Losing that many, especially the Chasing Hawk family, haunted him. There was nothing to do besides console the grieving. Jackson was determined it would be different next time.

Knowing the next target was New Orleans made it easier to switch priorities. General Gardner had focused on bolstering the defenses of the

Circle. He had hardened the outposts on both sides of the river, integrated the riverboats into the new navy, expanded the Marines, and worked on training as many as possible. With the bulk of the military personnel and advanced weapons, such as .50 caliber machine guns, mortars, and drones, in the Circle, deciding how much to send to New Orleans and how much to keep for defense was a tough decision. While day-to-day decisions were up to the General, overall strategic planning was Jackson's responsibility.

Planning became his life. Reviewing plans made by Gardner and his staff and approving budgets took most of his time. He wanted to be present for Rose, but his duties were all-consuming. Her grieving took on a quietness that dimmed the inner light that usually shone within her. He'd finally moved into her house. Nothing was ever said. Every time he came over, he brought more of his things until the hotel room was empty. He doubted she noticed, because she was surprised when he said he was moving his office to the Changleska administration floor in the hotel, freeing up the suite for guests again. It still felt like her house. He wasn't sure if it would ever feel like home to him. It wasn't Rose; he loved her with completeness without question. It'd take time. It was still hard for him to believe he now lived in 1793, even though it had been over a year and a half since Big Thunder.

A month after the battle, they'd interviewed all the prisoners, including the traitors who'd assisted the attackers in ways both small and large. An advisory committee recommended punishments ranging from community service for minor offenses to exile, being pressed into the British Navy, and hanging for fourteen of the worst cases. Those sentenced to exile were under house arrest until leaving for the new penal colony/farm community in the spring. The remaining eighty-six were waiting in the county jail. Despite interviewing all the prisoners, investigators obtained no definitive evidence that the United States had hired them.

"Without proof it was the Americans, a declaration of war would carry little weight," Mary had said in their last meeting, her tone clipped. "How other nations view Changleska right now could determine everything."

Jackson hadn't responded at the time, but her words stuck with him. She was right, and he knew it. Recognition meant legitimacy. Without it, they were just another rebellion in the eyes of the world. They'd need proof.

=..=

Jackson carefully reviewed the transcripts and watched the tapes of all the prisoners' interviews. He realized a professional had conducted none of them. Phil Gallo had never served in the military and was learning the craft of intelligence from spy novels and on-the-job experience. Sheriff Kenneth Harris had the most experience with interrogations, but coaxing a meth addict into revealing a dealer was a far cry from extracting military intelligence.

Very few of the National Guard or other veterans who came with Big Thunder had seen active combat duty in the Middle East. During his time in Iraq and Afghanistan, those in charge commonly used enhanced interrogation techniques. Getting accurate intel saved lives, especially when dealing with terrorist tactics. Jackson understood why these methods were now illegal. Torture was wrong and unjustified. Still, he also understood the rationale behind them. He knew how to push close to the line without crossing it. Unfortunately, he was the only one with that experience and would have to conduct the interrogations himself.

It had to happen soon. They scheduled the prisoners to be sent to New Orleans, but limited barge capacity prioritized troop movement.

After meeting with Sheriff Harris and Phil the previous week, he set his plans in motion. The jail held a handful of other inmates whose crimes fell outside the scope of restorative justice. Mostly violent alcoholics whose treatment hadn't worked. Their loyalty to Changleska was surprising, requiring careful monitoring to prevent retaliation against the political prisoners. One Native man, distantly related to the Chasing Hawks, had started several fights and had to be kept separated.

Jackson fed these local inmates a rumor that the other prisoners would be sent to isolated Lakota tribes. The inmates passed it along eagerly, embellishing it with vivid descriptions of mutilation and torture. They also spread word those who cooperated might avoid that fate.

After this softening period, Jackson selected several leaders and moved them into solitary confinement. He used the methods learned overseas: bright lights on through the night, food reduced to unseasoned mush, and periodic exposure to loud heavy metal music. No contact, no conversation. No human voice until he arrived.

The first interviewee was Samuel Centworth, an American in his early forties who looked worn and haunted. Compared to prisons of the eighteenth century, the earlier days of his incarceration had been nearly comfortable. These past two weeks, however, were another matter. Centworth had thought the previous interrogators were easy to manipulate and were done with him. His return to the interview room surprised him.

"Who are you, boy? Where's the other man I spoke to?" he demanded before Jackson sat down.

Jackson remained calm. "My name is Oliver Jackson. I'm an Executive Councilor of Changleska and the Minister for Defense."

"I heard they had a nigger running their military, and a squaw running the country. Hard to believe. No wonder your little uprising will fail. You've got no chance. Our army's coming."

Jackson didn't take the bait. "I have some simple questions. You didn't answer them before. Tell the truth now, and you'll leave solitary. Regular meals. Sleep in the dark. Cooperate enough, and we'll parole you and put you on a ship home."

"I'm not telling you nothin'. You don't know what it takes to run a real revolution." He looked tempted, but held back.

"Fine. I'm a busy man. You can go back to your cell. Maybe the Lakota will have better luck."

"Wait. Wait." He hesitated. "If I talk, I can leave solitary? And you'll give me your word of honor I'll be paroled and put on a ship home?"

"I give you my word you'll be paroled and put on a ship. If you cooperate fully." Jackson didn't mention which ship or where it was going.

Centworth broke. He gave them the evidence they needed. Benjamin Tallmadge was his handler, and funds went through him. Charles Cotesworth Pinckney was the general in charge of the operation and would lead the attack in New Orleans. He bragged Pinckney had twelve thousand men under his command. Jackson knew those numbers were inflated, but the rest confirmed their suspicions, now documented on tape and in writing.

It wasn't a smoking gun proving the United States had started the war, but it was closer than they d ever gotten. Jackson used the same method on the other three leaders, and they confirmed everything.

The interview with Leon Bauer was different. The jailers hadn't put him in solitary, but had observed him carefully, sending Jackson the reports.

Leon entered the interview room looking relieved to escape the monotony. Only books published before 1791 were available, but no other media.

Jackson introduced himself, although they might have met before when Leon worked at Omímeya. "I know you lied to the previous interviewers. You have heard from your cousin. This is your one chance to tell us everything."

"You know nothing."

"Louis Richter said something different."

In truth, Richter had said nothing, but he was a Hessian mercenary observed spending a lot of time talking to Leon.

"That motherfucker!"

"Come clean. We need the complete truth, every detail."

"Why should I? Aren't you going to give us all to the wild Lakota when the snow melts?"

"Not everyone. If you fully cooperate, we can parole you and put you on a ship."

"I don't believe you."

"You don't have to. Jail is boring. David Kim told me you were a gifted programmer. With so few programmers, it is a shame to have you doing nothing instead of working."

"David fired me for no cause. He said he was promoting me to Interstate, but it was because of my cousin. He revoked my security clearance because I wouldn't need it working there. That meant there was a lot I couldn't access."

Like porn, Jackson thought.

"At Omímeya, I worked on creating new programs. At Interstate it was only troubleshooting and maintenance. Plus, the perks were much better at Omímeya. It wasn't really a promotion."

Jackson had heard it all before. His jaw clenched, and a sharp comment teetered on the tip of his tongue. *So that justified contributing to all those deaths?* But he bit it back. He was trying to gain the man s cooperation, not derail the moment with anger.

"We cannot give you access to NewNet, but David said you could program some apps we need. You could work in the Sheriff's office from nine to five. You'd even get a better lunch."

Leon acquiesced; the boredom was driving him crazy. "Louis brought a letter from Karl. He said he lived in the palace of Francis II, the Holy Roman Emperor. Claimed Francis had given him lands and a villa with hot and cold running servant girls. He said I could get the same if I came with my computer and data. He also needed a screen for his and had a laptop that was password locked. But I couldn't get the data he wanted without a security clearance."

"Where is the letter now?"

"Burned it."

"Ok. I will keep my word. We will be in touch with a computer project." He had never spoken to David Kim about Leon, but he knew computer geeks. Being away from their tech was like a junkie without a fix. He knew how shorthanded IT was, having him working was better.

When he went home, Jackson felt hollow. He had what they needed. But he felt dirty all the same.

=..=

All the military planning meetings were becoming unwieldy, bogged down by too many people who had too much to do in too little time. Phone meetings didn t always cut it. Driving to and from Chamberlain was problematic in the snow. If he went, he had to bring his newly enlarged marine protection detail, which was a pain. Sometimes Gardner came to him, despite the hassle. Rose had suggested a four-day planning meeting at the resort. They could bring everyone from all the different service branches. People could bring their families and they could hold their promotion ceremonies. That'd be a win/win as the resort rarely booked rooms during midwinter weekdays, and it would offer an unexpected perk appreciated by families. By the week after the warning, everyone had completed their battle plans. They focused the agenda on reviewing and approving them.

Jackson s first meeting was with the new Air Guard. Coffee, prairie tea, and pastries were on the sideboard, and the map of the Mississippi corridor was on the overhead screen, with routes connecting Omímeya to St. Louis, New Madrid, and down to Oca Landing. A focused but tense atmosphere filled the room, and quiet energy preceding the big decisions was palpable.

Gardner leaned forward and began, "The runways and fuel depots at St. Louis and New Orleans are complete. New Madrid is still in process. We need a plan to use our air resources effectively. I'm looking forward to what you've come up with. I don't want to lose senior staff on a two-week barge ride, but I'm sure we could come up with other ideas besides transport. Where are we at?"

Cheryl Tigard, the new Air Guard Commander, wore a plain tan uniform with the patch of the newly formed Air Guard on one sleeve. She wore her hair pulled back tight, and looked every inch the cop she had been, and the commander she'd become since Big Thunder dropped her into the past with her police plane.

"The 206 is ready," she said. "Fully maintained, fresh plugs, instruments clean. We've done a few flights since last year, but started up the engine twice this month. She'll fly."

Gardner looked at her. "What about fuel?"

Kyle Ward spoke. "We finished testing. We've got about 5,200 gallons of viable AvGas left across the Circle. After a year, it's beginning to degrade. Some drums are already gumming up. We've sent some to the fuel depot already. The rest, if we don't use it soon, we'll lose it."

"And Unity Petroleum?" Jackson asked.

"Still months out from synthesizing anything clean enough for aircraft," Kyle replied. "They've got low-octane blends in prototype, but not for high-performance piston engines. No AvGas alternatives yet."

Gardner gave a tight nod. "Sounds like we've got a narrow window. You're saying it's now or never."

"Exactly," Cheryl said. "A single round trip to New Orleans and back burns around 160 gallons. We've got enough for maybe thirty flights if we don't push it. But that's in theory. If you want to use some now for intel, supply runs, or medevacs, now is the moment. It won't last."

Kyle added, "Even after the plant comes online, fuel for planes will still be limited. We need to look at lighter-than-air options like balloons and dirigibles. They work without burning gas."

Cheryl nodded. "There's an active forum on that. Some great ideas like reinforced envelopes, solar chargers, maybe hydrogen if we play it smart. Airships could give us long-range recon with almost no fuel. There's a hang glider forum; there are two here, if we can use them."

Jackson tapped his coffee cup slowly. "No place high enough in New Orleans to launch a hang glider. The rest will have to wait until we have time. For now, how fast can you be in the air?"

"Four hours. Less if I skip the preflight checklist."

Gardner said with a smile, "Don't skip the checklist. If you go down, we're not getting you back. We can replace the pilot, but you're flying the best plane in the world."

"Copy that," Cheryl said dryly.

Jackson asked, "Can the plane be configured to carry bombs or drop incendiaries?"

Cheryl sighed. "I investigated it. The short answer is no. There are no hard points. It can't fly low enough for precision drops or evasive flight under fire. There is no bomb sight or release system. If we had more time, perhaps something could be built."

Kyle asked, "What about the helicopter?"

Cheryl answered, "If you can figure out a way to get it down there, maybe, but that's a big maybe. It doesn't have the range to fly between here and St. Louis, much less to New Orleans."

They spent some time wrestling with the helicopter problem, working toward a possible viable solution. In the meantime, they planned their first run for the 206 with five members of the Signal Corps and their radio and communication gear. They scheduled ten more trips to follow, some with General Gardner and senior staff. Jackson wished he was going, but understood why he wasn't.

Jackson looked around the room. "Alright. Operation Tailwind is approved. First flight leaves at 0600 tomorrow."

He had other meetings with the navy, the marines, Indigenous war leaders, and various Guard units. They had a plan now. How well it would work, no one could say.

=..=

Jackson had slept little the night before the attack. In the last few days, reports from drone and reconnaissance flights had confirmed their worst fears: General Pinckney had indeed brought thousands of soldiers. The exact number remained uncertain. Some forces had arrived overland, others by various river craft, and still more by ship.

Gardner was in contact with the British regarding the impressment of eighty-four prisoners into the Royal Navy. They help draft parole documents consistent with the customs of the time. They planned to escort the paroled prisoners under guard to the British ships. There were too many for a single vessel, and the Royal Navy planned to transfer them directly to the ships where they would serve. Gardner made it clear there was nowhere to house them in New Orleans. The British needed to collect all of them at once.

They agreed to arrive on March fourteenth. Unbeknownst to the British, it was the full moon, the date Kimi predicted the attack. The British had maintained their position of neutrality, despite the compelling evidence shown to the ambassador. A few days before the scheduled transfer, four Royal Navy vessels anchored in the New Orleans harbor, waiting to receive the prisoners. Bristling with cannons, the ships looked intimidating.

When the American troop ships arrived and saw the British vessels, they mistakenly assumed a blockade was in place. Unaware the British were neutral, and unwilling to risk engagement, the Americans traveled many miles farther before finding a place to unload their men, which meant hundreds of soldiers arrived late to the battle.

The new Changleska Navy was quickly becoming a force to be reckoned with. *Spirit Wind*, the sloop captured from pirates, had been retrofitted with .50 caliber machine guns and rockets. She'd already taken four additional ships. In one engagement, she caught a smuggler vessel off guard at dawn, her crew cheering as the enemy surrendered without a shot fired. Each victory boosted morale and gave the navy a sense of rising momentum. The captured vessels now served under new names: *Morning Wind*, a small and fast cutter; *River Wind*, a shallow-draft brig for upriver missions; *Red Wind*, a gun sloop; and the newest addition, *Hawk s Wind*, a schooner named in honor of the Chasing Hawk family.

They positioned *Red Wind* and *Hawk's Wind* in the harbor to help sell the illusion of a British blockade. The other two were stationed at key points along the river.

The day before the main attack, the navy's river patrol boats, equipped with .50 caliber machine guns, had torn through dozens of enemy vessels carrying troops, sending shattered hulls drifting and smoke curling above the water, but the attackers kept coming. With the volume of boats and overland forces combined, they simply couldn't stop them all.

Jackson was frustrated trying to follow what was happening, listening to the shortwave in his office from Omímeya. Now the sun was rising, the radio was more unreliable despite the relays. He heard about events late, like the river boats attacking the troop transports, and now he could only get bits and pieces. There was something happening at Fort Charles. He hoped the flood traps worked. There was nothing he could do, no orders to give, only listening and waiting. Later that morning, he got a brief report about successfully repelling the forces attacking from the north. With a reminder to the staff to contact him if anything changed, he went to the gym for an hour to work off some of his anger and frustration. Afterwards, physically, he felt better, but mentally, not so much. He knew, like Gardner did, the Americans' major offensive would start tomorrow.

Upon arrival, they reached out to the local Indigenous tribes, inviting them to join Changleska. Today it was paying off. Chitimacha scouts had positioned themselves in the cypress thickets upriver for days. Their canoes hid in the reeds while the ever-present insects whined and the air stagnated, thick with humidity. At the first sign of American movement along the east bank, the scouts began sniping from cover. Houma hunters farther downriver set brush fires to obscure the shoreline, picking off soldiers as they panicked and scattered. The river patrols with the .50 caliber guns were still active, but ammunition was running low and they would need to return to base soon.

All that day, Jackson listened to reports and casualty lists. The worst of it came with the confirmation of looming ammunition shortages. They had already run out of many types and were low on others. Even with the Niokaska plant and what they'd brought from their time, it wasn t enough, not nearly enough. They had to win this next battle decisively. There wouldn t be enough ammunition to fight another.

Rose appeared in the evening, bringing Jackson dinner. She sat with him to make sure he ate and gave him keys to a room where he could try to catch a few hours of sleep, without asking questions or demanding attention. *God, I love that woman*, he thought as he drifted off to sleep.

As expected, the battle began at dawn. But contrary to what they had believed, Pinckney still had enough troops, even with all yesterday s losses, and the delays of the troops coming by ocean. Enemies surrounded Oca Landing on three sides.

Reports came in sporadically; at one point he glanced up to see many staff, some with tears in their eyes, crowding into the room where he was listening to the radio. Static crackled between reports, and long stretches of silence made the tension unbearable. Every voice coming through was strained, some breaking mid-sentence.

Then came the silence. Not just the usual static, but a long, dead void that stretched past anything Jackson had experienced. Even the background noise of distant gunfire had faded.

Someone in the room whispered, Have they breached the main house?"

A burst of garbled shouting crackled through the speaker, followed by a roar that might have been cannon fire or an engine.

"Repeat," the radio tech said urgently. "You're breaking up. Say again, Oca Command."

Then it came in clearer, broken but audible. "*Red Wind...* engaging east flank... holding line... *Hawk's Wind* coming upriver... repeat, air support inbound. She's letting loose on the western bank. They're using leapfrog fire from bow and stern, shelling clusters of infantry and pulling back before counterfire can lock on. Smoke is thick. You can't even see their line from here."

There were gasps in the room. Jackson stood, straining to hear.

A different voice, this one younger, came through the channel. "Chopper in sight. Coming over the ridge... I see it. I see it!"

Cheering erupted behind the transmission, scattered at first, then building.

Jackson didn t realize he had been holding his breath. He hadn t even been sure it would work, barging the helicopter down the Mississippi in pieces, hiding it under tarps, and reassembling it with a team of mechanics working through the night. It had started as a life flight helicopter, and the faded emergency logo was still visible beneath the repainted fuselage. They had rigged it with rocket pods, an old .30 caliber door gun, flares salvaged from an old mining cache, and electronics rebuilt with whatever components they could spare. Everyone had said the project was madness, but now it was in the air, flying, fighting, and saving lives.

An hour later, Gardner's voice came through the secure line. Jackson sat alone in the conference room, maps and empty coffee cups scattered across the table. Gardner sounded as exhausted as he must have looked.

"It was almost over," he said. "They were pushing hard from the north. We lost the outer barricades. I thought we were done. Then *Red Wind* came out of the fog, firing as she moved. Her cannons thundered over the river, sending splashes and shockwaves through the ranks of Pinckney's forward units. Didn't matter if every shot hit, it gave us cover and sent panic rippling through their lines."

He paused, taking a breath.

"Then that bird dropped out of the clouds like the angel of death. You should've seen it! It screamed over the treetops and lit up the enemy lines. One Guardian said it looked like a dragon made of smoke and steel. You could feel the air shift. People cheered before it even opened fire. Alston coordinated the southern perimeter and held them long enough for the gunships to make their pass. One of the freed slaves you met, Corporal Elijah Walker, was on the west barricade, coordinating with *Hawk's Wind*. He called in fire right when we needed it most. That saved us."

"I want names. All of them. Anyone who stood their ground today. They're going on the roll."

"You'll need a long list."

Jackson leaned back in his chair, the sounds of battle still echoing in his mind. For the first time all day, he allowed himself to hope.

Chapter Thirty-Two
Rose

ROSE WATCHED JACKSON standing near the sliding glass door in their bedroom, looking out toward the river. For the first time in months, the tension had melted from his frame. He looked like a Black Adonis, standing nude at the window in quiet contemplation.

At thirty-nine, his tall, lean body was honed by years of dedicated exercise, each muscle defined with the precision of a sculpture. His lack of pressure on Rose to exercise still surprised her. She often felt inadequate comparing herself to him, despite his repeated assurances he loved her plumpness.

Lying in bed, the afterglow of their lovemaking still warm in her body, Rose looked at this beautiful man and felt a swell of disbelief and gratitude. She wondered what karmic deed she had done to deserve him.

Their lives and work so intertwined, with mutual support, it felt like they were better together than apart. She could picture a future with him, not just surviving but building something lasting. What they had was not only love, but something sacred, forged by fire and time. In a world being remade, they had found each other whole.

She could see it, even with all the uncertainty ahead—a life they could shape together, not just weather side by side. She reached for her robe and crossed to where he stood, wrapping her arms around his waist from behind.

"I don't know what's coming," she said softly, her cheek against his back. "But I want to face it with you. All of it."

Jackson covered her hands with his. He didn't say anything, but he didn't need to. The warmth of his touch said more than words could.

It had only been a week since the Battle of Oca Landing. Yesterday the word came. The war was over. Washington finally relented. Despite the Americans' sound defeat, the death of almost all officers, including General Charles Cotesworth Pinckney, and the surrender of the few remaining forces in New Orleans, at first George Washington didn't concede. He wanted to continue the war. Normally, in this time, it would have taken weeks or months for messages to reach from battlefields to commanders. Washington's spies, listening to stolen radio transmissions, likely knew of his defeat, but to be certain, they sent an envoy with radio reports to confirm the surrender and casualty numbers. There were over 2,500 dead, 1,000 wounded, and 1,500 captured. The American force had numbered around 5,000, a mix of regulars and militia, who were unprepared for the modern tactics and firepower Changleska deployed. The highest-ranking remaining officer, a naval captain the sharpshooters couldn t reach, formally surrendered two days after the battle. Washington, Jefferson, and others had read about the future that was—how the US became a world power. They wanted the port, the land and technology. A few lost battles wouldn t stop them. Fortunately, Changleska had long prepared for this and had an ingenious contingency plan ready.

Rose found it amusing that the hippies came up with the plan that made such a difference. The hippies were a strong political group started from a bunch of people caught by Big Thunder at a permaculture conference. They were strong environmental activists, and the Gaia Committee was a major force in Changleska politics. Working with First Shield Command, they had planted agents all over Philadelphia where Washington lived now, as well as agents in New York.

It was two weeks after Washington's second inauguration when they got word he planned on proceeding with American war plans. That morning, simultaneously, the planned explosions occurred in the bedrooms of Washington, Jefferson, Hamilton, and other members of Congress known to support the war. In New York, the Custom House and the Federal Hall were targeted.

The explosions, mostly hidden in chamber pots because servants could place them unnoticed, set off stun grenades that released red paint and confetti messages reading, *No Greater Friend, No Worse Enemy—Changleska Coalition.* Although no one was hurt, the message was simple: we can find you anywhere. It worked. Washington backed down the next day. Changleska even forewent the usual reparations for the time and instead offered generous terms on port fees and technology transfers. They wanted the defeat to be lasting and as sweet as possible. Changleska sought to be the greatest friend and had proven they could be the worst enemy. They asked for the entire city of New Orleans, on both sides of the river, to become Changleska territory. Previously, only the western bank of the Mississippi had been included. Having the city divided proved too complicated. They granted a three-month transition period. Slave owners were furious over the loss of their "property," but given the wartime devastation common to this era, Washington knew they were getting off lightly.

Returning to work, everyone was jubilant. The heavy cloud of fear had lifted. Tomorrow was the Spring Equinox, and Rose changed their formerly muted planned ceremony into a big celebration. They planned a huge victory party, a formal dance, and other festivities. Despite the short notice, the resort would go all out, bringing in extra staff and preparing special food. Rose had already informed Jenny yesterday, and reviewing the updated plans was the focus of her first meeting today. It felt good to have something normal to focus on, like planning a party instead of preparing for survival in case of defeat.

She d shared the exciting news with Luke and Kimi the night before. She hadn t seen the girls much over the past few months. Kimi helped with the horses at her aunt s or stayed with her dad. Since she was no longer in school, where the bus could drop her off on Fridays and pick her up on Mondays, visiting on weekends rarely happened. Post-divorce custody agreements no longer applied; Kimi went where and when she pleased. Rose understood, but missed her. Kimi was still grieving, but knowing she'd given the warning that led to the victory that saved the entire Changleska Coalition would hopefully lift her spirits. Rose realized that in some ways, she was losing her daughter. She felt a bittersweet ache, partly proud in Kimi s strength and independence, and partly sadness that her little girl no longer needed her in the same way. At fourteen, Kimi had maturity and wisdom beyond her years. She was becoming her own person, needing her parents less. As much as Rose wanted to be there for her, there was a distance she didn t know how to cross. All she could do was keep the door open and hope Kimi would choose to walk through it.

Luke was rarely home, and she feared she was losing him too. They still had some teenage struggles, but he had matured. She still regretted all the years she hadn t been there enough. But this time, she didn t let the guilt take over. Her children were present with her when they were home, and they were all healing together.

Yesterday, she had suggested the girls invite friends to stay over after the party, and they agreed. Luke would be there, probably because Darla would be too. Now that Darla had started her apprenticeship to be an electrician, she worked weekends with her parents on Omímeya construction projects. Rose approved of the match. Darla was grounded, responsible, and had a quiet confidence that balanced Luke's impulsiveness. She wondered how much of modern teenage dating culture would survive in this time. The lack of birth control and the prevailing eighteenth-century norms were already bringing a shift toward early marriages and formal courtship, a stark contrast to the casual dating culture their teens had grown up with.

After the meeting, it felt good to get back to regular work. Although Rose didn't attend war planning meetings or political conferences, while she was aware of what was happening, her focus had been logistics. She and Kyle devised ways to add weapons and ammunition from the secret resort stockpiles without it being known where they came from. They repackaged items in nondescript containers, routed them through standard maintenance supply chains, and distributed them in staggered shipments to avoid suspicion. Jackson and General Gardner likely suspected, but both understood the principle of need-to-know and were too grateful to ask questions.

After Jenny, her next meeting was with Lou White Mountain, in his role as Lower Brule Tribal Chair, not as marine commander, his other job.

Rose stood and shook Lou's hand when he entered her office.

"Lou, good to see you up and about. You look pretty good after being shot."

"Not deep, just bloody. I'm fine. Your family?"

"Everyone is still grieving but okay, but are you as happy as I am to talk about something other than war?"

"You bet. I wondered if this day would ever come. We have a backlog of projects. Might as well start now."

"I see on the agenda," Rose said, glancing at her tablet, "tribal contributions and the landfill investment are top of your list."

"Yes, the Council understands why there was a pause in Omímeya's contributions to the tribe during the war. But now it's over, we are wondering when and how much it will be when it resumes."

"That didn't take long. We only found out yesterday. I'd thought the tribe's investments had been paying off."

"They have, but you know how it is. There's always more need. We need to build more Harmony Houses. We expect more people to return with PTSD and we want to be ready. Also, alcoholism is creeping back. There is a lot of drinking in this time period, and we need more treatment centers."

"Do you have a budget?"

Lou laughed. "Not yet. The war ended yesterday, and we've all had our hands full. I mostly wanted to feel things out and see if it was worth getting started on specifics. I know Omímeya did a lot for the war effort, but I also want to make sure we're not losing sight of tribal priorities."

Rose tried not to stiffen in response. "With the tribe owning twenty percent of Omímeya stock, we're not liable to forget. No one has received dividends. Capital expenses are too high. In a year or two, some of these investments will pay off, and the dividends will start rolling in. It'll take time to recover from all the war expenses."

"I understand. But I remember how much the old government fucked the reservations over, and I don't want to depend on even our own government to pay for social services in a timely way."

"It's hard to wrap your head around how much our world has changed. Lower Brule will soon be the wealthiest tribe in Ocheti Sakowin, and perhaps all of Changleska. Although the Miwok, and their gold fields, will give us a run for our money."

"Good to see you say 'us'. I know your dad was Yankton, but Kimi is Lower Brule, so it's good you know this is your tribe, and your responsibility." Rose felt a flicker of irritation. Lou's words pricked at old insecurities, ones she thought she had buried.

"Of course. Next item, the landfill. I remember a little; please elaborate."

"We need to expand the dump mine and the recycling plant. The county is earning real money from theirs. We need more workers, but not enough people are committing crimes to staff it. We need much more protective gear and recycling equipment. If we can get the copper wire, we can make more solar panels from discarded CDs. After the winter closure, we need to be ready. We're losing electronics every day, even plastic degrades in a landfill."

Rose knew this area of South Dakota had few recycling centers, and most things ended up in landfills. But when twenty-first-century items became valuable, landfills turned into gold mines. Something like a plastic dishwashing bottle became a bidet that cleaned better than toilet paper or a corncob. Since they hadn't succeeded in making plastic, what they didn't use as is, they melted for other purposes. They were finding all kinds of extremely valuable things people had thrown away, like appliances and electronics with parts worth salvaging.

"I agree. The dump is a priority since it's weather related. Mary will also hear from me about Changleska's contributions to the Harmony and Clear Path Recovery Centers. After all, Lower Brule tribal members are probably minority users of these services since the population boom."

Lou and Rose talked about the changes in population and other topics, and both left the meeting satisfied. Although they reached no specific agreements, it was clear Omímeya intended to support tribal priorities, invest in social services, and ensure equitable growth in the postwar recovery.

Rose loved numbers. Not the abstract kind you studied in calculus or quantum physics, but the useful kind: costs, kilowatts, calories, inventory lists, barrels of fuel. She enjoyed knowing how many people they could feed for how long with what they had, or exactly what it cost to power the second floor of Omímeya with geothermal and solar energy. She also knew how much money they were making, how much was being reinvested, and how much was quietly being held back by the board "for security purposes."

What she didn't know was how to solve the math of love and exhaustion and grief. That equation always came up with missing variables. It was like trying to calculate the shape of lightning from its sound alone.

=..=

After she got home that night, Rose was a little disappointed to find Jackson working late. The war wasn't over in a day for him. She had a surprise for him. The architect had brought her the plans for the remodel of her home. Although she and Jackson had discussed it briefly, he didn't know the extent of the proposed changes, many made specifically for him, so he would feel it was his home, too. Admittedly, the construction wouldn't be finished until late summer, but she hoped he would be pleased.

She lived in one of the original riverside cabins, built for weddings and hunting parties. The former General Manager had used her house to entertain guests, and it had some features the others did not, like a safe room. Designed for vacationers, they had nothing a normal house had, like a garage, mudroom, pantry, or storage space.

Right after Big Thunder, when the board met to discuss asset allocation, Phil had insisted the board receive the lion's share, in addition to big bonuses based on profits. Phil had been part of the consortium of Indian casinos that had planned and paid for Omímeya as a luxury bug-out shelter. He'd been involved before they broke ground, had seniority, and could have been CEO instead of Rose. Phil had decided he didn't want the headaches that came with serving as both CEO and general manager of the entire resort. Later, he became the Intelligence Chief, but he still wanted all the perks of a CEO. He had a larger salary than Rose and expected the same or better level of other benefits. Phil recommended giving Rose and all the board members titled plots of land for their personal residences, along with generous building allowances. Phil ensured Rose received the title to the Riverside Cabin she had been staying in after she declined the chance to build something new.

Other board members also got land and a building allowance. Wayne owned a house in Fort Thompson nine miles away. He commuted by electric truck but recognized he might want to be closer. The site he picked was not prime riverside property but a bigger site close to the triangle, the industrial park area behind the main building that held the geothermal plant. Kyle's girlfriend had moved in with him, and Rose expected wedding bells soon. He was working on a place right on the river, near her. Billy was going to build something nearby as well.

The architect spent time with Rose and her kids, spoke briefly to Jackson, and looked over the site. Between the building allowance from the board and her personal income, she'd told the architect money was no object. She couldn't believe she actually said that. There was a time when the idea of spending freely would have made her cringe. Now it felt strange and exhilarating, a sign of how much her life had changed. Rose was still coming to terms with the level of wealth she had and could expect in the future.

They would tear down the carport they had quickly erected last winter and put a large two-car garage in its place. They would build a small horse stable and corral shared with the neighboring property. There would be a mudroom, a pantry with space for a large freezer, lots of storage, and a small shop and tool room. In the back, leading to the deck, there would be a large room for a gym for Jackson. Above the garage would be an apartment with two and a half bedrooms and one bathroom. The half bedroom, the architect explained, was a bonus or craft room. He had seen all the girls' beads when he checked the place out. He picked another spot on the property to build Luke a tiny house. White River Farms had a company that built hemp tiny homes. Luke could either buy one of those pre-designed houses, or he could design and build his own. Rose loved these ideas and hoped Jackson would, too. She couldn t wait to show him the designs.

The architect s proposals reflected Rose s future position, the way her family was expected to grow and change, and the way her living space needed both function and beauty. He posed one deeply personal question, relevant to the space's design, that she couldn t answer. He asked her whether she and Jackson planned to have children. She honestly answered, I don t know."

She'd thought she was done having kids because she was immersed in a war that left little room for anything else. At times, she had felt guilty for choosing ambition over more time at home, but her responsibilities had grown so vast and important, there was never space to reconsider. But she was not yet forty. There was still time. She could afford all the help she needed. A part of her felt the empty nest looming, and knew she had enough love for another child. She had an IUD that was overdue to come out. It was a decision she'd put off. She smiled, thinking of having a child with Jackson and wondered what he thought. He had never expressed an interest in kids, but now she couldn't stop thinking about it. She wasn't making any decisions yet. But the idea was there, quiet and persistent. It had taken root in a part of her she hadn't paid attention to in years.

=..=

That night, well after dark, Jackson came home. Rose was in the living room with a mug of tea and the remodeling plans still spread across the kitchen table. He stood in the doorway for a moment, his shoulders slumped but his eyes warm.

"You're up," he said softly.

"I have something to show you."

She gestured to the table. Jackson stepped in, curious. As he bent to look, Rose couldn't help watching him, not the military man or the public figure, but the tired, beautiful person she loved.

He traced a finger along the blueprint lines. "You moved the gym to the back?"

"I thought you might enjoy having a space that opens to the deck. Quiet. Yours."

His eyes flicked up to hers. "You made room for me."

"It's your home too."

"When will this be completed?"

"Late summer, if all goes according to plan."

"We've had updates from the expeditions," Jackson informed her. "The northern team survived the winter. They're building a new outpost near a fur trading post that's half abandoned. California says mining is stable, but they're low on labor and ammo. The Southwest is making slow progress. There's been a lot of diplomacy, some interest, but no firm alliances yet."

They went out on the deck and stood together for a long time, gazing at the stars as the future whispered around them like a breeze through unseen trees. Standing in the night and looking at the stars. Somewhere out there, the other expeditions were still moving, still surviving. They had made it through a war. The next challenge would be building something that truly justified the cost.

Later, as Rose prepared for bed, Jackson's phone buzzed on the nightstand. He didn't open it right away. Instead, he set the phone down slowly, watching Rose as she pulled the blanket back on their bed.

"You should answer it," she said.

He checked the screen, brows knitting as he scanned the incoming message. "Security Council Meeting tomorrow, 9:00 a.m., regarding new intelligence about Karl Bauer." Jackson let out a deep sigh.

"Do you want to talk about it?" Rose asked.

"I thought we were done, war over, we can finally have peace, but now, we have a new problem. Karl Bauer."

"Is that the German from the first missing expedition? Wasn't his cousin involved in the communication blackout?"

"Yes, but this is not the worst of it. We believe he's pushing European powers toward war. Quietly. Strategically. If he's trying to save the Holy Roman Empire, he won't stop until Europe burns. Only he's not trying to change the past; he's trying to restore it."

Jackson returned a few minutes later, slipping into bed beside her. The silence stretched between them, heavy but not uncomfortable.

"Kimi had a dream," Rose said softly. "She said something's coming. Not bad. Just big."

Jackson exhaled slowly. "Maybe she's right."

They lay in the dark, the hush of the room broken only by the faint shifting of ice outside.

"Do you ever think about having a baby?" Rose asked, her voice barely above a whisper.

Jackson turned to her, moonlight catching the curve of his cheekbone. "I always wanted a child," he said slowly. "But I've been holding back. I didn't know if we'd survive the war, or even survive this world. And I didn't want to dream about something I couldn't have. Part of me wondered if it was too late for us. Too late to start again."

She reached for his hand beneath the blankets. "I don't know if I want it either. Not exactly. But maybe... I might. With you."

He closed his fingers gently around hers, steady and sure. "Then we'll figure it out. Together."

For a long moment, they lay in silence, listening to the wind stir the trees outside. The thought of a child no longer felt distant or impossible. It felt tender, fragile, but real. Something they could choose, rooted in love and built with intention. Not because time demanded it, or because they needed to, but simply because they could.

Outside, the ice groaned and cracked, loud in the stillness.

Beneath the frozen surface, the river shifted. The Earth was waking.

This concludes the story. What follows are the records left behind, the text of the treaty, a reality check, and the author's notes.

The journey continues in **Book Three** *coming Summer 2026.*

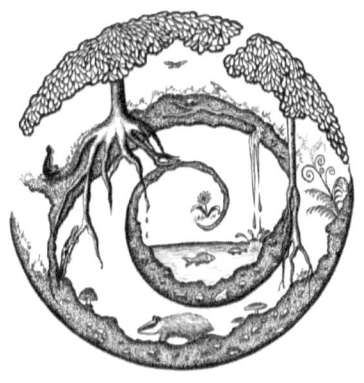

Part V
The Circle Continues

Echoes from the World of Changleska

Man did not weave the web of life, he is merely a strand in it.
Whatever he does to the web, he does to himself.
— *Chief Seattle (c. 1786–1866), Suquamish and Duwamish leader*

Selected Newspaper Articles, 1792–1793

Collected by the Changleska Historical Society

==•==•==•==•==•==•==•==

Charleston City Gazette and Daily Advertiser

Printed in Charleston, the Fourth Day of December, in the Year of Our Lord 1792.

Concerning Alarming Reports from the Interior. A strange alliance of Indians and Negroes hath formed a self-declared nation upon the upper Missouri. From accounts lately received by traders and frontier agents, we are informed of a confederation of peoples who now call themselves the Changleska Coalition. This body, by their own declaration, hath established a form of civil government without sanction of crown nor state, and have therein admitted persons of every race and sex into stations of authority contrary to law and the order set by Providence.

Accounts further speak of machines which move without beast, and dwellings lit without flame. These contrivances are not well understood and have led some to speculate that foreign agents or heretical arts may be involved. Within the territory, it is said, there exist factions that oppose this coalition, among them certain persons who assert that allegiance to the United States ought to be maintained. One such figure, Senator Clyde Folsom, is believed to have urged that rightful authority be restored and that negotiations commence for annexation into the Union under lawful terms. At present, it remains uncertain whether such efforts shall gain ground, or be silenced by the prevailing power. Let all who read consider well what danger may arise should this experiment persist and gain the notice of others discontented or unlearned in the proprieties of governance. We caution the reader to watch these developments with vigilance.

==•==•==•==•==•==•==•==

Aurora General Advertiser

Philadelphia, the Second of January, 1793

Strange occurrences from the Interior of the Western Continent. Several travellers of reputable standing, report that a gathering of considerable importance hath taken place within the territory claimed by those style themselves the Changleska Coalition. The location, known as Omímeya, is described as the seat of their government, wherein may be found structures of uncommon design and engines not familiar to our present understanding.

The gathering, convened as a general council, is said to include leaders of the Lakota and other Indian nations, and persons of African descent. Some accounts further mention the presence of observers from Spanish and British provinces, though their roles remain uncertain.

The governing body is called the Executive Council, consisting of seven ministers drawn from the various peoples now joined under the Changleska banner. Among them is a woman named Mary Landrau, who, by their custom, is referred to as the Chair, though her office more closely resembles that of a presiding minister or chief officer. One witness, whose remarks were recorded in a trader's ledger, wrote that she possessed "clear speech, firm command of the assembly, and a bearing suited to high office."

Subjects reported to be under deliberation include the establishment of trade with neighboring powers, the proposed purchase of lands presently under the authority of the Spanish Crown, and a declaration of natural rights, said to be extended to all persons without respect to race or station. Whether this new polity shall endure, or be recognized by the established nations of the world, remains to be seen. Yet those who have observed its proceedings speak with surprise at its order, the strange mechanisms in use, and the resolute character of its people. Further intelligence shall be published as it may be received.

==•==•==•==•==•==•==•==

Boston Gazette

Printed in Boston, the Tenth Day of February, 1793

On the Emergence of a Foreign Dominion in the Western Interior
Concerning recent accounts from multiple quarters of the interior and from letters received by reputable houses of trade, it is affirmed that a body of persons hath established a new and unlawful dominion upon the western plains, styling themselves the Changleska Coalition. Said body hath, by their own admission, renounced the authority of any established government, and is now governed by a council composed of men and women of mixed ancestry, including persons of Indian and African blood.

The said polity is further reported to maintain a standing force, wherein Negroes and savages bear arms, and engines of unnatural construction are employed in place of horse or oxen. Though no open conflict hath yet arisen, the matter is judged by many to constitute a threat not only to the peace of the frontier but to the integrity of the union itself. Among those who observe the situation with growing unease are men of rank and influence who caution that such insolence, if left unchecked, may give rise to sedition elsewhere. There is talk that foreign envoys have been received, and that treaties may be entertained without the knowledge or consent of Congress.

It is the opinion of this journal that the matter requires immediate and resolute action. The republic must not suffer a rival to flourish in its midst, under cover of inaction and delay.

==•==•==•==•==•==•==•==

The New-York Packet

Printed at New-York, this Twenty-Second Day of February, 1793

On Certain Movements Amongst the Militias of the Southern Provinces.
Rumours circulate concerning preparations in response to the western disturbances. It hath been conveyed by way of several letters out of the Carolinas, and by intelligence gathered from reputable men newly arrived from Savannah and Charleston, that certain companies of militia have been called to muster in the southern provinces. The occasion thereof, though not officially declared, is said to concern a body of persons settled near the upper Missouri, calling themselves the Changleska Coalition, whose designs are not yet fully known.

These reports allege that the said people have taken up arms and laid claim to governance independent of any crown or federal compact, and that their councils include Indians, women, and persons of colour. An arrangement most unusual and regarded by many with suspicion. Some speak of mechanical instruments and other artifices not commonly found among frontier settlements, though the truth of these claims cannot be confirmed.

Amongst the planter class, there hath arisen no small alarm, and it is believed by some that vessels and provisions are being gathered with quiet haste. Whether these stirrings shall come to action, or pass as another phantom of the frontier, remaineth to be seen.

==•==•==•==•==•==•==•==

The Orleans Gazette

Extraordinary Post March 17th, 1792

MOST ALARMING INTELLIGENCE from the Lower Mississippi!

A dreadful Engagement hath taken Place at the Outpost known to some as *Oca Landing*, a Settlement recently claimed by the so-styled Nation of Changleska. Reports are yet Confus'd, but sufficient Evidence hath been receiv'd to confirm a Battle of considerable Ferocity and Loss of Life.

It is declar'd by Persons of Reputation that the American Forces, under the Command of General Pinckney, did launch a grand Assault upon said Settlement from no fewer than Three Directions at the Dawn Hour. The Position was encircled, and the Fire of Muskets and Cannon did rend the Morning Air with great Violence.

An Officer lately arriv'd from the River states that a most infernal Machine, akin to a great Bird of Iron, did descend from the Clouds, belching Fire and Smoke upon the American Ranks. Said Device was fitted with unnatural Artillery and caused great Confusion in the Field.

Several Vessels of the Changleska Navy, including one call'd the *Red Wind*, were observ'd shelling the Eastern Bank with such Effect that many Companies broke Rank and fled in Disorder.

Casualty Lists are incomplete, but early Estimates number no fewer than 2,000 Men dead or grievously Wounded. Several high Officers, including General Pinckney himself, are rumour'd to have fall'n, though Confirmation awaits. Survivours taken by the Changleska are report'd to be in number no less than 1,500.

404

Though the Settlement remaineth in Changleskan Hands, it is understood that the Americans have not yet formally surrender'd. Reports reach us of Envoys riding under Flag of Truce.

The full Extent of this Catastrophe to the American Cause is not yet known, but the Mood in the City of New Orleans is one of Panic and Dismay.

More to follow as News arriveth.

==•==•==•==•==•==•==•==•==

Chamberlain Free Press

Surrender Confirmed by Council

March 18, 1793 By June Danner, Staff Reporter

Chamberlain — The Executive Council has confirmed that surrender terms have been formally accepted by opposing forces following the recent battle near Oca Landing. The decision was communicated by short-range radio to Omímeya early this morning and relayed to district leadership shortly thereafter. No further engagements have been reported, and security patrols have been recalled to standard posts. Casualty reports remain under review. Council officials declined to release full terms at the time of printing but indicated that no territorial concessions were made and that civil governance would remain unchanged.

Citizens are advised to continue normal operations and refrain from circulating unverified reports. The Free Press will publish full details as they are authorized for release.

Sources close to the Executive Council suggest that negotiations were concluded swiftly once opposing commanders recognized the strength of Changleska's defensive positions and the futility of continued resistance. While terms remain under seal, insiders report that humanitarian provisions were prioritized, including medical treatment for wounded prisoners and safe corridors for withdrawal.

District spokespersons emphasized the importance of unity during this transition period. "We remain vigilant, but today is a moment to breathe," said Executive Councilor Chair Mary Landrau. "The people stood together. Now we turn to healing, rebuilding, and ensuring our homeland remains secure."

Extract of a Letter from Lt. Col. Horace L. Wexley, His Majesty's Service, New Orleans – March 18th, 1792

To the Honourable Lords Commissioners of the Admiralty, Whitehall, London

My Lords,

I have made the following observations concerning the recent engagement at a place known locally as Oca Landing, a settlement held by the Changleska Coalition, a curious alliance of red Indians, freed negroes, and Americans.

On the 15th instant, General Pinckney commenced a full assault upon said position with several thousand troops, bolstered by artillery and, in the American fashion, a prodigious sense of their own inevitability. The result was a repulse most decisive.

The defenders, though fewer in number, demonstrated discipline and coordination unlooked for amongst such a gathering. Of particular note is the sudden appearance of a great contrivance, metallic and airborne, which discharged volleys upon the American flank with deadly precision. One might liken it to a flying furnace or mechanical bird. I assure your Lordships, it did sow confusion in the ranks, not unlike Minden, though with far less dignity.

I observed, too, what may be some new form of signaling, performed by handheld instruments which produced no discernible sound or flash. Orders seemed to be issued and received in silence, by means unclear to the eye. That women give instruction, and that these are obeyed without dispute, is among the more curious elements I have observed.

The American casualties are believed to exceed two thousand, with many more scattered or taken. General Pinckney's status remains unconfirmed. The enemy retains the field, and parleys are said to be underway.

It is my opinion that this Coalition warrants serious attention. Though composed of peoples long dismissed as savage or subordinate, they possess arms and understanding that suggest a most dangerous potential. Their refusal to abide by the expected order does not render them less formidable. It may render them more so.

I remain, Your Lordships' most obedient and humble servant,

Horace L. Wexley

Lieutenant-Colonel, Royal Engineers
On detached service to His Majesty's interests in Spanish Louisiana

==•==•==•==•==•==•==•==

The Boston Gazette

March 21, 1793

Strange Peace at New-Orleans: Surrender Without Treaty, and the Occurrences That Turned the Tide

From official dispatches passed in hours, not days, conducted not by courier but by a curious engine of unknown principle between officials near the frontier and those here in the capital, a feat not heretofore imagined. It is confirmed that the force calling itself the Changleska Coalition now holds the port of New-Orleans, following a three-day engagement that left General Pinckney slain and the American detachment in retreat.

Witnesses speak of uncommon contrivances and unnatural stratagems: a large mechanical craft, seen to rise and descend with fearful effect, laid waste to stores and batteries. Many say such occurrences, more than numbers or powder, turned the day. More startling still were the disturbances that followed.

In Philadelphia and New York, coordinated explosions were reported in the bedchambers of General Washington, Mr. Jefferson, Mr. Hamilton, and others. The blasts, set off by devices hidden in chamber pots, were likely placed by servants in league with Changleska agents. Though no one was harmed, they released red paint and slogans reading:

"No Greater Friend, No Worse Enemy. Changleska Coalition."

The insult, though bloodless, was grave. Many believe it, more than the battle itself, caused Washington to abandon war plans. By morning, he had agreed to receive Changleskan terms.

Among Boston's merchants and men of letters, opinions remain divided. Some call for renewed vigilance. Others suggest we witness a new order, founded not in Europe's image, but upon principles yet ungrasped.

Though the guns have fallen silent, this is no peace wrought by treaty nor by parity of arms. Rather, it is a peace imposed by those whose powers we do not yet understand.

If it be true, as some now whisper, that the age hath turned, then let all who cherish the Republic ask: What future awaits, when those beyond our borders write the terms of peace?

Founding Documents of the Changleska Coalition

Declaration of Independence

On September 21, 1791, representatives of the people brought by Big Thunder from another world gathered at the Omímeya Resort, in the Nation of Lower Brule, to declare independence from Spain. We claim the lands from the Mississippi River to the Pacific Ocean, the former borders of what was in our world, Mexico and Canada. These lands belong to the Indigenous peoples who live there. We recognize those tribes as sovereign nations, with inherent rights and responsibilities to their own people and to the Earth. From this day forward, we declare these lands to be held in trust for the good of all. We hereby create a new sovereign nation, the Changleska Coalition, to protect the land and the people who dwell within it. Our covenant as a nation is to protect the Earth and its interconnected bio-systems—waters, plants, and animals—from pollution, contamination, and exploitation, preserving them in health and wholeness for future generations.

The Constitution of the Changleska Coalition

Preamble We, the citizens of the Changleska Coalition, united by purpose, memory, and vision, establish this Constitution to protect our people, restore balance to the Earth, and govern ourselves with justice, transparency, and care for future generations.

Article I – Structure of Government: The Changleska Coalition follows a form of government rooted in Indigenous traditions of shared responsibility, consensus, and stewardship. The national government shall consist of a seven-member Executive Council, elected for seven-year terms, reasonably but not extravagantly compensated for full-time service. The Chair shall facilitate meetings and send agendas, with no additional powers unless emergency action is required and all other members are unavailable. The Council has the authority to remove any member for cause, using standards adapted from Lower Brule and Crow Creek Tribal guidelines.

Article II – Powers and Responsibilities of the Council: The Executive Council shall not originate laws. Its role is to vote to approve or deny proposals from citizen committees. All decisions are made by majority vote. If a proposal is denied, the Council must provide transparent reasoning unless it endangers national security. Rejected proposals may be resubmitted after one year.

Article III – Committees: Committees may be formed to address specific areas of national concern. At least two thousand people are needed to create a committee who can propose laws. Each committee may have up to eighteen members and must include:

Chair, responsible for guiding discussion and presenting proposals.

Secretary, to document proceedings.

Treasurer, to budget resources including funds, materials, and labor.

Article IV – Citizen Rights and Referendums: Any issue may be brought before the Council through a public referendum, bypassing committees, if approved by two-thirds of eligible voters. Referendums to change this Constitution must wait at least one year and require two-thirds approval to pass. After the first year, changes to the constitution may occur every ten years. Referendums to change laws must wait three years after a law is enacted and also require a two-thirds majority.

Article V – Citizenship: To become a citizen, be eligible to vote, serve as a Council, Committee, or Court member, and receive all the protection and collaborators of citizenship, a person must:

1. Be 18 years of age or older and either brought by Big Thunder within the thirty-mile circle or be born to someone who was, regardless of their original tribe, country, or county of birth. Dual citizenship is allowed. If not brought by Big Thunder, the person must have lived within the Changleska Coalition borders or a related community for two years.
2. Have sworn a sacred oath of the Covenant of the Earth before witnesses, of which one must be a citizen, and be duly recorded in the legal record.
3. Have agreed to support and defend the four freedoms and accept the four responsibilities freely, without reservations or purposes of evasion.

Oath of the Covenant of the Earth

"I solemnly vow, by all that I hold sacred, to safeguard the Earth and its interconnected bio-systems, including its waters, plants, and animals, from pollution, contamination, and exploitation. I pledge to preserve them in a state of health and wholeness for the benefit of future generations."

Four Freedoms *Every citizen has the freedom and right:*

1. To be free from slavery, torture, or rape. This includes the right to be free of discrimination based on race or ethnicity, religion, gender, sexual orientation, or political affiliation. Citizens have the right to justice, not to be subject to incarceration, cruel or unusual punishment, or death without the judgment of a court of law. Every citizen has the right to basic health care.

2. To worship or not worship as they choose. Everyone has freedom of religion or spiritual practice if they do not coerce or compel others to follow their beliefs.

3. To express dissent: This includes freedom of speech, via written or other forms of communication, freedom to gather, to engage in peaceful protest, and freedom to exit or travel. This freedom does not include the right to foment violence, insurrection, or treason.

4. To bear arms to protect themselves, their family, and their property. This right does not apply to those convicted of a violent crime, or who pose a danger to themselves or others as determined by a court of law.

Four Responsibilities *Every citizen has the responsibility:*

1. To protect the Earth for future generations, to use resources sustainably, and to stop those who would damage the ecosystem.

2. To protect their nation. All able-bodied adults from the age of eighteen to twenty-five shall be required to serve two years of military service either in an active or a support role. Those enrolled in either an educational or apprenticeship program may defer service for up to four years.

3. To aid in the care of those who are vulnerable, such as children and elders.

4. To support the financial stability of the nation by tithing ten percent of all gross personal income. Business income is taxed at a higher rate, determined by annual income and number of employees.

Treaty of Changleska, 1792
Articles of Peace, Recognition, and the Cession of New Spain

PREAMBLE:
In the spirit of peace, mutual recognition, and the pursuit of lasting friendship between sovereign nations, this Treaty is concluded and solemnly affirmed between His Catholic Majesty Charles IV, King of Spain, and the duly empowered emissaries of the Executive Council of Changleska, representing the independent and sovereign Nation of Changleska. This agreement serves to establish formal diplomatic relations, recognize territorial sovereignty, and enact the lawful cession of the dominions of New Spain, in accordance with the customs and laws of civilized nations.

The undersigned plenipotentiaries, having been vested with full powers by their respective governments, do hereby agree to the following articles:

ARTICLE I, RECOGNITION OF SOVEREIGNTY
His Catholic Majesty Charles IV does hereby recognize the full and independent sovereignty of the Nation of Changleska, its right to self-governance, and its authority to engage in diplomacy, commerce, defense, and administration over its own territories.

ARTICLE II, CESSION OF TERRITORY
All lands, dominions, holdings, and dependencies comprising New Spain, including but not limited to the provinces of Luisiana, Tejas, Nuevo México, California, Nueva Vizcaya, Sonora, Nuevo Santander, Coahuila, and all territories west of the Mississippi River formerly under Spanish jurisdiction, are hereby ceded in perpetuity to the Nation of Changleska.
Said territories shall pass with all appurtenances, ports, harbors, forts, settlements, and civil institutions therein, save where otherwise provided in this Treaty.

ARTICLE III, PROTECTION OF PERSONS AND PROPERTY

All subjects of the Spanish Crown presently residing within the ceded territories shall be afforded full protection under Changleska law. They shall retain the right to remain, remove themselves, or petition for lawful residency or citizenship within Changleska.

Private property, commercial enterprises, and lawful holdings shall be respected and protected under local law, subject to equitable taxation and civil regulation.

ARTICLE IV, FREEDOM OF RELIGION AND PROTECTION OF CATHOLIC INSTITUTIONS

Changleska affirms the right of all persons within its territories to freely exercise their religion without interference or persecution.

In special recognition of the longstanding presence of the Catholic Church, all churches, missions, convents, and charitable institutions of the Catholic faith shall be granted legal protection and permitted to continue their ministries in peace. Clergy shall be free to reside, worship, and carry out their duties, subject only to civil law and the public good.

ARTICLE V, NAVIGATION AND TRADE RIGHTS

Vessels and merchants of Spain shall be granted peaceful access to ports formerly under Spanish control, under terms of mutual benefit and subject to fair customs and trade regulations. A joint Commercial Commission shall be appointed within one year to negotiate a formal Trade Accord between the parties.

ARTICLE VI, NAVIGATION OF THE MISSISSIPPI AND TRIBUTARIES

Spain shall retain the right of peaceful navigation along the Mississippi River and its major tributaries, for purposes of commerce and lawful transit. No obstruction shall be placed on Spanish ships engaged in such navigation, provided they comply with Changleska's laws and customs regulations. Designated ports of entry shall be agreed upon through mutual consultation.

ARTICLE VII, TRANSFER OF ADMINISTRATIVE AUTHORITY

Within six months of ratification, all Spanish civil and military officials shall formally relinquish their posts to authorized representatives of Changleska. Administrative records, property inventories, and civil ledgers shall be delivered intact, and military garrisons shall depart in an orderly manner unless retained by separate agreement.

ARTICLE VIII, TRANSITION OF CIVIL JURISDICTION
Until Changleska's legal institutions are fully implemented, existing Spanish ordinances and civil codes may remain in temporary effect at the discretion of local authorities, subject to review and repeal under Changleska law.

ARTICLE IX, PENSIONS AND SALARIES FOR DEPARTING OFFICERS
The Spanish Crown may continue to grant pensions or compensation to civil and military personnel retiring from posts due to this territorial transfer. Changleska shall place no impediment upon such payments, though it shall not assume financial responsibility for them.

ARTICLE X, TRANSFER OF ARCHIVES, MAPS, AND SURVEYS
Spain shall deliver to Changleska full copies of all official maps, surveys, charts, censuses, legal documents, and administrative records relevant to the ceded territories. A joint commission shall oversee the timely and accurate transfer of such archives.

ARTICLE XI, ESTABLISHMENT OF A CLAIMS COMMISSION
To resolve potential disputes regarding property ownership, commercial contracts, or debts arising under Spanish authority, a Claims Commission shall be jointly established. Said commission shall operate for a period not exceeding five years from the date of treaty ratification and shall render decisions binding upon both parties.

ARTICLE XII, DIPLOMATIC RELATIONS
Ambassadors and consular officers shall be exchanged between the Kingdom of Spain and the Nation of Changleska within twelve months. Diplomatic correspondence shall be conducted in a spirit of mutual respect and peace.

ARTICLE XIII, LANGUAGE AND LEGAL VALIDITY
This Treaty shall be prepared and signed in both the Spanish and English languages. Both versions shall bear equal legal authority. In case of ambiguity, the matter shall be resolved through mutual consultation guided by the spirit and intent of this agreement.

ARTICLE XIV, RATIFICATION AND IMPLEMENTATION
This Treaty shall be ratified by the respective governments within ninety days of signature. Ratified copies shall be exchanged, and the treaty shall come into full force upon mutual ratification.

In witness whereof, the undersigned, having full powers, have affixed their signatures and seals in duplicate, at the town of Omímeya, this fifteenth day of November, in the Year of Our Lord Seventeen Hundred Ninety-Two.

For His Catholic Majesty Charles IV

Manuel de Godoy,

Prince of the Peace. Minister Plenipotentiary of the Spanish Crown.

Seal of the King of Spain

For the Nation of Changleska Coalition

Mary Landrau

Mary Landrau, Chair of the Executive Council (Signing on behalf of the full Executive Council)

Witnessed by the Executive Council of Changleska

Oliver Jackson, Minister of Defense
Richard Russo, Minister of Infrastructure
Duane Nelson, Minister of Communication
Theresa Martinez, Minister of Medicine
Shawn Caris, Minister of Human Services
Jerome Brown, Minister of Agriculture

Seal of Changleska Coalition

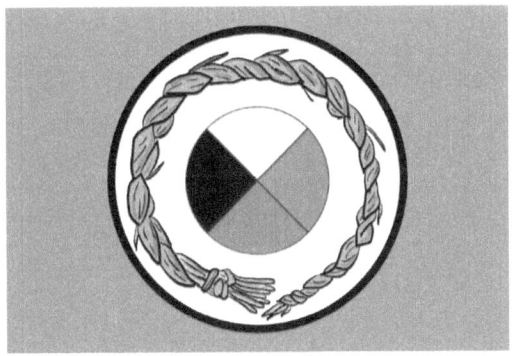

Changleska Coalition Flag

Part VI
Author's Notes and Reality Check

Context, credits, and where the fiction meets the truth

Action on behalf of life transforms. Because the relationship
between self and the world is reciprocal, it is not a question of first
getting enlightened or saved and then acting.
As we work to heal the Earth, the Earth heals us.
— Robin Wall Kimmerer (b. 1953), Potawatomi botanist and author of *Braiding
Sweetgrass* and other works on Indigenous knowledge and ecology

About the Author

Daphne Singingtree is an educator in plant medicine, midwifery, and emergency preparedness. At a young age, she became an herbalist, then later a midwife, an educator, and an author. She started midwifery in 1974, which led to an active practice in home and birth center settings until her retirement in 2002. Her influence extends beyond her practice, as she played a pivotal role in shaping midwifery education and accreditation.

Daphne is also an urban homesteader, promoting permaculture, and food resilience. She emphasizes the importance of emergency preparedness, not just for personal survival but also for the ability to aid others. She is the founder of Zaníyan Center, a nonprofit organization that promotes plants for health and a connection to the earth.

Her heritage includes Lakota from the Standing Rock Tribe, Spanish, and Scottish. She is the mother of four grown children and the grandmother of eight. She calls Eugene, Oregon, home, and is where she grows herbs, makes medicine, and is an activist for protecting the earth and water.

Other books by Daphne Singingtree
Circle for the Earth A Time Travel Saga for a Sustainable Future Birthsong Midwifery Workbook, the *Emergency Guide to Obstetric Complications*, and Training Midwives: A Guide for Preceptors, and the *Eagletree Herbs Guide to Medicine Making*.

Daphne's Great-grandmother Helen Brown (Fisher Woman)

Acknowledgments

Though a book may be written by one, it is rarely created alone. Writing my first novel was an adventure with a steep learning curve, and the help I received along the way made all the difference. While writing a sequel was smoother in some ways, the need for encouragement, advice, and practical support remained, and I'm deeply grateful to everyone who helped bring this book to life.

Special thanks to my dear friend Janet Russell and her husband Jerry for supporting the publication through the nonprofit Zaníyan Center.

I'm especially grateful to my beta readers: Yosama Sun, Sharon Cohen, Dawson Lewis, To my publishing team: Janet Russell, whom improved the text so much, Robert A. Mallane, whose invaluable advice gave clarity over many a muddy passage; and Elian Wren, who always knew the right reference, and kept my writing moving. To my publishing assistant, Mary Glo Cuda, not sure what I'd do without you. With AI increasingly doing art, I especially want to thank my human artists: Yosama Sun, Savanna Stamp, Van Halen Cunanan, D. A. Suraj, and Jo Fox.

Special thanks to my home helpers. Since my car accident, daily tasks have become more difficult and time-consuming. Their support allows me to keep writing. Thank you, Shari Arthur, Sharon Cohen, Brita Pastor, and Cindy Herzog. You are not just helpers, but friends and my everyday support system.

To my children and grandchildren, thank you for always standing by me, no matter what crazy thing I decide to do next. Writing a novel was just the latest of many, and you are my pride and joy.

Would you do me a favor?

As a self-published author, I rely heavily on reader reviews. They make a huge difference, and every review truly counts.

For more content, updates, and ways to offer feedback, please visit circlefortheearth.com. The *Circle for the Earth* series also has a private Facebook group where I share behind-the-scenes content and book updates. It's private to keep out spammers, but feel free to request to join.

Your thoughts and feedback help shape future books. You're welcome to email me directly at daphnesingingtree@gmail.com.

You can email me at daphnesingingtree@gmail.com.

What is Real?

Location

Expeditions continues the story begun in *Circle for the Earth*, centered on a real location in South Dakota. The 30-mile circle transported back in time encompasses the Lower Brule and Crow Creek Reservations and the nearby towns of Chamberlain, Presho, and others along the Missouri River. While the Omímeya Casino and Resort is fictional, the land base, terrain, and geography are real. The river loop described exists but is currently farmland. The hospital in Chamberlain is also real, although privately owned.

Historical Accuracy and Liberties

This is speculative fiction, but it is grounded in actual history. Dates, treaties, political figures, and social movements are as accurate as possible, with fictional elements woven in. Spain's declining colonial power, France's post-revolutionary instability, and the presence of Indigenous, African-descended, and Creole populations in Louisiana and the Caribbean are historically accurate.

The Haitian Revolution plays a role in the background of this story. While this book does not focus directly on Haiti, characters like Toussaint Louverture, a real historical figure, are mentioned. His leadership in 1791–1802 dramatically influenced global perceptions of slavery, colonialism, and African resistance.

Charles Cotesworth Pinckney was a real historical figure who served as a US diplomat and politician. His role in Expeditions reflects his known Federalist affiliations and historical presence in early American diplomacy.

Benjamin Tallmadge was a real historical figure and served as George Washington's chief intelligence officer during the Revolutionary War. He was instrumental in organizing the Culper Spy Ring. His appearance or mention in *Expeditions* reflects his known role in early American intelligence operations.

Some fictional political figures, such as Senator Clyde Folsom, are used to reflect 21st-century attitudes transposed onto the 18th-century landscape. The depiction of many legal structures, technological limitations, and cultural tensions is plausible or extrapolated from actual events.

Lakota and Reservation Life

The Lower Brule and Crow Creek tribes are real and located within the 30-mile circle. They do not currently operate facilities identical to those in the novel, but they operate buffalo herds, grow popcorn for Jiffy, have community programs, and have a small but very different casino in a different location. The details in this book are an amalgamation of many Lakota communities and not meant to represent any one tribe specifically.

While *Expeditions* references historical trauma, including the impacts of colonization and boarding schools, it also reflects Indigenous strength, autonomy, and cultural continuity. The language, governance models, and spiritual practices depicted have been drawn from real traditions, though adapted into a fictional world.

Technology and Infrastructure

Everything described in *Expeditions* including shortwave radio, mesh phones, Internet-in-a-Box, and Raspberry Pi computers is real technology that could be adapted for off-grid use. Communication networks described are plausible within the technological limitations of the time travel setting. All emergency preparedness methods, power generation, herbal medicine references, and permaculture principles are rooted in real-world practice.

Alternative energy sources, such as Kaplan wheels and biology-based energy sources, are all real.

Nikola Tesla (1856–1943) was a real inventor and visionary whose experiments in wireless energy and electromagnetic systems inspired many speculative technologies. In *Expeditions*, his theories are referenced by characters who had access to 21st-century archives.

Books for Inspiration
- *1632* series by Eric Flint
- *After Cilmeri* series by Sarah Woodbury
- *Lakota America* by Pekka Hamalainen
- *The Fifth Sacred Thing* by Starhawk
- *Emberverse* series by S.M. Stirling

Additional Resources - Radio groups, prep communities, CERT, and the open-source education movement

About Zaníyan Center

100% of all proceeds from this book go to support Zaníyan Center, a 501(c)(3) nonprofit organization dedicated to promoting health through plants and connection with the earth.

We offer workshops and publish educational materials that reflect our vision and values:
- The healing power of plants nurtures body, mind, heart, and spirit.
- Sustainable, resilient food systems are key to food sovereignty and long-term community well-being.
- How we birth, breastfeed, and care for the young shapes lifelong health and the future of the planet.
- Elders hold knowledge and wisdom that are essential for cultural survival, continuity, and care.
- End-of-life care be loving and dignified, and we honor the sacredness of the body after death.
- In a time of increasing disruption, we promote self-reliance, resilience, and preparedness rooted in community and connection to the earth.

At Zaníyan Center, we believe that connection to the land, reverence for life, and practical skills are essential for building a just and sustainable future.

Visit zaniyan.org for more information.

Tax deductible donations are always appreciated.